MISSION CRITICAL

MISSION
CRITICAL

MARK GREANEY

BERKLEY
NEW YORK

BERKLEY
An imprint of Penguin Random House LLC
1745 Broadway, New York, NY 10019

Copyright © 2019 by Mark Strode Greaney
Penguin Random House supports copyright. Copyright fuels creativity, encourages diverse
voices, promotes free speech, and creates a vibrant culture. Thank you for buying an authorized
edition of this book and for complying with copyright laws by not reproducing, scanning, or
distributing any part of it in any form without permission. You are supporting writers and
allowing Penguin Random House to continue to publish books for every reader.

BERKLEY and the BERKLEY & B colophon are registered trademarks of
Penguin Random House LLC.

Library of Congress Cataloging-in-Publication Data

Names: Greaney, Mark, author.
Title: Mission critical / Mark Greaney.
Description: First edition. | New York, NY : Berkley, an imprint of Penguin
Random House LLC, 2019. | Series: Gray man
Identifiers: LCCN 2018047590 | ISBN 9780451488947 (hardback) |
ISBN 9780451488961 (ebook)
Subjects: | BISAC: FICTION / Espionage. | FICTION / Action & Adventure. |
GSAFD: Suspense fiction | Spy stories.
Classification: LCC PS3607.R4285 M57 2019 | DDC 813/.6—dc23
LC record available at https://lccn.loc.gov/2018047590

First Edition: February 2019

Printed in the United States of America
1   3   5   7   9   10   8   6   4   2

Cover design by Steve Meditz
Cover photos: upper right: Bridge over river by Marchal Jeremy / Getty
Images; lower right: Shanghai China at night by chinaface / Getty Images; Man running
by Mohammed Itani / Arcangel; Riveted metal by Melinda Podor / Getty Images; Scratched
red wall by Dan Thornberg / Getty Images
Interior art: Black-and-white Paris map © Nicola Renna / Shutterstock.com
Book design by Kelly Lipovich

For Lauren Gilliland
November 27, 1984–
January 19, 2018
Rest in peace

ACKNOWLEDGMENTS

I would like to thank Joshua Hood (JoshuaHoodBooks.com), J.T. Patten (JTPattenBooks.com), Scott Swanson, Chris Clarke, Emily Field Griffin, Taylor Gilliland, Mike Cowan, Nick Ciubotariu, Tiffany Glanz-Dornblaser, Derek LeJeune, Igor Veksler, Larry Rice, the Memphis Greaneys, the Tulsa Greaneys, the Houston Greaneys, Jon Harvey, Bridget Kelly, Mystery Mike Bursaw, Michele Prusak, Jon Griffin, and Brandy Brown,

I'd also like to thank my agents, Scott Miller at Trident Media Group and Jon Cassir at CAA, along with my editor, Tom Colgan, and the remarkable staff at PRH: Grace House, Jin Yu, Loren Jaggers, Bridget O'Toole, Jeanne-Marie Hudson, Christine Ball and Ivan Held.

Valor lies just halfway between rashness and cowardice.

—MIGUEL DE CERVANTES

CHARACTERS

COURTLAND "COURT" GENTRY (AKA THE GRAY MAN; CODE NAME, VIOLATOR): CIA contract agent and former CIA employee, former member of Special Activities Division (Ground Branch) and the Autonomous Asset Program

MATTHEW HANLEY: Deputy Director of Operations, CIA

SUZANNE BREWER: Senior Officer, Programs and Plans, CIA

ZOYA FEODOROVNA ZAKHAROVA: Former SVR (Russian Foreign Intelligence) officer

DIRK VISSER: Luxembourg-based banker

WON JANG-MI (AKA JANICE WON): North Korean virologist and intelligence asset

VLADIMIR BELYAKOV: Russian oligarch

CHARLIE JONES: Nottingham-based crime boss

ANTHONY KENT: Nottingham-based criminal

ALEXI FILOTOV: Russian GRU (Military Intelligence) officer

ZACH HIGHTOWER: CIA contract agent, former CIA Special Activities Division (Ground Branch) team leader

WALT JENNER: CIA Special Activities Division (Ground Branch) team leader

CHRIS TRAVERS: CIA Special Activities Division (Ground Branch) officer

LUCAS RENFRO: Deputy Director of Support, CIA

MARIA PALUMBO: Senior Executive, Operations, CIA

MARTY WHEELER: Assistant Deputy Director of Support, CIA

ALF KARLSSON: Executive, Operations, CIA

DAVID MARS: London-based businessman

FEODOR ZAKHAROV: Former director of the GRU (Russian military intelligence), father of Zoya Zakharova

ARTYOM PRIMAKOV (AKA ROGER FOX): Russian mafia (Bratva) Vor (made man)

JON HINES: Bodyguard to Roger Fox

SIR DONALD FITZROY: London-based security consultant (retired)

The flight attendant standing at the top of the jet stairs slipped a hand behind her back and threaded her fingers around the grip of the pistol tucked under her jacket. Thumbing the safety down, she eyed the figure approaching confidently from the darkness beyond the lights illuminating the tarmac and wondered if she should go ahead and pull her weapon.

There was just one unknown subject in sight, so she'd settled on the handgun, but she had other defensive options available to her here in the Gulfstream IV executive jet. If there had been more threats she could have grabbed the loaded Colt M4 hanging by its sling in the coat closet next to her, and if things looked really dicey, she also had an M320 single-shot, 40-millimeter grenade launcher within reach.

The approaching man wore a black ball cap and a gray T-shirt under a dark brown jacket. He walked with purpose, but there was no obvious menace to his movements. Still, the copilot leaned out of the cockpit, a look of concern on his face.

"Is this our guy, Sharon?"

The flight attendant kept her eyes on the man as she replied. "If it is, he has trouble following directions. Our passenger was instructed to approach from the terminal, but this joker is coming out of the dark near the fence line."

"You want us to move the aircraft?" The engines were spinning; the

Gulfstream had been ordered to land here in Zurich and wait at idle on the tarmac for a single passenger to board.

Sharon said, "Negative. If this guy starts any trouble, I'll handle him. Just strap in and be ready."

"Say the word and we're outta here." The copilot returned to his controls.

The man emerging from the darkness kept coming; Sharon could see a backpack swinging off his right shoulder, but his hands were down by his sides, his palms turned towards her to show he was unarmed. He stopped twenty yards from the stairs and looked up at the woman.

With the turbines whirling there was no way they could talk at this distance. After a moment looking him over, she waved him up the steps with her left hand, while her right clamped down even harder on the grip of the SIG P320 9-millimeter. She pulled it out a fraction of an inch until she felt the click of her retention holster releasing the weapon, but she did not draw it completely free.

The man climbed the jet stairs. When he was within speaking distance he said, "Think you're my ride."

"How 'bout we confirm that, just to make it official?"

The man said, "X-ray, X-ray, eighty-eight, Whiskey, Uniform."

The woman thumbed the safety back up and pressed down on the grip, snapping the SIG back into its holster. She removed her hand from behind her back. "Confirmed. Juliet, Uniform, thirteen, Papa, Echo."

The man in the ball cap nodded.

"You had me worried, sir. You approached from the wrong direction."

A shrug. "I'm a bit of a rebel."

He was a smartass, Sharon saw immediately, but he gave a tired, friendly smile after he said it, so she let it go. She stepped up against the cockpit door to allow the man to pass into the cabin.

"Welcome on board," she said. "You must be something special; we were heading to Luxembourg on a priority movement when we were diverted here to pick you up."

The man shrugged. "Not special. Somebody at Langley wants a word, so I've been summoned."

The woman raised her eyebrows at this. "Well, good luck with that. Can I get a drink for the condemned?"

"No thanks. I'll be no trouble." With that he moved to the back of the plush Gulfstream, tossed his pack into a chair, and sank into the port-side window seat next to it.

The aircraft had seating for fourteen in the form of leather cabin chairs and an overstuffed leather sofa. A TV monitor inlaid in a rosewood front bulkhead showed their position here in Zurich, and bottled water rested in every cup holder in the cabin.

Sharon closed the hatch and leaned into the cockpit to speak with the pilot, and soon the aircraft began rolling. She moved back to her single passenger and sat down in a chair across from him. "We're to deliver you to D.C., but I'm afraid we have two stops to make en route. We'll land in Luxembourg, pick up our passengers there, and deliver them to an airfield in the UK. We'll refuel and get back in the air for the hop over the Atlantic. ETA at D.C. is around eleven a.m. local."

"Works for me."

"You really *are* no trouble, are you?" She stood, turned, and headed up to the cockpit.

The man looked out the window at the darkness.

The plane lifted into the night sky moments later, and Courtland Gentry, CIA code name Violator, drifted off to sleep soon after.

• • •

He only awoke as they touched down at Luxembourg City. Court knew the Agency preferred using smaller or even private airfields when possible, but the big international airport here in the suburb of Findel was the only paved runway in the tiny nation.

Just as in Zurich, the aircraft taxied and then stopped on the ramp, wide of any activity on the property.

Court looked idly out the port-side window for a moment with a yawn.

He saw headlights approaching on the ramp, and soon a pair of commercial vans pulled to a stop at the bottom of the jet stairs. The doors opened and a group of men began climbing out. Court glanced idly to the front of the cabin and saw the flight attendant standing in the open passenger doorway, holding an M4 rifle slightly behind her back, muzzle down but ready to whip it up at the first sign of danger.

She looked like she knew how to handle the weapon, which came as no shock to the CIA asset watching her. The Agency trained their transportation staff for anything.

Court himself was packing a Glock 19 9-millimeter, a .38 revolver, and a .22 caliber suppressed pistol. One on his hip, one on his ankle, the other in his pack, and he was ready to go for them if he sensed any danger. But the flight attendant seemed to have it all under control. She spoke with someone just outside the cabin on the stairs, then hung the M4 back in the coat closet and beckoned the man in.

Court closed his eyes and pulled his cap down; he was ready to get back to sleep.

· · ·

Forty-six-year-old CIA officer Doug Spano boarded the aircraft while his men waited on the ramp behind him for his all clear.

Once inside he spoke to the attractive woman at the door, and then he turned to look over the darkened cabin. Immediately he saw a man seated in the back, a ball cap pulled down over his face. Spano cleared his jacket out of the way of his sidearm and gripped it, and then without taking his eyes off the man, he addressed the flight attendant. "Who the *fuck* is that?"

"Agency personnel, sir. He's cleared."

"Not by me, he's not. This is a priority movement."

"So is he, sir. We were told to deliver your group to Ternhill and then to fly him on to Washington."

Spano grimaced in anger. Somebody had fucked up, and it was getting in the way of his op. He moved quickly down the cabin and leaned over the passenger in the dark. At first he thought him to be asleep, but the man lifted his cap, opened his eyes, and said, "Evening."

"Don't take it personally, sport, but I can't have you on this aircraft. Get Transpo to arrange another flight for you. I've got a priority mission you're encroaching on here."

The man seemed bored. He closed his eyes again. "Call Langley, extension fifty-eight twelve. She tells me to get off, I get off."

"You don't listen, do you?" When no response came he said, "Who are you with?"

"Coded."

If this man was, in fact, on a code-word operation, then Spano wouldn't be learning anything further from him about what he was doing on board.

But he didn't give a shit. "My op is coded, too, tough guy." He then changed tactics, opting for direct intimidation. "Not telling you again. Deplane. *Now*."

"Fifty-eight twelve," the man replied in a bored voice. He was positively unintimidated, and he rolled his head towards the window.

Doug Spano pulled his sat phone out of his jacket and stormed back up the cabin.

. . .

Five minutes later the CIA officer held the phone to his ear, and Court could tell from his body language that he was pissed. He came storming in his direction, and he handed the phone over.

Court took it and answered. "Hello?"

"Making friends as always, I see." It was his handler, Suzanne Brewer. She sounded annoyed, but Court couldn't remember ever hearing her sound different.

"Just being a good worker bee. You told me you wanted me on this plane."

"Well, yes, I need you here in Washington, stat. You're on that flight, but you need to relinquish any weapons."

Court paused. Said, "I'm not really the 'relinquishing weapons' type."

"Do it."

"Why?"

In an even more irritated voice Brewer said, "Because I *asked* you to, Violator."

Court sighed. "Okie doke." He passed the phone back to the CIA officer, who disconnected the call.

The man stood over him, obviously displeased by this intrusion on his operation. "Aren't you a Billy Badass? Gettin' to ride shotgun on a code-word op. Can't say I've ever seen *that* shit."

"I'll stay out of your hair, boss."

A finger came up, not quite in Court's face, but close enough to annoy. "Damn right, you will. You'll park your ass right here; we'll take the front.

You need to go to the lav, you *will* hit your call light and I'll send a man to escort you. Now . . . let's have those weapons. You'll get them back at Ternhill."

Court pulled his Glock, backwards and with his fingertips, so as not to be threatening, and he handed it over. The man took it, dropped the magazine, and cleared the round from the chamber, letting the bullet fall to the floor. He reseated the magazine and stuck the gun in the waistband of his jeans.

And then he looked back to the seated man.

Court gazed up at him. No expression, no movement.

"Secondary."

Court slowly lifted his right leg, ripped off an ankle holster Velcroed around his calf, and passed it over along with the .38 revolver tucked inside it.

He then looked back to the man standing over him.

As he expected, the CIA officer said, "Let's take a peek inside that backpack."

Court sighed, remained still.

"Don't make me send my four guys back here to pound it away from you."

Asshole, Court thought but did not say. He reached into his pack and removed the integrally suppressed Ruger .22 pistol stowed there. Again holding the base of the grip by his fingertips, he handed it to the man standing over him.

The CIA officer took the gun with a confused expression, then held it up to examine it carefully.

Court knew what this jackass must have been thinking right now. The Ruger Amphibian wasn't a pistol fielded by CIA case officers, security staff, or normally even paramilitaries. No . . . it was a weapon with only one obvious purpose.

It was an assassin's tool.

The CIA officer's eyes were wider now as he looked back to the man in the ball cap sitting in the dark. After clearing his throat nervously, he said, "Is . . . is that all?"

Court replied, "You're not getting my nail file."

The standing man recovered slowly, still holding the silenced pistol up for inspection. "I don't like this shit one bit."

Court yawned. "Dude, I don't know what your problem is, but it sure as hell isn't me."

The CIA officer turned away and headed up to the front. Court watched him place the .22 in the closet by the cabin door and then leave the aircraft.

. . .

A minute later Court looked on while the other men boarded. Two burly bearded guys, both with HK short-barreled rifles on their chests. Next came another large CIA man, and he held on to a smaller individual who shuffled into the aircraft with a black bag over his head, his wrists and ankles shackled. Behind them came the man who had disarmed Court along with one more bearded CIA officer.

The prisoner was led into a seat by the front and bracketed by two of the fit bearded officers.

In the back of the cabin, Court Gentry watched it all, and he recognized what was going on. They were taking this dude to the UK. Probably to MI6, British foreign intelligence. This was a rendition, a detainee handoff to another nation.

Before sitting down in the front half of the cabin most of the Americans gave Court "eat shit" looks. Court gazed back at them impassively, then rolled his eyes a little before closing them yet again.

The plane took off from Findel into a starry night.

CHAPTER 1

While an evening rain threatened outside, inside the well-appointed three-car garage gym a woman worked out alone. With her shoulder-length brunette hair tied in a ponytail, a blue American University T-shirt, and gray yoga pants, she did push-ups and crunches, pounded and kicked a heavy bag, and slung dumbbells, all before heading over to the climbing ropes.

The garage ceiling was just ten feet up, so the ropes weren't very high, but they were three feet apart and a challenge to climb. The woman grasped them both with gloved hands and began ascending, one hand grabbing and pulling while the other slid up the opposite rope to a higher position, then closed down in a viselike grip to heave her body higher.

Her arms and back and shoulders did all the work; she let her feet hang, swinging back and forth as she climbed, using her upper body for power. At the ceiling she shifted both hands to the same rope and climbed down.

Immediately she started back up again on both ropes.

While she worked out, a muscular bald-headed man in a Windbreaker and cargo pants looked in on her from time to time from his position on the driveway. He wore a Beretta pistol on a utility belt around his waist, as well as handcuffs, Mace, and a radio. Beyond him in the woods another man strolled with a rifle across his chest.

As the woman dropped down after her fourth time up the ropes she doubled forward and put her hands on her knees, struggling to catch her breath.

The bald man on the driveway chided her. "Suck it up, snowflake! Back at BUD's we had to climb a rope three times higher, five times, after about a thousand push-ups."

She faced away from him, but she took one hand off a knee and flipped him the middle finger over her shoulder.

The man looked at her rear end, covered in the yoga pants. "Anytime, sugar."

The woman ignored him, put her hands on the floor, and kicked her feet up into a handstand. In this position she slowly walked her hands the length of the garage, her arms straining. Steadying her body against the back wall, she did a few handstand press-ups.

A minute after this she unhooked the heavy bag from its chain and hefted all 120 pounds of it onto her shoulder. With it she ran across the three-car garage, from one wall to the other, spun, and ran back.

She completed the circuit ten times.

As the woman dropped the bag onto the ground for a moment's rest, she knelt again with her hands to her knees and her chest heaving. Through her labored breaths she heard a transmission through the walkie-talkie on the leering guard's utility belt. The muscular man responded through the radio, then called out to her.

"You ready, sunshine? I'll take you to your room to change first."

Zoya Zakharova grabbed her towel and her bottle of water, and she headed for the door to the safe house.

• • •

A minute later they walked down a long, brightly lit basement hallway. The security officer said, "Just you and me down here in holding tonight between twenty-two hundred hours to sunup. That means I have access to all the cams, *and* all the keys." He turned to look at her but she kept walking, her eyes ahead and her face covered with sweat. "I've also got access to a couple bottles of cabernet I brought in my kit bag. I could flip off any video evidence, come to your room after lights out, and you and I could have ourselves a pretty sweet evening."

Zoya kept walking. She answered him in perfect English, with no hint of any accent. "William, my answer was a polite 'no' the first ten times you propositioned me, and then a firm 'no' the next ten times. Do you really want to find out what comes next?"

"I can handle whatever you can dish out, sugar." He said it with a confident smile.

The brunette let out a little laugh as she walked. "You're something out of a bad movie."

"So . . . that's a maybe? Girl, you gotta be lonely cooped up in here for four months."

She did look at him now, eyed him up and down as they walked. "Not *that* lonely."

The man didn't seem to take offense, but he said, "You know, I defend you to the other guys, but they're right about you. You really *are* mean as a snake."

Zoya looked straight ahead as she headed to her room. "That's the thing about snakes, William. They aren't mean. They just prefer to be left alone."

Zoya showered and changed into jeans and a black George Washington University sweatshirt. Her hair was still pulled back, and she walked with William to a third-floor library in the nine-thousand-square-foot CIA safe house. Two more security men stood outside the door, and they opened it for Zoya, who entered alone.

CIA Programs and Plans officer Suzanne Brewer was already seated at the table in the center of the room, a pair of thermoses of hot tea positioned in front of her. A hand rested atop a thick brown folder. She was forty-one years old, with blond hair just past her shoulders, and wore a navy blue business suit that fit her lean frame perfectly. Her glasses were functional, not stylish, and she held the tip of a pen to her mouth, then took it away to speak.

"Hi, Zoya."

The younger woman sat down across the small table. "You're late, Suzanne. Of course I can't say how late, because I haven't been trusted with access to a clock, but it's dark outside. Usually you are here earlier."

"You have a date?"

Zoya reached for her tea. "Maybe."

Brewer replied, "I'd have to sign you out for that, and I haven't seen any paperwork." When Zoya did not respond she added, "Traffic was shit. Even more so than usual. Shall we begin?"

The brunette nodded, then looked out the window at the rain in the swaying trees.

Brewer turned on a small digital recorder lying on the table. "Tonight will be interview number ninety-four. Should just take a couple of hours, and then you can go back to your room."

"My cell, you mean?"

Brewer sighed a little. "The basement was designed as a holding center, true, but there are no bars. We lock you down at night, for your own safety, but during the day you have the run of the house."

"With security watching my every move."

"Ah, glad you mentioned the security. I'm told you've been surly with the guards."

"Not all of them. Just the ones who won't stop making passes at me."

Suzanne frowned at this. "Well, that's unprofessional of them. Who are they? I'll have them removed."

Zoya waved a hand in front of her. "Not necessary. They're harmless."

"If they're on my security staff I don't *want* them to be harmless. I also don't want them hitting on the guests."

Zoya sniffed. "Guests."

"Listen, we've been through this. This isn't a prison. It's a safe house. The guards are here to keep you *safe*. You are an asset in the making, and we're protecting our investment."

Zoya gazed out the window.

Brewer added, "Look. I wasn't going to tell you tonight, but since you're obviously in a mood, I will. I have some good news. You've been assigned an operational code name."

"How many guesses do I get?"

Brewer was confused. "I don't know what you—"

Still looking past Brewer to the rain, she said, "Anthem. My code name with CIA is Anthem."

Brewer blinked hard, and then her shoulders sagged. "Which one of these bozos around here let *that* slip?"

"I hear things. That's all."

The older woman closed her eyes in frustration now. "Idiots." Opening them again, she asked, "What else have you heard them say?"

"The short version is you and I have about the same approval numbers with the security boys here"—Zoya smiled a little—"and *I* come from an enemy service."

Brewer didn't seem to give a damn that she wasn't well liked by the detail at this safe house. Instead she said, "Again, Anthem, no one thinks of you as enemy. You came in willingly, you've endured months of debriefs, psych evals, testing, polygraphs. We're weeks away from cutting you loose so you can serve as a detached agent of our service."

Zoya nodded slowly, still looking out the window at the rain falling in the woods behind the house. "I have been well flipped."

The comment hung in the air a long time, until Brewer said, "I thought you'd like to know. I finally heard from Violator. He's fine."

Zoya stared back at her now. "You mean Court."

"Correct."

The Russian woman cocked her head a little. "Have I asked you anything about him in the months I've been here?"

"No . . . but I am aware of the feelings you two had for one another. Beneath your hard exterior I'm sure those feelings remain. I just wanted to tell you he checked in safe today."

Zoya nodded distractedly, then looked down to the folder on the table. "What do you have there?"

Brewer pulled out a sheaf of papers, facedown, and Zoya's dispassionate demeanor broke a moment as she looked at it in silence.

"You've been asking me to show you the file regarding the death of your father. I was hesitant . . . We have no questions or suspicions about the matter, so there's nothing we need from you. On top of this . . . the photographs and details in the file could be quite . . . upsetting, especially to the child of the victim."

"I am not a normal child of a victim, am I? I spent ten years in Russia's foreign security services myself, and my father was—"

"Your father," Suzanne Brewer interrupted, "was General Feodor Zakharov, the head of Russian military intelligence. Yes . . . you are an exceptional case, to say the least."

Brewer paused for a sip of tea, and Zoya took the opportunity to glance down again at the stack of papers.

The American woman lowered her thermos and said, "Here's what we've established from our debriefs. You were away in college in California when you learned he'd been killed in a mortar attack in Dagestan along with several other GRU men. After graduating UCLA you returned to Russia, following your late father into the intelligence services, but with SVR, not GRU."

After Zoya nodded, Brewer added, "Your father would have been proud of you."

The Russian woman did not return the smile. "Not for defecting. He was a true believer in the motherland. I'm a true believer in myself. Not the same."

Brewer kept looking at the Russian national for several more seconds, then tapped the file with the tip of her pen. "Again, this . . . information, these pictures. They will be disturbing to you."

"I can handle it. May I see them, please?" There was a small hint of emotion in Zoya's voice now, even though she tried to hide it.

After another moment's pause, Suzanne Brewer turned over the papers and spun them around on the table.

"Don't say I didn't warn you."

• • •

It was one thirty a.m. in the tony London neighborhood of Notting Hill when a sixty-two-year-old man with a thick dark beard and mustache lifted his head slowly and looked at his nightstand. He blinked out the fog, scanned the row of five mobile phones lying there in a charging cradle, and snatched up the one whose buzzing had woken him from a deep sleep.

He rolled onto his back again and rubbed his eyes as he answered in a heavy British accent.

"Who's calling, please?"

The voice was American English. Soft and rushed. "Mr. Black? It's me. It's Barnacle."

The man in bed sighed and rubbed his eyes. "I am in Europe, as you well know, which means it is the bloody middle of the night here. If this is about the matter we discussed yesterday, I assure you that—"

"No, it's not about that. Something's happened."

"I told you to calm down and—"

"You'll want to hear this."

The man in bed yawned. "Go on, then."

"Some time back you had me flag a list of files in our system, with orders to contact you immediately if they were ever accessed, updated, or shared with other intelligence or law enforcement agencies."

The man in bed sat up quickly, and he pressed the phone tighter against his ear. "I did, indeed. Something's come up?"

"Yes, sir. Forty pages were printed out this evening at six twenty-eight local time, about an hour ago. It's one of the personality files you asked me to monitor."

"There are dozens of personalities on our watch list. Which file was accessed?"

"A man named Zakharov. General Feodor Ivanovich Zakharov. He was the head of GRU, killed in Dagestan over ten years ago."

The man in Notting Hill rubbed his thick beard, grabbed a pen and notepad from his nightstand, and stormed towards the balcony off his bedroom to suck in some cool night air. "I recall the name. I don't believe you've reported that this particular file has been accessed since you and I began our partnership."

"No one has pulled it in years . . . until tonight."

"Who printed the file?"

"The login belongs to Suzanne Brewer. She's in Programs and Plans, but is basically working under Matt Hanley, deputy director of Operations. She's involved in some off-book activities, working on a sub rosa project called Poison Apple; certainly nothing I have access to."

"Interesting." Barnacle was a code name, just as Mr. Black was. Black was David Mars, and Barnacle was the name used for Mars's inside man at the CIA. A man who had begun selling information about code-worded operations to the highest bidder. Chinese, Iranians . . . and David Mars.

Barnacle added, "It gets even more interesting. This file wasn't printed out at Langley. It was printed out at an outside SCIF. That's a Sensitive Compartmented Information Facil—"

Mars answered in a bark. He was wide awake and engaged now. "I know what a bloody SCIF is! Where is it?"

"Yes, of course. Uh . . . we have a safe house in Great Falls, Virginia. Twenty minutes up the Georgetown Pike from Langley. We use it for long-term debriefs and high-value detainee holding, mostly. There's a vault on-site and it was printed there. I checked . . . The safe house is operational now, medium-sized security staff—indicates a guest who has been deemed moderate risk, either of flight or of external threat."

The man in London breathed into the phone slowly.

When he did not respond, the American said, "Mr. Black?"

Mars asked, "Can you find out who's being held there now?"

The man on the other end of the line was emphatic in his answer. "No. No way. If it involves Hanley and Brewer I'm sure it's one of their coded programs, possibly Poison Apple, which, apparently, is director-level sanctioned. And even if I tried to poke around a little, they'd suspect me. I'm hanging on by a damn thread as it is."

"I understand. Don't compromise yourself." A pause. "You've done well, Barnacle."

"Thank you." The man passed on the address of the safe house, and Mars wrote it down on the pad.

The American changed the subject. "What about . . . what about the other thing?"

"You needn't worry about it."

"Meaning?"

"Meaning he's being dealt with. Tonight, in fact. Relax, mate. We have a plan. Stick with it. Five more days and you're out."

"I can't wait another five days! Every time the door to my office opens I expect it to be counterintel. Every time I see headlights behind me I think I'm getting tailed by the FBI. Every single glance I get from a colleague here at the Agency makes me think the walls are closing in. I *have* to run!"

Mars's voice lowered an octave. "Watch your tone with me, old boy."

"Yes . . . of course. Sorry, it's just that—"

"The only safe way to extract you will happen next week, here in the UK. Just keep your bloody wits about you for a few days and you'll be safe and set. I have to ring off."

The man who called himself Black hung up the phone and leaned forward against the balcony railing. He looked down at Portobello Road, quiet at this time of night. After a moment of contemplation, he nodded to himself and dialed another number.

When it was answered he spoke again. "Fox? It's me."

A younger-sounding man with a British accent said, "Sir?"

"We need a team assembled. Tonight."

"We . . . we *have* a team on the way now to—"

"Another team. Not here in the UK. In the States."

"In the United States? *Tonight?*"

"Has to be. A location in Virginia, just outside Washington, D.C. Can you get it done?"

"What's the task?"

"I need a *complete* facility wipeout, so get men who have the mettle for that sort of thing. It's an Agency safe house."

"You're *serious*, sir?"

Mars did not reply.

"You've never ordered a wipeout in the States. Hell . . . you've never ordered a wipeout in Western Europe, either. But tonight . . . first at Ternhill and now in Virginia . . . both in the same night?"

"We are days away from our objective, Fox. You can expect an increase in all activity over the next week."

With a pause the man said, "Yes. I understand."

Mars looked back out onto Portobello Road, his eyes narrowed with determination. "We must protect our retributive strike from all threats, no matter what."

. . .

Zoya Zakharova read through each page of the file on her father's death slowly while Suzanne Brewer sipped her tea and looked on.

After five minutes of this, the American interrupted the quiet. "I have to ask. Are there some suspicions you have about what happened that you haven't revealed to us?"

Zoya shook her head as she read. "No. But I owe it to him to look. Someone from the family should know of his . . . his sacrifice." Now Zoya looked up. "It's my final duty to my father."

Suzanne Brewer looked at Zoya with suspicion, but said, "I understand."

The Russian woman with the American accent flipped a page and came to the first color photograph. It was of two men, both lying on their backs, face up, twisted among the rubble of what appeared to be some sort of automobile repair shop. Engine parts, tires, shop rags, and car parts lay on the ground near the bodies.

The man on the right Zoya didn't recognize, but he wore body armor and the combat uniform of a Russian artillery officer. His left hand and forearm were missing, his eyes were open but rolled back in his head, and blood covered his throat and the dusty concrete floor beneath him.

And the other man was her father. He wore a heavy coat that was half pulled off, and a tunic that was blood-soaked and ripped open, exposing his neck and right shoulder, as if someone had tried to render aid, but found the wounds to be unsurvivable. A fur cap lay next to his head, and his eyes were closed.

A jagged hole in his right temple had spilled blood down over his ear, onto a pile of shop rags lying under his head. His arms and legs were askew.

She leaned forward, absorbing every detail of the photo, running a fingertip slowly over her father's face and neck. All the while Brewer looked on, sipping her tea.

Finally Zoya turned to the next photo. A shot from across the same room showing the bodies on the floor in the rubble under a hole in the ceiling; Zoya had the expertise to recognize the impact of a high-explosive mortar round, fired with a delay fuse to penetrate the roof of the building before detonating.

In this picture she also saw three men standing around, looking over the bodies. They were all GRU officers; she did not recognize the first two, but the third she knew well. "Uncle Vladi," she said in Russian under her breath, but Brewer did not hear her.

There were more photos of the scene: a close-up of Zoya's father's clean-shaven face, placid in death. He looked younger than his forty-eight years, but he looked the same as Zoya remembered him.

After ten minutes more reading the notes, and several more returns to the photos of her father's body, she slid the papers back to the American CIA officer across from her. "Thank you."

Brewer had not taken her eyes from Zoya's face for the past twenty minutes. "Did you see anything worthy of note?"

The Russian shook her head. "It's just as had been described to me by my father's colleagues. A million-to-one strike by a mortar that killed the head of Russian military intelligence."

"Your father."

"My father. Yes."

"CIA never found out what a GRU general was doing there on the front lines in the middle of a pitched battle."

Zoya shrugged. "Neither did his daughter."

After a sympathetic look Zoya didn't buy as authentic, Brewer closed the file and slid it into a leather bag on the floor by her feet. "Very well. Shall we move on to tonight's debriefing?"

The brunette in the George Washington sweatshirt kept looking off through the window, but she answered. "It's not like I have someplace else to be."

"Me, either. Let's begin."

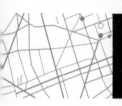

CHAPTER 2

Just before three thirty in the morning the CIA Gulfstream landed at RAF Ternhill, a nearly shuttered air base in the West Midlands of England owned by the Ministry of Defense but maintained primarily by civilian personnel.

Court sat up and rubbed his eyes, looking out the port-side window as the aircraft taxied up to three big silver SUVs parked next to a large refueling truck in a remote corner of the tarmac. Four men in ground crew coveralls stood by the truck, and as the plane came to a stop, a total of eight men in dark suits climbed out of the SUVs.

Court pegged these guys as MI6. He had done his own share of deliveries to the UK back in his days with the CIA's Special Activities Division, and he recognized the protocol.

Court was a singleton asset now, a contract agent of the CIA, not an officer. A somewhat reluctant and only occasional team player. But this had been Court Gentry's world once.

The out-of-the-way airport. The late-night rendezvous on the tarmac. The hooded prisoner with no clue as to where the hell he was.

The big guys in suits, guns at the ready, flitting eyes scanning the night.

Yes, he remembered this life, and he didn't much miss it.

.   .   .

Doug Spano stepped down the jet stairs and walked towards the three SUVs and the men standing around them. He noticed they had dispersed around the vehicles, a man at each wheel, keeping 360-degree security on the area, and this he was glad to see. He knew MI6 would be ready to deal with any threats.

The ground crew moved the fuel truck closer to the Gulfstream and a man pulled on a hose, taking it over to the belly near the starboard-side wing to attach it to the aircraft to start the flow of jet fuel.

Three other men climbed out and began helping with the hose.

Spano shook the hand of a balding man in a black suit who had stepped forward. "You're Palmer?" he asked.

"I am. And you must be Scott."

"That's me." They shook hands.

The Brit smiled. "I do love how you Agency Yanks only use first-name pseudonyms. It does make it fun and jocular."

Spano stayed on mission. "You've searched the ground crew?"

With a sigh the man said, "Of course we have, mate."

Spano nodded, then pointed back to the Gulfstream. "If you're ready for him, I'll have him brought down."

"Quite ready. Thank you very much, indeed."

The CIA officer waved to one of his men at the top of the stairs, and slowly the hooded prisoner was led out of the aircraft and down the steps.

.   .   .

In the back of the Gulfstream, Court continued looking out the window at the transaction, thinking about his past. The security cordon around the SUVs remained vigilant, eyes scanning the far reaches of the lights. The four men in the ground crew walked around the refueler, dealing with the hose.

Court watched the early-morning activity, only taking his eyes away when the flight attendant appeared next to him.

"Refueling should take about twenty minutes. We have some pretty fair schnitzel and potatoes we picked up in Munich earlier tonight. Will take me ten minutes to reheat them. Interested in a very late dinner?"

Court nodded. "Yeah, that sounds good." He glanced out the window again, ready to get back in the air, but then a trace of movement in the distance, beyond the lights of the SUVs, caught his eye.

It was an airport truck; on its side it said Lavatory Services, and behind it a catering truck appeared. Bringing up the rear was an unmarked black van.

The men pulling security saw the movement, as well, but there was a moment's hesitation in their response, probably while they conferred with the Americans to find out if these newcomers were here to service the aircraft.

Court spun his head back to the refueling truck. All four men were behind it, out of his view, and this fired off threat alarms and warning lights in his well-tuned combat brain.

He saw a pair of flashes from the darkness beyond the tarmac lights, and instantly a pair of men by the silver SUVs fell to the ground.

The refueling crew ran back into view from behind the truck. The men held rifles now, obviously pulled from inside their vehicle, and together they opened fire on the Brits and Americans on the tarmac as they advanced on them.

The booms and chatter of gunfire rocked the night.

More flashes from the darkness. The Lavatory Services truck and the black van skidded to a stop behind the refueling truck.

Court leapt to his feet and pushed the flight attendant down to the floor, shielding the woman with his body. He heard full-auto gunfire tearing into the fuselage now, puncturing windows, sending debris and bullet fragments throughout the cabin.

Another explosion shook the Gulfstream, and Court figured someone was taking out the SUVs with grenades.

"Get off me!" the woman shouted, and she crawled out from under Court and raced through the cabin. She pulled the M4 from the coat closet, flipped it to semiautomatic, and spun into the open doorway while raising it up to eye level.

Court began crawling up the aisle as more rounds pocked the skin of the Gulfstream just feet above him. He moved towards the door and the flight attendant as she fired a burst at a target.

Just five feet in front of him the woman cried out and crumpled down to the floor. The rifle spilled down the jet stairs to the tarmac.

Court grabbed the woman by the collar of her jacket and dragged her out of the doorway. Looking her over, he saw she'd been shot both through the left wrist and in the palm of her right hand, likely from a single round that caught her as her hands held the forward and rear grips of the rifle. Her hands bled freely and she writhed in pain.

As he knelt over her Court yanked a fleece hoodie off a hanger in the closet next to him and wrapped her hands with it.

"Gun?" he shouted.

"Small of my back," she grunted. Blood soaked through the fabric of the hoodie.

Court reached behind her back on the floor and pulled a SIG P320 from her skirt, then stood and stepped over her, racing past the open doorway and to the closed cockpit door.

As he passed the jet stairs he glanced out. In the near distance, not twenty-five yards from where Court stood, all three silver SUVs were in flames, and bodies littered the ground around them.

Two men in coveralls—members of the ground crew—had their hands on the hooded prisoner and were running with him towards the row of four trucks at the edge of the tarmac lights and bullets continued to strike the concrete and the SUVs while those CIA and MI6 still standing returned fire.

Court also saw two men from the refueler on the ground near their vehicle, submachine guns lying by their bodies.

He fired once into the back of each of the two men with the prisoner, sending them both face-first to the ground, then shifted aim towards the men in the catering truck, but a volley of fire zinged by him in the doorway, sending him to his knees. He turned away and crawled to the cockpit door and leaned in behind the pilot and copilot. "Move this plane!" he shouted, and then he noticed both men's heads hanging to the side. A pair of bullet holes in the windscreen told him the pilots had been taken out to keep them grounded, and it also told him there was at least one sniper with eyes on the cockpit, hiding somewhere out there in the dark. Court dropped below the glass, taking cover behind the pilot's seat, then reached up and unhooked the copilot from his harness. He grabbed the dead man, pulling him out of his chair and onto the floor.

Court climbed into his position, keeping his head down other than to steal a glance to orient himself at the airfield.

The turbines of the jet were spinning still, so Court found the brake release and then rocked forward the thrust levers twenty percent. Instantly the aircraft began to roll slowly on the ramp. He used the foot pedals to steer the plane down the taxiway, in the general direction of the terminal, a quarter mile away.

He backed off to ten percent power, then climbed out of the cockpit and returned to the open passenger-entry doorway, the pistol high in front of him.

A raging gun battle continued on the tarmac, but at least he was rolling away from it now.

He saw a man in coveralls behind the fuel truck, spinning around and raising a large rifle Court recognized as an L86A2, a light support weapon used by the British military. The man fired with discipline, short bursts towards the few men still in the fight in front of him.

Court did not hesitate. He lined up his front sight on the attacker who, with the Gulfstream's movement, was becoming a smaller target every second, and squeezed off four rounds from his SIG.

The man fell dead onto the tarmac, his rifle on top of him.

Beyond the body by the fuel truck Court saw that the hooded and handcuffed man was being pushed into the back of the black van by two more attackers. The catering and lavatory services vehicles were next to it, and several armed men had fanned out away from them.

Almost instantly more gunfire slammed into the Gulfstream near Court. He emptied the SIG at the distant threats but knew he was making more noise than hits because he was firing at a difficult angle back around the doorway of the moving aircraft.

When the pistol locked open, he rushed back to the cockpit.

The Gulfstream rolled on towards the taxiway and the darkness at twenty knots, a slow escape from the danger. Court knew there was nothing more he could do for the Americans back on the tarmac, nor for the MI6 officers.

He grabbed the medical bag off a small shelf just next to the cockpit doors and raced back to the injured woman. She was sitting up now, trying to reach into the closet.

Court knelt above her and began looking over her bloody wounds. "Both pilots are dead."

She looked out the door, and then back at him with confusion. "Then who the hell is taxiing the plane?"

"That would be me, I guess." He finished his examination of her injuries. "I know this hurts like hell, but all your fingers are still here and they're moving. Your wrist is broken, but you weren't hit through the nerves or the vein. You'll be fine."

She gazed down at the wounds with a detached expression on her face now, as if this were all happening to someone else.

Court pulled dressings from a sterile pouch in the medical kit and began wrapping the woman's wrist tightly. While doing this he said, "I need a sat phone and another weapon."

Her gaze rose from her shattered hands to the man kneeling over her. "Why?"

"I'm going after the prisoner."

"But . . . you're *alone*."

"That's kind of my thing, ma'am." Court tied off the bandages. "Weapons?"

"I've got more mags for the SIG in the go-bag in the closet."

"Anything else?"

She winced now, as if the pain was just beginning to reveal itself. "There's . . . there's an M320 in the go-bag with a bandolier full of high-explosive and tear gas rounds."

Court looked up to the closet. "A grenade launcher. Well, *that's* handy." He began bandaging her other hand.

Looking out the passenger door, he saw they were nearing the main buildings of the airfield. The G-IV rolled by a row of tied-down light aircraft, all bearing the markings of the Air Training Corps, a youth military group run by the Ministry of Defense to teach flying to the next generation of RAF pilots. This must have been some sort of flight training center for them, and immediately it gave Court an idea.

The woman said, "The go-bag has everything an officer needs. Surveillance gear, commo gear . . . *Shit*, my wrist hurts. Uh, medical equipment, surgical supplies."

Court again headed back to the cockpit to bring the wounded Gulfstream to a stop while the last few rounds of gunfire trailed off behind him.

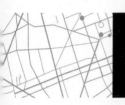

CHAPTER 3

The black van raced up the A41, heading northwest away from Ternhill airport. In the front passenger seat, a thirty-year-old man named Anthony Kent wiped sweat from his face while he conferred on the radio with his surviving teammates. The lav truck and the catering truck had been left on airport grounds, and the other men had climbed into a nondescript gray four-door. Kent had taken the opportunity to leave the van to check on those still alive, and now they'd resumed their escape out of the area.

Behind Kent in the back of the van, a black man with an unattended shoulder wound reached out with his good arm and ripped the hood off the prisoner.

With a British accent he said, "Name?"

The man seemed to be in a mild state of shock. He did not answer, only stared blindly for a moment.

"What's your *bloody* name, mate?"

The prisoner coughed. "Visser. Dirk Visser."

The wounded gunman pulled a sheet of paper from his pocket, pain evident on his face. On it was a color copy of a passport. He turned and shouted towards the front of the van. "It's him. He's not hurt."

From the front passenger seat Kent said, "Understood."

The man with the bloody hole in his shoulder put the hood back over the banker's head.

The other gunman in the back pulled off his ski mask to reveal a bushy red beard and a sweat-covered face. *"Fuckin'* hell! How many did we lose?"

Kent said, "Four men wounded, including Davy here. Six men dead."

"Six?" the driver shouted. *"Six?"*

Kent looked to the men with him in the van. "Martin's KIA. Saw him hit by a gunner firing out of the jet as it taxied off."

"Fuck!" the driver shouted now.

Kent added, "And Mickey took a bullet in the neck. Bled out right next to me."

All of the men in the van, the driver included, stared at Kent in disbelief now. The man on the floor in the back by the prisoner struggled to position a compress on his wound to stanch the bleeding. While doing so he said, "Martin and Mickey are both dead?"

The driver slammed his elbow hard into the door next to him. "Martin was in charge! Mickey was his second-in-command. The *fuck* we gonna do now?"

Davy said, "Kent here was number three. It's his bleedin' op." After a pause he said, *"Innit,* Kent?"

Kent realized only now that this was true. When Martin first met the men hired for tonight's job, he ranked them from one to fourteen, and Kent had been three, put in charge of the van and its crew.

Reluctantly he said, "Right. I'm in charge now." And then, *"Fuckin'* hell."

The driver said, "We were told it would be a quick hard hit and they'd all be put down fast."

Kent responded, "Yeah, well, we were just a mishmash of blokes thrown together for a hit. No bleedin' trainin'. No bleedin' coordination." He took a few calming breaths. "Still, we got the banker."

The driver shouted, "Who we now gotta protect shorthanded!"

Kent looked out the window a moment. "I'll call London. They'll send in another crew to help us out."

The driver said, "That's what I'm worried about. You know they'll send in some Russian gangsters. I don't wanna work with the bleedin' Russians."

"Dunno," Kent said, and then, "Probably." He slammed his own fist against the dashboard. *"Fuck!"* he screamed.

It was becoming clear to all in the van that Anthony Kent wasn't exactly leadership material.

After a moment he got control of himself and clicked his walkie-talkie, connecting him to the surviving team members in the other vehicle. "All right, lads, treat the wounded best you can. We're not goin' to the safe house. I have another place in mind. My turf, where I know the lay of the land. I can make a call and get us more blokes. It will be safer for us all there, but it's a two-and-a-half-hour drive, so keep eyes open for any surveillance."

"Two and a half bloody hours?" someone exclaimed into his radio.

Kent shouted back. "Those were government agents back there! Don't you think they're going to tear up the West Midlands lookin' for the shooters? We've got to put some distance between us and all that shite at that airport."

Kent pulled out his phone and made a call, and in minutes he had support on the way to meet him at his destination.

The ride in the van continued in tense silence.

. . .

After Court throttled back the Gulfstream and stepped on the brakes, he scrambled to the flight attendant, still on the floor in the cabin.

He helped her with her cell phone, then pulled the go-bag with the grenade launcher from the closet. His Ruger .22 was still there on the shelf, and he tossed it into the go-bag as well. He ran down the length of the cabin, hefted his own backpack, still on a chair in the back, and slung it over a shoulder.

The distant gunfire had trailed off to nothing.

Court nodded to the flight attendant as he stepped back over her, then leapt out of the jet and down onto the taxiway. The two backpacks made his movements uncoordinated and strained, but soon he began running over towards the flight line of tiny propeller aircraft. He recognized them all as Grob G 109s, an introductory power glider used as a simple trainer, and though he'd never flown one, he'd piloted more sophisticated piston engine planes and was confident enough in his abilities to get one of these tiny craft into the air.

He was just twenty yards from the closest plane when an electric cart came around from behind the row of aircraft and jolted to a stop in front of him.

A burly mechanic in his sixties sat behind the wheel. He shined a flash-light in Court's face. "What the hell is happening?"

Court said, "I'm going to need an aircraft. You have the keys to any of these?"

The man looked at Court as if he were insane. "I can't just give you a bloody glider, mate!"

Court started walking again towards the row of trainers. He said, "Trust me, you don't want me to take it from you."

The older man climbed out of his cart and pursued Court on foot. He grabbed him by the shoulder. Court turned back to him, sighed, then started to reach for the SIG, but he stopped himself. "A quarter mile down that taxiway there are a dozen or so good men dead and wounded. There are two more dead and an injured flight attendant in that G-Four. She needs your help, and *I* need to go after the assholes that did this to them. Can we work together on this?"

The older man looked out at the burning SUVs in the distance, to the Gulfstream, and then back at Court. "Who did this?"

"I don't have the first clue, sir, but I'm going to take one of these planes and go find out."

"I've been warned that when you CIA boys land your jets here I need to stay the hell away. I guess I now know why."

Court knew if the locals were aware the CIA was doing handoffs here, then it stood to reason that some bad actors could find out the same infor-mation.

It was quiet an instant, and then Court said, "The bad guys are getting away, and the good guys are bleeding to death."

A nod from the mechanic. "Tail number forty-three. Third from the end. I've got the keys on me, I just refueled it."

"Let's go." They climbed back in the cart and the older man drove.

As they approached the aircraft Court pointed to the northwest. "What road is that way that they might use to escape?"

"Loads of roads. Depends on where you're goin', doesn't it?"

"My guess is they want to get some distance fast, stay out of cities at this time of early morning because they won't be able to blend in like they would during the day."

"Ah, then they'll either be takin' the A41 northwest or the A525. With the A41 they'll be all the way to Liverpool in an hour. If they go east on the A525 it's quiet. Smaller towns to Stoke-on-Trent, and then they could do the A50. That would get them all the way past Nottingham, into the East Midlands."

Court realized he needed to get into the air as fast as possible to find the vehicles before they reached the decision point. Seconds later he climbed into the Grob G 109 self-launching motor glider, squeezing his backpacks in with him.

· · ·

At ten thirty p.m. at the CIA safe house in Great Falls, Virginia, the woman locked in the small and spartan room in the basement lay in bed on her back with her eyes closed.

Zoya had finished her debrief with Brewer just after eight, and then she was brought back to her room by William and locked inside for the night. She drank bottled water out of her mini fridge and watched a half hour of bad TV before stepping into the bathroom to change into sweatpants and a T-shirt.

She'd gone to bed just after that, and she'd remained still on her back the entire time, her eyes closed.

But she did not sleep. She thought about Court, a man she'd only known for days, a man she hadn't seen or heard from in months, but a man she was certain was the one person in this world she could trust. She missed him but knew there were two huge barriers preventing them from reuniting.

For one, she was locked up in this safe house till the CIA cleared her and put her to work for them. And secondly, Court was a freelance agent working from time to time at the behest of the CIA, and she was certain the two of them, both in the same line of dangerous work, would always be on the move, with security concerns that would mean they'd rarely, if ever, find themselves in the same place at the same time.

She forced herself to put the man she barely knew out of her mind and then she thought about her father. Another man she barely knew. He'd been gone fourteen years now, not that she'd seen all that much of him before that.

Her eyelids flitted as she thought about old memories of him, trying to reconcile the living man with the dead body in the photos she'd looked through tonight.

The memories were slow to return, but finally they did. She spent minutes lying there thinking about him, every little detail that remained in her mind over the years, like pulling an old photo album off the shelf.

. . .

William Fields reclined in his chair, his feet on his desk and his eyes on the wall of screens in front of him.

Or to be more precise, he monitored just one screen. Camera twelve, the device positioned in the upper corner of the holding room at the end of the hall.

He'd spent the last half hour watching Zoya lie in bed through the infrared vision built into the camera, her chest slowly rising and falling, her hands clasped in front of her while her five-foot-seven-inch frame lay still.

Watching Anthem nearly constantly through the night hours wasn't his mandate . . . He saw it rather as a perk of his job.

He had just taken a sip of Diet Coke when Zoya's eyes opened suddenly, glowing in the infrared. He'd thought her to be asleep, but now he watched with the can close to his mouth as she stared at the ceiling. He zoomed in on her face. Her eyes seemed to narrow, as if she were deep in thought.

She did not move for a minute more, and neither did the man studying her, but just as William started to take another sip of his soda she sat up, kicked her feet out of the covers, and rolled out of the twin bed.

She rose and walked towards the door to the room in her stocking feet. She pressed the call button on the wall by the overhead light switch, and instantly a tone sounded in the monitoring room. He watched her as she stood there, looking out the small viewing window at the well-lit hallway in front of her.

William kept his eyes on the screen as he tapped the microphone on his desk. "You rang?"

A hesitation, and then, "Yeah. Can you come here a second?"

Protocol dictated that the man in the monitoring room radio one of the men on the main floor to check on the guest, but William liked being alone down here, and he didn't think much of protocol anyway.

"Just a sec," he said, then grabbed his keys and headed out into the hallway.

. . .

Zoya peered through the window. Just across from her was a door to a small supply closet, and on her right were more holding rooms and then, down at the end of the hall, the monitoring room. The last door—this led to the stairs and the main house—was just beyond.

William appeared and began walking her way. He stopped on the other side of the window and looked in at her.

"What's the matter, hot stuff? Did you have a bad dream and wet the bed?"

Zoya glanced down nervously. "Uh . . . were you serious about the wine?"

William broke into a little grin. "I guess you're gonna have to call my bluff to find out."

She smiled coquettishly now. "I don't suppose one little drink is going to hurt anything."

He held a finger up. "The cameras first. Give me a sec." He started to walk away, then spun back. "And the vino. I'll grab the vino." William took off up the hall, not quite at a jog but close, and Zoya stepped back into the center of the room and took off her socks, rolling them into a ball and tossing them on the floor next to her. She pulled off her sweatshirt, revealing a white Lycra sports bra, then untied the drawstring in her sweatpants and pulled them down to the floor. Kicking them off, she stood there a moment, facing the door, taking slow, calming breaths, and waiting for her guard's return.

. . .

One hundred twenty yards away from the basement holding cell, a dozen men moved up a wooded hillside through a heavy downpour towards the lights of the building in the distance. When they arrived at the winding two-lane road in front of the big house, still much higher up the tree-covered slope, they broke up into four groups of three. One group stayed right there, taking up positions in the wet foliage, and the others moved off to the east and west.

They'd been ordered to close on the house from different directions to maximize their effectiveness.

All twelve men were *sicarios* of the Sinaloa cartel who lived and operated in Baltimore. Most of them had worked together before; most had killed in their duties, though none had ever done *anything* like this.

They'd been ordered by their leadership to hit this big house and to eliminate everyone inside.

The team had been warned that the location would be exceedingly well defended, but their leadership needn't have bothered with the caution. The *sicarios* assumed they were being sent in to assassinate members of a rival gang, so of course there would be men with guns ready for a fight.

The Sinaloans' weapons were individualized to their tastes; some carried AKs, some carried M4s, and one wielded a Scorpion EVO. Two of the men had venerable Uzis at their shoulders.

They all wore night vision goggles, most bought on Amazon or at Maryland sporting goods stores, and these helped them pick their way through the wooded five-acre property towards the main building.

When he was still fifty meters away from the gatehouse and the single sentry inside it, the team leader of the unit dropped into the wet leaves, flipped the bipod arms down on his M4, and lined up his four-power scope on the side of the lone man's head.

He triggered his radio headset. In Spanish he said, "In position at the south drive." In his ear he heard one of his men, this one sighting his M4 on a patrolling sentry in the back woods. "One target, west side. I've got him."

Another voice came over the radio. "North side, one subject. I'm on target."

When the eastern team reported no one outside in view, the team leader said, "*En tres . . . dos . . . uno.*"

An instant after the "*uno,*" the three men with targets fired suppressed, subsonic rounds from their weapons. Simultaneously the gate guard's head snapped to the side and he dropped down in the gatehouse while both sentries pitched forward into the wet leaves.

All twelve Mexicans rose in the woods and, still in teams of three approaching from each of the compass points, they began their assault on the safe house.

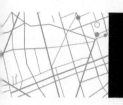

CHAPTER 4

Zoya stood all but naked in the center of the holding room as William peered through the glass with wide eyes. After taking a few seconds to recover, he unlocked the door. He fumbled with his keys upon entering, finally slipping them into a pocket with one hand while he held a pair of miniature bottles of red wine and two Solo cups with his other.

Zoya smiled, and William smiled back.

Entering the room he said, "Yeah," looking her up and down. Then, "*Hell* yeah." She looked down to the wine in his hand and he remembered it suddenly. "Right, vino. Gotta be honest, I've been holding on to these in my kit bag for the past month hoping you'd say yes."

As William took a bottle and a cup in each hand, Zoya Zakharova's smile remained, and she walked forward towards the man, her hand extended. She closed the distance between them and kept coming, reaching up and putting her hand behind his neck. William was clearly surprised by this; it looked as if she was going to kiss him.

But when her face was inches from his, her smile morphed into a look of primal intensity. Her legs sprang her up into the air and she swung her body around the security man, spinning high behind him by heaving herself up by the back of his muscular neck. Before William could react she had vaulted high onto his back, wrapped her legs around his midsection, and locked them together in front of his stomach, positioning her head above his.

The bottles and cups fell to the floor.

In a blur of motion Zoya reached forward around William's neck now, slamming her muscular right biceps into the carotid artery on the right side of his throat, and, bringing her forearm around to his left side, cutting off circulation through the artery there. With her left arm she pushed his head forward, into the pressure against both sides of his neck.

He tried to reach back and grab her, but she shifted herself left and right to avoid his grasp.

Spinning around with her riding on him, he grunted and reddened.

She leaned into his ear while he struggled. "It's just a blood choke, it won't hurt you."

The muscular thirty-year-old man slammed backwards into the wall, his hands pulling at the sinewy arms of the woman high on his back, desperate to relieve the pressure to his carotid arteries on both sides of his neck.

Zoya cried out in pain with the impact, but she did not release her vise grip.

A blood choke cuts off circulation through the carotid arteries to the carotid processes, which control the amount of blood in the brain. When the processes aren't supplied with new blood they assume that the body's blood pressure is too high, so they instantly flush the existing blood in the brain out.

An air choke, in contrast, involves closing off the windpipe long enough to remove the oxygenated air to the brain. This method is not only much slower, it's also the same method one uses to strangle someone and can easily cause damage to the windpipe and even death.

William rocked forward as his brain was starved of oxygen-rich blood, then shoved her back into the wall again. But this time he was weaker, and Zoya weathered this blow more easily.

"I'm sorry," she whispered again, and a second later William's eyelids drooped and shut, and he fell to the floor, unconscious.

Cutting off blood flow to the brain causes a victim to lose consciousness almost immediately, but the effects begin to reverse the instant the pressure is released on the arteries. Zoya knew this, so as soon as she let go of his neck, she rolled him onto his belly. Quickly she yanked the cuffs from his belt, pulled his thick arms behind his back, and shackled his wrists.

Already he was moving; his eyes opened and he shouted, "Bitch!"

Zoya grabbed her rolled-up socks and shoved them into his mouth, then whipped the drawstring out of her sweatpants and tied it tightly around the socks and the back of William's head.

She rolled him onto his back now; he stared up at her, his eyes filled with a mixture of rage and disbelief.

As he watched, Zoya put her jeans and sweatshirt on.

She pulled the keys out of his pocket but left his gun in its holster. Then she turned away without a word, stepped into her shoes by the door, and ran off up the hall after locking the holding room behind her.

. . .

Zoya used William's keys to get out of the basement, and on the first floor she moved slowly and silently through an unoccupied den. She heard voices in the large entryway of the building: the hollow footsteps of men walking slowly on a hardwood floor. She suspected they were just patrolling the interior of the house, making their rounds.

She turned away from the sounds and headed for the kitchen, off which she had seen a large laundry room with a door to the rear of the property.

She stepped up to the door moments later and looked out the window, checking to make sure there was no one guarding it on the outside. A paved walkway ran from the door and along the house; a grassy hill continued up into the woods, and the darkness, along with the rain, made it hard to see anything beyond the reach of the lighting on the walls of the building.

She started to open the door, preparing herself to get utterly soaked, but she stopped quickly and ducked down below the window when she registered movement in the woods at the edge of the landscaping lights.

What was that?

She jolted in surprise when gunfire kicked off behind her at the front door of the safe house. Zoya spun and looked through the kitchen. She heard men shouting, glass breaking. Dropping down to the floor, her back against the door to the outside, she knelt there, bewildered by what was happening.

These weren't security men after her. No, this was clearly an attack on the facility.

She made the determination to make a run for the trees, but just as she started to climb to her knees, the window above her head shattered in. She dropped even lower now, well out of view of anyone outside, looked up as glass rained down on her, and saw the butt of an AK-47 as it broke out the remainder of the window.

The door out of the laundry room was only four or five steps away, but she'd be visible to the man with the gun the entire time. When she saw a hand reach through the broken window, searching for the inside door latch right by her head, she realized the armed attacker had taken his hand off the trigger of his rifle, and he probably wouldn't be able to get a shot off at her if she moved quickly.

This was her only chance.

She scampered across the floor in a low crouch, slid through the door-way on her butt, and scrambled into the kitchen. She heard a shout behind her but couldn't understand what the man said.

Every single knife in the kitchen had been locked up in a cabinet, stan-dard protocol for the safe house. Zoya had William's keys, but there were at least a dozen on the chain, and she didn't have time to go through them, so she shot through the kitchen and into the den, fully expecting to find a portion of the CIA guard force there now, because the gunfire seemed so close.

But the den was empty. She now realized the shooting was coming from the foyer of the house, out of view, and between the bursts and shouts she heard radio calls and movement in the kitchen she'd just left behind.

A massive stone fireplace anchored one side of the den, just next to the hallway to the kitchen, and Zoya leapt up onto the hearth, then pulled herself onto the mantel, six feet up. She rose to a crouch, facing the door-way, just as a man with night vision goggles high on his head stepped into view, his AK-47 at his shoulder.

Behind him was a man wielding an Uzi, moving close behind his partner.

Zoya dropped down on the second man, taking him by the neck and using her momentum to wrench him backwards, sending them both to the floor. Before they'd even landed on the hardwood she had her hand around the trigger guard and grip of his Uzi. The man in full combat gear landed on top of the Russian woman, but she lifted his Uzi along with the arm holding it and squeezed his trigger finger down with her own.

This sent a burst into the legs of his partner in front of him, who spun and fell to his knees. Zoya pressed the man's trigger finger again, and the 9-millimeter rounds slammed into the wounded man's head, finishing him instantly.

She hip-thrusted the man on top of her to the side, yanking the Uzi from him as she did so. She pressed the muzzle against the man's ribs and fired a burst of three rounds into him at contact distance.

More shooting cracked off on the southern and eastern sides of the house. Zoya climbed to her feet and moved for the door off the den to the backyard, but she stopped herself, turned around, and ran for the stairs back down to the basement.

Downstairs Zoya raced into the security monitoring room and found the "master on" control for the basement's surveillance system. She activated it, then rushed up the hall, past the door to the utility closet, and to her room. She unlocked the door and found William still on his side, unable to sit up.

His eyes widened when he saw Zoya standing there with an Uzi in her hand, but she slung the weapon around on her back and grabbed him by the shoulders. She dragged him across the tiled floor and out into the hall; he shouted through the socks in his mouth the entire time, but she ignored his muffled curses. Pulling him into the dark utility closet, she heaved him around and behind the massive hot-water tank there. She sat him up, his back to the heater, and got close to his face.

"Listen to me. The safe house has been overrun. It's too late for you to help; all your mates are dead or dying. The attackers won't find you in here if you don't make any noise."

His eyes went even wider, and he tried to shout again.

"I'm saving your life, William."

She drew the HK pistol from his holster and rose, opened the door and, after checking to make sure the hallway was still empty, stepped out of the utility closet, locking the door behind her.

There was only a smattering of gunfire, still at the front of the house, when Zoya made her way back to the rear door off the walk-in pantry. This time she looked out carefully and saw a single man in black moving to the door to the den, fifty feet off her left shoulder. He held his carbine with one hand, and he seemed to be trying to raise someone on the radio with the other. She wondered if he was on the squad with the two men she'd killed in the den and was on his way to investigate their radio silence.

When he disappeared from view, she stepped outside and began sprinting through the heavy rain, down the hill for the tree line.

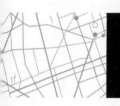

CHAPTER 5

Court leveled off at one thousand feet and began scanning for the highway that led northwest away from Ternhill. While he searched the night, he dialed his phone with his right hand, activated the speaker function, and put the device in his lap.

Just then he saw a black van, followed closely by a gray four-door sedan. He banked to position himself behind them, slowed the aircraft, and descended to two hundred feet for a better look.

Court felt through the go-bag he'd taken from the Gulfstream now. Inside he found just what he was looking for—a pair of binoculars. He brought them up to his eyes and scanned the highway below.

In seconds he was certain he was following the correct van, and the gray four-door behind it clearly seemed to be part of the operation, as well.

After several rings the call was answered. "Brewer." Her voice was clipped and businesslike; Court imagined she was still at work, though it would be nearly eleven p.m. in Virginia.

"It's Violator. The aircraft has been overrun on the ground at Ternhill. Multiple shooters . . . maybe a dozen or more. They took the detainee."

Brewer stammered a moment, then said, "What . . . *what* detainee?"

"The other Ops guys on my plane . . . it was a rendition team. They had a prisoner on board, they delivered him to MI6, and now they're dead or wounded on the ramp and the prisoner is in the back of a black van leaving the area with a gray four-door sedan in convoy."

Brewer was slow to understand. "Who are they?"

"How the *fuck* should I know? I was just along for the ride, I wasn't read into any of this shit."

Another pause. "Okay."

"So . . . do you want me to stay on him? We need this guy?"

Brewer said nothing.

"Hey!" Court shouted. "What do you want me to do?"

She hesitated a moment more, then said, "This isn't my op. I don't know anything about—"

"Make a decision!"

Brewer answered quickly. "Stay on the detainee."

"Roger that."

"I'll contact London station and inform them of the hit. I just—"

Court could hear another phone ringing in the background on the other end of the line.

"Violator, stand by."

Court looked down at the satellite phone incredulously. "You're actually putting me on *hold* right now?"

She did not answer him; instead he heard her speak into the other phone—"Brewer"—and then she muted her call with Court.

He scanned the highway ahead with his binos again. He knew the sun would be up soon, and he imagined that the two vehicles carrying the surviving gunmen and the CIA prisoner must be on their way to a safe house or layup position.

He flew a slow wide circle behind the killers, the little aircraft bouncing in the early-morning air.

"Take your time, Brewer," he mumbled to himself.

After five full minutes she came back on the line. Her voice was unsteady, confused. "Uh . . . Violator, I . . . I have to let you go. You keep after the prisoner, and we'll notify London station about Ternhill. They'll take care of it."

"You're telling me there's something *else* going on that's bigger than *this*?"

"Uh . . . I don't . . . Yes, actually. We're . . . we're having a situation here. I need to get back to you."

"You realize I'm the only link between you and the assholes who just killed a half dozen agency personnel, right?"

"You're a singleton. This is what you do. You'll . . . you'll be fine."

"What the fuck is hap—"

Court stopped talking when Brewer hung up. He stared down at the phone in his lap in disbelief.

Below him the two vehicles turned to a highway heading east, racing on as the first glow of morning appeared on the horizon.

. . .

David Mars sat at a walnut desk in the home office of his large Notting Hill home, facing three seventy-two-inch plasma televisions on the far wall of the room. CNN, RT, and the BBC all broadcast morning news here in London, and Mars normally kept an eye on all of them.

But he was especially tuned in today.

He'd just taken another call from Fox informing him that the team at Ternhill had recovered the CIA prisoner and were proceeding to the next waypoint on their journey. They'd lost several men in the process, but they'd managed to remove their dead from the scene.

Dirk Visser was a compromise to Mars and his organization. Mars had no reason to believe that the Dutch banker who worked in Luxembourg knew his identity, but he was the private banker of his traitor high within the ranks of the CIA. The American had been passing intelligence to Mars for the past several months, and Mars had been wiring money to Visser via shell companies. Somehow the CIA had managed to tie the account, and Visser, to the leaker, although Mars could not conceive of how this came to pass.

Visser had been snatched by the CIA, and Mars knew that the moment he talked, Mars's source in America could be identified. The American traitor did not know Mars's true identity, but he certainly knew enough tangential facts about him to pose a definite compromise.

And Mars was especially concerned about threats now. The most important operation of his life was just days away. Too much was on the line;

Mars would destroy cities if it meant keeping a lid on his operation for just one more week.

Initially, the man in Notting Hill just wanted to have Visser taken from the Americans and the British to be squeezed to find out if he'd said anything. But now the stakes had risen. The revelation from Barnacle, the American traitor, that a detainee at an Agency safe house in Virginia knew something about a particular name from the past increased the threat against Mars's operation exponentially, and Mars knew he had to do two things.

One, remove the compromise in Virginia, and this was under way right now.

And two, find out how and why the name Feodor Zakharov had been resurrected from some dead Agency file and printed for review by black ops personnel.

Could Visser have somehow passed Zakharov's name to his American captors?

Mars had to unravel this mystery quickly, so he ordered Fox to have the banker held until Fox himself could go and interrogate him to see what he knew.

This was all he could do about the problem in Britain for the time being.

One of his phones rang, and he snatched it up. In his exquisite British accent he said, "Yes?"

"It's Fox."

"What's going on?"

"It's not good, sir . . . They *did* wipe out the facility, and they confirm there was a detainee being held there, but she somehow managed to escape in the melee."

"*She?*"

"The clothing in the holding cell belonged to a woman."

"Did they find out who she was?"

"I needed a crew of cutthroats quickly, so I used a dozen men from the Sinaloa cartel. They knew how to kill, but sensitive sight exploitation is beyond their skill set. They suffered four KIAs, and four more injured, and as soon as they cleared the building of hostiles they exfiltrated the area."

"The bodies?"

"Left at the scene. They're *sicarios*, not Marines. No code with those guys. Still, don't worry about that. It will look like a cartel hit, no comebacks on us."

Mars kept looking at the televisions in front of him. Finally he said, "The woman who escaped. I trust you have people looking for her?"

"I do, sir. Not the Mexicans. I have others canvassing the area."

The man in London demanded hourly updates and then hung up the phone.

What is happening? he asked himself with welling panic. He racked his brain, trying to think of some woman who might have known something, *anything*, relevant to today about a long-buried GRU director.

Nothing came.

. . .

Suzanne Brewer arrived at the Great Falls safe house at one a.m., pulled up to the front gate, and saw a small group of FBI men and women standing around a body, shining lights in the nearby wet grass. She showed her credentials to a police officer controlling access to the property and was instructed to park her car next to a row of ambulances on the driveway. She walked the rest of the way up the hill to the house; the rain continued softly, and the air around her was cool and misty.

By the time she got to the front door she could see the devastation. The porch was pocked with bullet holes and the windows around it were completely shattered. She entered the building through the open door, passed more FBI whom she ignored, and found a group of CIA officials standing between a pair of bodies.

This safe house was run by CIA Support, the dead were Support security personnel, and no one in the building other than Brewer knew just who Anthem was and what the Agency was doing with her. This was part of a code-word operation so only those with the code word knew, and this meant Brewer and her boss, Deputy Director of Operations Matthew Hanley.

And no one else on Earth.

Hanley himself had created an initiative, code named Poison Apple, that handpicked former singleton operators to work as off-the-books contract agents for the CIA. There were only two agents in the program now, and Anthem was on her way to becoming the third, though she was former Russian intelligence, not American. The DDO had put Brewer in charge of Poison Apple and the agents who were part of it, despite the fact that he knew she didn't want to be anywhere near the operation at all.

Looking around at the dead, Brewer wished she'd managed to defy Hanley and be long gone from this assignment before this happened. She assumed Anthem was somehow involved with all this killing. Nothing else made sense. There was no hint of any Russian wet operations here in the United States, nor was there the slightest clue that the Russians knew Zakharova was in U.S. hands, and even if they did know, she couldn't imagine the Russians going to such lengths, even to recover a former operative.

The turning of Zoya Zakharova from a Russian spy to an American asset had been Brewer's job, the focus of her attention for roughly four months now. That she had been duped, that the woman about whom she'd passed glowing progress reports to the deputy director of Operations had killed CIA security men here at the safe house and then escaped into the United States, made her sick to her stomach.

She looked down at the men. "Ricketts and Jarvis," she said. She knew all the guards here because she had been to the property nearly every day since Anthem arrived.

Jay Seekins, the assistant to the deputy director of Operations, stood in the group in the foyer. He hadn't been here at the time of the attack, but he lived close by in Reston. One look at him told Brewer the man was obviously in a state of shock. Still, he had the wherewithal to eye her with disdain. He knew nothing about Poison Apple or Anthem, and it bothered him that an upstart from Programs and Plans was read in on the operation, while he, the number two man behind Matt Hanley, was not. "What the *fuck*, Suzanne?"

Brewer ignored the comment. "What have you learned?"

Seekins shook his head, his eyes all but unfixed. "Don't know yet. Man at the guard shack out front is dead. Two more dead in the woods. Two more dead here. We found a total of four bodies of unknowns, all armed, clearly hostiles killed in the raid."

Brewer didn't care about any of that. "What about the guest?" she asked.

"The guest is gone, along with William Fields, a security officer. He was on duty down in holding at the time of the attack. We found one more security officer on the second floor, Halperin. He's alive but wounded. He's been transported, but he might not make it."

"Have you watched the CCTV recordings yet?"

"Negative. Was paying my respects to the fallen up here before heading back down to monitoring to do that."

Suzanne had no desire to pray over dead security guards. "Let's go." Seekins followed reluctantly. They passed through the house, stepping through the two bodies of Americans inside the front door. Walking into the den, they encountered two more dead there. From their off-the-shelf night vision gear and other non-CIA-issued equipment, it was clear they were part of the attacking force.

Seekins said, "All the unknowns are Hispanic fighting-age males. I'd guess cartel *sicarios*. Sinaloa is the biggest group around the D.C. area, but that's all just preliminary guesswork on my part."

Brewer was barely listening. Instead she bent over one of the bodies. "Was this man disarmed after death?"

Seekins stepped up to her. "What do you mean?"

"His pistol is in his holster. I assume he was carrying a primary weapon."

"This is how we found him. Only the sidearm."

"The sidearm still on his hip, right? Can you imagine him walking around through this shootout with no weapon in his hand?"

"Would be strange. What are you saying?"

Suzanne's chest heaved inside her raincoat, and she blew out a sigh. "I'm saying we can assume the guest is now armed."

"Mother of God," Seekins muttered. "This just keeps getting worse."

They continued to the stairs to the basement.

• • •

In the monitoring room Brewer herself operated the playback on the computer while four other CIA execs stood around. The FBI men were upstairs and had the good sense to know the second the CIA showed up that they needed to secure the crime scene and wait for instructions.

She put all twelve camera feeds on the property up onto a sixty-five-inch plasma on the wall, displayed in a grid, backed up the master recording three hours, and then fast-forwarded the video, expecting to see the beginning of the attack.

But at ten forty-five p.m. on the holding room camera she saw Zoya climb out of her bed and go to the door. William appeared soon after, then left again.

Seconds later the three cameras in the basement flipped off. The others continued recording the house and the grounds outside.

Seekins said, "The security guy shut the cameras down in holding. The hell he do that for?"

On the cams outside and then at the front door Brewer watched the attack begin. It was a large group of men, closing from all directions, and they seemed competent enough, but perhaps not terribly well coordinated.

Anthem appeared in the kitchen and moved to the den. Brewer watched the Russian woman leap down from the mantel, disarm one of the hostiles with her bare hands, and then kill them both. The entire engagement took fewer than three seconds.

"Holy Christ," Seekins muttered. "What *is* she?"

Brewer said nothing; she just watched the Russian woman climb back up to her feet, heft the Uzi, and return to the basement.

Seconds later the camera feeds in the basement resumed. Fields was on his back in the cell, bound and struggling to sit up against the bed. What appeared to be a dark liquid was spilled all over the floor around him.

"What is all that?" Brewer asked as her eyes remained glued to the video.

Seekins said, "There are two airplane bottles of cheap cabernet broken on the floor of her room."

After no more than a few seconds, Anthem entered the holding cell from the hallway. She slung the Uzi over her right shoulder and grabbed the security man under his arms, began dragging him out of the room.

Switching their gaze to the hallway camera, Brewer and the men standing with her watched while Zoya opened the supply closet and pulled the big man inside. Seconds later she returned to the hallway, this time alone, and began running for the stairs.

A minute after this a pair of hooded men with M4 rifles entered the hallway. They bypassed the utility closet door and assaulted the holding room. Finding it empty, they rifled through the clothing they found there, then left the basement at a jog.

Brewer and Seekins exchanged a glance with each other, and then they ran out into the hall and down to the supply closet, just across from the holding cell. It took a few calls with their walkie-talkies to have a set of keys brought down, but once the door was finally opened, Brewer stepped in. At first she saw nothing, and then she moved around the water heater.

William Fields sat there with his hands behind his back, a gag in his mouth. He stared up at Brewer, and she gave him a look designed to let him know that it would have been better off for him if he'd been killed with the others.

She pushed the drawstring down to his neck and ripped the socks out of his mouth.

The first words out of Fields's mouth conveyed to Brewer that he knew exactly the situation he was in now.

"I want a lawyer."

She knelt down in front of him. "How about, instead, I give you a deep dark hole in some Supermax prison for the rest of your piece-of-shit life?" She waited a few beats, then added, "Unless you tell me what went down tonight. Every last damn bit of it."

A CIA officer leaned into the utility closet. "Ms. Brewer? Matt Hanley and Marty Wheeler are upstairs in the library. They'd like to speak with you."

She stood back up and looked to Seekins. "Keep Fields's cuffs on. I'll get everything he knows out of him after I talk to Hanley."

CHAPTER 6

Matt Hanley was the deputy director of Operations for CIA, having served in this role for only a few months. He was in his fifties, six-two and heavyset, with a broad face, shoulders like a defensive lineman, and blond hair heavily flecked with gray. Poison Apple had been his brainchild; he ran it outside normal operations channels and, just as had been the case with Fields, Brewer could see from Hanley's worried expression that he understood how much trouble *he* was in right now.

Marty Wheeler served as the assistant deputy director of Support for CIA. At fifty-one, he was short with a white shock of hair and a weatherbeaten face from his decades as a yachtsman on the Chesapeake Bay. Hanley outranked Wheeler, but the two men had been close friends since serving together as Green Berets nearly thirty years earlier.

Like Seekins, Wheeler didn't know anything about Zoya Zakharova specifically, only the fact that there was a guest at the house, and Brewer wondered how the hell she could talk to Hanley with him standing right here.

Hanley said, "What happened, Suzanne?"

"Coordinated attack on the facility, sir. Jay thinks the dead hostiles might be Mexicans."

A new man stormed into the room without knocking. Brewer looked up and then stood, unable to mask the surprise on her face. "Deputy Director Renfro."

"Suzanne," the man said. He turned to Hanley, who stood next to a built-in bookshelf. "Matt."

"Lucas," Hanley replied coolly, not even looking his way.

Brewer could tell by both men's greetings that they were no fans of each other.

Lucas Renfro was the deputy director of Support for CIA, Marty Wheeler's boss, and Hanley's equal in rank, if not stature, as the Operations end of the intelligence community was more highly regarded than the Support end. Renfro had been a CIA congressional staffer for years; everyone in Operations thought of the fifty-five-year-old as more of a politician and less of a career intelligence official, and Brewer was surprised to see him here in this slaughterhouse in the middle of a rainy night. Especially considering the fact that Wheeler, his capable second-in-command, was already on scene.

Lucas Renfro addressed Brewer exclusively. "I came as soon as I heard. What the hell happened?"

She filled him in on the attack but left out any information about the woman being held on the property.

She wasn't surprised that Renfro picked up on this.

"And the guest?"

Brewer glanced to Hanley for the all clear to answer, and when he gave her a frustrated nod, she said, "Escaped, sir. Not with the attackers. At present we don't know the guest's location."

He shook his head in frustration, then asked, "Why would the cartels hit this facility?"

"Must be a mistake on their part. Bad intel," Brewer said.

"Are you sure about that?" Renfro demanded.

Hanley sighed. "Well, Lucas, unless your Support Directorate has a sideline gig running drugs out of the safe house, then I can't imagine what interest the Sinaloans would have here." The big man took a breath, then added, "This just happened, and we just arrived. You'll have to give us a little time."

"While the guest runs free in the city? Am I safe to assume that you had the guest in secure holding for a reason? What's his threat level? Who is he?"

It was clear to Brewer that Renfro knew nothing about what was going on here at all, not even that the guest was female. Like Wheeler, he wasn't read in on Poison Apple, but obviously a lot of Support personnel knew that a woman was the lone guest at the Great Falls safe house.

But Brewer imagined Renfro wasn't one to sully himself by talking directly to his facility security people.

When she didn't answer his question, he repeated himself. "Who is he?"

She glanced again to Hanley, and Hanley said, "We can't get into that."

"For God's sake!"

Hanley changed the subject. "You've heard about the flight at Ternhill?"

"Only just. You lost some men, I hear."

Hanley nodded. "Doug Spano was killed."

"Shit." Then Renfro added, "You've got a leak in Ops."

"Bullshit!" Hanley replied, hardening up again in an instant. "You've got a leak in Support! You are in charge of Transpo *and* Facilities, we've had three aircraft compromised in the past four months, and now we've had a domestic facility overrun!"

"All four incidents involved *your* operations, Matt." Renfro didn't rise to Hanley's level of vitriol. "Besides, the inspector general ran an inquiry into Support after the first two aircraft incidents and found nothing. If I were you, I'd look into your off-book activities, because the IG isn't able to do so. *That's* where you'll find your leak."

Hanley fumed a moment, then said, "Lucas, Marty . . . can you excuse us? Suzanne and I need to talk."

Renfro didn't look happy, but he motioned to his subordinate and they both stepped out of the library.

When they were gone Brewer asked, "Why are they here?"

Hanley sat down at the table in the middle of the library, then looked around. "Cams? Mics?"

Brewer fought an eye roll as she sat across from him. *Of course* she had no recording devices running while they were talking. "All off."

Hanley said, "You know why. This facility is the domain of Support. They aren't read in on Anthem, or Poison Apple, but they are responsible for this place, and this place got wiped out. Hell, FBI is here, and they don't know what the hell is going on either."

Brewer said, "It will make finding Anthem a lot harder if Support is nosing around."

"I'll talk to Wheeler, he'll back off. Renfro, on the other hand, is always a pain in the ass. If he learns anything about Poison Apple then he could make a *lot* of trouble for us."

"Agreed."

Hanley changed gears. "When you called you said Violator was in pursuit of the prisoner in the UK. Any more word?"

"No, sir. He hasn't called back, and I've been too busy here to reach out to him."

"These two situations *can't* be related, can they?" he asked.

"How can I answer that, Matt? I don't even know who the prisoner on the Gulfstream was."

"A banker. We picked him up in Luxembourg yesterday. He managed a private account that wired a total of three hundred thousand dollars' worth of Bitcoin in three payments to a computer terminal at the Agency. All three payments coincide with the three compromises to Agency aircraft over the past few months."

"So you are saying this banker knows the identity of whoever is passing information about Support activities to everyone who has targeted the three Agency flights before tonight, and . . . and whoever the hell snatched the prisoner tonight? He facilitated payments directly to the traitor?"

"It looks as straightforward as that, yes."

"Why would the traitor use a computer here at Langley?"

Hanley replied, "There is only one reason. He or she is trying to frame someone else."

"So you are saying you know whose computer received the Bitcoin?"

"I do, but I'm not going to tell you, because I am certain this person is innocent."

"But—"

"The person implicated is innocent, Suzanne. We have to find the real culprit. End of story," Hanley said flatly.

Brewer didn't press. Instead she said, "If this leak came from the Agency, why were we handing the witness over to MI6?"

"The director ordered me to deliver him to the Brits because the nominating entity of the private account was in the name of a business registered in London. He was trying to keep this as aboveboard as possible in case we had to turn this all over to the FBI for a criminal prosecution of the Agency employee, but . . ."

His voice trailed off.

"But what?"

"I asked you to recall Court Gentry to the States because I didn't want to see the traitor arrested."

Brewer understood slowly. "You were . . . you were going to task Violator with *deleting* an Agency employee?"

"He'd have done it, too." He shrugged his big shoulders. "But now he has to find the banker and get him away from the men who took him, because the banker's our only link to the traitor."

"Sir . . ." Brewer drummed her fingers on the table. She looked across to Hanley, seated where Anthem had sat six hours earlier. "I'm just going to say it. Poison Apple is a ticking time bomb. Both assets in the program now, Violator especially . . . are highly unstable. Completely untethered. Anthem isn't even an official member, but she was weeks away, and already she detonates."

Hanley leaned forward in his chair and put his thick arms on the table. "I know you don't like your assignment, Suzanne. I am aware you'd much rather be on the seventh floor making executive decisions, or on Capitol Hill influencing legislation, or at some embassy as chief of station. Not here with me, handling hard assets on the sharp end of the spear. I know you don't believe the risks in these initiatives are worth the potential reward. But you're here for a reason. My confidence in you to put a lid on all this remains, even though you have reservations about the sub rosa project I've put you in charge of. I'm *not* reassigning you, so get that out of your head. You're stuck with me for now, because you're the right person to run Poison Apple." He added, "You might just want to consider making the best of it."

She looked down at the table. "Yes, sir."

"Now," Hanley said. "We have to send a description of Zoya out to local law enforcement. But do *not* release a photo."

"Why no photo?"

"I'm not ready to burn Anthem just yet. We don't know what happened."

Brewer didn't like it. If she saw Anthem on the street on her way home to her house this morning, her first inclination would be to run her over and end this debacle. But she said, "I'll give the description to FBI. They'll get it to local authorities. We'll find her."

Hanley nodded. "That's not all we need to do. We need to find the mole."

"That's not Operations's role."

"True. Not officially. But Operations is paying the price for a leak in the building. We had two ops burned hard tonight. Add that to the list of compromises over the past few months. First thing tomorrow we're going to come up with a new strategy to figure out who is wrecking these Agency operations."

"But . . . how?"

"We do it off book. There are a finite number of people who've had access to all the intelligence that has been leaked. We ID all of them, and then go to work on each one."

"Waterboarding?" Brewer joked.

But Matt Hanley did not smile. "If it comes to that," he said, and Suzanne Brewer silently cursed the day Hanley had manipulated her into working for him.

CHAPTER 7

FOUR YEARS EARLIER

The sail of the submarine broke the black surface of the Sea of Japan twenty-five minutes behind schedule. It was after four a.m. now, which meant the infiltration would have to be expedited if it was to be completed under cover of darkness.

Japanese shore defense radar operators saw no trace of the small sail on their screens. North Korea's Yono-class miniature subs were only twenty meters long, and they were exceedingly stealthy, which was exactly the reason this vessel had been chosen, even though it was designed for coastal operations and not the water it had just crossed.

The Yono was armed with torpedoes and capable of delivering up to six special forces troops or other personnel on intelligence missions, but there were drawbacks to the vessel. Submerged, the sub only made an average of 10 kilometers an hour, which meant the 445 kilometers of open ocean between the North Korean port of Wonsan and this stretch of Japanese coastline had taken two full days of arduous travel.

This submarine and its crew of four had been given the mission of delivering three passengers to the Japanese mainland, and as it now bobbed in the water five kilometers from shore, four dark silhouettes climbed out of the sail hatch and onto the deck. One man quickly inflated a small black boat with a compressor, an outboard motor appeared from the sail and was placed at the stern of the boat, and in seconds the four were churning through the night towards twinkling lights in the distance.

They carried no weapons; in fact, they brought with them nothing more than the clothes on their backs.

As they approached the sandy beach they saw a flash of light, and the sailor piloting the boat adjusted his course to point the bow at the signal.

This was Ishikawa Prefecture, in the center of the mainland on Japan's west coast, and one of the closest points to North Korean waters. There were cities and towns all over this part of the mainland, but this small stretch was particularly rural, known for white sandy beaches and forests of black pine trees dotted with campgrounds popular with weekenders from as far away as Osaka and Tokyo.

Forty minutes after setting out from the submarine, three of the four climbed out of the raft and into the low water, then began walking through the gentle surf.

They saw movement in front of them: three other dark silhouettes stepping off the sand and into the water. The trio of new arrivals from the submarine continued walking, and soon all six converged in ankle-high seafoam. They bowed to one another without speaking or breaking stride, and then the three from the shore pushed on towards the dinghy and the three from the submarine headed ashore.

The dinghy returned to the submarine while the new arrivals walked to a road ahead, barely visible as thick clouds drifted in front of the fingernail moon above.

Two of the three were men, sent on this mission as a small but well-trained protection detail for the woman between them. Kim Dong-Woo and Nam Jun-Ho were security officers of the Reconnaissance General Bureau, the intelligence directorate of North Korea, and in addition to speaking English fluently, they also had nearly three decades of military and intelligence experience between them.

The woman was Won Jang-Mi, and she was the oldest in the group at thirty-six. This mission was all about her, and that meant Kim and Nam's job was to keep her alive, even take a bullet for her if it came to it, because Won Jang-Mi was a leading North Korean scientist, and she was a well-trained intelligence asset, which meant she was precious to the government of the DPRK.

Won had served as a deputy department head at the Pyongyang Biological Technology Research Institute, a dual-use organization that claimed to develop pesticides and herbicides for the North Korean agricultural community but in truth served as the center of the Hermit Kingdom's robust chemical and biological weapons program.

Her specialty was pneumonic plague and hemorrhagic fever, and tonight was the beginning of the mission North Korean intelligence had been grooming her for for seven years when they started teaching her Western languages and South Korean customs, while at the same time fortifying her programming in the divine supremacy of the Dear Leader of North Korea and the assuredness that the West was scheming to destroy her nation.

Won was a true believer; she planned on following all orders from North Korean intelligence to the letter, and she was certain her actions would help save her tiny nation from the threats it faced from the rest of the world.

Minutes after stepping onto dry land the three moved through the Oshima Beach Resort, a simple campground and cabin complex in the trees, within sight of the coast. There were a few tents set up, presumably with campers sleeping inside, but the three of them walked directly to cabin number four.

Upon entering they saw luggage left for all three of them, and inside the roll-aboards, the briefcases, and the large purse, they found all the clothing, accessories, papers, computers, and phones they would need to turn themselves into three innocuous-looking South Korean business executives. Three sets of passports, driver's licenses, and credit cards lay on a bed, alongside three more sets of clothing, one for each of the infiltrators.

The IDs and other documentation belonged to the three who just climbed aboard the dinghy. These were sleeper agents who'd been planted years ago in South Korea to establish their legends, and each possessed a passable resemblance to Won, Nam, and Kim.

There were three envelopes on the table in the kitchenette. Inside each one was a plane ticket from Osaka to Athens, along with a visa to allow entrance to Greece.

Won, Kim, and Nam changed, then packed their own clothes in a laundry bag left for them, and within twenty minutes of their arrival they headed back outside.

Parked next to the cabin was a Kia Rio, a four-door South Korean car with a hatchback. The keys were behind the fuel door cover, left there, like all the other items at the cabin, by the three North Korean sleeper agents who were now on their way home. They put their luggage and the laundry bag in the vehicle, Nam took the wheel, and Kim climbed into the front passenger seat after making sure Won Jang-Mi was comfortable in the back.

At five forty-five in the morning they began driving south towards Osaka. Along the way they tossed the laundry bag over a bridge and into a swiftly moving river.

. . .

They parked the car at Itami International Airport, just north of the city center, brought their luggage through security, had their documents thoroughly checked by customs and immigration, and by eleven a.m. were slipping into their seats in the main cabin.

Greece was not their destination but rather a way station; from here they made their way to Tehran, Iran. Won spent the next six months working in the biological warfare research field, exchanging her expertise with the top scientists in the Islamic Republic and in turn learning from them. She concentrated her research on coming up with new and potent ways to alter plague spores to increase their lethality, and to weaponize the diseases via aerosol to maximize their impact.

From there she and her protectors moved to Syria, again studying the aerosol distribution of bacteria and viruses, although the Syrians themselves concentrated their efforts on the chemical agent sarin. Still, the Syrians had become experts at spreading the chemicals quickly and efficiently via bombs and rockets for use in their brutal civil war, and Won received "on the ground" training in the techniques and technology.

After Syria she was ordered by her control officer in North Korea to go to Russia. Pyongyang and Moscow had worked out a joint deal that saw her taking a position at the 33rd Central Research and Testing Institute, a closed military research laboratory in southwestern Russia near the Volga River.

Here she worked perfecting her craft and honing her skills in maximizing the effect of various nerve, blister, choking, and blood agents. The Russian doctors, scientists, and technical experts knew what they were doing, and she learned a lot in a short time.

Another focus of her work was on counterbiosecurity. It was her job to learn what detection and prevention means the nations of the West had in place to stop or lessen the effects of a bioterror weapon. The Russians had studied the same thing since the Cold War, and although they didn't have the infrastructure in place any longer to develop and produce large quantities of bioweapons, they did have some knowledge about how the West would, and would not, be able to combat an attack.

The Russians also had the strains of all the bacteria stored for testing, and their safety measures were far superior to what Won had worked with in North Korea.

She made valuable contacts in this secret industry both in Russia and in other nations. There were international treaties against biological weapons, of course, but Russia, Iran, Syria, and, to a lesser extent, Cuba all had programs, and they all had scientists willing to work with a North Korean expert of Won's caliber.

She saw nothing wrong with her work from any moral standpoint. The United States, Canada, the United Kingdom, and many other Western nations all did research on bioweapons of different types, so why shouldn't North Korea be allowed the same rights?

Plus, she had grown up hearing stories of the Korean War, American soldiers eating North Korean children, and the constant imminent threat of American nuclear attack.

The West was evil, pure and simple. Every fiber of her being believed this.

She had been sent by her nation on this mission to learn everything she could to make weapons of mass destruction out of the biological strains, and she had been indoctrinated for her entire lifetime in the task to ensure that she would not falter on her trip to the West.

Won had been given no operational mission by Pyongyang beyond studying her field of expertise abroad, so that she could return with this knowledge to North Korea. But with each passing year of her training she had become more and more convinced that the work she was doing would never be implemented in the field, and she felt it was utterly crucial that North Korea attack the West with a first-strike bio attack, both to damage her nation's enemies and to show the world her own personal skill in her work.

Her greatest fear was that someday she would be recalled, and then she would go home and return to her life at the laboratory, never given the chance to act against her enemies.

The Russians benefited from her knowledge as much as she benefited from theirs, and they recognized in her, after months of subtle vetting, a potential that they could put to use. Their foreign intelligence service, the SVR, was notified about the potential foreign asset and her skill set, and though they had no plans on the horizon to infect anyone with a biological weapon, they kept tabs on her.

CHAPTER 8

PRESENT DAY

Court flew high and far behind the two-vehicle caravan, following it to the east into the sunrise along the A50, staying well out of sight to avoid any detection.

The vehicles passed to the south of Nottingham just after eight a.m., and around eight thirty they pulled off the highway and onto a two-lane road that headed due south. After a few minutes they entered a dense wood in the center of flat farmland, and Court circled high above, certain he'd see them exit soon after.

But the van and the sedan did not reappear.

There was a large collection of redbrick buildings at the southern edge of the forest, and at first he saw no evidence that anyone was around at all. The complex appeared abandoned, but it was impossible to know for sure from one thousand feet.

Shortly before banking back to the north, though, he noticed two vehicles parked next to the main building on the dilapidated property. He couldn't make them out other than the fact that they were sedans, but he wondered if whoever had arrived in those cars could be part of all this.

The tiny aircraft Court flew was simple and slow, but it did have one advantage. He could put it down quickly and quietly, and he could land it pretty much anywhere. He found a straight stretch of road that ran along the far side of a wheat field from a farmhouse and barn; he could see no evidence of anyone close by, so he cut the engine and descended, guiding the glider to a bouncy but serviceable landing just after nine a.m. Once safely stopped, he climbed out and rolled the plane onto an adjacent farm track, the wings pressing through the wheat.

It was a breezy and cool morning; dust and chaff surrounded him in a brown cloud as he hoisted his two backpacks onto his shoulders.

He pushed through the wheat surrounding the farmhouse and came out of the crops just behind the barn. A small and dirty M2R pit bike sat unlocked near the rear door. Court thought it probably belonged to a kid; the engine was only 90cc. It was caked with hard dirt, and the tires looked like they were about to go, but it had over a quarter tank of gas in it and would help him quickly close the mile distance between himself and the area where the van disappeared.

He felt a little bad about taking some kid's bike, but not *that* bad. The men who'd slaughtered a large group of U.S. and British intelligence officers this morning were close by, and Court would do *anything* in his power to bring them down.

He walked the bike into a narrow irrigation track through the wheat field, kept going until he was almost on the other side, and then fired it up. It turned over roughly, but in seconds he opened the throttle and raced in the direction of the woods he saw on the northern side of the building complex he'd spied from the air.

Once on a path in the thick woods he shut down the bike, then climbed off and pushed it along. As he did this he put his Bluetooth earpiece in and dialed Brewer's number. Court found it unfathomable that she hadn't been back in touch with him yet, and he was glad he wasn't involved in whatever it was that had her so occupied, because it must have been one hell of a clusterfuck for her to put the slaying of several CIA officers on the back burner.

He found himself a little surprised when she answered, as it was three a.m. on the east coast of the U.S.

"Brewer."

Court spoke softly, though he was hundreds of yards from the far edge of the woods. "It's me. You get a handle on your situation?"

"Everything is under control," she replied flatly.

"You sure?"

"Was just about to call you for a sitrep."

"Sitrep to follow. But first . . . what's the tally at Ternhill?"

Brewer said, "I just spoke with London station. We lost three officers and two pilots and suffered four serious injuries. MI6 didn't fare any better. Three dead, three injured. It was a massacre."

"You *do* remember I was there, right?"

She replied, "Yes, Violator, I do. Now, you."

Court said, "I'm in the East Midlands now, I know that much. Haven't stopped to check exactly where yet. The subjects holding the prisoner are here, for now, at least. I'm heading closer to pinpoint them."

"Very good."

"Send me a team and we can end this."

Brewer said nothing.

"No?"

"Unfortunately, that's not going to happen."

Court felt anger welling in the pit of his stomach. "Why the hell not?"

"You're in the UK. *They* have jurisdiction."

"Then send me some Brits. They can jurisdiction the shit out of these fuckers once I get our prisoner back."

Again she made no reply.

"Brewer?"

"Listen. We don't know who told these people that there was a CIA flight landing at Ternhill delivering this prisoner. If it was someone on our side, then you're better off without anyone else at the Agency knowing where you are and what you're doing. But if the compromise came from MI6, well, we don't want to run the chance we alert any opposition by informing them."

"What *aren't* you telling me?"

She sighed, audibly. "The Brits are convinced they have a mole, same as us. Perhaps more than one."

"You've got to be kidding."

"They have let us know that they are working to ferret out their leaker, but we have to assume they are as exposed as we are."

Court continued pushing the little pit bike through the trees. "Why did the attackers go to the trouble to do this at the airport? If they waited until the MI6 team was on the road with the prisoner it would have been much simpler for them, and they would have faced half the opposition."

Brewer said, "I've been wondering the same thing. Perhaps they were missing some piece of intel that forced them to hit the plane to make certain they achieved their mission objectives."

"Like they didn't know for sure if the prisoner was being dropped off or if other people were being picked up," Court said.

"Maybe," allowed Brewer. "That might make finding out who did this a little easier on our end. Anyone involved in the code-word op itself would know it was a drop-off. But anyone in Support would only know that the plane was scheduled to pick a group up in Luxembourg and make a scheduled stop in the UK before proceeding to the U.S."

Court said, "And that would make it less likely the compromise came from the British."

"Possibly."

"What do you mean, *possibly*?" Court said. "Brewer, this is *our* leak, not theirs. Do I need to remind you that this isn't the first time an Agency transport has been compromised recently?"

That was true. Just a few months earlier Gentry himself had been on a flight to Hong Kong that Chinese intelligence clearly identified as CIA. Brewer had been involved in that compromised operation, as well.

He noticed Brewer's hesitation in admitting it, but finally she responded. "True. And your case isn't the only one. This has happened other times."

"That's terrific. Here's a thought. How about you stop putting me on Agency aircraft?"

"Fair enough. Actually, the reason I was recalling you to the U.S. was to help us in our hunt for the traitor."

Court instantly knew what this meant. He wasn't an investigator, and he wouldn't be brought into the States to run a surveillance operation. No, he was an assassin. If Brewer was bringing him in, she was bringing him in to kill an Agency employee . . . in the United States.

"Has the person been identified?"

"Not yet. Hanley wanted you here and ready."

"Roger. Well, as soon as we get this end taken care of, I'll happily go after the asshole responsible for all this. Is the compromise limited to aircraft? That would definitely put the traitor somewhere in Transpo."

Again, another pause. Court was getting used to Brewer's reticence about giving him information. Finally she said, "It is not limited to aircraft, unfortunately. It seems to be slightly more broad."

He didn't know what the hell that meant, but he *did* know he wasn't going to get anything more out of Brewer on the subject.

"I need to know who this prisoner I'm going after is."

"He's a Dutch banker, working in Luxembourg."

"Since when do we perform extraordinary renditions on Dutch bankers?"

"He has information about the owner of a private account. We think that owner is the CIA employee who has been passing intelligence to bad actors." She added, "He is the only person we've identified who possibly knows who the traitor is."

"This banker has at least a half dozen armed men around him. What do you expect me to do?"

"Your best, Violator."

"Meaning?"

"Meaning we still don't know for sure the British aren't involved in this exposure over there. Until we *do* know for sure, you're on your own."

"Such a blast to be working with you again," Court said, and then he disconnected the call.

Court thought, and perhaps not for the first time, that sometimes it almost seemed like Brewer *wanted* him to die.

• • •

I wish he would hurry up and die, Brewer thought.

She hung up the phone on her end and put her head in her hands. She wanted out of this. She couldn't blow the lid on Poison Apple; she was too inexorably tied to it, thanks to Hanley's maneuvering and blackmail, to survive the inevitable fallout should the media learn about the program. But if the program failed, or perhaps even if one of the assets failed spectacularly, then Hanley would have little recourse but to shut Poison Apple down.

If Violator died, Hanley would abandon Poison Apple; she was certain.

Brewer would do what she could to limit support for the asset and cover her ass with good handling when she saw no other way to avoid it, but she would always have her eyes out for a time when she could make this whole problem go away with some sort of incident in the field that ended Hanley's dangerous program.

But Violator simply refused to play by her rules. He was quite possibly the best singleton asset in the world, and she chalked it up to her bad luck that he was so good and she wanted him to fail so bad.

But he was a man not afraid to risk it all, and she was a woman not afraid to throw him into peril, time and again, in hopes that someday her luck would change.

And for that to happen, all she needed was for *his* luck to change.

. . .

Court saw the silhouette of vehicles ahead of him, parked together off a dirt road under a thick canopy of fir trees. He recognized them as the van and the sedan he'd been tailing across the Midlands, so he drew the SIG pistol he'd taken from the Agency flight attendant and approached warily. Behind the van and the car he saw bloody gauze and sterile pads lying in the pine needles on the ground as if they'd fallen out of the backs of the vehicles as men climbed out.

Court didn't know if the prisoner had been hit in the melee, but he hoped like hell all the blood meant some of the men involved who'd survived the airport would be unable to fight here if it came down to it.

He looked inside the sedan and found it empty other than some blood smeared on the wall and flooring. But when he opened the back of the van he found six dead bodies lying in a heap.

He quickly picked through them for a moment looking for identification, weapons, or cell phones, but they had been stripped of everything save for the clothes on their backs.

It occurred to Court this might explain why no one came out of the woods while Court circled above. Stripping a half dozen dead and dealing with wounded surely would have taken them some time.

He followed a sporadic blood trail to the south one hundred yards, to within sight of the edge of the trees. Leaving the bike there, he crawled forward. Directly in front of him he saw a small gravel lane, and in front of it a massive redbrick monstrosity that looked like something from the nineteenth century.

Several smaller buildings of the same red brick were all around.

Scanning both the main structure and the outbuildings, Court determined everything in the area had been abandoned for some time. He thought the main building was probably an old hospital; half the windows were boarded up and the other half fully broken out. These he began peering into, and soon he saw a shadow of movement in an open window on the top floor. Further inspection revealed a man just inside, using the darkness of the room to keep himself undetected from the outside, although Court's trained sniper's eye managed to pick him up.

In the darkness of the room he couldn't tell much about the man, but he certainly seemed to be a sentry watching to the north. A scan of the other run-down redbrick buildings in the area revealed no more activity, so he returned his focus to the structure that looked like a hospital.

Soon he saw a second man step out of a doorway and stand there, looking out across the open land to the trees. He was fit, black, with a bloody dressing on his shoulder, and he wore a pistol in a drop leg holster.

Definitely the right place, Court thought. He reached into the go-bag for his binoculars, and as he did so his hand ran across the M320 grenade launcher. For a moment he fantasized about dropping a few rounds of "forty mike-mike" into the hideout of this group of killers, but he knew he had to make an effort to recover the prisoner alive.

He pulled out his binos and settled in, quickly detecting two more men walking around the western side of the hospital towards a large garage.

Shit, he said to himself. If there were four men in sight, that likely meant there were a lot more he couldn't see.

He backed into the woods and opened the go-bag. Inside he found prepackaged food and water. He broke both open while looking through the other items. He chewed on a protein bar and drank water from a bottle while he pulled out climbing ropes, which he put to the side, along with fire-starting materials and water purification equipment.

He found a smartphone in a waterproof case. He knew it would be loaded with all manner of communications and tracking software, as well as encryption and decryption applications. His own phone had a few commercial apps for clandestine work, but this one would be far superior.

The good thing about his own phone, however, was that it was virtually untrackable. In contrast, with this device from CIA, he knew that as soon as he turned it on the Agency would know where he was, something that, for most of the past five years, would have utterly terrified him. Before his recent détente with Langley he'd lived off grid as a burned asset, targeted by the very organization he now served. His truce with the Agency was only a few months old, and in that time he'd caught himself more than once missing the simplicity of working alone, an assassin for hire, only taking contracts that he believed served the greater good.

Now his life had returned to taking orders, need-to-know-only briefs, and impenetrable ambiguity.

He put his concerns out of his mind and turned on the phone, then slipped it into his cargo pants, along with a cable and a spare battery.

He found a headlamp, which he left in the bag, along with another bottle of water. He then pulled out a tiny case that contained a pair of earplugs. They were electronic noise reduction devices, but they also enhanced softer sounds to twelve times their normal volume. He immediately turned them on and placed them in his ears. The ambient noises around him were cacophonous; birds, the strong breeze, a distant train approaching along the track behind him.

He tapped the earplugs and the enhancement function turned off, and then he slipped them back in their case and into his pocket.

He loaded the M320 with a high-explosive round, slipped it into the go-bag, and then threw in his suppressed pistol, the toolbox, the binoculars, two extra magazines for the SIG, and the climbing rope. He left everything else, including his own backpack and the bike, in the woods and began crawling towards the east.

CHAPTER 9

Former Russian spy Zoya Zakharova hadn't hitchhiked in the United States since her college days in California, but after hiding in the woods and then walking aimlessly through backyards for nearly two hours, at four a.m. she managed to thumb down a Honda Civic driven by a middle-aged woman on her way to her job at a call center in D.C. Zoya fed her a story in flawless and unaccented English, a tall tale about her boyfriend kicking her out of his house with only her clothes and shoes, forcing her to leave her purse and phone behind and walk home to her apartment in D.C.

The woman offered to give her a ride home and Zoya directed her to an apartment building just a few blocks from Union Station.

As soon as the woman drove away, Zoya headed for the station, but she did not enter. Knowing cameras would be prevalent there, she found a place to sit on a bench next to the Christopher Columbus Memorial Fountain that was shielded from view behind it by a concrete wall.

She focused all her attention on the front of the station.

At this hour there was only a trickle of commuters leaving the station, and Zoya eyed them all. She also noticed a strong police presence in the area, mostly patrol cars. She wondered if they might have been looking for her, but her tradecraft kept her away from both law enforcement and any suspicious unmarked vehicles that might be from CIA or FBI.

It took her almost a half hour to find a target. A bearded man in an expensive leather jacket came out of the station and began walking down the street, heading towards Louisiana Avenue. Zoya rose to her feet and followed, lagging just behind him while maintaining good situational awareness.

The man spoke on his cell phone and pulled a black leather Tumi roll-aboard behind him. He stopped at a street corner with several people waiting there in the dark for the signal to change, and Zoya moved next to him.

She had trained in picking pockets ever since she was a little girl, so she knew what she was doing. First, she'd profiled him as a man carrying cash, and she'd already identified the location of his large folding wallet, in his inside right coat pocket. In addition, the man was focused on his phone call, making him an easier mark.

At the corner he kept talking, his eyes on the crossing sign while he waited there.

Attention steers perception, Zoya had been trained. The man wasn't thinking about the wallet inside his jacket, nor the woman standing next to him. She nonchalantly moved in front of him, squeezing tight through the group of people standing there, from his right to his left, and while she brushed close in the small crowd her left hand rose, snaked inside his jacket, raised the wallet from the pocket, and smoothly lowered it out of his jacket and down to her waist.

She never even slowed down.

A block and a half away she checked her loot. As she expected, the wealthy-looking man in the leather jacket was a fan of cash. There were three crisp hundred-dollar bills, a small fold of twenties, and a few fives. Just over $400 in all.

Good, she thought. This was enough to get her moving.

. . .

The eastbound turning lane off Route 123 into CIA headquarters was infamous. Here, on January 25, 1993, a Pakistani national in the United States on forged papers dumped ten rounds from his AK-47 into cars waiting to turn into the agency, killing two CIA employees and injuring three more.

Suzanne Brewer wasn't thinking about the turn lane's history now, even though she sat in the middle of it in her Infiniti sedan, right on top of where the attack took place. She knew all about the murders, for sure, although she'd been in high school when it happened. As a CIA officer she had spent much of her career protecting the Agency from threats and had exhaustively studied the 1993 attack, all the way up to the 1997 arrest in Pakistan of Mir Qazi and his 2002 lethal injection for his act.

Right now Brewer had other, more contemporary events on her mind. With two attacks on personnel in the last eight hours, the former facility threat expert wanted answers, but that wasn't her job anymore. Now she was Hanley's working dog. An indentured servant to the deputy director of Operations in charge of managing sub rosa, off-book assets.

She made the turn into the HQ at five a.m., anxious to have a couple of hours in the office before attending the crisis center meeting at seven about Ternhill and Great Falls.

She'd just begun heading up the drive when her phone rang, and she answered it over the car speakers.

"Brewer."

"It's Matt. How soon can you be in my office?"

"Parking now, sir. Ten to fifteen?"

"Ten would be better." Hanley hung up, and Brewer groaned aloud in her car. If he was already here in his office, wanting to speak with her in person even before the seven a.m. meeting, then it was a safe bet he was scheming something, something she would likely be tasked with carrying out.

. . .

Suzanne Brewer walked down the hall to Matt Hanley's office thirteen minutes later. Heavy throngs of men and women passed by, the noise level higher than usual here on the seventh floor, and there was a sense of urgency to the scene.

This had nothing to do with Ternhill or Great Falls, Brewer knew. Instead, everyone up here was busy because of what Brewer saw as a stupid and pointless conference they would all be attending in Scotland in a few days.

Everyone on the floor, virtually all of the executives along with dozens of mid- and upper-level subordinates, would fly to the UK on Saturday. They'd spend a day at the U.S. embassy in London prepping with members of the CIA station there, and then they would fly or take trains north to the Scottish Highlands for the annual three-day Five Eyes conference, to be held in a completely restored and massive fifteenth-century castle overlooking Loch Ness.

The intelligence agencies of the five English-speaking nations of the world—the United States, Canada, the United Kingdom, Australia, and New Zealand—were known collectively as the Five Eyes. They shared all manner of intel product between one another, and they worked together whenever they could. The Five Eyes conducted a regular cycle of conferences, each year in one of the five nations. The previous year had been in Wellington, New Zealand; next year it would be in Toronto, but the United Kingdom had host duties for this year's gathering.

Senior operational, analytical, and executive staff from the intelligence agencies of all five participating nations would get together, some four hundred spies, spymasters, and IC experts in all, and they would attend briefing after briefing about the ongoing and emerging threats facing the Five Eyes' interests.

Brewer wasn't going to Five Eyes this year, and she saw it as perhaps the only perk of working on Poison Apple. Sub rosa initiatives weren't discussed with the partner nations, so she saw no reason to go and rub shoulders with colleagues from other services to whom she wouldn't be able to say much of anything.

Brewer passed by Jill, Hanley's executive assistant, with a nod, and entered through the open door of his office.

While the rest of the floor seemed to be almost frantically preparing for the mass exodus, Matt Hanley appeared relaxed, looking over papers with a glass bottle of apple juice next to him.

She sat down while Hanley finished reading the page in his hand. She knew Matt himself had become somewhat legendary in his ability to get out of attending the conference in years past, usually due to critical deployments, but now he was the new top dog of CIA ops and would be one of the senior attendees at the event in Edinburgh.

"You've had a night," he said as he looked her over.

"More like a nightmare."

"Any sleep?"

Brewer knew he wouldn't take pity on her and cut her any slack if she told him the truth, that she hadn't even put her head down on a pillow, so she responded with, "I'm fine, Matt."

"I want to start working on the potential moles today."

Brewer nodded thoughtfully. "And by working on them you mean . . . *what*, exactly?"

"Watching them. Leaning on them."

"I can assemble a surveillance team from operational and technical staff, but as far as leaning on them—"

Hanley interrupted. "We put a Poison Apple asset on them. Outfitted with rules of engagement that will unease the potential traitors, cause them to make mistakes, reveal themselves. Tickle the wires, just to see what happens."

Brewer said, "Violator is in play in the UK right now. Anthem wasn't even operational before she snuck out of the safe house during a massacre. So am I to assume you are talking about Romantic?"

"That's right. He's perfect for this job. Where is he?"

"He's in the D.C. area. I have him in training, won't be difficult to get him here."

"I want him heading this way within the hour."

"Sir . . . I don't know about him coming into the office."

Hanley said, "Of course not. You'll meet him somewhere off site, tell him what we need from him."

Brewer hesitated. "Are you sure about this, Matt? Sure about sending an off-book asset, especially one like Romantic, to intimidate high-ranking Agency colleagues?"

"The only thing I'm sure of is that my people are dying, and nobody is doing shit to stop it. That changes now." Hanley added, "Romantic will be happy for the work. Especially because it involves being an asshole to Agency suits."

"The problem will be keeping him on a leash." She then asked, "Who are the suspects?"

Matt Hanley said, "Assuming the event last night in Great Falls was part of the same compromise, that removes the Transportation Division–only suspects. Those who knew about Great Falls and all four of the aircraft movements that were compromised make for a very small subset."

"How small?"

"Besides you and me? Four people. Two in Operations, and two in Support."

When he said nothing more, Brewer pressed. "I'll need the names, Matt, won't I?"

Her sarcasm was ignored by her deputy director. Instead he just said, "Marty Wheeler, Support."

Brewer had known Wheeler for the past three years. Moreover, she knew he and Hanley were friends. He'd shown up at the safe house earlier in the morning. She wrote his name down but said nothing.

"Got it."

"Maria Palumbo, Ops."

Brewer knew Palumbo well. She was new at the HQ here in McLean, having spent virtually all of her career in embassies around the Middle East, Asia, and Europe, but Brewer had worked at many of the same facilities. Palumbo had been in harm's way more times than Brewer, and Brewer couldn't imagine her betraying her own organization.

Hanley said, "Number three is Alf Karlsson, also in Operations."

Brewer only knew the handsome first-generation Swede socially; they'd never worked together at all. She said, "He had knowledge of all the events?"

"Yes, like the others."

She wrote down the name.

Brewer asked, "Who is number four?"

"Lucas Renfro."

Brewer's mouth opened in disbelief. "The *deputy director* of Support? That's ludicrous. He's a department head. Thirty-five years in the U.S. intelligence community."

Hanley said, "We have to investigate all leads."

"Investigate." She said the word with an air of dubiousness.

"Renfro doesn't like me. He wanted to be DDO, is pissed I got it. Plus he is by the book to a fault. I am not. That gives him motive. He knows I have sub rosa activities, and he wants to put a stop to them."

"By passing secrets to the Chinese and the Russians and whoever else? I don't believe that for a minute. Sure, he wanted the promotion you got, I don't doubt that. But there is no way he would turn traitor just to see you fail."

Hanley said, "Nothing else makes sense, Suzanne."

"With respect, sir, *anything* else makes more sense."

The big man sighed. "I know you are doing this under duress." She thought he was about to throw her some sort of lifeline. But instead he said, "Just do it anyway."

"Right." She looked at her notes with the names. "I guess I need to tell Romantic where to start."

To this Hanley said, "I'll tell you where to start. He can check them all out, but I want him leaning on Lucas Renfro, *hard*."

Brewer looked up to her boss. "This is beginning to sound personal."

Hanley shook his head. "He's an asshole. Never heard it said that assholes can't also be traitors. In fact, I'd say there's likely a positive correlation."

Brewer stood and headed back to her office.

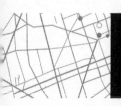

CHAPTER 10

TWO YEARS EARLIER

Won Jang-Mi sat at a computer monitor in a windowless room, but through the walls she could hear the whipping snowstorm. Winters in this part of Russia could be harsh, more brutal than anything she'd ever seen in her native North Korea.

Every day she walked from her apartment in the dreary town of Shikhany, boarded a special bus, and then sat quietly for the fifteen-minute ride to Shikhany-2, the Russian Defense Force military base where she worked. She'd been here for four months already; she appreciated the good facilities and her intelligent colleagues, but she didn't really know why she was in the middle of a snow-covered forest studying viruses with Russians.

She wanted to be an operative, not some glorified foreign exchange student.

A knock at the door of her tiny room surprised her. She usually was left alone here and did most of her talking with her Russian colleagues in the lab or conference room.

"Enter," she said in her rapidly improving Russian.

A man in his thirties whom Won had never seen came in. She stood and shook his hand, giving off a hint of discomfort while doing so.

"My name is Alexi Filotov," he said.

"Dr. Won Jang-Mi."

Behind him, the colonel who managed the entire facility leaned into the doorway.

"Doctor," he said. "This man is with the government. He would like to speak with you about your work. I thought you could take a few minutes."

"Certainly," she said, confused about what exact part of the Russian government the stranger in the suit worked for, and just what he wanted to know.

The director reached in and took the door latch, then closed Won and the man in the tiny dark room, which only increased Won's misgivings. She suffered from severe social anxiety, and even shaking hands was a difficult task that she'd had to master to leave her nation and head to foreign lands, all of which were full of men and women who always seemed to want to touch one another.

When they touched her or even moved close to her she found it sickening, but she weathered the close contact with this man and asked, "How can I help you?"

"I have been hearing good things about your research here. I am not a doctor, so you will have to keep things simple with me. But I would appreciate an explanation of what you are doing."

"I have a specific specialty, Mr. Filotov. I am willing to talk about this, as my government has told me to collaborate in any way I can."

"And what is your specialty, Jang-Mi?"

The woman bristled. "Jang-Mi is my given name. Won is my surname. I would prefer you simply call me 'Doctor,' Mr. Filotov."

"With apologies, Doctor." The two sat in the only two chairs in the room.

She said, "I am an expert on category A organisms. Do you know what those are?"

Filotov nodded. "Go on."

Won detected a certain perfunctory nature to the man's tone.

"Is this something that interests you personally, professionally, or perhaps you are a government functionary merely ordered here to find information?"

Filotov did not deny his motivations. "Very much the latter, Doctor. I have been assigned to meet with several biological warfare experts around the nation. No disrespect, but frankly it is boring work. My country has focused its energies on chemical weapons for more than thirty years. The state of our biological research, as you are probably well aware, is in shambles."

Won would not admit it, but the facilities here were far superior to anything she'd ever seen in North Korea.

Filotov added, "But then I heard about you. I am hoping you will have some technology, some insight, some knowledge that goes beyond what I've been hearing from my own countrymen for the past several weeks. North Korea, from what I've been told, has been pursuing bioweapons aggressively."

Won said, "We have. All different types and strains. My specialty, however, is weaponized plague."

The Russian reached into his jacket. "May I smoke?"

"It's your country."

He lit a cigarette; he still didn't seem terribly interested in this encounter, and Won was already looking forward to getting back to work, hoping he wouldn't shake her hand again on the way out.

Filotov said, "I know next to nothing about plague, I'm afraid."

Won began a short primer. "In the history of mankind, plague has been the second-largest killer of all epidemic diseases, behind only smallpox.

"The Black Death of the fourteenth century that killed between seventy-five and two hundred million people in four years was bubonic plague, which targets the lymph nodes. Pneumonic plague, in contrast, targets the lungs.

"The bacteria that causes plague, *Yersinia pestis*, is relatively easy to acquire around the world. It is something an expert can grow in a laboratory, and is easily disseminated by aerosol delivery or other means. Further, there is a very high lethality rate when using pneumonic plague as opposed to the more easily treated bubonic plague, and secondary spread—infected hosts infecting others before they die—is not only possible; it's all but assured."

Filotov took another drag on his cigarette. "It's a weapon."

"A magnificent weapon, when carefully produced, maintained, and distributed by an expert. As opposed to toxins, most biological weapons, plague included, consist of living organisms, and this means they can reproduce once dispersed." Won was in her element now; her social anxiety and general insecurity were forgotten, because she was speaking about the only subject she had really focused on since her early twenties.

Filotov said, "What are the effects?"

"Would you like me to show you?"

He thought she was kidding. When her deadpan expression revealed she was not, he asked, "What do you mean?"

She motioned to her computer. "I am in possession of a video of a test we ran four years ago in my country. Would you like to see it?"

"A test on . . . on *what*?"

"On human beings."

The Russian's eyes went wide. "Very much so."

She cued up a file on her screen. "This video has never been shown outside Pyongyang. It has never been shown outside my research laboratory, to the best of my knowledge."

Filotov said, "I am honored."

She looked back to him. "You might find it disturbing."

Now the Russian smiled and took another drag. "I sincerely hope I do."

She hit play on the device, and the screen displayed a group of men and women in white prison uniforms, standing in orderly rows in the center of a concrete prison yard. Walls and barbed wire were evident behind them, and armed guards ringed the group.

"Who are the test subjects?" Filotov asked.

She hit pause. "Political prisoners in the DPRK. We gave them Western-sized rations for six weeks to build their strength to approximate the enemy population. We also gave them more access to sunlight, more sleep, more water, more medicine. The majority of these subjects were quite healthy when the test began, although, frankly, they were not nearly so healthy as the average Westerner, so I suspect the test results ultimately were skewed in the direction of slight exaggeration of outcome."

"How many prisoners were used?"

"We used one hundred for the primary test, which I thought to be excessive, but I was overruled. The demonstration could have been made just as easily and the results nearly as statistically significant with twenty men and women."

Filotov said, "One hundred is a good even number. Please, continue."

The screen showed the prisoners, still in the prison yard, in two lines walking through a small concrete building, not much larger than a potting shed.

Won said, "Here they are being administered the agent I personally designed. My strain of bacteria has been altered to allow increased pathogenicity, meaning a stronger effect from the spores, and a shorter incubation period, meaning less time before the effects become fatal. Furthermore, my strain allows more time before symptoms present, an average of four to six-and-a-half days. This will give the hosts time to infect others with secondary pneumonic plague before their own sickness even registers."

"That is impressive, Doctor."

The video showed the inside of the small building now. Nozzles jutted from the walls and ceiling. She said, "It is sprayed in aerosol form but it is odorless and completely invisible. The sound of the expulsion of the agent would have been evident to the prisoners, but there was no way they would have been able to discern what was happening to them."

She added, "After they were exposed, they retired to their cells. The guards were given daily courses of antibiotics, so they would not have to wear protective gear and skew the test results by making it obvious the population had been infected.

"If antibiotics are not administered in the first eight hours and continued through a course of a week or more, the patient has little chance of survival." With nonchalance she added, "This population was administered no antibiotics whatsoever."

A new camera angle, again of the concrete yard, and again all the prisoners were lined up in rows. Won said, "Here they are at the end of day one. No symptoms evident, even after twenty-four hours. The same at the end of day two. This is to be expected with normal strains of pneumonic plague."

The video image changed to show a woman in a prison uniform, obviously in an infirmary or clinic there at the labor camp, having her blood pressure taken by someone in a full hazmat suit. She was coughing into a paper towel.

"On day three, hour fifty-five in the trial, a single subject showed symptoms. This is a sixty-one-year-old woman who had already spent ten years in the labor camps." Won glanced to Filotov. "Chronically malnourished, unhealthy, notwithstanding the weeks we attempted to strengthen her and bolster her immune system. I assessed her health as that of the average eighty-five-year-old Westerner."

She played the video a few seconds more, and there were more men and women in the clinic now being evaluated. Some lay on gurneys; others remained standing.

"On day four there were seven showing symptoms. The sixty-one-year-old woman was unable to get off the stretcher without help. The others had coughs; two presented with fever. Again, these were the older and the less fit."

Filotov watched more film: the sick lined up in a darkened hallway, guards walking among them.

"On day five sixteen prisoners had fallen ill. Our first subject was wholly incapacitated at this point." The monitor displayed the woman on a hard floor mat, convulsing and vomiting. "We quickly took the fifteen who showed symptoms but were still ambulatory and put them here, in a second prison yard."

A similar space to the first was shown, and a large group of men and women stood at attention in the middle of the concrete floor.

"This location is sequestered five hundred meters from the first. Our aim here was to check the efficacy of secondary pneumonic plague. As in the primary trial, one hundred subjects were exposed."

The fifteen men and women showing symptoms from the primary trial entered the yard, the prisoners were dismissed from their rows, and soon they were all intermingling.

Won said, "It is not an airborne disease. For someone to become a secondary patient, they generally must be within two meters of a host subject who is showing symptoms. Coughing, for example. Still, the West is a generally crowded place. Plague can be an insidious beast."

"I have no doubt, Doctor."

"On day six, twenty-six patients in the primary trial showed symptoms. On day seven, that number had grown to seventy-one. The woman who presented first died on this day, along with another subject."

The grainy video continued, showing the dead woman and rows of prostrate sick, lying in the open yard.

Filotov leaned towards the screen, entranced by the power of the microscopic bacteria.

"Day eight," Won said. "By now eighty-eight showed coughing, fever, vomiting. There was morbidity in some extremities: the onset of gangrene. It was really quite impressive."

The camera in the prison infirmary showed blackened fingers and toes on many of the patients.

"By day nine all one hundred of the primary subjects had developed symptoms of plague; nine had died. By day ten, the number of deaths had risen to fifty-one."

The Russian leaned back in his chair now. "Ultimately, of the one hundred primary subjects, how many died?"

"All of them died, Mr. Filotov. The longest lived fifteen days, which was something of a miracle, but he was twenty-one and very healthy before he was infected."

"And of the one hundred secondary subjects? What was their mortality rate?"

"Sixty-three dead, so sixty-three percent. My prediction had been between fifty and seventy-five percent, so I was quite satisfied with my analysis."

"One hundred sixty three out of two hundred."

"Yes, but those secondary subjects would have—if they were in an uncontrolled population—caused tertiary infections in others." Won smiled. "It is hard to predict what the mortality rate would be in that population, but it is also difficult to overestimate the danger of plague when released."

Filotov said, "I will level with you. I am an intelligence officer. I am no scientist. But my organization would like to know one thing. Do you have everything you need to weaponize this on a larger scale?"

She nodded. This filled her with excitement, although she still took this conversation as theoretical, because Filotov had not mentioned any specifics.

"Is there any question that your weapon will work?"

"There is one gap in my knowledge on the subject, which prevents me from answering that question with specificity."

Filotov sat up straighter, obviously surprised to hear this from the woman who seemed so completely self-assured about her expertise. "And what would that be?"

"The DPRK knows very little about existing biodefenses set up by the

West. Do Western nations have security measures intact to respond to an attack, are hospitals in major cities prepared, are enough oral and IV drugs staged to combat a mass casualty event, are there protocols to identify the origin of a devastating plague outbreak? I simply do not have as much of this information as I require."

"And where could you go to obtain this information?"

Won shrugged. "Two places that I know of. Stockholm and Atlanta. Stockholm is the location of the European Centre for Disease Prevention and Control, and Atlanta, Georgia, in the United States, is the location of the CDC, America's Centers for Disease Control and Prevention."

Filotov took some notes. "If we could help you obtain a position at either of these locations, would you be able to fill in these knowledge gaps you speak of?"

Won replied with a little confusion. "I don't work for Russia. I work for—"

Filotov waved a hand. "Our two nations have shared interests in the knowledge you could obtain. We could speak with officials in your country, and work on this together."

She thought it over. "I do not want to go to America." Won smiled now, and she did not smile often. "But I will go to Sweden if you can arrange it, both with the center there and with my leadership back home."

Within months Won left Russia and moved to Stockholm, taking a job as a researcher at the European Centre for Disease Prevention and Control. The Russians secured the job for her, secured her cover identity, secured the money she needed to set herself up in the European capital. The North Koreans, for their part, allowed Won Jang-Mi to go.

The Russians and the North Koreans both wanted to know everything about biosecurity in the West, and Won had the same goal as her masters.

She needed to understand the protective measures in place, so that she and her plague could find a way around them.

Two years to the month after wading ashore on a moonlit beach in Japan, she sat down at the desk in her new office in Stockholm.

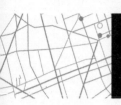

CHAPTER 11

The abandoned hospital just south of the hamlet of Rauceby had originally been built in the 1890s and served as a mental asylum until World War II, when it was employed as a "crash and burns" unit for the RAF. After the war it reverted to its original role, run by the National Health Service, serving until the 1990s, when it was shut down for good.

Now the wards, halls, offices, laboratories, treatment rooms, and nurses' quarters were abandoned, suffering mightily the decay of time. Vines snaked in through windows and mold grew along the tile flooring. Some furniture and fixtures remained, but everything else was rotting or rusted, mildewed or broken.

Graffiti adorned the walls, mice and bat shit were piled everywhere, and green newts clung to the walls.

It was an empty, hollow shell, with dusty shafts of light beaming left and right through broken windows along the long corridors and high-ceilinged rooms.

Anthony Kent stood in one of these shafts in the large and hazily lit dining hall, itself in the center of the massive former sanitarium. A rotting wooden stage loomed at the far end of the hall, and in front of that three men stood around in light jackets with weapons slung over their shoulders. In the center of the group was a man seated on a chair, with a black bag over his head.

Kent knew absolutely nothing about the prisoner, other than the fact that he was a big prize that someone had paid a lot of money to recover, and thus many poor sods had died in the process.

The Englishman looked at his watch. He was waiting for a call, and he prayed it would come soon, so he could be done with this wretched day.

Anthony Kent was a highwayman for the Nottingham Syndicate, a family-run criminal firm that specialized in extortion, shipping and transportation theft, and prostitution all across the East Midlands. The majority of his work involved hijacking trucks, usually in brazen but straightforward armed robberies, stealing everything from beer and liquor to medical supplies to be resold on the black market. In addition to this he also served as one of the Nottingham Syndicate's chief enforcers, abducting enemies of the group and beating them back into line.

And this was how he knew about the abandoned hospital.

This building in which he now stood had been home to some of his most brutal actions as a mob enforcer. While not officially a safe house of the group—Kent knew he'd be killed by his boss for taking this prisoner to some actual safe house and connecting the Nottingham Syndicate with the attack on MI6—this ruined building had served for years as something of a torture chamber. Certain that he and the survivors of tonight's attack would be safe here, he'd made the decision to drive across the middle of the island nation to be back on his own turf, where he knew the lay of the land.

All six of the other survivors of the airport shootout were members of different gangs across England, and like Kent, sent on this job by their employers, who had been hired to provide crewmembers for the operation. Kent had heard a rumor that this entire affair had been set up by a shadow man in London, and his boss had been paid a quarter of a million pounds. Kent himself would be paid seventy-five thousand for all this . . . but at the moment he felt that he'd drastically undercharged for his services.

The one good thing that had happened since they opened fire at the airport was the arrival of more help. When Kent called his boss, the man who'd sent him on this mad endeavor, and told him they'd lost six of their number and he was heading to this abandoned hospital to lay up, his employer told him he would have reinforcements waiting for him. And, true to his word, when Kent and his men arrived they found six armed men, many of whom Kent had worked with in the past. He'd wasted no time in positioning the new arrivals around the building for security, and this allowed him to breathe his first sigh of relief in hours.

Still, he knew he was in over his head. He wasn't a leader; he wasn't a soldier. He'd killed, multiple times, but had never been involved in anything remotely as large-scale as what had happened in Ternhill this morning.

His phone rang and he snatched it out of his pocket. It was the inbound helicopter telling them they would arrive in twenty minutes. He hung up and notified his men outside to make one last concerted scan of the area to ensure that all was clear.

Kent walked over to the prisoner now but addressed the men guarding him.

"Chopper is twenty minutes out. Look alive, lads."

Dirk Visser's head turned to the voice. Through the bag and in accented English, the banker said, "You're in charge here?"

The Englishman said, "I guess I am, yeah."

Visser said, "Look, friend, thank you for rescuing me. Now I just want to go back home. Why am I still tied? Why am I blindfolded? I have nothing to do with—"

Kent snapped back, "I'm not your fuckin' *friend*, mate. Don't talk to me, don't talk to anyone at all. Just sit your arse there and wait. You'll be getting a ride out of here soon enough."

"A ride? A ride to where?"

"Dunno. But I'd hazard a guess you're gonna get a talkin'-to here before they take you away." He looked around the room. "God knows this bloody place has seen its share of interrogations."

. . .

Court moved across the property carefully, passing a derelict chapel and scooting along behind a low brick wall, half broken by time and the elements. He crawled through the tall grass, remaining low enough to avoid detection, and made it to within one hundred feet of the eastern wall of the target building. Here there was one more building between himself and the old hospital.

He decided to look in to see if he could move through the building next to him instead of around it. Fighting his way past brambles and some broken old hospital beds smothered in vines, he arrived at a window and looked in.

A sign on a door inside said Viewing Room. He wasn't sure what he was supposed to view on the other side, but whatever it was, he figured it was probably not much to look at considering the poor condition of the structure.

He stepped through the window, carefully measured his footsteps around broken glass, and made his way into the room. He passed through the door of the Viewing Room and found the space behind it completely empty other than papers and plaster on the floor. In front of him, however, he saw three doors, each with a faded sign attached.

Female, Postmortem, and Male.

He was standing in the middle of an abandoned mortuary.

He entered through the middle door and found himself in Postmortem. There were broken lab tables and another stretcher, and to the right was a doorway to a flight of stairs that went down into darkness.

Court took the stairs, sensing there was some sort of underground access to the hospital itself. He pulled the headlamp out of his pack and flipped it on the red light setting because red light does not cause pupils to shrink like white light does, so he could retain some of his night vision. Before him he saw a tunnel that did, indeed, lead off in the direction of the large building at the center of this property.

The tunnel was rank with mold and ankle deep in water and trash, but with the dim red light from his headlamp leading the way Court moved out, slowly so as to make as little noise as possible. He didn't think there were enough people on this property for them to post a guard down here, but he knew he couldn't be sure.

The passage had been built wide enough for a gurney to be pushed along; obviously it was designed to move bodies from the hospital to the morgue. Black-and-green lizards shot along the walls and ceiling while Court negotiated the decades of trash along the floor.

Halfway up the tunnel he could see that it ended at a pile of garbage in front of a metal door. Court continued to within twenty feet, covered his headlamp with his hand, and used the faint light that shone through his fingers to make his way over the pile. He turned the light off now, opened the door enough to squeeze his body through, and after this he stood silently for a full minute, listening for any sounds. Eventually he put his earplugs back in and turned them on.

Court flipped on his headlamp, back on its red light setting.

He stood in a dusty basement, so he made his way to the stairwell at the end. Court climbed, exceedingly careful with every footfall.

At the top he realized he was in a former medical ward of the hospital. Porcelain sinks lined the wall; metal tables and trays and shelving units lay twisted and turned.

The broken window in the room looked out to a courtyard of high weeds, and a small road beyond that snaked through several other buildings in the complex. There was what looked like an old army barracks, a water tower, and a massive parking garage.

He also saw the two cars he'd noticed from the air, parked there behind the building, and was surprised when he recognized the models. One was a Dodge Charger; it was matte gray and appeared to be at least ten years old.

The other was a twenty-five-year-old black Mercedes Benz SL-500 sedan. Assuming the Mercedes to be the V8 model, and certain the Charger was a V8 Hemi, Court knew he was looking at two muscle cars, something of a rarity in Britain, and he worried this meant the men from Ternhill had received reinforcements.

He looked out into a corridor illuminated by shafts of light through the windows. Here he turned on his hearing enhancement again, and he immediately recoiled at the sound.

A helicopter was approaching. It changed pitch, and this told him it was in the process of landing.

He worried the prisoner would be spirited out of the area before he could make a play for him, and he also realized the opportunity that the noise of the landing helo gave him. He knew from the windows that he was in the east wing of the building, so he moved into the corridor, turned to his left, and began hurrying as fast as possible, staying out of the dusty sunlight as he went.

· · ·

Six men climbed out of the Airbus H145 helicopter from London and began walking quickly towards the west wing entrance of the hospital.

Their eyes scanned the entire property as they moved, and the man in the center of the group did not seem pleased at all about the surroundings.

Roger Fox was thirty-nine years old, with reddish brown hair styled neatly and a trim goatee. He told people he'd been educated at Princeton, in the United States, and he wore a charcoal suit made by Savile Row's Henry Poole along with a Rolex Cosmograph Daytona.

Four men in his security component carried submachine guns under their light jackets, but they did their best to hide the weaponry as they advanced on the building, unsure about this location and its proximity to wandering eyes.

The fifth man in the group was Jon Hines, Fox's personal bodyguard. As always Hines walked just behind him, a half step back. At six feet, nine inches tall, he wore two hundred sixty pounds of sinewy muscle like an athlete.

Like a weapon.

Hines was English, forty-one years old, and a former boxer. He carried an FN pistol on his hip under his jacket, and he knew how to use it, but all seven of the men he'd killed in his life to date he'd done with his bare hands, and he'd never once drawn his gun in a fight, simply because he'd never seen the need.

· · ·

Anthony Kent stood in the doorway of the west wing; he waved the group over to him. As the group converged the Englishman looked around, trying to identify the man he'd spoken with on the phone, although he had no idea what he looked like.

It was hard to take his eyes off the massive frame of muscle in a suit looming just behind the smaller man in the goatee, but when the smaller man extended a hand, Kent looked to him and extended his own. "Mr. Fox?"

Fox shook Kent's hand without smiling. In a British accent he said, "Yes. What the hell is this place?"

"It's safe," Kent said. "Been comin' here for years for a wee bit of quiet."

Fox stepped with Kent into the building. His men bracketed them front to back.

"The prisoner?"

Kent said, "We have him inside, haven't told him anything."

"Has he offered anything?"

"No. He's scared."

"Good," Fox said, and he pushed past the smaller Englishman. His men did the same, and Kent followed.

"Have to say it, sir. I was worried we'd been workin' for the fucking Russians. Nice to see that a proper Englishman is in charge. Don't much care for the bloody Russians who've taken over London with their flash and their mess."

Fox made no reply.

Kent went ahead, directing them through the west wing into the large room with the stage. The entourage walked up to the three in the center of the room standing over the hooded prisoner. Fox did not acknowledge the three, only reached over and yanked the bag off Dirk Visser's head.

The man looked up at him, sweat dripping from his face.

"It's him," Fox said, then added, "Kent, take your men out into the corridor. I'd quite like to speak with my new friend here alone."

The four Englishmen did as ordered. This was the man paying their wages, after all.

When the British were gone, Fox looked down at Visser. "I'm from London, and you might not yet know why I am here. I will tell you what I am *not* here to do. I am *not* here to fuck about. We know CIA picked you up in Luxembourg, which means they know you are the banker tied to a particular account at your bank that is of interest to us."

"Yes, that's right," Visser said, helpfully. "The British or the Americans have a mole in my bank. It's the only thing that makes sense. They identified the account and recognized I was the one maintaining it, converting amounts to Bitcoin and then transferring them to the U.S."

"What have you told the CIA in the time you've been their captive?"

"Nothing! I haven't said a word. And I won't say anything. Not to the Americans, the British. I'm just a banker, I've done nothing wrong."

Fox knelt down slowly, all the way to Visser's face. "I told you I wasn't here to fuck about. I know there's more. I know you have been doing some looking into the owners of the shell company that made recent deposits into the account you manage."

The banker cocked his head, a genuine show of surprise. "What do you mean? I know nothing about the depositor. I don't know if it's a shell or not, nor how the shell is run. But I know how it works, normally there is no true principal as a signatory to the articles of incorporation. It's all done by nominating agents, lawyers working for lawyers, shells within shells. Even if I wanted information about the company, I wouldn't be able to get it." Visser smiled a little. "That's how everyone stays safe."

"Yeah, and yet here you are," Fox said. "Not too bloody safe, are you, mate?"

"Yes, but I haven't told anyone—"

"I'm going to say a name," Fox interrupted. "When I say it I want you to tell me where you heard it."

A half nod from the seated man.

"Feodor Zakharov."

Visser shook his head slowly. "I don't . . . think I have ever heard that name. *Should* I know him?"

The man in the goatee stood back up now and looked to the huge man standing with him. Still to Visser he said, "Two nights ago the CIA picks you up. Then last night the CIA looks into a fourteen-year-old file of this man, a man known to us."

"He is . . . he is somehow involved with the account I manage, or the company that deposited into the account?"

Fox looked up at Hines. "Jon? Will you remind Visser here that *I* am the one asking the questions?"

The big man instantly fired an open hand out. The whack of palm against face echoed through the cavernous main hall.

Stunned and in pain, Visser looked back up at the men looming over him with terror in his eyes, as if he just now realized the danger he was in.

Fox said, "You told them about Zakharov. How did you know? Who else did you tell?"

"I swear to you, I don't even know that name. Perhaps there is a mole in *your* organization. Perhaps they found out some other way."

"No, Visser. No other way. You talked."

Hines's hand whipped out again, slapping the man even harder, and this time the banker screamed.

CHAPTER 12

Court heard a distant scream echoing through the massive hospital. He'd been moving through a nurses' break room, carefully bypassing a man patrolling up the hallway with a flashlight. He stopped in his tracks, and when the next scream came he was able to identify the sound as coming from up the hall to the west. He moved to the doorway and lay down, waited until he heard the footsteps of the patrolling sentry begin climbing a staircase nearby, then scooted on the floor until his head was outside in the hall and he was facing in the direction from where the screams came.

One hundred feet up the hall he saw a group of four men standing in a wide shaft of window light in front of double doors opposite from the main entrance to the hospital. He tapped his audio-enhancing earplugs and immediately began picking up the whispered conversation of the men as it echoed off the tile and plaster in the long empty space. Court had missed the beginning of the conversation, but he quickly got the impression that the helicopter he'd heard land had dropped off a group, and they were now with the prisoner through the door that was behind the four men in sight.

Another scream from the room behind them told Court that the newcomers were really working this guy over.

So, Court recognized now, this was not a simple rescue of a man held by the CIA. These people wanted something from this banker just as much as the Agency and MI6 did.

Sucks for him.

Court tuned into the conversation, desperate to pick up more intel about what was going on. A man with a thick British accent said, "Look, Kent. It's not that we don't trust you, it's that we don't even *know* you. You might have been pegged as the man to run the crew if Martin and Mickey weren't around, but none of us know this Fox bloke, either. I don't trust him."

The man being addressed said, "Same as you lot, I was sent by my boss to do this job. And now he's fuckin' furious at whoever set this shite up. I either get this sorted, or I end up buried in a bleedin' ditch somewhere. I don't know Fox, just met him when he climbed off the heli. I do what I'm told, and I was told to run things if the first two men went down. Hopefully these sharp-dressed fucks will take that Dutch geezer in there and we'll be done with this. You can go back to Southampton, Bristol, London, wherever, spend your money, and try and forget this ever happened."

Court lifted his phone, activated the camera, and zoomed it in all the way, centering on the group of men. He stabilized his arm against the door frame and took two dozen pictures in just a few seconds, using a light-enhancing mode.

He hoped Brewer would use facial recognition analysis to identify some or all of the men, but what he really needed now was to find a way to get to the prisoner.

No, Court thought. *I can't extract the banker until I know more about my opposition.*

He cursed Brewer in silence, although he knew this wasn't her fault.

. . .

Jon Hines smacked Dirk Visser across the face for a third time, and this time the Dutchman fell to the floor. The big man grabbed him by the throat and slammed him back down on the chair without a word or a sound.

Hines enjoyed beating people up. As a kid he'd been the biggest and strongest, but his overbearing mother called him a "clumsy oaf" and tried to put him in ballet. He made it five minutes in his first class till the stares and snickers got to him—he was twelve and six-one. He left and went straight to the boxing gym next door.

He had no money on him, and his mum wasn't returning to pick him up for an hour, but when the trainers set eyes on the massive child, they smiled at one another and put him in the ring for a free session.

He told himself that if he could move like the American champ Mike Tyson, then his mum wouldn't pick on him. And if he could fight like Mike Tyson, then *no one* would pick on him.

He was a star at the gym from day one; his mum relented and paid for his lessons, and he became a fixture there, a pet project for the trainers.

Throughout his teen years he grew even bigger and continued with his boxing. He also studied judo and karate, but when he was eighteen he joined the Army, serving as a light machine gunner in the Royal Anglian Regiment.

He boxed in the infantry, of course, but he fought dirty, always. After three years, he left to try his hand as a prizefighter in the robust boxing system in the UK.

His career never took off, as he remained hampered by his inability to follow the rules of the sport. There was no one who could go toe-to-toe for long with the quick and skilled giant of a man, but Hines was constantly having points deducted for rabbit punches, low blows, stepping on his opponent's feet, and hitting them after the bell. He either won his matches quickly with knockouts or lost them on point deductions or outright disqualification.

Eventually his untamed aggression became too much, even in a sport where men were scored on their ability to hit one another in the face.

Since he failed as a boxer, he began working for a loan shark in Portsmouth. Here, there *were* no rules about low blows or rabbit punches, but even in this work he managed to step out of bounds. He accidentally beat a man to death and then was promptly arrested and convicted.

He was sent to HM Prison Wakefield, the toughest correctional facility in the nation. The complex was known as the Monster Mansion for all of the high-profile lowlifes incarcerated there.

Hines was sentenced to six years behind the fence, and with only five months remaining in his sentence, he ran afoul of a pair of young, muscular Russian inmates over a prime seat in the TV room. The six-nine Hines had taken a chair in the front of the room to watch a heavyweight fight, and the two brothers complained that they couldn't see the screen. Hines ignored them for the entire two-hour run of the program, then quietly stood and walked into the bathroom.

The brothers followed, with a young Russian entering behind.

Everyone in the prison knew Artyom Primakov, and they knew that he was a member of the Vory, a made man in the Russian mafia. He'd been arrested for possession of forged documents and sentenced to four years, and was set to be deported back to Russia upon his release.

When Hines saw the dangerous Primakov, he said, "You've got fuck-all to do with this, mate. I know who you are, but I don't give a toss. I will beat you down, just the same."

Primakov just smiled, then motioned to the two young toughs to get to work on the big blond Englishman.

Hines then proceeded to dismantle both of the hard men, barely breaking a sweat as he cracked orbital bones, jaws, and ribs, and left them on the floor covered in blood.

Then Jon Hines looked up at Primakov, his red swollen knuckles still tightened into fists.

Primakov began to clap. "Marvelous. Well done. But what now, friend? The five remaining months of your sentence just turned into another ten years for your actions of the last ninety seconds."

Hines moved forward, raising his fists.

"Unless," Primakov continued, backpedaling while he talked. "Unless I get you out of it. I could have one of my other men take the blame for this."

Hines slowed. His rage and adrenaline were in control, but his brain had, at least, heard what the Russian gangster said.

"Why the fuck would you do that?"

"Two reasons. One, the obvious. So you don't break my neck. And two . . . you were attacked, you were only defending yourself, but the guards won't see that. The British legal system will condemn you. I don't think that is fair, do you?"

● ● ●

The truth was that Primakov realized he couldn't let an asset like Jon Hines get away, so he ordered one of his men, a lifer in prison for a homicide in London, to confess administering the beatdown.

Jon Hines was released from prison five months later.

Primakov was still on the inside, but he made contact with some associates in his organization, the London brigade of the Russian multinational criminal organization known as the Solntsevskaya Bratva. Soon, the big former boxer was employed as a security officer for senior members.

Primakov was sent back to Russia, but he made his way back into the UK on a new, improved set of forged papers, claiming his name to be Roger Fox, a subject of the United Kingdom. Unlike his last visit to the UK, when he posed as a Russian immigrant, now his English was flawless and spoken in the common multicultural London dialect.

And Jon Hines became his bodyguard, a permanent fixture at his side.

．．．

Visser's nose snapped with a crack during Hines's next hit. This time the big Brit used a closed fist and, although it wasn't a very hard punch, it was perfectly placed and an exceedingly efficient application of force.

The banker's head went down, and he continued mumbling something about his innocence in all this, but Fox was not listening. Instead he looked to Hines. "Put him in the helicopter. Mars can decide what to do with him."

"Yes, sir," Hines replied, and then he hoisted the man up and onto his shoulder, carrying him like a sack of flour.

．．．

Court remained on the filthy floor, his eyes just past the door frame into the hallway so he could observe the men he'd been listening to. He remained confident they wouldn't be able to see him in the darkness some hundred feet away, not with the tiny profile he'd given them.

He watched as several men stepped out of the doorway next to Kent and his three subordinates. In the middle of the group was a huge figure—Court thought the man must have been at least six-six—and he carried a smaller man who was clearly either dead or unconscious over his shoulder.

Court assumed him to be the prisoner he'd last seen on the Gulfstream a few hours earlier.

There were nearly a dozen men plus the prisoner at the other end of the hall, but the group immediately turned to the left, away from Court, and they began walking towards a doorway that Court assumed led to the western side of the property.

The four who'd been in the hallway turned to follow them.

The sound of the helicopter spinning up again filled Court's earplugs, forcing him to shut them off.

Court decided to get a look at the tail number of the helo. To do so he could either pursue the men or find a window on the southwestern side of the building that would give him a vantage point to the area outside the west wing. This meant crossing the hall, and he knew he couldn't wait for the group to leave to do it, because if he couldn't get eyes on the helo from here, he'd have to take the time to find another vantage point.

He quickly glanced across the hall, still listening to the sounds of the men walking away off to his right. He looked to the left for any flashlight beam that would alert him to a sentry, but it was too dark to see into the stairwell across and to his left.

The hallway floor between Court and the room on the other side looked clean of obstructions, so he began moving slowly and silently.

On his third step across the hall he heard a sudden noise to his left. The echo of footsteps on the tile at the bottom of the stairs was unmistakable.

And the footsteps were quickly followed by a voice.

"Bloody torch is dead. We pullin' out now?"

Court turned to see the silhouette of a man approaching through the dimness, a rifle held low in his arms.

Quickly the sentry's gun began to rise, so Court swung his suppressed pistol up and fired twice. The Ruger made a quiet but easily audible *thump, thump* sound, and the ejecting brass from the weapon clinked along the floor, echoing down the length of the hallway.

The sentry fell back in a heap on the stairs.

One hundred feet behind Court, eleven men turned in the direction of the echoes. A flashlight's beam shone on him even before he began moving again for the room across the hall.

He took off in a sprint, then dove into the room and crashed into an upturned desk just as a pair of gunshots pounded the thick air behind him.

CHAPTER 13

Kent had fired one of the two rounds, but he was certain both he and Davy had missed the target moving through the dusty dim. "Get him!"

Two of Kent's men began running up the hall, flashlights in one hand and pistols in the other, but Fox shouted at Kent as he and his group hustled in the other direction. "*All* of you go after him! He cannot leave here alive!"

Kent turned away and followed the rest of his men up the hall, staying far to the back of the pack. "Everyone move to the south side, ground floor, east of the entry. One subject. Take him out but watch your crossfire!"

Kent didn't want to get shot by his own men any more than he wanted to get shot by the hostile.

• • •

Court's grand scheme to learn something about the helo went up in smoke as his opposition began getting word from their leader that an interloper was inside the wire. He knew men would be collapsing on him now from all over this massive old hospital, so he raced back to the east through doorways that connected the administration office to a long narrow room lined with broken file cabinets.

His goal was to get back down to the tunnel, but basement access was on the far side of the east wing, and he had a lot of ground to cover.

He pumped the air with his arms as he sprinted, his SIG pistol in his right hand and his red headlamp shining on his forehead so he could see his way forward even though it could be seen easily by others in the darkness.

He heard the helicopter behind him lifting into the sky, but there wasn't a damn thing he could do about the captured banker.

Instead he just kept running for his life.

He sprinted to a doorway, raising his handgun when he heard the squawk of a radio on the other side. Court knew that with the light on his head and the noise generated on the flooring by his frantic pace, he wasn't likely any stealthier than whoever was in the next room with a walkie-talkie blaring, and the man there would hear his footsteps even if he did not yet know if Court was friend or foe.

Court moved to the wall, dropped to his knees, and quickly spun into the doorway, mindful of the sound of others approaching from behind him. Just feet away he saw a man with a bloody dressing on his thigh, and the man saw him at the same time.

The gunman lifted his submachine gun and pointed it in Court's direction.

Court fired, dropping the man onto his back with two rounds to the chest.

Up and running again, he had not made it far at all before he heard more gunfire, close and on his left. The wall next to him began to pock with bullet holes, fired from the other side by an automatic weapon. Plaster and paint sprayed across the glow of his red headlamp's light.

This forced Court down into a crouch as he ran. He returned fire blindly into the wall, then felt a powerful tug, nearly toppling him. He was certain he'd been hit at first, but quickly realized his backpack had taken a bullet instead of his body.

More bursts of fire chased him back across a hall in the east wing, and then, when he made the turn to head towards the stairs to the basement, he found himself facing down another pair of men with flashlights and guns, just a dozen feet away.

As gunfire pounded his ears, Court dove to the dusty floor of the abandoned building, sliding on his hip towards the gunmen. He took one down like a bowling pin as they collided, then shot the second man three times as he spun and took aim on Court's prone body.

The sentry on the ground with him had lost control of his gun and it fell away, but he quickly pulled a short, hooked, fixed-blade knife out of a sheath on his belt and drove it down at Court's face while Court still had his weapon pointed in the direction of the other enemy. Court parried the first strike with his left hand, and the man knocked Court's gun arm back and lurched to stab again.

Court rolled quickly onto his stomach. The knife cut through air above him, and then the blade slammed into the backpack, burying itself into a plastic bottle of water.

Now Court rolled onto his backpack, bringing his left arm out as he whirled back around, and he executed a spinning backfist that connected with the jaw of the man above him. With the *thunk* of bone on flesh, the man's head snapped to the side, a tooth flew out of his mouth ahead of a spray of blood, and he slumped to his side, on top of his dead colleague.

Court rose to his feet as more men approached from behind. He fired back behind him as he ran the opposite way, quickly getting himself out of the line of fire by racing into the stairwell down to the basement.

As he entered the tunnel to the mortuary seconds later, he could hear the footsteps and shouts of what sounded like at least a half dozen men running through the basement behind him. He ran in a crouch through the tunnel, using his red light freely now, a necessity to avoid tripping through the trash-filled water or banging his head on pipes hanging from the ceiling that ran the length of the passageway.

He knew that in moments there would be bullets racing through the narrow shaft and he'd be a fish in a barrel, so he pulled off his pack, yanked out the grenade launcher, and spun back around. He dropped to his knees in the murky sludge just as the first flashlight beam shone on him, and he raised the weapon.

A *crack* of unsuppressed gunfire, the *ping* of a bullet hitting a pipe feet from Court's head, and then Court pulled the trigger, arcing a 40-millimeter grenade back up the small tunnel to the entrance to the basement. With a jarring boom and a ball of fire it detonated, and Court was back up and running again, reloading the single-shot break-open-barrel weapon, this time with a tear gas round.

He made it all the way to the mortuary end of the tunnel before the gunfire behind him resumed, and here he dropped again into the ankle-deep water, spun back, and fired the launcher once more.

The tear gas round didn't generate the sound or the flash of the high-explosive shell, but he knew it would make the poorly ventilated, claustrophobic tunnel impassable for the next hour or so. When it detonated halfway down the passage he raced up the stairs into the postmortem room of the mortuary, then ran through the building, throwing his M320 back into his wet pack and retrieving his pistol from his waistband.

He exited through a window of the mortuary, then sprinted for the woods with his gun, shifting left to right with his eyes as he scanned for targets, unsure if anyone was up at ground level with eyes on him.

• • •

A minute later he was back on the little pit bike, racing through the woods at a breakneck pace. He was aware that the men behind him were in possession of two vehicles that could run him down in seconds, and the last thing he was going to do was buzz out onto the highway on top of this two-wheel toy.

He needed a car, and he knew where to get one.

As he'd flown over the area most of an hour earlier, he'd spied a golf course with a parking lot adjacent. It was just on the eastern side of the forest, so he took his bike all the way to the wood line, then ran from there onto the property.

He climbed a fence, dropped down into the parking lot, then crouched between cars while he watched a lone valet near the entrance to the clubhouse. An older man with a set of clubs on his shoulder stepped up to the valet and handed him a ticket, and then the young man grabbed a key out of a box next to him and began running off into the lot.

Court had spent dozens of hours watching valets in his career, and as was usually the case, this young man had not bothered to lock the key box.

Court stowed his pistol under his jacket, rose, and walked confidently up to the valet stand despite his filthy clothes, soaking backpack, and soiled face. He nodded politely at the man standing there. Without a word he reached into the key box. He settled on a set of Audi keys, hoping to snag something that was both fast and low-profile in his surroundings.

Walking through the lot he pressed the key fob, and a beep to his right directed him to a 2005 Audi S4 sedan. It wasn't particularly fast, certainly not like the two cars he saw back at the hospital, but he didn't think he'd have much trouble blending in with a fifteen-year-old four-door.

A minute after that he was on the A17, heading west. While he drove he opened his backpack and checked his gear.

He realized quickly that a large hole had been cut in his bag from the knife attack, big enough for the two spare pistol magazines to fall out somewhere, likely in the tunnel. Checking the mag in the pistol, he found he had only six more 9-millimeter rounds, plus the one in the chamber. The Ruger .22 was still in the backpack, but he was down to his last five rounds with no spare mags for this weapon, either.

"Shit!" he shouted to the empty car, then glanced up at his rearview to check his six.

"Shit!" He shouted it this time because the gray Charger he'd seen at the hospital was in the center of his rearview mirror, growing by the second. He'd been concentrating so much on his gear in his lap and the road ahead that he'd failed to notice the vehicle closing the distance with incredible ease. The Mercedes followed behind the Charger, and from the speed of both vehicles he was now assured they were both, indeed, V8 models.

As he stomped on his gas pedal, he saw armed men rising out of both sides of the Charger's backseat, and they each pointed a weapon at Court's Audi.

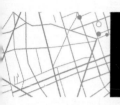

CHAPTER 14

Court ducked down and looked ahead now. The traffic in front of him was light, but there was enough in both lanes to where he knew he couldn't devote all his attention to the approaching cars behind him.

He heard the crack of gunfire now, and his head turtled down even more.

This A4 was the 3.1-liter V6, the top-of-the-line engine in the series for the year it was built, and it produced 255 horsepower. This wasn't bad for a fifteen-year-old luxury sedan, but it was nothing like the Mercedes and the Dodge behind him, which he assumed to both have in excess of 400 horsepower.

Court brought his car up to one hundred miles an hour, but more snaps zinging by his driver-side window told him the men after him weren't backing off.

He swerved left and right, willing the old Audi to go faster, and knew it was just a matter of moments before he would be overtaken.

His rear window cracked as a handgun round pierced it and buried itself into the dashboard over the radio on Court's left.

He couldn't outrun his pursuers; he had to fight them, but there was no way he could target them effectively with his pistol while facing the other direction.

Snatching up the SIG, he wedged it tightly between his seat and the door on his right, with the grip just rising above the leather upholstery. He then grabbed the Ruger by its long silencer, and this he tucked under his left thigh on the seat.

Another bullet hit the back window, and then a third shattered it fully, passed through the car, and spiderwebbed the windshield. Court calculated the distance to a pair of civilian trucks ahead of him and waited for an oncoming car to shoot by on his right. He put his right hand on the two o'clock position of his steering wheel, and his left hand grasped the emergency brake handle between the seats.

At eighty miles per hour he pulled his foot off the gas and drew it all the way to the seat so he wouldn't be tempted to step on the foot brake, and then he yanked the hand brake up as hard as he could, locking the rear wheels.

Once in his high-speed skid he turned the steering wheel to the right slightly, moving his hand from two to four o'clock, and this spun the vehicle hard to the right on screaming and smoking tires.

As the 180-degree turn reached the halfway point he used his thighs to hold the steering wheel in position and let go with his right hand. He reached down between the seat and the door and drew his SIG Sauer. In front of him he saw farmland streaking to the left in a blur, and then the road he'd just driven down.

Just two and a half seconds after locking the brake he was now facing the matte gray Dodge Charger, which itself was smoking its brakes to arrest its closing speed.

Court shoved his pistol to the windshield in front of him and, less than twenty-five feet away from the oncoming vehicle, he opened fire, dumping round after round after round into the driver-side windshield. As he did this he shoved down the emergency brake and shifted the transmission into reverse with his left hand.

As he continued to fire the last of the 9-millimeter rounds he stomped on the gas, and his stolen vehicle lurched backwards, gaining speed with every yard as the tires whined and white smoke billowed.

When his pistol went black on ammo he tossed it onto the passenger-side floorboard and retrieved the Ruger, then emptied it into the windshield of the Charger while still flooring it in reverse, only looking into the rearview to fine-tune his backwards vector when he threw the silenced .22 onto the floor next to the nine.

The gray four-door Charger fishtailed and then lurched to a stop in the middle of the road: its driver dead, the vehicle stalled out. The Mercedes behind it had to slam on its brakes and then negotiate its way around both its partner vehicle and oncoming civilian traffic.

Court brought the Audi up to fifty in reverse, reached his right hand across the steering wheel and took it on its left side, then looked through the windshield. As the Mercedes began catching up to him again he took his foot off the gas and threw the steering wheel as hard to the right as he could, letting it go and beginning a reverse 180 on tires that wailed again in protest. The Audi spun to the left, the world a blur to the man behind the wheel, but as soon as his grille faced forward on the highway again, Court shifted the whirling car into drive, grabbed the wheel to stop the turn, and stomped the gas pedal to the floor. Within seconds he was back to one hundred miles per hour, weaving through traffic in both directions, heading east.

But it wasn't over. The Mercedes had him beat by over one hundred horsepower, and it would overtake his A4 within moments if he didn't find a way to stop it.

Court looked down at the backpack in the seat next to him. The stock of the grenade launcher was exposed, and quickly he had a plan.

As with the pistols, there was no way he could effectively target the moving car while facing the opposite direction, but if he faced the car, he might just be able to stop the threat.

He didn't think there was any way these assholes chasing him would be dumb enough to overshoot him if he swerved and slammed on the gas, and they would be ready to defend against another 180, but he had another idea in mind.

He let go of the steering wheel, checking the alignment of the wheels. The Audi ran true, straight up its lane, with no pull either left or right.

He set the cruise control for ninety, and the car began to slow slightly, and then he grabbed his backpack and put it in his lap. He removed the M320 and loaded it with an HE round one-handed but left the rest of the bandolier of grenades, along with the other gear inside the pack. He unhooked one of the shoulder straps just as a fresh string of gunfire from behind him tore into the front passenger seat.

The men after him were having trouble keeping their aim steady at these high speeds, but they were closing on him faster now, and it would not be long before they couldn't miss either the tires or, if they chose, the back of his head.

Court wrapped the strap over the steering wheel, then reclasped it to the backpack. He put the pack down between his knees. It hung from the wheel, keeping it extra steady with its weight.

He let go of the wheel now and checked the Audi's trajectory, adjusting the pack once to realign the vehicle with the center of the lane just after rocketing past a slower-moving Toyota.

More gunfire raced up the road on his left, tearing asphalt, just as an oncoming car flashed by to his right. Court unbuckled his seat belt, lowered his seat back, and pulled himself rearward into the back, careful not to disturb the backpack that had taken the wheel of the speeding sedan.

Still more rounds impacted the rear of the car. Court imagined they were close enough now to where they were trying to shoot out the tires, and he thought it likely the Audi would run off the road if they did so.

He reached into the front passenger seat, pulled the M320 back to him, and then spun around to face his pursuers.

The old silver Mercedes was there, in front of him, just forty or so yards back. Two men hung out of it, both with submachine guns in one hand while they held on to the door frame with the other. Court recognized Kent from the hallway of the hospital, leaning out of the front passenger side.

Both subguns flashed, and bullets slammed into the Audi, forcing Court down to the floorboard, but the second they stopped he rose back up, balanced the M320 on the rear seat back, and pointed the muzzle at the center of the Mercedes. He raised his aim an inch, accounting for the high trajectory of the weapon, and then, with no further hesitation, he pulled the trigger.

The launcher bucked in his hands.

The high-explosive round left the M320, passing through the already shattered rear window, arced back up the highway forty yards, then penetrated the windshield of the oncoming vehicle. It detonated, and the explosion ejected both men hanging out of the windows onto opposite sides of the road.

The silver sedan's gas tank detonated. It drove on like that for fifty yards before skidding hard to the right, running off the road and rolling end over end for twenty-five yards through an uncultivated field.

Court was thankful, but he held his applause; he was in the backseat of a car with no driver, racing towards traffic at ninety miles per hour and, just as he started to move back to the front seat, he heard the telltale *thump thump* of a blown tire below him.

He dove forward through the seats and turned off the cruise control, then directed the vehicle out of the oncoming lane.

He climbed back into the driver's seat and pulled a U-turn, racing on the flat tire back to where Kent lay in the road.

Court skidded to a stop next to the still body, climbed out, and ran up to him. He saw that Kent's right leg was all but severed at the thigh; blood poured out of his ripped pants leg.

Kneeling down, Court began running his hands through the man's clothing.

"Hang on. Don't you *fucking* die! You *better* not die, dude."

Court found what he was looking for. He pulled Kent's phone out of a front pants pocket and examined it. It was an iPhone 8, which caused him to look back up to Kent's face. It was white as a sheet and his eyes were slowly rolling back into his head.

"No!" Court shouted, then dropped the phone onto the highway and began applying chest compressions. "Come on, Kent! Hang on!"

The first passersby came running up, their vehicle parked in the road to the west. A husband and wife, both in their sixties, appeared next to Court. The husband had a small first-aid kit he'd taken out of the boot of his little car.

The woman said, "We've called for an ambulance! The others are dead. What can we do to help?"

Court didn't answer; he just kept pumping Kent's chest, virtually as hard as he could, while watching the man's eyes.

The husband said, "He's bleedin' from the leg, mate. We need a tourniquet!" The man began ripping off his belt.

Court kept up the compressions, ignoring the massive wound in the man's leg, and finally he saw Kent's eyes flicker. They were unfixed, but he was definitely alive.

The husband said, "Let me get in there and put this around—"

Court stopped the chest compressions.

"Keep it up, mate. He's not going to make it unless—"

Court lifted the phone off the ground, grabbed Kent's limp right hand, and held his thumb to the home button.

"What the hell you doin'?" the husband asked.

Almost instantly the phone unlocked.

He opened the phone, used Kent's finger again to allow him to change the password on the device. Court pushed "1" six times, confirmed it by repeating it, and then rose from his knees and stood over the horribly wounded man. The husband was still kneeling, working on the makeshift tourniquet on Court's right, the woman busy opening the first-aid kit on his left.

Court looked down to Kent lying in the road. "You can die now, mother-fucker. Don't need you anymore."

The two Brits looked up at him in shock, but Court didn't notice. He'd already turned away, heading back towards the Audi.

The iPhone Touch ID sensor uses the capacitive signal from the owner's finger to unlock the device, and the signal only comes from the electric pulses made by a living body. Court knew if Kent was dead he'd have a hard time getting into the man's phone, and since he'd not accomplished much of anything in the last several hours as far as recovering the banker, he knew he needed to risk going back to the injured killer to try to get it.

Sounds of sirens seemed to appear from nowhere, and they grew in all directions.

The Audi was virtually dead now, both the front and the back glass were shattered, and the right rear tire was shredded with pieces lying all along the highway behind, so Court left it and continued sprinting to the east, pulling out the CIA phone and cables from his pocket as he ran.

Behind him smoke and fire roiled from the Mercedes in the field along the A1, and somewhere behind that there was a gray Charger, presumably out of commission in the middle of the highway and filled with dead or wounded. Ahead Court saw a gas station a quarter of a mile off, and he made for it as fast as he could as the effects of adrenaline began to wear off. He felt the exhaustion taking hold, but he pressed on, hoping he could get the hell out of there before every single police officer in the East Midlands arrived at what must have been the biggest violent crime committed in this part of the UK in decades.

He wasn't happy about what had happened, not psyched at all about killing multiple carloads of men. It was not that he felt bad about the shooters, not in the least, but he understood he'd pressed his luck with all the gunplay, and only by undeserved fortune had he survived.

He told himself he couldn't just continue bouncing from one gun battle to another, one car chase after the next, from impossibly close call to impossibly close call.

He was good, many said he was the best, but Court knew better than to believe all the hype about his skills. He was well aware he was operating on borrowed time, and if he continued shooting it out with every bad actor he came into contact with, time would run out sooner rather than later.

As he ran through a trash-strewn field near the gas station he slowed, stopped, and then dropped to his knees.

He vomited the contents of his stomach onto the dirt, puked again until he retched, and then climbed heavily up to his feet. He felt drained, ill, worn through, and defeated.

He'd gotten nothing out of this morning save for the phone. He had to get some actionable intelligence from it, and that meant he'd have to work fast.

Court shook away his doubt, his recognition that his next move might be his last, and he began walking again towards the gas station.

He glanced at his watch. It was time to steal his fourth vehicle of the day, and the day was still young.

CHAPTER 15

Suzanne Brewer sat in her office more pissed off this morning than usual.

She'd come into the office early to prepare for her seven a.m. meeting regarding the disappearance of a protected code-word asset during an attack on a CIA safe house. The meeting went as she'd expected; no one there was read in on Anthem, per Matt Hanley, and Hanley hadn't bothered to attend. So Brewer took the heat from ten execs from Support and Personnel, none of whom knew any of the victims from the night before in Great Falls, but all of whom would find themselves roped into the inevitable hot wash and cleanup of the incident.

Every one of these execs was already feverishly working on the upcoming Five Eyes conference in the United Kingdom, with most of them flying out within the next couple of days. Great Falls was a disaster even without the impending trip, of course, but with their schedules already full, to a man and to a woman they all held Brewer accountable for their added stress.

Brewer had spent the majority of her career focused on threats to the Agency, working in the Middle East during the global war on terror, all over Asia, and back here stateside at the CIA's sprawling complex in McLean, Virginia, so a facility compromise investigation was nothing new to her. Still, the scope and scale of the attack, especially considering it happened inside U.S. borders, was entirely unique.

As was the fact that she herself would be coming under scrutiny about what happened. Had she correctly assessed the threat to the asset? Had she arranged for enough security?

Her stomach churned as she thought about the potential comebacks on her about this whole debacle.

Her secure mobile rang and she grabbed it without looking. She expected it to be one of the teams canvassing northern Virginia and D.C. for Anthem, but instead she heard Violator's voice.

"The prisoner was exfiltrated by helicopter."

Shit. The other matter was running into yet more difficulties as well. Brewer had back-burnered Violator's situation; nobody could place any blame on her about some detainee she didn't even know being recovered by an unknown enemy force, but she was still Violator's handler, so she knew she was stuck with him and his problems.

"Tell me you at least got the tail number of the helo."

A pause. "Didn't get it. I got a phone off the shoot-team leader. I'm downloading all the data to my device and will upload ASAP."

"Tell me there's more."

"A little. Apparently the shooters were from different gangs around the UK. They were brought in for this hit by a guy named Mr. Fox."

"A pseudonym, probably. Useless."

Court sighed. "The name of the shooters' leader was Anthony Kent. He only became the top dog when the two guys above him got fragged at the airport. None of these men had worked together before, apparently."

"They killed a lot of intelligence professionals. They certainly seemed like they knew what they were doing," Brewer said.

"Yeah, they caused a lot of damage, but their hit wasn't clean like a well-trained outfit. Ternhill was an ambush; they had all the advantages, but they still lost a half dozen dead. Here in the East Midlands I took out that many more."

"You are saying you engaged them *alone*? Was that smart?"

"Would have been smarter if I'd stayed in Zurich and didn't get on your damn plane!"

Brewer drummed her fingers on her desk. "That tail number from the helicopter would have been helpful."

She heard nothing for several seconds. Then Violator replied. "You know? Maybe I need you to come show me how it's done. How about next time *you* hit the building filled with armed assholes while I hang back at my desk and bitch about your performance?"

Brewer didn't respond to this. Instead she asked, "Is that it?"

Court sighed into the phone. "There's an abandoned hospital where the interrogation took place, just a few miles behind me now. Look into it and see if it's tied to some group. They didn't just stumble on this place. They came straight here."

"Understood. What are you going to do?"

"I'm going shopping." The line went dead.

· · ·

Zoya Zakharova had been waiting for fifteen minutes at the front door of the Nordstrom Rack on 12th Street in D.C. when the doors opened at nine a.m. She bought a pair of jeans, a T-shirt, a zip-up jacket, two casual tops, a pair of slip-on flats, and a new pair of running shoes. She headed across the street to a Starbucks to change in their bathroom, stuffing the clothes she had been wearing, her shoes, and the shopping bags all in the trash.

At nine forty-five a.m. she sat at a computer terminal at the Northwest One Neighborhood Library, doing research on the Internet. She jotted down pages of information with paper and a pen she borrowed from a high school kid and, while she did this, she shot her eyes up and around the room every few seconds. She knew CIA had robust facial recognition technology, and she'd not been able to avoid all the cameras on the streets or in the library, but she also knew CIA was not supposed to use their tech inside the United States.

Still, she came from Russia and had worked in their government, so she knew how a government's intelligence services could be easily and efficiently turned around on its own people. She couldn't be sure the same was not happening here in the States, so she remained ever vigilant.

She had planned four different escape routes out of the library if the walls started closing in on her, and she was ready to fight if the men who'd attacked the safe house the evening before reappeared.

But no one came to take her away, and she continued with her work.

And by ten thirty she knew where she needed to go and what she needed to do.

She was a woman on a mission, a highly trained asset with a plan.

First things first, though. To accomplish her operation she had to get out of the United States and into Europe. This wasn't going to be easy, since she had no passport or identification, but she knew a way.

It would take all her abilities of manipulation and deception to pull it off, but she'd been a student and a practitioner of high-level social engineering since she was a child, so she knew she could get it done.

CHAPTER 16

FOUR MONTHS EARLIER

North Korean virologist Dr. Won Jang-Mi stepped out of her office at the European Centre for Disease Prevention, her lunch swinging from a plastic bag in her hand. Stockholm was in the midst of winter and the temperatures were below freezing, but in her heavy down coat and knit cap it wasn't unbearable. On sunny days like this Won liked to take her lunch alone outside on one of the wooden benches just behind her building.

Her two security officers had returned to North Korea when she moved to Stockholm; there was no rational overt reason for the woman to have men at her shoulder all the time, and they could hardly reveal they were her bodyguards. Since then, she had been alone for nearly two years, except for during her workdays at the center. This sequestration of herself from others was one third due to the tradecraft ingrained in her by the North Korean intelligence apparatus, one third due to her absolute hatred of the West, and one third due to her crippling social anxiety that made personal relationships here, or anywhere, nearly impossible.

The other change made when she'd moved from Shikhany, Russia, to Stockholm twenty months earlier, under orders from North Korean intelligence and with the help of Russian intelligence, was replacing her Korean given name Jang-Mi with the Westernized "Janice."

Now Janice Won sat down on her bench after wiping it off with a hand towel she kept in her bag for that duty.

She tightened up her coat at the neck and looked at the dirty picnic table.

Won had suffered her entire life with obsessive-compulsive disorder. Each evening she laid out every bit of her clothing, her shoes, and all her accessories on a table or sofa or chair in a perfect representation of how she would wear them the next day. She impulsively washed her hands, and washed all utensils and flatware twice before meals and twice more after meals.

Even with her OCD, eating out here was better than eating in the cafeteria with all the Westerners, so she sat down.

Won had grown up with icy winters in North Korea, and more often than not there was no fuel for the tiny coal-fired furnace in her home. Sweden's bitter cold reminded her of her past in this one regard, but the two nations had nothing in common when comparing North Korea with Sweden's opulence, and its calm, happy people of diverse ethnicities.

No, other than the seasonal chill, Pyongyang and Stockholm were as different as two worlds could be.

As she bit into her sandwich she thought about her life here. Won excelled in her work. She studied Western preparedness for a biological outbreak of a size and scope she knew she had the power to deliver. The Russians wanted this information, ditto the North Koreans, and Won was perfectly trained and placed to provide it for them.

She sent in her periodic reports, kept at her job, and served her masters.

But Won had another goal. Not under orders from Russia or the DPRK, no, this was a quest of her own making. She wasn't here to collect data to give to Russia or North Korea.

No, she wanted to act.

She wanted—she *needed*—to release bacteria in the West to punish them for their crimes against her homeland.

And this was why she was particularly distraught today. The North Koreans had recalled her a week earlier; she'd remain here in the West for only another three weeks, and then she would make her way back to Pyongyang, where she was all but certain she would spend the rest of her life in a laboratory working on theoretical schemes that would never come to fruition.

She normally had the picnic table to herself for lunch in winter, so she was surprised when a man sat down next to her and crossed his legs, gazing out into the street. She gave him a quick sideways glance and found him handsome and exceedingly well dressed, but somewhat severe looking. He wore fine Western clothing under his fur coat, but she pegged him as Slavic; two years living in Russia had taught her certain characteristics.

The man turned and looked at her while Won bit into her sandwich.

"How are you today?"

He spoke English; it sounded like a British accent to her, and he seemed relaxed.

But Won did not like small talk with strangers. "Fine, thank you," she said, and took another bite of her sandwich.

"You are Dr. Won, are you not?"

Her heart began to pound. This stranger was initiating contact, and she'd been trained to report this to her control immediately. She quickly went on guard, told herself she had to remember everything the man said as well as his appearance. This was the first time in her travels through the West that any suspicious unknown Westerner had initiated a conversation.

She put down her sandwich and swiveled to face him. "How can I help you?"

He extended a hand. "My name is Roger Fox. I am an engineer working at the aerospace center up the street."

She did not believe this for a second. When the hand remained in the air in front of her, she took it with a slight grimace, because of her loathing of human touch.

"And how do you know my name?"

"I believe you and I have a mutual friend."

"Oh?"

"Alexi Filotov."

Won remained on guard, but at least she thought she understood what was going on now. Filotov was Russian GRU, military intelligence; this she had determined after the day she showed him the video of the pneumonic plague strain trials conducted at the prison in the DPRK.

She had the common sense to know that this man in front of her was telling her he was affiliated with Russian intelligence in some capacity.

Guardedly, she said, "I have not seen Filotov for some time."

"He sends his regards."

"Fox," Won said. "That's not a Russian name."

The man in the goatee smiled. "And Janice is not a Korean name, but it helps you fit in."

"Why do you need a pseudonym?"

He smiled more broadly now. "Necessary for my purposes, Janice."

"And what are these purposes? Nothing to do with the aerospace center, I imagine."

"You are perceptive. The truth is I have been sent to extend to you an invitation for a short trip."

Won returned to her lunch. "I've seen enough of Russia, but thank you."

"Not Russia. London. Ever been?"

Won turned away from the sandwich inches from her mouth and stared at him for several seconds. "I suppose if you know Filotov it would be easy for you to know where I have and have not been."

Fox gave an apologetic bow. "Yes. I've seen your file with FSB. Sweden is the only Western nation you've visited."

"You have me at a loss. Perhaps I should speak with Filotov before—"

Fox said, "Talk to him, certainly. But hear my offer first."

. . .

Won did speak with the FSB officer back in Russia via encrypted messaging, and even though Filotov claimed to have no clue who this Roger Fox was, he said he would check with his higher-ups. He reported back that Fox was, indeed, known to Russian intelligence. He lived in London, and Filotov suggested she go there to hear him out.

This was something she could not do without North Korean approval; in fact, she had a responsibility to report this contact with the Russian agent, even though the North Koreans knew she was on a joint mission set up by Moscow. But Pyongyang had ordered her home and she was certain the Russians would only want to talk to her in London if they had some sort of need of her talents.

She decided then and there not to seek approval from her handler in Pyongyang. She would go on the trip, and *then* report what she'd learned.

The following morning she was picked up by Fox in a Mercedes, along with a giant of a man, who seemed to Janice to be Fox's personal security officer. Soon the three boarded a private jet and flew to Farnborough Airport, thirty-five miles southwest of London. Here a black Mercedes SUV with a driver picked them up and drove them out of the airport grounds.

As soon as they pulled onto the highway, the huge blond in the front passenger seat turned around and handed something to Fox. The Russian turned to his guest.

"Dr. Won, we ask that you wear this blindfold for the duration of the trip. For security reasons, I'm certain you understand."

Won did as she was told, taking the nighttime mask and placing it over her eyes.

The vehicle stopped an hour later and she was escorted carefully across a gravel driveway and into a building. A maze of corridors and steps came next, and by the time Fox helped her into a chair she was utterly disoriented.

Finally her blindfold was removed, and she found herself seated at a table in an opulent dining room. Outside the window she saw a beautiful expanse of lawn, several acres in size, surrounded by a well-manicured and extravagant-looking garden.

Fox was there, seated next to her. A bearded man in his sixties sat across from her at the table, but he stood as soon as she saw him and bowed.

Fox made the introductions. "Dr. Won, this is my employer, David Mars."

Mars extended a hand. "A pleasure, Doctor. I trust your journey was both comfortable and uneventful." He poured tea from a service for all three of them, then sat back down. "It's green tea, from Korea, in honor of your visit today."

Mars sat close to her, leaning closer still. Won did not like having her personal space violated, so this intrusion disquieted her, although the man still smiled at her like they were long-lost friends.

He said, "Your nation has served you well with your operation to move you into the West, and you, in turn, have served it quite admirably over the past three and a half years."

"Who are you? You aren't Russian, either."

"I trust the fact that Fox has been cleared by Russian intelligence will put you at ease, but I will tell you something about me. I represent interests here in the United Kingdom, interests that I believe coincide with your own."

"How would you come to know of my interests?"

When she stole another glance at Fox, Mars said, "I have your file from GRU. It's all there."

She nodded slowly.

"We also know you've been recalled by Pyongyang."

Won's eyes narrowed. "There would be nothing in my file about that. The Russians are not privy to my orders directly from Pyongyang."

Mars sipped his tea. "You put your flat up on the market; you've not been shopping for another residence. You haven't taken on new assignments at the Centre for Disease Prevention; it certainly seems as though you are winding your time down in Sweden. We don't see evidence that you are moving to another job in the West, and Russia did not recall you, so we can only assume your birth nation has asked you to return home."

"You are spying on me. I do not think my birth nation will like hearing that."

Mars shrugged now. "They don't know you are here. I doubt you'll be telling them anything I tell you."

Won realized this man knew more about her than she did him, or the reasons he was interested in her at all. "I think you should tell me exactly why I am here and why you know so much about me, Mr. Mars."

"I want to use your talents."

"In what way?"

"I want to build you a laboratory, here in the UK, and I want you to create a weaponized version of pneumonic plague."

Won cocked her head. "For what reason?"

Mars smiled, then pulled his chair closer. She could not help but find his smile surprisingly warm and charming, for a Westerner. "I understand you, Janice. You and I think alike. You want to matter, you want to utilize your life's work, you want all the years of toiling for a cause to be *about* something. Not something theoretical. Something tangible. Something real." He paused. With unmistakable passion, he clenched his fist in front of his face and said, "So do I."

Won said her next words as a statement. "You are planning a biological attack."

"Yes. Real world, against the West. I am thinking aerosol delivery will be the most efficient, but I will leave that to your expertise."

Won was utterly confused. "But . . . why would *you* attack the West?"

Mars smiled. "I have my reasons. If you agree to work with me, at some point I am sure you will learn them. But Fox is my liaison with Russia, and Fox is your insurance that this operation is sanctioned by one of your two masters."

Still baffled by this, she said, "But not the other. Pyongyang has given no instructions to—"

"They have not, and they will not. And this is the best part for you, and for them. Your nation will in no way be implicated by what happens. You can act, you can make the difference you have been longing to make, and your nation will remain safe from harm. We will go to unimaginable lengths to keep your involvement a secret."

This seemed almost too good to be true to Janice Won. She fought to maintain some objectivity, some skepticism. But in the end she failed. Considering it a moment, she said, "I would need a sample of *Yersinia pestis*, the bacterium that causes pneumonic plague."

Mars waved a hand in the air. "You have it back in Stockholm. For testing and research."

"You think they will just let me walk out of the lab with it?"

"Yes. Yes, I do. We will provide you with equipment to safely and secretly remove and transport it. We will help you do it. Once you have it, you will come here, and we will be ready for you."

"What is the target, specifically?" she asked, but Mars immediately shook his head and poured more tea for himself and Fox. Janice Won hadn't touched hers.

"That is information you will receive at the right time, and not before."

Won made no decision immediately; she spent the night in the massive home, then left blindfolded on the way to the airport the next day. Fox and his bodyguard returned with her to Stockholm, gave her a number, and told her to call it when her decision was made.

But her decision *was* made. Russian intelligence wanted to use her skills to attack the West, and this would only implicate Russia in the action. She saw it as a perfect opportunity to strike a blow that would help her nation without worry of reprisals *against* her nation.

She knew she could not tell any of her North Korean handlers about Mr. Mars and the trip to London, or about the laboratory and the theft of bacteria from the lab.

No, she realized she had to become a rogue agent to protect her country from being nuked into dust in retaliation for what she would do.

CHAPTER 17

PRESENT DAY

Two and a half hours after the rolling firefight ended on the British highway, Court drove a stolen station wagon on the A15, heading north, just to
get away from the gun battle. He'd taken plates off a Renault parked in the
service lot at the gas station and then put them on an old Volvo nearby. He
hot-wired the Volvo and now he was passing through the town of Lincoln,
waiting for Brewer to get back to him with some answers.

He parked the Volvo on a street a block from the main train station,
then took off on foot, spending a few minutes on a simple surveillance
detection route to slip anyone who might be following him. He made a
cover stop at a café, and another at a bookstore, and saw no hint of a tail.
After this he wandered into a shopping mall, used the ATM to get some
local currency, then entered a men's clothing store. He'd tossed his jacket
in a rubbish bin during his SDR, and his T-shirt wasn't that dirty or
stained, but his black jeans were soiled through. Still, he didn't garner any
notice from the shoppers around him.

He excelled at moving low-profile throughout the world.

He picked out two full sets of clothes, along with new hiking boots,
sunglasses, and other accessories. He changed in a bathroom off the mall's
food court, and by one p.m. he was back outside, walking down the street.

When his phone rang he was most of the way through a rolled-up Turkish pizza he'd bought from a street stand, walking along the River Witham. He quickly downed the last few bites and answered his phone, sitting down on a set of steps that went down to the waterline, far enough away from the footpath to where no one could hear him.

"Any luck?" he asked, knowing Suzanne Brewer was the only person with this phone number.

"Some, but the tail number of the helo would have provided us more answers."

"Will you *please* stop whining about the damn helicopter?"

Brewer blew out a little air of frustration, then said, "Three of the four men in your pictures have been identified, all from British criminal databases. Nigel Halton from Southampton, Kevin Ball from Bristol, and Anthony Kent from Nottingham. They've all been to prison, they all seem to work for different criminal firms in the UK, but other than that there is nothing that puts them together."

Court said, "Tell me about Kent."

"Well, he's employed as a truck driver and has four convictions for theft. Two more charges were dropped. He's linked to a criminal firm based in Nottingham, which is only about forty miles west of the abandoned asylum. The group is called the Nottingham Syndicate."

"Never heard of them."

"Theft, extortion, a few killings, but only of rival gang members or police informants. They are pretty low-scale for a takedown of a dozen intelligence officers."

"According to what I heard, Kent was ordered to join this outfit to do this job. His criminal firm isn't running this show."

"Well, it's a fair bet the man in charge of the Nottingham Syndicate knows who hired his man."

Court nodded. "Who is he?"

"His name is Charlie Jones. He's the top guy in the Nottingham underworld, apparently."

"You got all this from the Brits?"

"Yes. Thank God for the Five Eyes. If you were in Germany or France, we'd only have access to our own resources without a formal request, which means we likely wouldn't know much at all."

"Where do I find Charlie Jones?"

"We don't know for sure, but something interesting popped up. Kent's phone was a burner unit, and location services were turned off, but he did make two calls, both to the same number, both after the ambush at Ternhill."

"And you got the address?"

"Again, thanks to a database we have via the Five Eyes network. It's a pub in Nottingham."

"He lives in Nottingham. He's English. The fact that he made a call to a pub doesn't really blow me away."

"Well, this is not his corner pub. It's twenty-five minutes' drive from his flat. We looked into the place and saw that the local police have tied the location to the Nottingham Syndicate."

"Address?"

"Forty-three Angels Row. Checking archived cam footage in the area, we have seen Jones go in there most every evening around six. He usually stays till eight or nine, then goes elsewhere for dinner."

"I'll go check it out."

"Good," she said. "Look, you got away with killing on British soil in an abandoned hospital and on a remote highway, but if you shoot up a pub in a major city, you're going to get photographed and picked up."

"What do you care? You'll just disavow me."

"Yes, I will," she responded. "So try not to go crazy in there."

"Yeah."

"All right, if there's nothing else, I have to get back to work."

"Back to work? This *is* work, Brewer."

"I have an off-site meeting I'm pulling into now. Have to go."

She disconnected the call.

. . .

The CIA contract agent operating under the code name Romantic climbed out of his pickup truck and walked through the parking garage, heading directly for the champagne Infiniti sedan parked in the darkened corner. As he neared the driver-side door he heard it unlock.

Romantic was six feet, two inches tall, powerfully built, with blond hair liberally flecked with gray that he wore slicked back. He had a brownish-blond beard that was trimmed into a short point below his chin, and dramatically cut sideburns. His grizzled skin around his facial hair showed the effects of a half century of sun and more stress than ten average men. He wore a denim shirt, thick canvas work pants, and well-worn roper boots.

He looked more Texas than D.C., which made sense, because he was born and raised near Dallas.

Zack Hightower had begun his career with the U.S. government in the Navy, as a SEAL, and then he was recruited into the CIA's Special Activities Division. There he spent years as a team leader of a group of paramilitary operations officers tasked with running renditions, hits, black bag jobs, and other tasks around the world in furtherance of American interests.

He was the team leader of Task Force Golf Sierra, the SAD–Ground Branch unit known infamously in the shadowy deep corners at Langley as "the Goon Squad." One of his subordinates had been a young Courtland Gentry, and that had led to Zack's downfall several years earlier.

Hightower had fallen out of favor with the leadership in the National Clandestine Service and spent a couple years bumming around Virginia and West Virginia as a hunting guide before being scooped back up, dusted off, and put back into service as a contract agent working for the Agency.

No, *not* working for the Agency. Hightower worked for Matthew Hanley specifically. Hanley, through Brewer, directed Zack through Poison Apple, just like Court Gentry, though neither Violator nor Romantic had ever heard the name of the code-worded program they were a part of.

Gentry and Hightower were used as cleanup men to deal with special problems that the CIA couldn't run the risk of being tied to. Zakharova was being groomed for the same program, although her status as an asset at present remained in serious doubt.

Hightower sat down in the front passenger seat of the Infiniti. "Howdy, Suzanne. Aren't you looking particularly lovely today?"

Brewer responded to this with "You're late."

"And as delightful as ever, too." He looked at his Luminox watch. "I'm in training. Ninety minutes ago I was rappelling down a twelve-story building in Chantilly when my phone rang. Left the rigging right there and raced over, hoping you'd have something real to do." He grinned. "Cut me a little slack, it's eight after."

"So you're ready for work, Romantic?"

The man grimaced. "I fucking *hate* that code name, you *do* know that, don't you?"

"I believe you mentioned it. Every time I've spoken to you since it was assigned, as a matter of fact."

"Court gets Violator, I get . . . I get . . . *Shit*, I can't even say it."

"Luck of the draw. Grow up."

"What about 'Night Train'? That would be an awesome code name. You've got the juice to make that happen, don't you?"

She ignored him and repeated herself. "Ready for work, Romantic?"

Zack sighed. "Yeah. Always. Where am I off to this time?"

"Tysons Corner."

Zack cocked his head. "Uh . . . We're *in* Tysons Corner, Suzanne."

In a deadpan voice she said, "Well, would you look at that? You're doing great so far."

Zack smiled. Suzanne didn't have a sense of humor unless she was trying to be insulting. He could tell she was annoyed, perhaps not at him, he hadn't done anything, but she was annoyed nonetheless.

Brewer said, "There's a compromise at the Agency, which certainly seems to be stemming from someone at Langley. It's been narrowed down to four individuals who had relevant knowledge of all the ops that were betrayed. Only four. Matt wants you to put some pressure on these individuals to try to provoke a reaction." Brewer shrugged. "If they react, if they run, then we have our culprit."

Hightower raised an eyebrow. "What kind of pressure are we talking about?"

"Psychological." She turned and pointed a finger at him. "Psychological *only*. Let them know they are under suspicion. Intimate, by your actions, that you are not constrained by the justice system or CIA counterintel protocol. But do *not* initiate bodily harm."

"Scare the fuck out of them, is that it?"

Brewer nodded. "That *is* it, exactly."

"No sweat."

She handed him a packet of papers; he looked inside quickly but didn't take them out.

"Who do I start with?"

Brewer did not hesitate. "Hanley thinks it's Renfro, but go after all of them equally. I don't care where you begin."

Zack gave a quick nod. "Renfro. Never liked that prick."

"When have *you* ever worked with Lucas Renfro?"

He shrugged. "Don't know him. Just getting into character." Zack Hightower smiled. "If he's the traitor, I'll crack him like an egg."

"I have no doubt about it, Romantic."

"Any chance you could just call me Zack?"

"Negative," she said, and she fired up the engine, giving Hightower the not-so-subtle hint that their clandestine meeting had come to an end.

CHAPTER 18

Washington Dulles International Airport lies just west of D.C. and flies to all corners of the world. On the northern side of the property, a row of hangars and office buildings off Airport Drive sat quiet now at midday as planes lifted into the sky behind them. Zoya Zakharova leaned against a tree on the landscaped edge of the nearby parking lot, watching a 747 take off behind her target, the last small corporate aviation office in the row.

When the Lufthansa flight banked to the northeast, she returned her gaze to the door of the office. The place looked closed, but she had expected this because she knew the proprietor worked alone, and since it was lunchtime she'd steeled herself to be patient.

To her surprise her wait only lasted ten minutes before a Toyota Camry pulled into the lot and parked by the single metal door next to the hangar bay. Zoya lifted the cheap binoculars she'd bought a half hour earlier and centered them on the man who climbed out.

The man went to the door and unlocked it, entered, then shut it behind him. Zoya considered waiting a few minutes to get a better lay of the land, but she understood that her plan had a higher chance for success if no one else was aware of her presence here, and since she didn't see anyone around, that meant she had to take advantage of the situation that presented itself now.

She walked across the parking lot and tried to open the door but found it locked.

The same man she'd seen climbing out of the Camry opened it a moment after she knocked, surprise evident on his face at seeing such an attractive woman. In a barely discernible Slavic accent he said, "Well, hello there. How can I help you?"

"I'd like to speak with you about a charter."

He nodded with a smile. "Come in then, please."

She followed him inside, up a staircase that overlooked the hangar floor. There, in the center of the space, she saw a Cessna Citation Sovereign, a mid-range twin-engine jet. Next to it sat an old and simple Cessna 152 trainer.

They continued on to the office.

The room was small and cramped, full of books, papers, small aircraft parts, and other odds and ends. On the wall were dozens of photos, each one of a different man or woman standing in front of the 152. As he cleared paperwork off a plastic chair so she could sit down, he saw her looking at the pictures. "When I'm not flying charters, I am a flight instructor. Each time one of my students completes their first solo, I take a picture."

"I see," she said.

"But you are not here for that, you said. You wish to charter the Sovereign?"

"I do."

"Where are my manners? I'm Arthur Kravchek." He stuck out a hand and she shook it.

"Kravchek? That's Polish, isn't it?"

"Yes, it is."

She shook his hand. "My name is Irina."

A bemused look crossed his face quickly, but then disappeared as they both sat down.

"And where are you from, Irina?"

"I am from the Russian Federation."

Something flashed in the man's eyes now, Zoya saw clearly. It wasn't fear; it was more like confusion.

"May I inquire as to where you heard about my company?"

She leaned back in her chair a little. "I'll cut right to the chase. I was sent by Yasenevo."

The pilot stared back at her.

Yasenevo was a district in southwestern Moscow, and it was also the location of the headquarters of SVR, Russian foreign intelligence.

It was clear the man knew this, because he blanched slightly.

As she'd expected, he said, "I don't know what you are talking about."

"Kolya Aslanov sent me. I know this is outside the norm, but we are in a critical and immediate need of your . . . service."

Now he squinted at her. "Kolya? You are on such friendly terms with Nikolai Aslanov, SVR's deputy operations chief, that you call him by his diminutive?" He looked her over. "The Americans know who Aslanov is. How do I know you are not FBI? That this isn't some sort of setup?"

Zoya smiled coolly. "You just confirmed that you work with Russian intelligence, Arkady. If this were a setup, my team would have your face in the carpet and a knee in your back already. But look around; it's still just you and me."

Zoya's utter calm and confidence was a put-on. She had to sell the fact that she was working for Russian intelligence although she was all alone, operating without a net.

The man hesitated. "You'll have to do better than that."

She switched effortlessly to Russian.

"All right. For starters, your name is not Arthur Kravchek, it's Arkady Kravchenko. You are Ukrainian, not Polish; you flew MiG-29s in the So-viet Air Force, were recruited into the SVR as a foreign contract agent in the nineties, then emigrated to the U.S. twenty years ago for the express purpose of ferrying goods and personnel covertly for Russian intelligence. Your charter company was set up by us, and you have been moderately successful in your aboveboard endeavors here in the U.S. Five years ago you were arrested for transporting heroin from New Mexico to Chicago, but your lawyers got you off on a technicality. SVR dropped you for risking exposure, but"—she leaned forward—"we still own you, Arkady."

Kravchenko remained on guard. "Tell me . . . who was my handler at Yasenevo?"

"Aslanov himself, in the old days. Then, when he was promoted, Yuri Popov took you."

The sixty-year-old Russian nodded slowly. "Fine, you're SVR, and Asla-nov sent you."

Zoya fought a sigh of relief. She remembered Kravchenko from an operation she'd been on early in her career, and she knew Aslanov had run him and other pilots in the United States, Europe, and Asia before Popov took over in the role. She'd also heard about Kravchenko's drug charges. The fact that SVR had fired him was a guess but an educated one. She couldn't imagine they would face exposure with an agent moonlighting as a drug mule.

Zoya had come because she needed to get out of the country, and she knew there was no chance in hell he, or anyone, would agree to fly her if they were aware she didn't have any money or any papers, she had no Russian support, and she was now a fugitive from the Americans.

"So," he asked. "What is it that you want?"

"I want to get on your plane, and I want you to fly me to London."

Arkady made a face. "How the hell am I going to do that? My Sovereign has older engines, and not nearly the range. Five thousand kilometers to an empty tank. London is well over six thousand, seven depending on the weather and the route I can get approved."

Zoya flashed a disappointed smile. "Don't take me for a fool. We will conduct a ferry flight. Shorter hops. We can stop in Newfoundland or Greenland or Iceland or Scotland. They have airports, last I checked."

He turned and looked at a map over his shoulder but did not study it for any length of time. He turned back and shook his head. "No. I'm too old for this shit."

"Yasenevo is counting on you. And you really don't want to disappoint them."

"Are you threatening me?"

Zoya's smile now was pleasant, belying the words that came next. "Not just yet, no."

His face, demeanor, and tone remained defiant, but he said, "When do you want to leave?"

"Tonight."

He laughed angrily. "For *fuck's* sake, woman, I have a charter to San Diego in the morning."

"Cancel it."

As she had hoped, the man's defiance seemed to dwindle. After an audible groan he mumbled, "I regret ever working for you people."

"A lot of people say that once they have taken SVR money, contacts, and connections to set up their civilian careers."

A new thought popped into his head and he raised a finger. "This flight will be sixteen, eighteen hours, at a minimum with all the stops necessary. I don't have a copilot."

"An aircraft the size of your Sovereign does not require a copilot."

"But . . . you can't expect me to fly all the way nonstop. Go and find someone with a longer-range plane."

Zoya countered with, "You don't have to fly nonstop. I'll take over when you need breaks."

He raised an eyebrow. "You're a pilot?"

"Yes."

"Multiengine rated?"

"*Nyet.*" She smiled. "But I'm a quick learner."

"How many hours of flight time?"

"One hundred, give or take."

He sneered at this. "In singles. You aren't nearly qualified enough to—"

Zoya said, "I can watch over autopilot for you while you rest."

The man said nothing for almost a minute. Then, "Seventy-five thousand dollars. Half in advance."

"Forty thousand. Nothing in advance."

"You're a crazy bitch, aren't you?"

"I'm just someone with the full weight of the Kremlin behind me, so I know I can set these terms. The round-trip flight will cost you less than ten thousand. Thirty thousand profit for a day of flying is a good deal for you. Plus, Yasenevo will be in your debt. We know you've been having money troubles."

Zoya knew nothing of the sort, but she was playing a hunch looking at the man's disheveled office and expensive aircraft, an aircraft she was certain he didn't own outright.

He nodded slowly. "I guess you won't want to come in contact with customs and immigration."

"You're very clever, Arkady."

"How am I supposed to—"

"I will board the flight after you go through departure immigration at the airport here. We will land in the UK at night, I'll exit the aircraft on the taxiway, and you'll continue on to the terminal alone."

He groaned again, rubbed his face, then finally said, "Be back here at eight p.m."

Zoya shook her head. "I'm not going anywhere. Except to London. Now."

CHAPTER 19

Court Gentry walked to the front entrance of the pub on Angels Row at seven p.m. He had a plan, but it was thin, and he was banking on his improv skills seeing him all the way through. He was unarmed now, with all his guns and his grenade launcher left in the dead Audi forty miles east, and his forged passport and wallet jammed in a new backpack he'd stuffed into a storage locker at the main train station.

He'd spent the last hour working on his accent. His strategy involved him convincing a group of Englishmen he was English, and even more specifically a resident of a particular region. He'd sat by the canal watching YouTube on his phone for examples of the accent and dialect, and he thought he was ready, but he knew well that he wouldn't be certain he'd pulled it off till he saw the reactions from those around him.

He was determined not to get into yet another gunfight here, to use social engineering to complete his task instead of his considerable martial skill. It was going to be tough pulling this off, but impossible if his American accent gave him away.

Feigning supreme confidence, he opened the door to find a meager crowd inside, which seemed unusual to him considering this was at the end of the workday, when many Brits tend to stop off for a pint on the way home. He picked a stool at the center of the bar, waited for the bartender, and scanned the room through the mirror on the wall.

He saw no more than a dozen in total in the room; all male, all aged between their twenties and fifties. It was a decidedly blue-collar crowd and, even though he saw no overt malevolent looks from anyone, he'd been in more than enough bar fights to recognize the kind of establishment where one might touch off at any time with just a little provocation.

He ordered a pint of Carling lager, and was just a few sips through it when the bartender leaned over to him.

"Not from around here." It sounded like a statement, not a question.

"No," Court said; his British accent sounded fine to him, but he knew he couldn't be sure he was pulling it off just yet.

The bartender cocked his head. *Shit.* Court halfway wanted to throw his beer in the man's face and make a run for it, but he didn't move.

"Think you got business here, do ya?"

"Yeah. I think I do."

"What kind of business?"

Court took his elbows off the bar and sat up straighter. In a voice loud enough to be heard by other men sitting around him he said, "The kind I'll only talk to Charlie Jones about."

The few hushed conversations around him all stopped.

The bartender made a face, then snickered. "Not how it works, mate."

"Maybe not for you lot, but he'll want to talk to me."

A voice from down the bar said, "What's a bloke with a Hampshire accent know about Charlie?"

Nailed it, Court thought to himself. He'd once spent two weeks in Southampton with CIA watching over a ship docked there, photographing the comings and goings because it had suspected ties to an al Qaeda financier. Nothing ever came from the op, as far as Court knew, but he'd spent his time in cover listening to and attempting to replicate the local dialect. He'd forgotten more than he remembered about his time there, but by using YouTube to refresh his memory, apparently he'd done a good enough job to at least trick a couple of guys in a pub a couple hundred miles away.

Court said, "I don't know anything about Charlie Jones. Don't care. Kent sent me."

He saw a flash of surprise in the bartender's face, but before he said anything, Court heard a voice just behind his left ear.

"Kent, you say?"

He turned to find a thick man in his fifties with horrifying teeth inches from his face. He said, "Kent hasn't turned up. You know anything about that?"

Court replied, "Take me to Jones and I'll tell him."

Just then a short fiftyish man in a tweed jacket and a black driving cap entered the bar bracketed by a pair of large goons. He took his hat off, nodded seriously to a pair of men sitting near the entrance, then strode up to the bar.

He'd only made it a few steps before he locked eyes with Gentry. He slowed an instant, glanced around, then continued forward.

The man behind Court said, "Charlie, this bloke says Kent sent him here to talk to you."

The man raised a single eyebrow. "Did he now?"

Court started to stand from the stool to shake the man's hand, but a strong arm clasped his shoulder and held him where he sat.

Court nodded. "He did."

"When did this happen?"

"This morning." After a pause, "Right before he was killed."

It was clear to Court that Jones knew Kent was dead, but some of the other men in the room turned to him in surprise.

Jones sat down at the bar, facing the bartender. A steel mug with some sort of cocktail in it appeared, and the man in the tweed coat took a slow drink. Without looking he said, "Where you from, friend?"

"Southampton," Court responded, and then he held his breath. He'd heard Kent mentioning the city as being the home of one of his team members. If the different men on the crew really did not know one another, he took it as likely that the boss of one of the men wouldn't know the other individual players, either.

Charlie Jones sipped his drink, as if in thought.

Finally he asked, "You were there, this morning?"

"I was. At Ternhill. Kent took charge when Mikey and Martin went down, and then he brought us all the way to the old hospital."

"Don't know Mikey. Don't know Martin. I know Kent." And then, "Keep on."

"We handed over the prisoner to the Russians, and they flew him out, but there was a bloke in the hospital watchin' us. We chased him out to the highway, but he shot up my car and blew up the other. Kent was in the other. He didn't make it."

He felt certain no one had made it out of either of the two vehicles, but there would be no way Jones could know this for sure.

"Why did Kent send you here?"

"He was ragin', same as me. Someone got a lot of blokes killed today, sent us in with bad information. We were overmatched, outgunned, we had no bleedin' preparation for what we went up against. He told me he was going to find out who set this up and burn them for it. He said if he went down and I made it, that I should come to you and you'd tell me who hired him for the job."

"Southampton, you say? I take it you work for Tony Palace."

Court didn't miss a beat. "His son, Reggie." Court had looked into the Southampton underworld before arriving at the pub, expecting to be questioned about the leadership of the organization he claimed to work for. He'd found that their largest criminal firm was ostensibly run by an eighty-year-old gangster named Tony Palace but in fact had been taken over by his forty-five-year-old son, Reggie.

Court thought he was selling himself well but knew he had to remain sharp and not let his guard down for an instant.

Jones said, "Reggie ain't his dad, is he?"

"No, sir. He's a right bastard. With all the coke he does he's fucking useless most of the time. Can't be bothered about real problems, even if it throws his own men into danger."

Court had read that the man had been arrested for cocaine possession more than once. The rest of it he was winging. He'd spent most of two decades freestyling his way through background stories, and he was damn good at it.

Jones said, "I know Reggie Palace. How about I call him right now, make sure you are who you're sayin' you are?"

Court shrugged. "He'll just tell me to get me arse back down to Southampton, won't he? That's not what you want."

"It's not? What is it you and Kent cooked up? What do you want from me?"

"The name of the bloke who reached out to you about this in the first place."

"And what will you do with that?"

"I'll give him a talkin'-to."

The man seemed unsure, but then he stood, headed across the pub alone, and sat in a booth on the far wall.

Court was confused, but once there, Jones motioned him over. Grabbing his Carling, he complied. He was halfway across the floor before two men grabbed him and roughly frisked him, causing much of his beer to spill. Finding no weapons or microphones, they let him proceed and he sat down across from Jones.

Jones leaned forward, speaking softly now. "I'm askin' meself why I'd pass along important information like that to some geezer I don't even know. Never heard of. Workin' for a bastard that I don't respect."

Court said, "Because all this today happened on your turf. To your men. All the other firms sent one man on this op. You sent one, and then, when Kent came here, you sent him two carloads more, didn't you?"

"What of it?"

"Your losses make me suspect you want payback for this shite same as me. Maybe more."

"You're right. Seven of my men killed today. Good men, all. And you were the one tosser who walked away with your life. How *is* that?"

Court said, "Dunno. But I do know I'm going to find the people responsible for sending us into that bleedin' buzz saw, and I'm going to put this right."

Court could see both indecision and skepticism on the older man's face. Finally he said, "You and Kent had yourselves some sort of pact to avenge the deaths of a load of blokes you just bloody met for one op?"

"For me, it's not about the other blokes on this op. I react poorly when people try to send me to the slaughterhouse. Kent and I didn't have a plan. I just told him I wanted the name and I was sure my boss wouldn't give it to me. He said he would ask you." Court shrugged. "Then he died, on your turf, along with six more of your crew. I'm betting you wouldn't mind someone not attached to you in any way to dealing with the bastard who caused all this."

Charlie Jones sat and drank in silence for a minute. Court sipped his lager, waiting. Finally the leader of the Nottingham criminal firm said, "I don't know who set the whole thing up. But I do know who I talked to. A solicitor in London. He works for some interesting chaps. Russians, mostly. Underworld, all."

Court nodded. "A name?"

Another long pause from Jones before, "Tell you what. A couple of my boys will take you to an inn, right down the street. You stay here tonight, and I'll do some lookin' into you. I find out you are with Southampton, and were there at Ternhill and Rauceby today, then I'll tell you what you want to know."

"I don't have time for that. If I'm going after the men that did this I have to do it now."

"If you want the information from me, you have to play by my rules, lad. I'll talk to you in the morning about what I learned."

Court said, "You're not gettin' my bloody name, Jones. Palace finds out I'm doin' this and I'm in loads of bleedin' trouble."

"Don't need your name. Got your description, don't I? I know blokes in Southampton who will tell me if a dark and angry shooter who looks like you works for Reggie Palace. Don't worry, lad. I can be discreet." He shrugged. "I hope you check out . . . I *want* someone's bollocks for what happened to me boys."

Court started to protest again, but he realized it was futile.

A minute later there were four firm hands around Court's biceps and he was being led back outside, then turned and walked towards a small and simple inn at the end of the street. He knew his scheme would fall apart if Jones took even a couple hours to dig into him, and he couldn't let that happen. He had no real doubt he could make short work of these guys, even though he could plainly see the butt of a 1911 pistol inside the jacket of the man on his left.

But he had to remain in character, even for just a short time more, to increase any slim chance his plan had for success.

The check-in process for the inn involved one of the heavies with Court stepping behind the counter and pulling a set of keys off a shelf while the front desk clerk looked on silently, and seconds after that the three men began walking up a staircase. Court was led to a room at the end of a hall; the door was opened by the guy with the .45, while the other grabbed a chair by the tiny elevator door and dragged it over. Court entered his room, gave a nod to the men who led him there, then closed it, just as the one man sat down on the chair, facing the stairs and elevator.

Looking around the simple space, he realized the room had no balcony. There were two windows, one on either side of the bed, and while they weren't large, they opened to the side. He peered outside and down the street, then stepped out onto the windowsill in a crouch.

He used a drainpipe to climb down to ground level and was clear of his two minders a minute and a half after they locked him in his room.

It took him another thirty to steal a locked Vespa scooter from behind a theater in the city center. As he putted off back in the direction of the pub, he wondered if he would end up stealing or commandeering every vehicle in the UK before this damn operation ended.

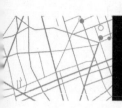

CHAPTER 20

Charlie Jones left his pub at nine, walked out to his Jaguar, and folded into the backseat. His driver and his bodyguard climbed into the front, and together the three men headed west through town, towards a restaurant Jones frequented.

It was only a ten-minute drive, and the crime boss spent the time on his phone, calling people who knew people in Southampton. He was determined to find out if one of Reggie Palace's men was missing and, if so, if the man fit the general description of the man he'd met tonight.

Jones liked the thought of having a "dead" man working for him, untied to his syndicate, unaffiliated with his town. If this stranger checked out, Jones had decided he would give him the information about the bastard who'd set this up and see what he did with it; if the man did manage to pull off some sort of retribution for Jones's dead crew, then Jones would want to talk to this fellow again.

There was always a need for a proxy asset in organized crime.

Charlie Jones and his bodyguard climbed out of the Jaguar at the entrance to the restaurant and stepped inside. As had been the case with the pub, the people at the restaurant knew him well. They kept a table for him, and he in turn watched out for them.

He was taken to his table in the back of the room, while his bodyguard took a stool at the bar—his regular perch—and ordered a soda water. The bodyguard faced the door, monitoring anyone who came in to see if they posed a threat to his protectee.

. . .

Jones's driver stood outside by the Jag, smoking a cigarette and thumbing through text messages on his phone.

He didn't hear anyone walk up behind him on the darkened pavement, so he was surprised when a voice coming from not three feet away said, "Hey, mate, got a light?"

The bodyguard spun his head around to the voice and straight into a vicious right jab to his face, knocking him out cold.

. . .

Court scooped up the man and dragged him quickly up onto the stoop in front of the carpet store. Once out of view from the restaurant on his right, he knelt over the man, reached into his coat, and fished around for a weapon. As had been the case with the heavy who'd escorted him to the inn, Court saw that the driver had a .45 caliber pistol in a shoulder holster. And while the old 1911 model pistol wasn't Court's first choice for combat, it was certainly a supremely lethal and imposing weapon.

He pulled the pistol, jabbed it into his pants under his shirt, then headed around back to enter the restaurant from the kitchen.

. . .

Charlie Jones put down his mobile phone and fumed.

He'd spent the last ten minutes on a conference call between a friend in London and his contact in the employ of Reggie Palace, head of the Southampton criminal firm. This man claimed to have direct knowledge of the gunman Palace had sent up to Ternhill, and from what he relayed to Jones about the man, none of the details seemed to match at all.

For starters, the actual gunman sent by Southampton was forty-seven years old. He was tall, well over six feet, with black hair streaked with gray.

But the man Jones had met tonight claiming to be the lone asset from Southampton was of average height, with brown hair, and he appeared to be under forty.

Jones sipped his pinot noir. His salad was placed in front of him but he did not touch it.

"*Dammit,*" he said softly. It was settled now. No, the man locked in the inn back near the pub wasn't who he said he was. He was some sort of infiltrator, here in possession of a great deal of knowledge about what had happened in Ternhill and Rauceby, but he was definitely *not* who he claimed to be.

Jones shook his head at the audacity of it all.

He reached for his mobile again, ready to call his employees waiting back in the inn near the pub, to instruct them to beat the man to death and then throw him in a ditch on a country road.

But as he started to lift the phone a hand appeared over his, gently holding the phone down.

The man connected to the hand sat down at the table, and when Jones looked up, he realized it was the stranger.

For a man unaccustomed to feeling fear, Jones found the tightening twinge in his chest especially unsettling.

The local crime boss turned to his man, who was positioned far across the room. But the bodyguard was facing the entrance, not his boss, and it was evident now that the stranger had slipped in from the kitchen in the back of the dining room.

Jones spoke softly, but sternly. "I call out and he pulls his gun. It'll be over for you quick, lad."

The stranger lifted Jones's napkin off the table, took it back to his lap, and wrapped it around the .45 pistol he pulled from under his shirt. He put the napkin and the gun back on the table, its barrel pointing at Jones.

In his best impersonation of a Southamptoner he said, "Does his gun look anything like this? Probably so, since I nicked this one from your driver out on the street."

Jones turned to the window, then back to the man in front of him. "Where is my driver now?"

"He's resting."

An eyebrow twitched as Charlie Jones realized he was beaten. He recovered and said, "I talked to some mates in Southampton about you. Men with the firm down there. They say the bloke they sent to Ternhill was forty-seven years old."

The stranger said nothing.

"C'mon, then. Let's have it."

"Have what?"

"The secret to that youthful skin of yours."

It was a joke, but the stranger made no reaction to it.

Just then, the bodyguard at the bar scanned back in the direction of his boss. His head began to turn back to the front door, but then it snapped back to the table across the room. He rose to his feet quickly, obviously astonished to see the stranger from the pub now seated with Jones.

Court grabbed the napkin-wrapped pistol and held it under the table. Calmly he said, "You're gonna want to wave him back to his stool, Charlie."

Jones did so. The man hesitated, then sat back down, but opened his coat and put his hand inside, his eyes locked on the stranger.

Court eyed the bodyguard back, matching the man's malevolent stare. Without taking his eyes from this threat, he said, "I'm just here to talk."

"I was *bleedin'* right not to trust you."

"No, sir. You were wrong. I'm *exactly* who I said I was. I'm the bloke who's gonna exact some payback from the people who got all your boys killed."

"But you ain't from Southampton, are ya?"

"I'm from one of the other firms. I won't be sayin' which."

Jones closed his eyes a moment, a look of frustration on his face. "I knew something was off about that accent of yours."

Court found himself momentarily crestfallen; he thought he should have been awarded an Oscar for his performance. But he made no outward reaction.

Jones sipped his wine, but Court could see the man's nerves. Court had been unnerving people for decades, after all, so he knew the cues.

The Brit said, "Why should I help you now?"

"Because I'm the guy you want fighting for you, and I'm also the guy you don't want fighting against you. You give me the name of this man in London, then I get up and walk out the door. You don't see me again. You don't ever learn my name. You just sit right here, live your life, and know that sooner or later, the people involved with all this will pay for what happened to your men. Hell, if you want you can take credit for it, tell all your mates you were the one who exacted retribution for your seven employees."

Court shrugged. "Or don't . . . I don't give a toss either way."

Charlie Jones finished his glass, then poured more wine from the bottle. He didn't offer any to Court. While this was going on the front door to the restaurant opened, and Jones's driver rushed in, his eyes searching across the room to the table where Court and Jones now sat. There was a panic-stricken look on the man's swollen face that did not diminish when Jones waved the man over to the bar to sit next to the bodyguard.

After he'd downed several more sips, Jones continued. "I don't like you, mate, but I *do* like your style. I'll give you what you're after. The solicitor's name is Terry Cassidy. He contacted me, put me in touch with the bloke who paid me for Kent's involvement. A bloke who didn't give a name, but he was an Ivan, for certain."

"He was Russian?" Court clarified.

"Aye. I should have known from the start. I know fuck-all about the plan, the reasons behind it, who the prisoner was. Never met the Ivan face to face. All done over the phone."

"Terry Cassidy knew to come to you for a shooter?"

"Shooters and muscle. He's a middleman. You know the score, lad. You lot, head knockers, I mean, aren't bringing in the money unless you're bashin' in faces or pullin' out pistols. I farm out me boys for the goin' rate. Last night was a bigger scheme, I knew that much, so I got triple for poor Kent."

Court asked, "If this guy was Russian mob in London, why did he hire muscle from a crime firm in Nottingham?"

Jones waved a dismissive hand in the air. "They do it all the time. The Russian mafia likes to hire proper Englishmen to do some of its dirty work. Keeps them off the radar of the Yard and the Met."

Court nodded, reached across the table, and shook Jones's hand. It occurred to him that if Jones had any inkling that the man sitting with him had killed all seven of his people this morning, Court wouldn't be leaving this bar alive. "Thank you, sir."

"What you gonna do now?"

He downed the last of the wine in Jones' glass. "I'm getting up and going out through the kitchen, and I'm hoping your lads don't shoot me in the back."

"I'll see they behave. Then what?"

"Then I'm going to London."

"Yeah? Well, if I learn you talked, I'll start callin' around. I'll find out who you're with, where you are. I'll come at you with everything I got. Do we have an understanding?"

"A perfect understanding, Mr. Jones. Thank you very much, indeed." Court stood and headed for the kitchen. Every step of the way he felt more certain someone was about to stop him, to grab him, to pull a weapon on him.

But he made it to and through the door, and five minutes later he was running an SDR through the streets of Nottingham, making sure he was clean before he grabbed a train to the capital.

• • •

The Cessna Sovereign jet lifted into a cloudy Virginia sky at four thirty p.m., with a flight plan filed for Greenland and a stop in Newfoundland along the way. Zoya Zakharova sat in the copilot's seat, doing her best to acquaint herself with the gauges, dials, and computer screens.

With only 110 hours in single-engine fixed-wings, and not a single minute flying multis, she was by no means an experienced pilot, but she knew that with a little familiarization with the cockpit she'd be able to monitor systems when Arkady Kravchenko took breaks throughout the crossing.

By leaving America, she'd slipped the noose of CIA and FBI, who would be searching the D.C. area for her, and she'd managed to avoid the hit team that showed up at her safe house just as she was in the process of escaping.

But neither of these facts was involved with the initial reason for today's clandestine exodus.

No. Something had occurred to her while lying in bed back in her holding room, obsessing over the photos of her father in Dagestan. Something that caused her to break out of American custody, to impersonate an active SVR officer to reboot a defunct asset to help her get out of the country.

Something that forced her to travel to London. *Now.*

She'd been so mission focused since the moment she'd sat up in her bed in her holding room, the realization of what she'd seen in the file Brewer handed her only then occurring to her, that she had barely stopped to think about the deeper meaning of what she'd learned. But facing over fifteen hours in the air her thoughts returned to the photos.

And now, just like in the holding room, an icy chill shot down her back.

Zoya Zakharova was thirty-three years old, but she fought against emotions that brought her back to her childhood. She tried to shake them off, but the ramifications of all this for her were just too big.

She didn't know how everything, how *anything*, would play out in the coming days and weeks on this quest she had begun late last night. The odds were long, to be sure. But she had to push forward because she knew one thing now that she did not know before she saw the file on her father.

She now knew, beyond any shadow of a doubt, that her father did not die fourteen years ago in Dagestan. He was alive in the photo, it had been staged, she assumed he was alive now, and she knew where to go to find out answers about where he was and what he was doing.

Her emotions threatened her mission; this she warned herself of as she watched the nose of the Cessna break out of the clouds and into sunshine over the Chesapeake Bay. She'd have to fight to keep those emotions in check. But as she evaluated herself right now, taking notice of how she felt, she realized her main reaction to what she had learned, that her father was alive, was telling.

She felt no elation. She felt no excitement. She felt no hopefulness.

No. She'd just learned her father was alive, and right now she found herself fighting against an overpowering sense of dread.

CHAPTER 21

FOUR MONTHS EARLIER

Janice Won moved to the United Kingdom, using the same name she used in Stockholm, and through David Mars and Terry Cassidy, she started a company, on paper, at least. Her firm, Biospherical Research Labs, specialized in laboratory research of infectious diseases, ostensibly under contract with the National Health Service. Mars purchased a real firm under Won's offshore corporation name, then sold it for parts, although the firm retained all its licenses and contracts so it could purchase items without raising eyebrows.

Won spent the first couple of weeks in an office in Soho, London, not a laboratory, and here she drafted a list of items she needed and a list of requirements for a lab to grow and weaponize the *Yersinia pestis* bacteria she'd successfully taken from the lab in Sweden. She also read through résumés of lab assistants Mars had selected as suitable, trying to find one or two people to help her, although they would think they were working for the front company, and they would never see the weaponized version of the spores.

Won was busy, but she was frustrated at the pace of one element of her preparation. To date she had not been given the information she requested from her new employer. She didn't yet know the size and scope of the attack David Mars had in mind, or the distribution of the intended victims. She didn't know if she would be attacking a football stadium, a sprawling metropolis, or a single building with her spores.

She found it ridiculous that she was having to base her needs on wild guesses about her objective, but Mars took her requests and went to work finding her a laboratory without giving her any more information.

It only took him a few days before he met with her in Soho. "Your lab will be in a private building next to Edinburgh University in Scotland. There is an existing facility there, no longer in use. It was built for medical research, but with some work it can be turned into a suitable lab for you. I have contacts in the local police; you will be well protected there, just as long as you use good operational security and don't ever let out what is going on."

"I have been trained, Mr. Mars."

"I know you have, Doctor. I'm sorry."

"Why Scotland?"

Mars shrugged. "Why not? Quite lovely people up there. You'll like it."

• • •

Two weeks later Won was in her new facility, watching refrigeration technicians restoring the long-dormant coolers in the old laboratory to operational condition. The rest of the equipment she'd ordered had already been installed: the fermentation vats, the freezers, and the spinners. While the lab was smaller and simpler than where she'd worked in Sweden or in Russia or even in Iran, it was a lot more advanced than where she'd done most of her work in North Korea.

Her two assistants had begun working with her. One was a twenty-six-year-old British woman of Pakistani descent, a registered nurse who had worked extensively with infectious disease, and the other was a twenty-four-year-old female Portuguese laboratory tech in the UK looking for more lucrative work.

Won's company, run by David Mars, paid them well, and Won worked them both hard.

As the refrigeration men left, David Mars and Roger Fox appeared in her lab, again showing her how personally invested they were in the attack that she would help prepare. Mars and Won stepped into her office off the lab floor while Fox looked around and Hines shadowed him.

Mars said, "I trust the laboratory meets your needs."

"Very much so. The two assistants are . . . adequate, as well. My only question remains—"

"The target?"

"Yes. I know you won't tell me specifically, but to determine the ideal recipe for the agent, to choose and construct the proper delivery vehicle, I must know *something* about where this is to happen. Is it a city block? A sports stadium? What's the weather in this location? There are so many variables that must be accounted for before I can even begin work on this."

Mars nodded, drummed his fingers on the table a moment, and then said, "The location is here. In the United Kingdom, which means you will have to prepare for any weather conditions save for extreme cold and extreme heat. The target is a building. Large, sturdy, well fortified and protected."

"A building like a grocery store, or a building like a shopping center?"

Mars said, "A building like a shopping center."

Won waited for something more, then said, "I assume there will be a narrow time window when this must take place."

"You are correct in your assumption."

"How much time do I have before the attack?"

"Ten weeks."

Janice Won gasped. "That is not much."

"You told me the spores will grow quickly."

"It . . . it can be done. But why didn't you approach me sooner?"

"Because . . ." He hesitated, and Won noticed an unease in the normally composed man in front of her. "Because I only became sufficiently motivated to enact this attack a few months ago. Believe me, I reached out for a virologist as soon as the idea came to me."

Won recognized there was a clue here about this mysterious Englishman's motivation, but she could not discern it. "I see. I hope you understand I will need more information as time draws even closer. Very soon, even."

"I do understand," Mars said. "I will feed you intelligence about the target, the defenses, everything, well in advance of the mission."

Won wasn't satisfied, but she went back to her work. She had much to do today to set up the perfect conditions here at the lab before she could take the small amount of spores she'd stolen from Sweden and cultivate and weaponize them, and she had no time to waste.

PRESENT DAY

A sleek corporate helicopter descended through the darkness towards a landing pad at a country estate an hour's drive west of London.

The AgustaWestland AW109 had been purchased the year before for six million U.S. by an offshore business owned by David Mars but untraceable to him. It was a chic craft with a plush interior, a range of 600 miles, and a top speed of 177 miles per hour.

Mars sat behind the pilot while a trio of Israeli security officers, all armed with subguns and pistols, sat to his right and behind him. He looked out the window on his left at the estate as they descended; its impressive landscape lighting throughout the grounds shone brightly in the overcast night on a backdrop of rolling hills dotted with other multiacre mansions.

Upon landing, Mars and his three body men climbed out and turned away from the thirteen-thousand-square-foot home and instead walked towards an immaculate horse barn. A half dozen beautiful Arabians ran around in the lighted paddock outside, but Mars did not look at them. The barn was statelier than many mansions, but Mars did not register this.

He marched on towards the open barn door, his security detail surrounding him.

Inside it was utterly spotless, but again, David Mars just walked along, single-minded of purpose.

His men stopped halfway down the hall, but Mars proceeded to the far end of the barn and stepped up to two men standing outside a closed stall door.

Mr. Fox wore a blue polo and khakis. He held a mobile phone in his hand.

Next to him, Fox's bodyguard, the colossal Englishman Jon Hines, wore a white undershirt, drenched in sweat, and boxing gloves on his hands.

Mars opened with, "Visser's talking?"

Fox shook his head. "Only to swear he doesn't know anything."

Mars looked to Hines now, and Fox understood. "Jon did as much damage as he could possibly do without killing the poor bastard. At this point I have to wonder if Visser is telling the truth."

The older man shook his head. "No. Nothing else makes sense other than that the leak came from him."

Fox replied with, "Yes, sir."

They entered the stall and Mars found Dirk Visser sitting in a chair, his arms bound at the elbows and wrists behind him. He was ashen faced, except where the deep bruising around his eyes and nose colored his skin with blues and grays.

Mars saw the man staring, not at him, but at Hines. He was utterly terrified.

"Good evening," Mars said. When the man did not react he shouted. "Do you know who I am?"

Visser's head turned, half hung, but his eyes scanned Mars's face. "No . . . no, sir. I don't."

Mars nodded. "Where did you come across the name Zakharov?"

Visser closed his eyes and tears pinched out the sides. "I told your colleagues, sir. I don't know a Zakharov. I have many Russian clients, yes. It is possible I just don't recognize the name because he works for one of the smaller entities I manage."

"No. He doesn't work for anyone. He's dead."

Mars pulled up a folding chair waiting for him and sat down in front of the detainee. "Here's the problem, old boy. Feodor Zakharov was the top man in Russian military intelligence, a twenty-five-year career going back to the Soviet Union. He dropped off the map, killed in battle, and CIA put his file on a shelf and forgot about him. That is, until just one single day after they picked you up. Now the Yanks are looking into him quite closely, and I, Mr. Visser, am not a man who believes in coincidence."

"Who . . . who is he?"

"His name is related to some transfers into an account you manage. Transfers that were converted into Bitcoin by you."

The Dutchman squinted through his swollen eyes. Sweat dripped from his lashes. "If he . . . If he, died, sir, then how is he related to the transfers?"

David Mars sat up straighter in the chair. "His name is tied to a shell corporation involved in the transaction you managed."

"I don't understand. How would I know who is tied to a shell?"

"Jon, please remind our friend again about who is asking the—"

"No!" Visser shouted. "I get it. No questions. Don't hit me!"

Jon Hines held back.

Mars next asked, "How did you know about Zakharov?"

"I never heard the name before—"

Mars stood up from the man, took a half step back, and looked at Jon Hines again. The former boxer snapped out a jab in a blur that connected with the seated man's right eye, swelling it instantly.

Mars said, "You are being difficult, which means this is going to take a while. I am annoyed to have to stand here in a barn and ask you the same thing over and over, but I'm certainly not as put out as you are going to be about your obstinance."

For the next hour Visser was asked over and over about Zakharov, with Hines punching him, breaking ribs, and turning his head into a bloody pulp.

He revealed nothing.

Finally Mars left the stall and walked outside the barn. Fox and Hines followed along, with Hines only now taking off his boxing gloves.

Mars looked to Fox. "He's good. But the question remains unanswered."

Fox said, "We must at least entertain the possibility that whoever the woman at the safe house was, she knew your name from some other way. She tipped off the Agency, and she isn't affiliated with Visser."

Mars said, "I've been here a long time and, to date, there has not been one compromise to my operation. Days from the culmination of my life's work, and this security leak happens. We've been careful, exact. I must know why CIA is looking into a long-dead GRU general now." Mars looked up at Fox. "Perhaps I have a traitor in *my* midst."

Fox sniffed at the older man's comment. "Do you think I'm working for the Central Intelligence Agency? What, I was turned by the allures of the West?" He looked down at his $5,000 suit and brushed the sleeve with his arm. "I have all the allures of the West I can handle right now, Mr. Mars."

Mars smiled a little at this. No, Fox wasn't a traitor.

Fox said, "There is someone else here in the UK who knows the truth about Zakharov."

Mars's eyes narrowed a moment. Then he shook his head. "No . . . if there is one man I trust, it's him." Mars looked to Fox. "You'll come back with me to London. I'll sleep on this tonight and decide what to do in the morning."

Jon Hines had been standing silently next to them. As Fox and Mars turned for the helo he spoke the first words in some time. "And Visser, sir?"

Mars looked back over his shoulder, directly at Hines.

"Dump his body in the Thames."

"Understood, sir."

Hines turned back towards the barn, not bothering to put his gloves back on. He could snap the little banker's neck with ease, and that way he wouldn't hold up the return flight to London.

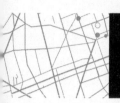

CHAPTER 22

The aircraft carrying former Russian SVR operative Zoya Zakharova flew south over England above a sea of gray clouds. The pilot, Arkady Kravchenko, had been silent for over an hour, but now he spoke up.

"Forty-five minutes from landing. Pay me now."

Zoya was in the right seat, right where she'd been most of the sixteen hours of their flight time, and she replied, "I'll pay you in forty-five minutes."

Kravchenko growled softly. "No. We'll fly around up here until I get the money."

"Not a good idea."

"I assume you don't have it in cash. You can wire it from my laptop to my account in the Caymans."

Zoya just looked out through the windshield for several seconds. Finally she spoke with nonchalance. "There is no money."

She glanced over to the pilot after a few more seconds. The Russian had reddened, his muscles were tensed, but Zoya could tell he'd known the entire time this might happen.

"You aren't with SVR, are you?"

She shrugged. "I *was*. At present I am a free agent. I needed a lift. Don't feel bad, you did a fine job. Next time I talk to Yasenevo I'll put in a good word for you."

He reddened even more. "I will turn you in to the British when we land. Tell them you hijacked me."

"I'll be gone before we get to the ramp, and you'll have no proof. And we both know you don't want to draw attention to yourself after this."

The man thought a moment. "I'll contact Yasenevo directly. They'll know you're here in the UK. They'll track you down."

Zoya answered in a tone that conveyed boredom with the topic. "You do that."

For the next ten minutes it was silent in the cabin. Then Kravchenko said, "I'm going to the bathroom once more before landing. You have the controls." And then, "But don't touch a damn thing. Leave the autopilot on and just sit there."

She reached over and handed him a Bluetooth earpiece. "If I have any problems I'll call you."

He put it in and she slipped one into her ear, pushing back her headset a bit to accommodate it while also allowing the microphone to pick up her voice.

* * *

Kravchenko slid back his seat, climbed out, and headed towards the cabin.

He walked to the rear, opened the lavatory door, and stepped inside. Immediately he looked back up to the cockpit. He saw the brunette woman in the copilot seat, her attention focused on the gray outside the windshield.

"I'll just be a minute," he said, and her reply came over the Bluetooth. "No need to rush."

Still looking her way, Kravchenko spun out of the lavatory and moved across the cabin to the galley at the rear. He stepped in, again shielding himself from the woman at the controls. Quickly he reached for an access panel on the wall there and upon opening it he put his hand below the manual cargo-door override lever and felt around for a moment. Quickly his hand found what it was looking for, and he pulled out a small, stainless steel, .38 caliber revolver.

After he checked the cylinder to ensure that it was loaded, he spoke aloud into his Bluetooth. "I will give you some advice, young lady. Don't cheat a Ukrainian, then threaten a Ukrainian, and then just let him get up and go retrieve a weapon. I'm sure you'll agree it was very stupid of you to allow me the opportunity to get my gun."

Her voice answered, but it was not over his earpiece. Instead she was right behind him. "Not if I needed to find out where you were hiding it."

Kravchenko spun around quickly and was surprised to find the woman there. She grabbed him by the throat and slammed his head up against the wall of the galley, while ripping the pistol from his hand.

After a couple more rough shoves against the wall, he crumpled to the deck.

Zoya picked the pistol up off the floor.

. . .

Minutes later Kravchenko's hands were tied behind his back and he sat in one of the cabin chairs. The plane flew on autopilot, with no one at the controls.

The Ukranian man looked up at the woman standing over him with the pistol in her hand. "How are you planning on landing this plane, bitch?"

"With your help, of course."

He laughed angrily.

"I wouldn't be laughing. You're on board, too, remember?"

"You aren't rated for twin engine, and you don't know anything about this aircraft."

She moved him into the cockpit and put him back in the left seat, with his hands still tied behind his back. She pulled out the ear buds and put his headphones over his ears, climbed into the copilot's position, and put on her own set. After a deep breath she took the controls.

It was quiet in the cockpit for a long moment other than the hum of the aircraft's engine. Outside the windshield she saw nothing but impenetrable gray.

Finally, she said, "Start talking, man."

Kravchenko remained silent.

Zoya looked to him, saw the resolution on his face, and realized she had to snap him out of it. She reached over, flipped off the autopilot, and immediately pushed the yoke forward, and the Cessna jet began to dive.

"What the hell are you—"

Zoya said, "You're right, no way I can land this without you, so let's just go ahead and end it."

"You're fucking crazy!" Kravchenko shouted. "Level off! Reduce throttle! Put the fucking autopilot back on!"

Zoya maintained the dive for a few seconds more, wanting to put enough fear in Kravchenko to where he wouldn't defy her again. Then she pulled back on the yoke, throttled back to slow her speed, and reengaged the autopilot. All the while the man in the left seat shouted at her.

"What's wrong with you? You're a crazy bitch!"

Zoya replied, "Yes, I am. Better not do anything to make this bitch even crazier right now, Arkady."

Twenty minutes later she was lined up on the runway lights at London Luton, north of the capital. It was three thirty p.m., and heavy rain fell. Zoya hoped this meant she'd have an easier time slipping away from immigration and customs when the plane arrived.

She checked her altitude and speed and glanced over to Kravchenko. "How am I doing so far?"

He did not answer.

She smiled, an attempt to hide her nerves and indecision. "I'm disengaging autopilot."

She waited for him to say something, and when he did not she shrugged and turned it off. She controlled the aircraft with the yoke now, her eyes constantly scanning gauges.

When Kravchenko did not speak for a full minute, Zoya began to worry that the man was going mute again, but finally he said, "Too fast. Too high."

Zoya reduced throttle and increased her descent. "Teamwork, Arkady. I love it. I'm feeling a little less crazy already."

The sixty-year-old Russian gave her no more trouble; he talked her down to a safe landing, then complained about her too-slow application of reverse thrust and her too-fast application of the brakes. Soon they began taxiing towards the fixed-base operator where the immigration and customs ramp was located.

Zoya told Kravchenko to use his foot pedals to taxi the plane, then she climbed out of her seat and cut his hands free with her knife.

She knelt down behind him, holding the pistol, muzzle down, with a hand resting on her thigh. "Now . . . two things you will not do. You will *not* notify local authorities about me. If you do, it will become evident to them very quickly that you are an agent for Russian intelligence."

From the look on his face she could tell he would comply with this. He didn't need the aggravation.

"And two," she continued. "You will *not* notify anyone at Yasenevo. Right now you are nodding your head in agreement, while inside you are planning on ratting me out. But again, you won't. You have no idea what's going on here. It's big, bigger than you can imagine. This means the second you tell SVR you transported me from the U.S. to Europe, you will become one big, fat, loose end to a complicated situation that they will want to sweep under the rug."

She patted him on the head with the muzzle of the pistol. "Nobody wants to get swept under the rug, do they?"

Zoya Zakharova stood, slipped the pistol into her backpack, and opened the door to the aircraft. She leapt to the taxiway and sprinted off into the rain.

Kravchenko climbed out of his seat and shut it, lest the customs and immigration people here at Luton find it odd that the aircraft had flown from America with an open hatch. Cursing all the way, he continued taxiing to the ramp.

• • •

Suzanne Brewer found herself where she didn't want to be: back in front of Matt Hanleys's desk, watching him read something, waiting for him to address her. She didn't know what he wanted, specifically, but was certain it was information on one or all of the crises she was dealing with at the moment.

When Hanley put his reading material down, he looked up at her. "How you doin'?"

"Working all three situations with Poison Apple, as I'm sure you're aware."

"Busy time," Hanley said, and this caused Brewer to cock her head.

"Indeed, sir." When he said nothing she added, "Is there something I can do for you?"

"You're gonna hate it."

Brewer groaned inwardly. *I already do.*

Hanley said, "I need you to go to the Five Eyes in Scotland."

The Programs and Plans officer didn't even try to hide her eye roll. "*Seriously?* It's a couple of days away, Matt. And my workload at present is off the charts. I am completely snowed under with—"

"You can work Poison Apple from over there. We'll be at the embassy in London and then we'll have access to the SCIF at the venue in Scotland. I just need you there making an appearance."

"Can I ask why?"

"It's getting around the office that I have you working on something sub rosa, and that's not terribly sub rosa, is it? If I keep you cooped up in your office all the time, without having you out and around the others in your pay grade, then it's just going to bring more scrutiny down on you, and me, and the initiatives we're working on."

Brewer said, "But I have a war room down on three working the Anthem hunt here in the States. I can't just shut it down and go to Scotland."

"You can and you will. You won't find Anthem if she doesn't want to be found. She's probably halfway back to Moscow by now or, who knows, maybe she's on her way back to Southern California where she went to college so she can meet up with a long-lost boyfriend."

"That seems incredibly unlikely considering what we know about—"

"The point, Suzanne, is that the minute Zakharova slipped the noose around Great Falls, she was in the wind, and she is one hell of an asset who can stay off grid as long as she wants." He smiled a little. "Remind you of someone else we both know?"

"An equally insubordinate singleton who also contributes to my ulcer? Yes, someone comes to mind."

"Look," Hanley said, leaning closer over his big desk in a way that was intimidating, though Brewer didn't think he meant it menacingly. "Our best assessment is that Zoya ran from the safe house because people came to kill her and we couldn't protect her. *We* failed *her*, not the other way around. She doesn't trust us now, but I'm hoping at some point she'll reach out to us, and we can get her back in the fold."

"You are very optimistic, Matt."

"Or just desperate. I'm not sure which."

It was silent for several seconds. Then Hanley said, "I'm going over in one of the jets. You'll fly with me, the director, Renfro, a couple of assistants, and the director's security detail. I'm also bringing Jenner and his crew over as my security."

Brewer knew that Walter Jenner ran the Special Activities Division's best paramilitary operations team. She said, "There are six guys in Jenner's team, and you're the DDO. Do you really think that's enough?"

Hanley smiled a little. "It's enough to protect me, anyway, so stay close and you'll be fine."

Brewer was furious that Hanley was now adding more to her plate. She excused herself to go back to work, because it was going to be an even rougher day than she'd envisioned.

CHAPTER 23

Court climbed out of the Tube station at West Kensington and found himself in the middle of one of London's many ethnically diverse neighborhoods. It was also an area with a lot of hotels, which meant tourists, and good access to two Tube stations: Baron's Court and West Kensington.

He saw a sign for a basement flat and walked the street to check it out from a tactical standpoint; then with a burner phone he'd bought in Nottingham he called the number on the sign. Within an hour he was in a leasing office a mile away, signing papers, proffering a CIA passport Brewer had insisted was firewalled from any alias database at Langley and set up only for him.

Court had no way of knowing if this was true, but he deemed it worth the risk because he needed a home base in London while he set up surveillance on Cassidy. He rented the place for a full month but was hoping to start eyeballing the solicitor's office within a few hours and get what he needed here in London within a couple of days. A daylight infiltration of a building for the purposes of establishing a surveillance hide was, to put it mildly, suboptimal, but he liked his chances.

It was nothing he hadn't done a hundred times in much less permissive environments than London, England.

By ten a.m. he stood alone in the little furnished flat. It was nicer than most places he stayed, but security-wise it was good enough. Down a narrow set of metal stairs, an iron gate led to a short passageway between the laundry room and the door to the flat, and the wooden door itself was well made and secure.

He judged the conditions suitable, if not ideal.

Soon he was out the door, heading on foot to the nearby neighborhood of Earl's Court. He'd make his way up onto the roof of the building near Cassidy's office and see what he could see. If he couldn't get much good intel, he'd have to go ahead and perform a sneak-and-peek, but only through surveillance would he know the camera angles and force structure, if any, inside the building. This took time to do right, and Court was anxious to get started almost immediately.

He figured if the man was, in fact, somehow affiliated with elements in the underworld, then there was at least a fair chance he kept a pretty secure work environment.

He had a plan for this afternoon and tonight, but he was not ready to act just yet.

No, right now he needed some gear.

. . .

Zoya Zakharova rented a tiny flat in London's West End, with a small supply of cash and a large supply of bullshit. Her story was that she'd lost her passport, she was a Croatian national who'd been told she'd have to wait up to three days for her embassy to get her the paperwork she needed to go back home, and she couldn't afford anyplace else around.

The Pakistani couple who owned the small and poorly kept Soho building took pity on her, and they handed her the keys to a tiny attic room.

It was a fourth-floor walkup, dingy and dark with two bare lightbulbs illuminating the entire studio. There was no furniture, not even a chair or a table.

She put her bag down in the middle of the room, sighed, and turned back for the door.

She purchased a sleeping bag at an army surplus store in the Arch Gallery, along with eating utensils for one, an olive green cold-weather balaclava head and face covering, and a few other personal items. She stopped at a hardware store to pick up some tools, a home goods store for a towel and a washcloth and a thick rubber welcome mat, a sporting goods store for a yoga mat in a canvas case, and a food market for provisions on her way back to the flat.

Back inside she stacked her food on a moldy shelf in the kitchenette: a few bags of crackers, protein bars, canned tuna, and bottled water.

In the tiny and foul-smelling bathroom, she put her toothbrush and toothpaste on the rusty vanity and tossed the bath towel and the washcloth over a hanger.

She unfurled the sleeping bag in a small closet next to the bathroom door, changed into track pants and a sweatshirt, then sat down cross-legged in the closet with a protein bar in one hand and her phone in the other. She scanned the Internet on her mobile phone as she alternately chewed and sipped water, looking at maps and satellite images, solidifying her plan of attack for the evening.

At four p.m. she climbed into her bag, pulled her .38 pistol close to her, and closed her eyes.

She was exhausted with the travel of the past two days, but still it was hard to sleep, because her mind continued to race with thoughts of her father.

. . .

After a call to Brewer and a two-hour wait, Court climbed out of the Tube at Clapham High Street Station and walked to a raised parking garage a block away. It was misting in advance of some real rain predicted later in the day, but Court just wore a gray T-shirt and jeans, and he walked with his backpack over one shoulder.

He made his way to the corner of the top level of the garage and found just a few cars parked there. The one man in sight stood next to a silver Volvo S60.

Court walked up to him in a relaxed fashion but with his arms out a little from his sides. The man was young, perhaps twenty-five, with red hair and a short beard. He was dressed in a black raincoat and dress slacks. He had a nervous look to him that caused Court to glance around the area to make sure there were no other dangers lurking about.

Sometimes, Court knew, people showed excessive nerves when they knew something was about to go down. Other times, however, especially with newer members to the intelligence game, some folks just couldn't hide the trepidation of the moment and do their job in a cool and calm manner.

Court knew this kid was CIA, which meant they were ostensibly on the same side, but Court had had his own issues with CIA for a long time, and he would never let himself trust them again. Though he approached non-threateningly, he had a plan to draw his weapon and put three rounds in this asshole's face and neck if he saw any clear sign of threat.

Court passed the redhead by and walked to the wall of the rooftop parking space, then turned around with his back to the wall so he could see everything in front of him.

This done, he said, "You're backwards."

The young man cocked his head. "What's that?"

"You parked your car with the nose against the wall. You can't get out of here without putting it in reverse. Slower. Limited visibility."

When the man said nothing, Court added, "Basic tradecraft, ace."

The young man looked at his car, and his face fell a bit with the realization that this obviously seasoned asset was correct.

He now looked both nervous and annoyed.

Looking back to Court he said, "Yeah, well, you violated protocol, yourself. You're supposed to be wearing a green shirt."

"It's at the cleaners."

The young man didn't appreciate the humor. He reached for his car door. "Well then, I guess it's time to back my ass outta here."

Court smiled and said, "Romeo, Papa, November, seventy-four, Tango, Alpha."

The man stopped reaching for the door and stood back up.

"Alpha, Quebec, Uniform, eight, three, Yankee."

Court raised an eyebrow. The man just stared back at him.

Court said, "Almost there, double-oh seven. You missed one."

The young man's eyes hazed over as he thought. Softly he said, "Alpha, Quebec, Uniform, eighty-three, Yankee . . . *shit!*"

"Calm down, kid. It's fine. Call your control and they can—"

"No!" the man said quickly. "He'll ship me off to New Guinea for fucking up something so simple."

Court said, "Close enough for government work. Let's just let it go. You know *I* passed the ID check. If you have the items in your car I'll take them off your hands and nobody ever has to know you forgot 'Juliet.'"

The young CIA case officer snapped his fingers angrily. "*Fucking* Juliet. Damn."

Court had moved on. "The equipment? You've got it?"

The redhead popped the trunk of the little Volvo and Court looked in. Lying there in an open case was a short-barreled HK rifle with a variable-power Nightforce scope, a suppressor, a laser designator, and a flashlight. The weapon was already loaded with a polymer magazine, which Court dropped with the mag release button to check the ammo. Two more loaded magazines lay next to it.

The young man said, "A .300 Blackout, as requested."

"Subsonic?"

"As requested."

"Well done, then."

The young man pulled out a backpack that had been lying next to the rifle case. "Electronic surveillance kit, high-end binos, night viz shit, more ammo for your rifle, a Glock 19 with night sights and a high-lumen light, extra mags. A Glock 43 in an ankle holster, and a Benchmade Infidel stiletto. Some climbing and rappelling equipment, as well."

The kid still seemed nervous, but he stretched out a little smile. "Whatever you're up to, it's gonna be badass. You need a wingman?"

Court zipped both bags tight and left them in the trunk. "Better you spend your time working on memorizing your ID checks." Court stepped up to him, then stopped and slapped the young man on the shoulder. "Just messing with you. Anybody who tells you they've never fucked up an ID string is lying through their teeth. Forget about it."

He then put a hand out. "Keys?"

The CIA officer handed over the keys, and Court took them. "Always back in, front grille towards the exit. That'll save your life someday."

He climbed behind the wheel of the Volvo and drove off, backing half the length of the roof before executing a J-turn and disappearing down the ramp.

The young American stood there in the parking lot and watched him go, and only then did he realize nobody had said anything to him about the asset taking the car.

"Dammit," he said aloud.

CHAPTER 24

Zoya slept fitfully, freakishly in tune with any noise in her building or even in the street below, but at ten p.m. she climbed right out of her sleeping bag, propelled on by her intensity. She rolled the bag tight and tied it, left it in the closet, then did twenty minutes of intense yoga in her underwear so as not to foul her clothes with her sweat.

After a shower she ate a quick meal of tuna fish, drank some more water, and then dressed as if she were a jogger.

Once in her track pants and formfitting pullover, she took several tools purchased that day at the hardware store and taped them to her back and ribs with liberal amounts of duct tape. That way they wouldn't rattle when she moved in a stealthy fashion, and she wouldn't have to worry about a backpack.

The .38 she tightened into her drawstring pants; she felt confident the leather holster would keep it in place, even if she had to climb or run.

Over this she slipped on her black Nike raincoat, and then she grabbed the yoga mat carrier. She rolled the thick rubber welcome mat she'd purchased earlier in the day, forced it inside, and slipped the case over her shoulder.

A few minutes later she walked towards the underground station and, although there were no real crowds at eleven p.m. on a weeknight, even here in central London, she managed to slip the billfold out of the back pocket of a man climbing up the stairs next to her as she descended. She then walked confidently to the turnstiles. Reaching into the wallet, she pulled out the man's Oyster card, and she held it over the reader and was allowed in.

On the train she stole a look into the wallet. She pulled out seventy pounds and crammed them into her pocket, thumbed through the man's credit cards but left them where they were, then flipped through a small group of wallet-sized photos.

In the first picture the man she'd just robbed sat with his wife, their little daughter in his lap. They were all smiling, even the two-year-old girl.

Zoya looked at the father, at the daughter, and she shut her eyes tight, barely holding in her emotions.

She closed the wallet and slipped it into her pocket before she opened her eyes again and wiped them with the cuff of her jacket.

Calm down, Zoya, she told herself. *This is just a job. Just a job.*

・ ・ ・

Shortly before midnight she climbed out of the underground at Victoria Station and zipped her waterproof jacket tighter as she reached ground level because a steady, tepid rain had begun to fall. She started jogging a route she'd memorized by looking at maps, both at the library in D.C. and then on her phone the evening before.

She entered Belgravia, one of the nicest and most expensive parts of London, though from the street this was difficult to tell. The back entrance to Buckingham Palace was just a few blocks ahead of her as she turned off Belgrave and onto Chester Street, but she wasn't infiltrating the queen's residence. Instead she quickly made her first right onto Wilton Mews.

It looked like a nondescript row of buildings on both sides of a street barely wider than an alleyway, but Zoya had done her homework, and she knew that every home and every flat in every building on this tiny street cost in the tens of millions of pounds and were packed with all manner of high-end technology.

She passed by an archway and made a sharp left into an alley off Wilton Mews. From here she ran through the darkness until she came to a brick wall on her left.

From Google Maps she saw that on the opposite side of this wall was a back garden for the mansion at 1 Milton Mews. She leapt into the air and grabbed hold of some vent pipes affixed to the brick wall. Scaling her way up to the top, she encountered a row of three-inch-high razor-sharp spikes.

Zoya unslung the yoga mat carrier off her back, put it between her knees as she held on to the pipe with one hand, and reached inside. From out of the tube she pulled the welcome mat. Zoya carefully draped the mat over the top of the brick wall, covering the spikes. She climbed the wall, used great effort to distribute what weight she did have to load there as evenly and lightly as possible and, on the far side, she dropped down into the backyard, crouching between perfectly manicured topiaries.

Zoya pulled the knit balaclava down over her face.

It was a narrow garden, only ten meters to the opposite brick wall, but long. There was a back wall, the same size and with the same metal spikes as the other two, and to her left was the rear of the house.

The house itself was wide and three stories high, but even though the rear garden was not expansive, it did have one feature that stood out.

A single-lane swimming pool, glowing and shimmering blue with the underwater lighting, started right in front of her and continued all the way to the back of the home, twenty meters away.

She looked over the house for a while from where she squatted in the landscaping, trying to figure out a way in, but as she eyed the long swimming pool she saw that it butted up to the home itself, and there was a clear window in the wall there.

She could tell by the odd design that it was an indoor/outdoor pool, and that meant there would be some sort of access below the water line for swimmers.

A pair of guards walked across the wraparound balcony on the third floor, strolling lazily together, and she heard notes of idle conversation. The black mat and the rope on the top of the wall behind her were not hidden, but it was dark there and the color of the mat and cord matched the dark brick wall closely enough.

She waited for the guards to make their slow circuit out of view, then ran across the lawn and made it to the wall next to the pool. By staying low she could avoid being seen from the window next to her, but she glanced through it to see that she had been correct. The interior section of the pool extended into a large dark room with a hot tub and several chaises. A spiral staircase led to a door one level above, and there appeared to be a changing room on the far end of the pool.

The only real light in the room came from the glowing indoor pool itself.

She crouched at the back door, preparing to pick the lock, but before she'd even begun to do so, a man entered the pool room. She watched him through the glass on the second-floor mezzanine; he looked out into the night through the floor-to-ceiling windows.

Zoya froze and made herself small. Here in the darkness she was banking on the man taking her for one of several planters on the patio next to the lap pool.

The man was security; he had a tiny Czech-made submachine gun hanging from a strap over his neck. Zoya thought he'd turn away after a moment, but instead he sat down on a recliner overlooking the pool, kicked his feet up on it, and lay back. Here he began looking through his phone.

Der'mo, she said to herself. *Shit.*

After watching the man get comfortable for what appeared to be a leisurely break, she adopted a new plan. She pulled off her pack and the other items taped to her, leaving them there on the patio next to the pool. Then moving slowly in the darkness, she stripped down to her black sports bra and panties.

She slipped her folding knife into her bra, then gently and slowly rolled into the water next to her.

Grabbing her lock-picking kit with a telescoping metal shim from the patio next to the pool's edge, she took a deep breath and went underwater.

The pool was well lit, so anyone looking her way, either outside or inside, would be able to see her as she worked on the lowered Plexiglas door separating the indoor portion of the swimming pool from the outdoor portion.

Zoya could see through the Plexiglas that it was held in place by a simple lever latch above. She opened the thin metal shim and slid it up.

It took some work, but in under a minute she had the latch lifted. She pulled up on the divider; it slid freely now, and she swam under it before gently lowering it and locking it once again.

She came to the surface now and began swimming languidly through the water as if she didn't have a care in the world.

She made it all the way to the pool stairs before the reclining guard saw the movement. He all but leapt from his resting place, reached a hand inside his jacket, and then stopped himself.

Zoya stepped out of the pool, water cascading off her hair and skin, her bra and panties soaked, and her guise and mannerisms completely calm.

The man lowered his hand. He was above her on the mezzanine, and he looked at her several more seconds before speaking down to her.

In broken English with a Russian accent he said, "What you doing here?"

Zoya looked up at him, unashamed and proud. In Russian she spoke with defiance, "What does it look like I'm doing?"

She saw the flicker of understanding on the man's face. "You are here with the boss?"

She walked over to a towel rack. With a half sigh she replied in Russian, "Of course he couldn't last ten minutes, and I still had a lot of energy to burn."

A smile crossed the man's lips, though he tried to hide it.

Zoya toweled off while the man leered at her. He thought she was a prostitute, which had been her aim, and so far her plan was succeeding.

The exit to the room was off the balcony, so she climbed the stairs barefoot, still drying her wet hair with the thick towel.

As she passed the guard she looked him up and down. With a little smile she said, "Next time, maybe, I will find some other way to exercise before bed."

The Russian bodyguard grinned. "You're a little slut, aren't you?"

Zoya smiled till she walked through the door, and then her smile disappeared in an instant and she rolled her eyes.

Seconds later she roamed the halls, looking for her target's bedroom.

She turned in the direction of where she thought she'd find her target, to her left down a long hall, and she started moving barefoot across the carpet.

There were at least two more security men inside the house; she heard them talking and watching TV to her right towards the den as she turned left to ascend the stairs.

She picked her way up a quiet staircase, turned left towards the master, and listened carefully for any noises.

One minute later Zoya stood in front of the bedroom door, hesitating a moment.

She knew the man she was coming to speak to. Or once did, anyway. He'd never married, never had children, and somehow he had been so steadfast in this, even long ago, that she thought it unlikely this had changed in the intervening years.

He should be alone right now at one a.m., but she had to allow for the possibility that he was not. She pulled out her folding knife and opened it before reaching for the door latch.

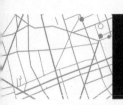

CHAPTER 25

Zoya took three full minutes standing still so that her eyes could become accustomed to the darkness, and when they finally did she began moving silently in her bare feet towards the four-poster bed in the middle of the room.

When she saw a single figure in the bed, she slowed down a little more but continued forward.

Standing over the lone form, she looked around. She slid open the drawer to the side table next to him but found it empty other than a few pill bottles and a pair of reading glasses. She walked around to the other side of the bed; it was unmade but empty, and she smelled the strong scent of a woman's perfume and the faint scent of sex.

Looking away, she checked the nightstand there, as well.

She sighed silently in frustration.

Finally she reached under the pillow on the unmade side of the bed, and pulled out a pistol. It was a Czech-made CZ P-01, a compact aluminum-framed semi-auto, and Zoya immediately flipped off the safety and moved it out of the man's reach.

This done, she climbed slowly into bed next to the form there and inched her way over, and this caused the man to stir. He reached a hand out and it landed on her breast. He started to smile and squeeze, but when Zoya pressed the blade of the knife up against the man's fleshy throat, hard enough to cut him superficially, his hand let go and his eyes opened in surprise.

He pulled his hand away and began sliding it under the pillow next to him.

In Russian Zoya said, "You make any noise and you die. Then I shoot my way out of here with the gun you had hiding under your pillow."

The man tried to look at her, but it was clearly too dark for him to make out facial features.

"You are a woman."

"And you are perceptive. I will kill you just the same if you try anything. Do you understand me?"

"Yes, yes, of course. No noise or you chop off my head. I've got it."

"Very good. Now . . . slowly, I want you to turn on your bedside lamp, Vladi."

Upon hearing the diminutive of his name, Vladimir Belyakov reached out and grabbed the lamp pull.

When the light flickered on, he blinked hard, as did Zoya, both struggling to becoming accustomed to the light. But after a second he turned to the woman next to him in bed with her knife still pressed against his jowls.

Belyakov was sixty-five years old, short and fat with dyed black hair so thin across the top as to be useless, but still rather thick on the sides. Zoya hadn't seen him in over ten years, and he'd certainly aged, but she expected he would have no problem recognizing her instantly.

She was wrong.

After several seconds staring at her, he said, "I'm sorry, madam, but I am hopelessly farsighted. Can I put on my glasses?"

"They are on the top of your nightstand. Your hand goes anywhere else, and I sink the blade up under your chin, through your tongue, and into the roof of your mouth. Then I twist."

He reached for his glasses slowly and put them on. While he did so, Zoya lay down closer to him, keeping the knife where it was but positioning her body where they could both speak in whispers.

The man stared at her for several seconds more. "Is that . . . It *can't* be. Zoya?"

"Hello, Uncle Vladi."

"You're . . . you're *alive*?"

"I think you have your answer. It's been quite a while, hasn't it?"

Belyakov seemed absolutely poleaxed. "I . . . I should say so. Moscow. Ten years ago, was it? Your graduation from SVR. One of the proudest days of my life, even though I was only a friend of the family."

"But a close friend, Vladi. You always were. You looked in on me when you were home and my father was away. There were entire years I spent more time with you than I did with Papa."

Belyakov nodded a little, but not too much, because the knife was still in place. Drops of blood had already made their way down his throat.

"It is wonderful to see you. You do know everyone, *everyone*, thinks you're dead," he said.

"Do I *look* dead?"

"You . . . you look more beautiful than ever. But why are you in your underwear? Why are you all wet?"

She didn't answer. Instead she said, "I need to talk to you."

"My dear, we can talk without you sneaking in here, crawling into my bed, and threatening me. Why on earth have you come to me in the night like this?"

"You were my father's best friend. You told me you were there, that night, in Dagestan, when he died."

Belyakov blinked in genuine surprise, as if he'd had no idea why Dagestan would possibly come up. "I was."

"Killed by rebels, I think you told me."

"Indeed. Shariat Jamaat, they were called at the time. They are still around, but go by Vilayat Dagestan now. We kicked their asses back then; they still haven't recovered."

"A lucky mortar round did him in?"

"Why are you asking all this? Yes, of course, as I told you at the time." He looked away again, shut his eyes for a moment. "Please, Feo was my best friend, and your papa. Let's not dredge up such painful memories."

"They aren't *that* painful, Vladi. Papa and I have something in common. Everyone thinks *he's* dead, too, but he's not, is he?"

The short man squinted through his glasses, a dumbfounded look on his face. "*Sto?*" What? "Don't be ridiculous, of course he is."

Zoya just stared him down.

"My darling, what is going on? Why would you think—"

"I've seen the pictures purporting to show his body. Classified photos from GRU. But he was alive when the photos were taken. They were staged."

"I was *there*, Zoya!"

"I saw you in the photos, so I *know* you were there. And that means you are lying about what happened, and *that* is why I am here."

"Look—"

She interrupted him. "Look at these." She pulled down her sports bra to reveal the top of her breasts. "They are faint, but they are there. They're called stress hives. I get them when I'm anxious. I *always* have gotten them, since I was a kid. Right here."

This was a lot for Belyakov to process, she could see in his eyes. He stared at her upper chest, right into her cleavage. Zoya did seem to have several very light but unmistakable pink splotches there.

She continued, "In my line of work, of course, anxiety is something I learn to manage, but I've never been able to fake out the hives. If it's a stressful enough situation, they will appear."

"But what does that have to do with—"

"My father had the exact same condition. Higher on his neck, on the side, but just as noticeable as on me. When he would have a bad day at work my mother would say to my brother and me that if Papa had the red rash on his neck, we should leave him alone and wait for him to come to us."

Belyakov waved her statement away with his hand. "I was on the scene within moments after the mortar round hit. If you say I was in the photo, then you see. It had *just* happened. Perhaps the hives stay on the body after death. You haven't died before, so you don't know."

"The rash disappears when the stress is relieved, within seconds. Nothing relieves stress quite like death, Vladi. He was alive in the photos, and anxious, which I can believe if he had to feign his own death in the middle of a combat zone."

"But—"

"And the other body next to him, *that* man was dead. His blood had congealed, not much, but a little. He might have been dead thirty minutes, an hour at most, but I've seen a lot of bodies, Vladi, and there is no way both men were killed by the same mortar round."

"This is all fantasy, my darling. I understand why you want it to be true . . . but it simply is *not* true."

Zoya pressed the knife tighter against his throat. But this did not change his story. "Feo is dead. Your papa is gone, darling. Kill me, too, if you must, but that won't bring your dear father back to life."

Zoya leaned closer to the older man now, right in his ear. "I always liked you, but even as a little girl, I knew you were his bitch. Did whatever he told you to do. After he was declared dead, you left GRU and went into the oil business. Made billions. That only happens with state approval. The Kremlin set you up here in London, and there must be a reason why they did that. I never put it together until I saw you in the picture and realized my father was alive. You are still connected to him somehow, still connected to the Kremlin, and London holds the key."

"Crazy talk. Asinine. We Russians leave Russia and come here when we have the means to do so because the Kremlin wants to take our riches from us. This is the only place we can protect them from the greedy Siloviki who run the *Rodina*."

Zoya shook her head with certainty. "I've been following your career since you left military intelligence. No way you're working against the Kremlin. You were always a loyal servant, both to my father and to the *Rodina*. Nothing has changed, except your bank account and your location. Now that I know my father is alive, I am wondering why you are here with so much money, and what it is you are doing." She added, "Are you still his bitch?"

"What am I doing? I am raising horses, I am donating to charity, I am buying property all over the world, I am fucking a different hooker every night, if you must know. What I am *not* doing is spending my money helping your dead father."

His voice had grown louder with each word, and Zoya slapped him hard against his face to shut him up. His glasses flew off onto the nightstand.

Momentarily stunned, he reached for them and put them back on.

When he turned back to the bed, the knife was gone from Zoya's hand, but the Czech pistol was there in its place.

"You fire that gun and my twelve-man security team will be on you in an instant."

"It's a six-man security team, eight perhaps, if two of them are somewhere sleeping, and the safety of London has made all of them slow, fat, and lazy. I, on the other hand, am still Russian, and I am fast, lean, and hungry for the truth."

"Truth? *What* truth? A fantasy is what you're after."

Zoya reached over him, to the table and to his mobile phone. Handing it to him, she said, "Open it."

He did so and handed it back to her.

Zoya kept the gun on the man who had been like a second father to her, but she scrolled through his contacts, his text messages, and his phone calls. She looked first for her father's name, although she knew both he and Belyakov would have been too smart to use it. She checked a few of the many aliases he used, the diminutive of his name, but found nothing that looked relevant.

She scrolled through text messages, some in English, some in Russian, and stopped at one from the day before. It was an exchange with a man named Terry Cassidy, and it was in English.

I have some things I need to get out of your safe, Belyakov wrote.

In Berlin at the moment, came the reply. Return tomorrow. Can this wait till Wednesday or do you need to go to my office without me?

It can wait. Lunch Wednesday? Belyakov replied.

Excellent. You do your business with the safe and then we'll walk over to the club.

Zoya looked at Belyakov, wanted to ask him about Terry Cassidy and his safe where Belyakov held items, but knew better than to tip him off to her interest. She pulled up a random text message to hide what she'd been looking at, locked the phone, and threw it on the bed. "Fucking useless."

The Russian expatriate oligarch cocked his head. "Was that English, Zoya?"

Shit. Zoya realized she'd switched to English accidentally. She faked a smile. "As Papa always told me, own your cover."

Belyakov smiled a little, too, at this. "Why, Zoya? Why do you come with weapons to find your father? If you think he is alive, what threat does he pose to you?"

She hesitated for several seconds, and started to say something twice, but each time she stopped herself. When she did finally speak, she did not answer his question. "I will leave you now, Vladi, but I can come back at any time. When I go, I want you to call him, tell him I was here, and tell him his daughter only wishes to see her papa. Will you do that for me?"

Pleadingly, the old man said, "How *can* I do that, Zoya Feodorovna? He is buried up in Mytishchinsky. You've been to his damn grave, girl." The Federal Military Memorial Cemetery was in the Mytishchinsky district, on the outskirts of Moscow to the northeast.

Zoya said, "You're right, I *have* been there. And I knelt down and wept over the grave of a man I've never met, because whoever is buried in my father's plot at Mytishchinsky is *not* my father."

Belyakov sank his head back into the pillow. "Come back tomorrow, in the light. You and I can have breakfast together, and we can talk more."

Zoya did not answer; she just climbed off the bed, the pistol still level at the prostrate man's chest, and backed off into the dark.

· · ·

Seconds later Belyakov heard the bedroom door shut softly.

He started to reach for his alarm button to alert his security team, but he thought against it. Shooting Zoya Zakharova would cause vastly more troubles for him than it would solve. No, better she got out of here safe and sound.

Belyakov did, however, reach for his mobile. He scrolled through his contacts and tapped the one for David Mars.

Mars lived in Notting Hill, also here in London, and it took him several rings to answer the phone.

With a hoarse and tired voice, Mars said, "Vladimir? What bloody time is it? Why are you calling me so damn late?"

"We need to meet, very first thing in the morning."

"What is it?"

"I . . . I can't . . . Not on the phone."

"Come here for breakfast, then."

"No," said Belyakov. "The old place."

"*The old place?* How much vodka have you drunk tonight?"

"The old place."

Mars hesitated. Then said, "All right. Seven a.m.?"

"Yes. That will work." Belyakov hung up the phone and rubbed his eyes under his glasses.

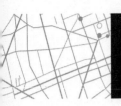

CHAPTER 26

St. James's Park was a major tourist attraction in central London, and right in the center of it was a bit of espionage history. The Tin and Stone Bridge had been used by British intelligence officers to meet local contacts for years, and the placid area with good sight lines meant it was also a common meeting place for others looking for quiet, candid conversations.

At seven a.m. there weren't many tourists out, but a few men and women walked through the park on their way to work.

Russian billionaire oligarch Vladimir Belyakov arrived at the Tin and Stone Bridge first, holding his umbrella above him to keep his tailored business suit and raincoat dry. He sat on a green park bench, looked to his two security men who stood closer to the pond in front of him, and continued scanning in all directions.

Light rain trickled from the hoods of their open raincoats.

Belyakov himself scanned the area to make sure no one was around in eavesdropping distance, and then he spent the next moments thinking about what he was going to say.

Well before he'd decided on a suitable script, he saw David Mars walking across the bridge. There were three men with him, including that British beast Jon Hines looming behind, and the younger man with the goatee and the Savile Row suit walking next to Mars. The third man, Belyakov assumed, was one of the security officers who accompanied Mars wherever he went.

Vladimir Belyakov focused on the one called Fox. He had no idea of the man's real name but was well aware that he was tied to Russian organized crime, and as erudite and dapper as he appeared, he no doubt dealt a lot of death and woe to those who got in his way.

Mars's Israeli bodyguard, Fox, and Fox's British giant and bodyguard held back twenty yards or so, while Mars walked all the way up to the bench and sat down next to the short, balding sixty-five-year-old. The men did not greet each other; instead they just looked out towards the narrow pond in front of them.

Mars spoke first. He sounded annoyed. Rushed, as if he had other places to be. "This bench, this bridge. It's always bad news when we meet here. Usually I am the one needing something from you. But now . . . *dammit*, Vladi, I've got a lot on my plate. What the hell couldn't be handled via our encrypted phones?"

"I needed to be face-to-face with you for this."

Belyakov balanced his umbrella against his shoulder and turned to face Mars, which was hardly the protocol for a clandestine meet.

Mars saw this in his peripheral vision. "Vladi, turn back around, damn you."

The Russian oligarch ignored him and kept looking his way. "What I'm about to tell you will be difficult to hear, David. Someone broke into my house last night. Held a knife to my throat. A gun to my head."

Still looking ahead, still annoyed about Belyakov's pivot to face him, Mars said, "Someone? Who?"

"Someone who knows the name Feodor Zakharov."

Mars sat back on the bench slowly. He blew out a sigh. "A woman?" he asked.

"*Da*. How did you know?"

Mars turned fully to Belyakov now, his own umbrella low and the rain dampening his dark hair and his coat. He was giving up on the tradecraft, because his partner in this meet had already done so. "I've been looking for a woman who knows. She was in America two nights ago.

She either told the CIA, or they told her. This *must* be her. What did she look like?"

"David . . ." Belyakov spoke through a dry throat. "I am—"

Mars looked in the Russian's eyes now, any last vestige of protocol gone. "You *recognized* her, didn't you? You know who she is."

"I do. David . . . it was . . . it was Zoya."

David Mars blinked once, hard, then grunted angrily. "What the *fuck* were you and your hooker drinking last night, Vladi? You know as well as I do that Zoya was killed by the Americans four months ago in Thailand."

Belyakov shook his head. "Apparently the Thailand story was disinformation. She's not dead. Far from. I swear."

David Mars looked away, out through the rain to the swans in the pond, swimming languidly. His eyes were unfixed, but quickly they began filling with tears.

From twenty yards away Fox stared at him, but Mars ignored the younger man.

His voice broke a little as he spoke. "Is there any way you could have been mistaken? Or that this was some sort of a trick by the Americans?"

Vladimir Belyakov pointed to a long, shallow cut on his thick neck. "She was close enough to do this to me. She was in my face for five, ten minutes. Of *course* I know Zoya when I see her. Even after all these years."

Mars wiped tears away with his shirtsleeve. "Did she . . . did she seem all right? Is she hurt?"

"Same old Zoya. Somehow she broke into my Belgravia home that I spent millions to secure. She had to be a world-class operative . . . a gymnast even, to get through my security. I'd say she's as healthy as ever."

David Mars wiped away more tears now, and he smiled. After several seconds he spoke hoarsely. "My beautiful . . . beautiful . . . little Zoyushka. She is alive."

Belyakov put a hand on Mars's shoulder and switched to Russian. *"Da."* He spoke softly now. *"Da,* Feodor Ivanovich, your precious daughter is alive and well."

The man who had called himself David Mars for the last fourteen years let his umbrella drop into the path, then put his face in his hands and wept openly.

. . .

It was a full minute before he got hold of himself, and Belyakov just sat there the entire time, averting his eyes from his old friend's emotion and watching the ducks and swans.

Fox, Hines, and Mars's bodyguard had taken up positions around the bench, but they all stole glances at the last scene they ever thought they'd set eyes on. David Mars broken down in tears.

Finally Mars wiped his eyes with a handkerchief, picked his umbrella back up, and covered himself with it, although he was all but soaked now. He said, "What . . . what was she doing there? With you?"

"She wanted me to tell her about you."

"What about me?"

"She knows you're alive, Feo."

"But . . . *how?*"

"Somehow she saw the photos of you back in Dagestan. The ones used to prove your death on the battlefield. The ones we staged with you lying next to that poor bastard colonel who caught the mortar round . . . what was his name?"

Mars answered distractedly, as if this were not an important point to Belyakov's story. "Sokolov. Field Artillery."

"Yes, right. She saw your pictures, and she said something about hives. What the fuck, David? You get welts on your neck when you're nervous? How did I never know this?"

David Mars brought his right hand up to his neck and rubbed the exact spot Zoya had indicated. "She knew to look for them."

Belyakov waited for a response, but when none came he said, "Those files were sealed by GRU as soon as your death was announced. I don't know how she saw them, but she did."

David Mars, once known as Feodor Zakharov, now understood without question that Zoya, his only daughter, was the woman in the CIA safe house he'd ordered raided two nights earlier.

She was alive, which made his heart soar, but only until he connected the rest of the dots. She *had* to have been working for the Americans now. They'd made it look like she'd died in a raid on a yacht off the coast of Thailand, they'd brought her back to America, they'd brainwashed her and turned her, and now they were directing her back out, sending her to find her own father, whom they'd determined was alive and in play.

Belyakov said, "I know where she's going next."

"Where?"

"Terry Cassidy's office. Tonight, would be my guess."

Now Mars's face turned dark. "You told her about Cassidy?"

"Of course not! She got into my phone. I had been exchanging texts with him about getting something from his safe. Just some bearer bonds, but the text was there. I *know* she saw it, she is too careful to miss it."

"You *do* know what's locked in that safe, don't you?"

"Of course I do. And that's why you need to stop her. She's your daughter . . . but she's . . . she's *different* now. More dangerous."

Mars nodded, stood, and began walking away without another word.

Belyakov stood himself and pursued him. "You are planning something. Something I know nothing about. We've been comrades for forty years. Friends. I've always been there with you, been there *for* you.

"Tell me, David . . . Feo . . . What's all this about? What's your endgame?"

General Feodor Zakharov, aka David Mars, looked up to the gray sky, and rain washed his face. After a time he said, "You don't understand. Nobody understands but me. There *is* no endgame in the Cold War. It is a permanent conflict of ideas, of soldiers, of spies. I have devoted my life, I have devoted everything I have, everything I am, to the great battle against the insipid forces of the West. They fought back, they took so damn much from me, but I will reap my vengeance soon, Vladi."

"I don't want anything to do with your personal war, Feo. I did not sign up to—"

"You have connections to Moscow still."

"Of course I do. Only by the Kremlin's good graces have I been so successful."

"But, Vladimir, you are forgetting the most important thing about Russians living abroad." Mars stepped close. "As long as your nuts are in Moscow, the Kremlin can squeeze whenever they want."

Belyakov felt the menace from his old friend and colleague. "And you are the Kremlin?"

Zakharov shook his head. "No. I am just a man in the middle, passing on helpful advice to an old friend."

"This operation you've cooked up on your own. I don't believe any of it is sanctioned."

David Mars said, "The *Rodina* will benefit, and they will benefit more if they don't know what I'm doing."

Belyakov blew out a worried sigh. "That's a dangerous game, comrade."

"For dangerous times, comrade." General Feodor Zakharov walked off without another word, and this time Belyakov did not follow.

. . .

David Mars continued towards the bridge, thinking about resolve now. He was a hairsbreadth away from the culmination of his life's work. He could not let *anything* interrupt it.

Not even his little girl.

He steeled himself for what he would have to do in the coming days.

His men formed around him, and together they walked back over the bridge and climbed into a waiting limousine. Once they were all inside, Mars said, "Mr. Fox. I need you to take Hines here along with a crew of two . . . no, make it three good men to the offices of Terry Cassidy. Take the Israelis. They are good. I expect they will encounter an intruder this evening. Is all that clear?"

"All but the rules of engagement when they find the intruder."

"The intruder will be taken alive. No exceptions." He turned to Jon Hines and pointed a finger his way. "*Alive.*"

Hines replied, "Right, sir. Alive. Very well."

Fox hesitated, then added, "It would help if you could tell us something about our target."

Mars turned to Fox. "My daughter is not dead. She went to Belyakov, and he led her to Terry Cassidy's office. She'll go there next, looking for answers about me." Despite his fury and his concern, he smiled a little. "And if you don't stop her, she'll find the safe, and she'll crack it like it was nothing." He smiled even more now, and his eyes filled again with tears. "I taught her well."

. . .

Zack Hightower had spent the first couple hours of the day tailing Maria Palumbo, a CIA officer and one of the four who was a potential source for all the recent Agency compromises.

To be precise, tailing wasn't the correct term. He was using an old FBI tactic known as "bumpering," an overt surveillance measure used to cause a subject to flee or make some other desperate choice that might tip off the surveillance professional that the subject being followed was indeed checking for a tail and had something to hide. Police departments all over the country did the same thing, but referred to the tactic as jamming.

It was the opposite of covert surveillance, really. Zack wanted Palumbo to know he was tailing her, watching her, tracking her every movement, and he hoped this would reveal to him that she was, indeed, the mole.

But Palumbo didn't bite. At all. After Zack picked up on the fact that she'd noticed the tail just after dropping her kids off at school, she began a series of idle turns throughout Chantilly, clearly looking to see what Zack in his black Chevy Suburban would do.

Zack stayed tight on her ass until she pulled into the parking lot of an Au Bon Pain for breakfast. He parked just out front and watched her eat a muffin and sip coffee while talking on her phone, occasionally stealing glances outside at Zack's car.

At nine a.m. she threw away her trash, put down her phone, and then stood there, hands on her hips, staring at Hightower. He stared back through his Oakleys unfazed, enjoying exerting sanctioned pressure, even though he had not a clue if this woman had done anything to warrant this stress.

He got the feeling something was wrong in the pit of his stomach about thirty seconds before the flashing lights broke his staring contest with Palumbo. He looked in his rearview and saw three blue-and-white squad cars from the Fairfax County Police Department pulling up. They blocked him in expertly. He figured Palumbo had called CIA security and told them about the tail, and they alerted the local yokels.

Zack sighed, pulled out a set of fake credentials from the folio given to him by Suzanne Brewer, and rolled down his window.

Palumbo drove off while Zack got a talking-to. He had a legend and a story ready; he thought this woman had sideswiped his wife's vehicle outside their kid's high school the day before, and he was just trying to get a look all the way around her car to see if there was evidence.

It was good enough for Fairfax County PD, and within fifteen minutes he was driving off, heading towards his next target.

Palumbo was a bust. There was no way, Zack thought, that anyone could be so cool as to quickly call in an unknown contact to CIA security if they were, in fact, spying for a foreign entity.

He'd mentally scratch her name off the list, and then move on to the next in line: Assistant Deputy Director of Support, Marty Wheeler.

· · ·

At lunch Zack Hightower stood in line at Whole Foods on P Street in central D.C., holding a plastic bottle of some sort of green sludge that he had no plans to consume. The woman in front of him was hot enough for Zack, for a mom, anyway, and he was stealing glances at her ass as she leaned over her baby in the shopping cart to hand him a toy. But Hightower was on duty, so he broke his gaze off her backside and returned it to the man in front of her.

Marty Wheeler paid for his salad and his can of cold green tea, and he headed over to the dining area in the front of the store. Zack watched him intently while the woman checked out, and then Zack bought his green shit and walked over next to Wheeler. The CIA assistant deputy director of Support sat alone at a long table with four chairs on each side, and although there were plenty of other tables around, Zack plopped down across from him at the far end.

Wheeler looked up, smiled and nodded to the fit and intense-looking man in the beard, and then returned to his salad.

Zack opened his drink and, despite himself, he took a sip.

"For fuck's sake," he said, then sealed the bottle back up.

Wheeler glanced up at him again and cracked a smile, but soon he was looking at his phone.

Zack followed the fifty-one-year-old out to his car after lunch, walking just fifty feet or so behind him, then climbed into his Suburban, parked two down from Wheeler's Mercedes C-Class in the garage. Wheeler pulled out onto P Street and turned left, and Zack stayed on his bumper.

This continued until Wheeler pulled into a parking lot a block from the U.S. Capitol. Zack parked nearby, in sight of his car, then followed the man on foot towards the Capitol building.

Zack sighed. He got nothing out of Wheeler, not even a recognition he had a tail.

This dude was either as pure as the driven snow, completely oblivious, or incredibly well trained at countersurveillance. Zack knew he couldn't write him off like he had with Palumbo. He'd need more intel on Wheeler before deeming him clean, but he wasn't going into the Capitol building to get it.

Zack headed back to his car. There were two more on the list. Alf Karlsson, who he'd been told had already flown to London in advance of the Five Eyes meeting in Scotland in a few days, and Lucas Renfro, the deputy director of Support and the highest ranking of the four on the list.

Renfro had been at Langley all morning, where Zack couldn't touch him, but he told himself he'd go position himself to follow the DDS when he left work. He'd lean on Renfro for a while to see if he crapped his pants, because his first two tails of the day had been wholly unsatisfactory, particularly for a man who enjoyed scaring people.

CHAPTER 27

A steady rain pelted the canvas painter's tarp lying over Court Gentry's body, creating a soft relaxing sound that made him want to take a nap. But he kept his eye in the sight of his rifle and ignored the moisture from the wet flat rooftop that soaked his clothes.

He was as close to invisible as one could be in cloudy daylight in the center of one of the leading capital cities in the world. On this fifth-floor roof he was just slightly above the other buildings, all but shielding him from below and through the windows of their lower floors, and the tarp was close enough in color to the roof itself—both were covered with white paint—that someone would have to come up here and walk around for a while with the intention of spotting him to do so.

Court fought his desire to nod off and looked through the four-power scope above his suppressed rifle, centering it on a window in the building across the street. This was Terry Cassidy's private office. Court watched the man as he sat at his desk, alternating phone calls with typing on his computer and chatting with assistants.

It was only noon, but Court had been in position since before the man arrived for work that morning, and while doing so he'd been getting a feel for the security of the location. There were guards in the lobby, cameras all around, the windows looked secure, and there was no adjoining rooftop access.

The only way over that Court saw was either to infiltrate with a stolen ID or to somehow get across the street with a cable and access the roof.

Alternatively, he could scale the outside, perhaps, and make entry far away from the guards and hardest access points.

It wouldn't be easy.

As he slowly scanned the two windows of Cassidy's office, his earpiece buzzed. He tapped it to open the call.

"Yep?" he said softly.

As expected—as always, in fact—it was Suzanne Brewer. "You weren't supposed to take the Volvo. London station is pissed."

"That's what I like about you, Brewer. You've always got your mind centered on the important stuff." When Brewer said nothing he sighed. "I'll return it when I'm done."

Brewer snorted out an angry laugh. "The last car you misappropriated is probably *still* on fire up in the East Midlands."

Court smiled at this. "I'll be super careful with this one. Government property and all. Look, I see where your priorities lie, but I'm out here tryin' not to get a bullet up my ass, so if you could help me out a little instead of busting my balls, I'd appreciate it."

"Fine. First, your mission to locate and recover Dirk Visser is over."

"Why is that?"

"He was located and recovered. Out of the Thames, in fact. It looked like he'd been run over by a truck, but Scotland Yard is looking into the exact cause of death."

Court sighed, then moved on. "What do we know about a lawyer in London . . . I guess they call them solicitors here, named Terry Cassidy?"

Court could hear Brewer typing. It would be just seven a.m. in Washington now, and this woman was sitting at a computer, either at Langley or at home.

He doubted she had a life beyond work, and wondered if she and he actually had more in common than he'd imagined.

After thirty seconds Brewer said, "Terrance Albert Cassidy. Aged forty-three, born in West Sussex. Divorced. Father of—"

"I don't need his Wikipedia page. I need to know who he runs with, who his clients are."

More tapping on the computer. "He deals in offshores, cryptocurrencies, that much we know. No known ties to any criminal element that I see, but I'll keep digging."

"Shit," Court said.

"Here's something. He travels to Russia regularly."

"Moscow?"

"Yes. Always. Every month or so."

Court said, "I guess I'm going to have to go in and take a look at his office tonight. Keep digging, see if you can find anything relevant about his contacts, clients, known associates in general."

"Understood."

She started to speak again, but Court noticed something through his scope and disconnected the call in his ear. He then concentrated fully on Cassidy, who had stood up from his desk and walked over to a painting on the opposite wall of the room. He reached a hand behind the frame, slid it up high, almost out of reach, and then he pulled the painting open like a door. Behind it Court clearly saw the dial of a safe built into the cherry-paneled wall.

The solicitor worked the dial for several seconds, swung the latch, and opened the small door to the safe. Inside he pushed a button, and a section of wall, from the floor to six feet above it, slid open a few inches.

Cassidy pushed this up, then stepped into a large vault.

Court was no expert safecracker, but with the right audio equipment and enough time, he thought he'd have a fair chance to get into this vault on his own. He put down his weapon with the four-power scope and hefted his ten-power binos, and through these he was able to determine the make and approximate model of the door to the vault. He jotted down some notes on a waterproof pad next to him, then continued scanning the office.

Cassidy reappeared seconds later, locked the safe, and replaced the painting by closing it on its hinges. He then returned to his desk.

Court knew then and there he would need to enter the building tonight. But to do so he wanted a lot more intel about the property and those in it, so he settled himself in for a long day of watching in the rain.

. . .

Gorik Shulga pulled up to his office at Gateway Shipping and Air Freight in south London just after lunch, climbed out of his Renault, and entered through the open warehouse door. In front of him were dozens of forty-foot shipping containers and CONNEX boxes, all either just off ships and out of customs or else in the process of being loaded with export goods for overseas.

He was thirty-six years old, reasonably good-looking with a serious brow and dark brown hair, but his suit was off the rack and a little loose fitting, and he walked with a bounce in his step that made it hard for others to take him too seriously.

He greeted a couple of his shift leaders and walked down a long hallway to the administrative section of the forwarding company.

He entered his office and dropped his keys on his desk, then took off his raincoat and hung it on a coat rack. He'd just begun to turn around when he heard the hammer clicking back on a pistol.

Shulga knew enough about guns to feel sure he'd heard the cylinder of a revolver turn, as well, because although Gorik was officially the manager of this freight forwarding concern in London, in truth he worked for SVR.

"Who's there?" he asked in English, still staring at his coat on the rack in the corner in front of him.

But the reply came in Russian, and it was a woman's voice, one that sounded faintly familiar to him. "I'm not going to hurt you, Gorik. Not unless you really, *really* want me to."

He raised his hands, cursed himself for not checking the corner of his office as he entered, and said, "Well, can I take a look at you before I decide?"

"Turn slowly."

Gorik Shulga turned *very* slowly. He saw a woman seated in the wooden chair across the room, and the pistol pointed at his chest. When he took his eyes off the gun and put them on the face of the brunette woman, his head snapped back in surprise. "Sirena? Is that *you*?"

Zoya Zakharova's code name with SVR had been *Sirena Vozdushoy Trevogi*, which meant *Banshee*, but it had been shortened operationally to simply Sirena.

"*Da.* It's me. How have you been, Gorik?"

"I heard you were dead."

"Not true."

"I heard you turned traitor on your nation."

"Not true, either."

"I heard you were booted out of SVR."

"That, actually, *is* accurate."

"You killed an SVR operative in Thailand. Utkin. Is that right?"

"*Da.*"

"Well, Sirena, I'm not Oleg Utkin. You will find me harder to kill."

"If it comes down to it, I doubt that."

"Why is that?"

"Because, Gorik, Utkin had a gun to my head and I still managed to kill him. And now I have a gun pointed at *your* head. Want to see if you're faster than a speeding bullet? Oleg wasn't."

Shulga offered no protest. Instead he sat down in front of the Russian woman with the small pistol pointed at him.

Zoya said, "I always liked you. You were one of the good ones. Slower-witted than many of the others, but sweeter."

He raised an eyebrow. "Thanks . . . I guess," he said.

"I would feel terrible if there were some misunderstanding now and I had to shoot you."

"And I might even feel worse."

Zoya smiled. Repeated, "I always liked you."

"Not enough to let me get that black dress off you that night in Venice, as I recall."

Now Zoya gave a tired little laugh. "You were drunk, and we were in the middle of an operation. Under different circumstances, you might have succeeded."

"What do you want?"

"Stuff."

"Stuff? What stuff?"

"Tools, gear, kit, supplies."

"You are out of SVR. Why would I give you anything from the London cache?"

"I would have thought the answer to be obvious." She waved the gun back and forth in front of her face.

Shulga said, "Oh. Right. Killing two SVR officers won't get you into much more hot water than killing just one."

"Exactly. Listen, I know you have three forty-foot sea containers of cached SVR weapons and other gear here on your warehouse floor. You and I are going to walk down there, I'm going to take a few items, and then I'm going to leave. At that point, you have three choices. Either you alter some paperwork to make the equipment disappear, or you make it look like you were robbed overnight by some unknown subject, or you tell SVR your security was shit, Sirena the burned dead officer got the drop on you, and then you outfitted her with enough equipment to conduct an intelligence operation."

Gorik's face turned gray.

"Yeah," Zoya said. "You get the picture, don't you?"

"I don't know what you think you're doing, Sirena. You're crazy. You always were off in your own little world. Motivated by something other than our nation. Some . . . some desire to make your dead father proud. Well . . . I don't think he'd be so proud of you now."

Zoya did not respond.

"So . . . who *are* you working for?"

"If I were working for anyone, I wouldn't be here stealing equipment from you, would I? I have a personal interest in a delicate situation, and I need to figure some things out on my own."

"With guns and knives and bombs?"

She raised an eyebrow. "You've got bombs?" When he didn't answer, she said, "Kidding. I'll need a pistol and ammunition. A couple of fixed-blade knives. But what I really need is surveillance tech, climbing gear, audio equipment for safe cracking, that sort of thing. You can lose that sort of equipment and cover for it."

"I can't cover for a lost gun," he said flatly.

"Give me one of your local purchases. One you haven't logged with Yasenevo."

He made a face. "What are you talking about?"

"Come on, Gorik. We came up the ranks together, until you topped out at thirty. I'm sure you remember I used to run foreign caches at the beginning of my career. I know how the game is played. You have official equipment, and you have unofficial equipment, black market shit in case you need to pass it out to a proxy. Give me one of those guns, the rest of the gear I ask for, and you can paper over this entire day."

Gorik just eyed her for a long time. "What do I get in return?"

Zoya rolled her eyes. "Again, dummy, I'm pointing a gun at you. You get to live." She added, "Doubt you'd have ever figured out how to get my dress off if I let you try back in Venice."

. . .

Twenty-five minutes later Zoya Zakharova left Gateway Shipping and Air Freight with a backpack on her back and a second, smaller backpack strapped around her front. Gorik was back in his office, and Zoya put the odds at fifty-fifty as to whether he was already on the phone to Moscow.

She hoped he wouldn't make that call, of course, but to tip the scales in her favor if he did, she decided she would speed up her work even more here in London. She'd go to the office of Terry Cassidy this evening. She'd find that damn safe and, she hoped, whatever was inside would help her figure out her next move.

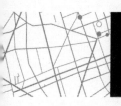

CHAPTER 28

ONE MONTH EARLIER

David Mars arrived in Edinburgh with Fox, Hines, and a full security crew of six men who knew how to dress, act, and move as if they were not a security crew. They wore civilian attire, and nothing that screamed "Tactical Tuxedo." Their weapons remained perfectly concealed. HK MP7s with folded stocks under arms or in instantly accessible gym bags over their shoulders, and various makes and models of pistols carried under their shirts in the appendix position. As Fox, Mars, and Hines headed along Lauriston Place, past buildings that made up part of the University of Edinburgh, the UK-born-and-trained security detail commander walked ten yards ahead. The principal was flanked by two armed protection agents, and two more walked twenty feet behind the trio but not in any set formation. A sixth man was one hundred yards ahead, looking for threats but in a low-profile manner.

Mars, Fox, and Hines finally entered the building that housed Janice Won's research lab, passed through an unmarked door, and took an elevator to the third-floor lab. While three of the detail remained outside to keep their eyes open for trouble, the security commander and one of his men came with the protectees. The point man was already in the lab, checking over everyone there.

Won was there, in the middle of the laboratory, at a stand-up desk with a laptop computer. Around her two technicians worked on one of the fermentation vats, monitoring temperature and moisture via gauges on the side of a cylinder that looked like a large high-tech oil drum.

"Good morning, Doctor," he said as he crossed the room. "How lovely to see you."

Won did not return the smile, but she did shake his proffered hand. He always felt her do this with reticence, and he remembered reading in her file that the Russians had found her to be psychologically damaged and unable to form intimate relationships or even friendships. Something from her childhood, Mars imagined, but he didn't really care.

He said, "We just wanted to drop in and see how you are getting along with the task of growing the spores from the material taken from Stockholm."

She replied curtly. "We will speak in my office first."

Mars raised an eyebrow at Fox but followed her compliantly.

A minute later the two sat alone in the small and spare office, cups of steaming tea in front of them. Mars didn't love green tea, but his English manners, learned in the last thirty-five years of his sixty-two years on Earth, obliged him to sip it.

He tried a little small talk but, as usual, Won was mission focused in the extreme.

She interrupted his comment on the weather to say, "Regarding the development of the plague spores, it is impossible for me to give you a progress report, with completion percentages and time projections, because I do not yet know how much developed *Yersinia pestis* is needed for our operation."

"Understood. Perhaps just let me know the percentage increase in the bacteria you have grown. I can make a layman's estimation from that and—"

Janice Won interrupted. "No. I am a scientist, Mr. Mars. I don't want a layman's estimation. I need firm information to do my job. I need *more* information."

"What are you telling me?"

"I am telling you it is no longer negotiable. You reveal the target to me, now, or I leave this project."

Mars was not a man to take ultimatums quietly, even if they were reasonable, as he had to allow that this one was. But he caught himself from
lashing out. He saw Won as a crucial and powerful weapon, but one that
needed to be carefully handled to prevent a misfire.

Despite some misgivings he said, "Doctor . . . you are quite right. It's
time." He put the tea down on the table and sat back, crossing his legs. "Do
you know what the term Five Eyes refers to?"

The younger woman made a face of frustration. "You *do* know I have
training as an intelligence operative, don't you?"

Mars held a hand up. "My apologies, Doctor. I did not mean to be pa-
tronizing. Well, you are probably also aware that Five Eyes has a conference each year in a different location, but you might not know that this
year it will be here, in Scotland. First there will be a series of meetings in
London, but only among the principals and their deputies. Then they will
join their larger staffs at a thirteenth-century castle and resort property in
the Highlands, just south of Inverness."

Won nodded slowly. "How many people?"

"There will be over four hundred intelligence officers, executives, security personnel, and administrators, meeting each day at the property.
Many are staying there, but all the hotels and rooms to let in the area are
filled, as well. Each of the five nations will have a full array of representa-
tives in attendance."

Her eyes widened with the recognition of the opportunity before her.
"Who, specifically, will be at this location?"

"As you are probably aware, the U.S. intelligence community contains
sixteen separate agencies, and key members of all of them will be represented. CIA, NSA, FBI, Homeland Security, Office of Naval Intelligence,
and so on and so forth. One hundred seventy attendees at the conference
will be American. The British have ninety attending. Canada, New Zealand, and Australia have smaller contingents, but it is not the sheer number of people at the castle that is important."

Won knew what he meant by this, because this was Won's field of expertise. "No, it's the access these people have to their coworkers when they
return to their respective countries *after* the conference."

"Precisely," said Mars. "Think about almost two hundred or so members of the U.S. intel community leaving the conference and returning to Langley, their foreign stations, military bases, wherever. If they are infected with the disease, they would not show symptoms for days, giving them plenty of time to intermingle unknowingly with their colleagues. They will be hosts for this quickly spreading weapon."

When she spoke again Mars was fascinated by her nimble mind's instant transformation into utter mission focus. "We don't need to worry about the bacteria. We will have more than double what we need for this task. I have this under control. We must talk about the proper means of delivery and distribution of the bacteria. This castle will have some sort of natural ventilation we can use. Aerosol delivery would be best and most efficient, but we'll have to find a way to ensure that no one detects anything amiss when the attack happens. We have to infect the population without them realizing it."

Mars was pleased that he had revealed more information to Won, because now he could concentrate on the op fully. He said, "Too true. We can't shell the building with mortars filled with plague, because they would realize they had been attacked, and doctors would simply give all the attendees antibiotics."

"Exactly," she said. "The virus needs to incubate in the body for only eight hours, and *then* it is terminal. Only heavy antibiotics—Cefalexin, for example—administered within that short window can save the infected patient."

Won added, "We can use a crop duster. It is an effective means of delivery, assuming they use them in Scotland."

"They are all over the Scottish Highlands," Mars said. "Used to keep back the heather and bracken that grows insidiously there."

"I will have to check the weather conditions, and you'll need to find a good pilot. Precision will be required."

"I am already working on that. Now, the location of the Five Eyes conference is Castle Enrick, on Loch Ness. The location is rented out for conferences, but the rest of the time it is a five-star hotel. My agents and I have stayed there at different times over the past two months looking for vulnerabilities. If you like, you and I can stay the night, as well."

Won immediately snapped back, "In separate rooms, I assume?"

Mars flashed a glance to Fox. "Certainly, Doctor." Fox smiled, his way of showing Mars that this woman was nuts. Mars said, "Don't worry, Dr. Won. This entire enterprise is not just a means for me to get to know you better."

She did not react to this. "How soon can this be arranged?"

"How does the weekend sound?"

"Excellent," Won said, and for the first time in the conversation she smiled.

PRESENT DAY

The London rain stopped long before the sun went down, and by eleven p.m. the summer air was cool and misty.

Court found himself on a different roof closer to Terry Cassidy's office now, right next door to the one he'd spent six hours on earlier in the day. He'd chosen this building because it was directly across from ductwork that ran up the length of his target location, and although the aluminum piping looked wet and not exactly sturdy, he thought he could use it to his advantage. He had a climbing harness and gloves with him and had decided his best bet was to go down and cross the street out of sight of the guards in the lobby, and then make his way up the wall and move all the way up to either the rooftop to access the door there or, better still, find some breachable window along the way.

He was taking his time, though. There was always more tactical intelligence to pull off a target before acting, and many an operation had failed because someone had decided they knew enough to push ahead when they were, in fact, missing the one critical piece of information that spelled the difference between life and death.

He had his suppressed and subsonic short-barreled rifle up here with him, but it was zipped in its case. He had no plans to shoot anybody tonight, but he'd wanted the weapon on hand in case organized criminal elements who were clearly working with Cassidy were present and this whole thing went south.

He'd climb carrying only his Glock, which wasn't much firepower, but slinging the .300 Blackout SBR up the side of a building on his back, using the thin aluminum and wet masonry as foot and handholds, would be no fun at all.

He'd left the Glock 43 back at the apartment, not wanting to be encumbered by anything strapped to his ankle while he climbed.

He took a break to eat a bag of raisins he'd brought with him, and to drink his last bottle of water. He bit into a protein bar, chewed a moment, then shoved the rest into his mouth.

He picked his binos up one last time before descending and gave one final slow scan to the building across the street when his night vision image stopped and froze on the northeast corner of the structure. There he saw a figure dressed in black, stepping over the third-floor balcony and then crouching down by the door latch there.

Where the hell did he come from?

It seemed to be some sort of a burglar, or someone with the exact same plans he had: to snoop on one of the offices inside.

This was opposite to the end of the building from where Cassidy's office was, but there was no way he could penetrate the building now that there was some other jackass in there, potentially tripping off alarms or otherwise drawing attention to the place.

No, he'd have to sit tight and watch.

"Asshole," he muttered as the figure opened the latch and disappeared inside the building.

* * *

Zoya Zakharova had performed a grand total of twelve minutes' reconnaissance on the building before walking across a darkened portion of the street away from the lights of the front lobby, leaping up onto a thin iron pipe along the wall, and then pulling herself to a first-floor windowsill. From there she free-climbed up to the second story, which in Europe meant she was now three floors above the ground. It had taken her all of forty seconds, and after vaulting a balcony railing and dropping behind it, then picking a simple latch lock and slipping into what appeared to be an office break room, she squatted in the corner and listened for noises.

There was a patrol of two guards; she heard them talking as they passed, and then a stairwell door opened and she heard two pairs of feet descending. She stood and went for the door, then began skulking up the hall. She had two stories to climb, and to do it she moved towards the stairwell on the opposite side of the building from the one the guards used.

. . .

"Where are you, you stupid son of a bitch?" Court muttered to himself on the roof across the street. He continued to scan with his binos, looking through every window he could see, desperately trying to get some sort of a fix on the intruder.

While doing this he tapped his earpiece, placing a call to the one number in his phone.

Twenty seconds later he got an answer. "Brewer."

"No chance you have someone else doing a sneak-and-peek on Cassidy's building, is there?"

"No chance, whatsoever. I assumed you could handle that by yourself. Was I overly optimistic?"

"Well, I *could* have, if some random dipshit didn't just scale the side of the building and climb in through a balcony door."

"You're kidding. What if he's going for the safe?"

"Then I guess I'll smash him over the head when he gets out of there, and I'll take whatever he took out of the safe. My concern, though, is that he fails and this makes it impossible for me to get in there until their security relaxes again."

"Right," Suzanne Brewer said. "What do you need?"

"Wait one," Court said, because he scanned Cassidy's office and saw the masked figure moving through the darkness there, staying away from the window but not out of view from someone with night vision equipment.

The figure looked over the room, began opening drawers in wooden file cabinets and thumbing through them, and then opened up a computer there on the desk.

"Shit. Subject is in Cassidy's office. Definitely hunting for something."

"A safe?"

"He's rifling through the desk."

"Keep watching and reporting what you see."

The figure moved to a paneled wall behind the desk and began feeling around. He was thirty feet away from the painting the safe was hidden behind, and Court doubted there was any chance he'd find it.

The person in the office then went back to the file cabinet and fidgeted with his mask for a moment, lining up the eyeholes to read some papers in the file. After several seconds of this, the figure reached up and pulled the knit mask off his head.

Shoulder-length brunette hair tumbled out of the balaclava.

Court blinked in surprise. The figure was facing away from him, kneeling in front of the bottom drawer in the file cabinet, but Court put the subject's height around five eight, and he noticed the lean frame did seem to have some feminine curves.

Was he looking at a woman?

Court said, "Brewer?"

"I'm here."

"Uh . . . here's a twist. The target is a—"

Just then, the person squatting turned towards the door to the office. Through Court's night vision binos and their ten-power magnification, he could easily see the face of Zoya Zakharova and the look of alarm on it.

Court felt a muscle spasm in his low back and the burn of fresh adrenaline and dopamine in his system. He'd thought about this face in front of him nearly constantly for the past four months, told himself he'd probably never lay eyes on it again, and now the face was here, right in front of him.

And expressing imminent danger.

Brewer spoke. "I lost transmission. Do you have me, Violator?"

Court didn't answer; he just bit his lip while he watched the former Russian operative close the file cabinet, spin around, then crawl behind the desk.

"Violator, how do you copy?"

After a long pause Court said, "The subject . . . the subject in Cassidy's office, is identified."

"*Identified?* Identified as who?"

"It's . . . it's Zoya."

Clearly Brewer could not process what she was hearing. "*What* did you say?"

"Zoya."

"Zakharova is . . . she's *there*? In the UK?"

"In the lawyer's office. Right now. Hiding, looks like she thinks she hears someone coming."

Brewer said, "What the hell does any of this have to do with her?"

"Lady, don't ask me. I haven't got a *fucking* clue what's going on with any of this shit. Just tell me what you want me to do."

CHAPTER 29

Suzanne Brewer sat at her desk on the sixth floor of CIA's Langley Head-quarters, her phone to her ear. Her eyes were closed while she tried to process the new and utterly dissonant information her agent had just passed on to her.

Anthem was in play in London. *But for whom? And how did she get there?*

Her first inclination was to tell Violator to shoot Zoya Zakharova in the head from standoff distance right this moment. But she was no fool; she knew there was no way he would comply with the order. Instead she said, "Just watch her."

Through the phone she heard her agent speak in a challenging voice. "I thought you told me she was at a safe house somewhere."

"She was. She . . . escaped. A couple days ago."

Violator said, "I talked to her before you brought her over to the States. She *wanted* to go. She *wanted* to work for you. What the hell were you do-ing to her that caused her to escape?"

"*We* weren't doing anything. She was on her way to becoming an asset. She was doing great, only weeks from operational status."

"Until one day she just walked out the front door?"

"Yes. Well . . . not exactly. The safe house was hit by armed hostiles. Her motives remain unclear because from the surveillance cameras we see that she was in the process of escaping even before the raid began. There is no way she knew she was in any danger when she made the decision to run, unless she'd been tipped off somehow that gunmen were coming. We don't think they were there to rescue her, because of her actions against them."

"You are saying she killed one, aren't you?"

"Two, in fact."

Court then asked, "Who were the attackers?"

"Mexican *sicarios*, although we assume they were working for someone who ordered them to eliminate Zoya. But we don't know who, and we don't know how they knew Zoya was there."

She heard the sigh through the encrypted phone line. "Let me help you with that. You have a *big fucking leak* at CIA."

Brewer sighed. "Thank you, Violator, but we are well aware of that much, at least."

"And people like Zoya and I are exposed and vulnerable. What the hell are you guys doing about it?"

"We're working on it. We have it narrowed down to a few possibles."

Violator said, "So . . . again, what do I do about Zoya now?"

To herself, the woman at the desk in McLean, Virginia, said, *Shoot that bitch, shoot yourself, and then I'll run over Hightower with a bus.*

But to Violator she said, "Do nothing. Let this play out. Then follow Anthem when she leaves."

"What the hell is Anthem?"

"Her code name."

"Right." A few seconds later he spoke again. "Well . . . shit."

"What?"

"She's not going anywhere. The office lights just turned on and a bunch of dudes with guns are in there looking for her."

To this Brewer just repeated herself. "Let it play, Violator."

• • •

On her knees behind the desk, Zoya drew the Walther pistol she'd taken from Gorik Shulga earlier in the day, and she hefted it for use. She was about to rise to her knees and fire, when a voice in Russian called out to her.

"Zoya Feodorovna Zakharova! We mean you no harm. We only wish to speak."

She did not recognize the voice at all; it was definitely not Vladi Belyakov or Gorik Shulga, the only two native Russians, as far as she was aware, who knew she was here in London. *What the hell is going on?*

"I have several armed men with me. If you exchange fire with us we will have no choice but to defend ourselves. But we would rather do this peacefully."

Zoya looked at the glass window, fifteen feet to her left. She could run for it, shoot a hole in it, then dive out, but then she'd fall several floors to her death.

Not an option. Engaging multiple armed men didn't seem like good odds, either, especially because they clearly had her pinpointed to behind the desk, as the office held no other obvious hiding places.

She did the only thing she could think to do. *"Khorosho," Fine*, she said, and continued speaking Russian. "I'm sliding my pistol over the desk, and I'm standing up slowly with hands raised. Does that work for you?"

"As long as you play no tricks, that works fine," said the Russian voice. She heard him speaking English softly, conferring with others, which surprised her.

These obviously weren't SVR personnel. So who *were* they?

She put the Walther on the mahogany desk above her, then slid it forward, all the way over the side. It bounced along the wooden floor.

The Russian man himself now said, *"Khorosho."*

Zoya stood straight, all in black, her dark hair sweat-soaked and matted from the balaclava she'd dropped on the floor behind the desk. Her gloved hands were away from her body, and she looked across the bright room at five men. Three had dark hair, rifles pointed at her chest, and combat gear; one was an impressively tall and broad blond-haired figure in a leather jacket who seemed to be unarmed; and the fifth was a younger man wearing a dark goatee and a nice suit. He had a small pistol in his left hand, down by his side.

This man spoke to her in Russian, the same voice she'd heard before. "Step out, please."

She had knives on her, but she wouldn't go for them, and she had a revolver in an ankle holster, but she wouldn't make a move for that, either. No, they had her. She'd comply and see where this went.

"Who are you?" she asked the Russian. "And who are they?"

"My name is Fox. I work for someone who wishes to speak with you."

"Fox isn't a Russian name."

"It's the name I'm prepared to give you."

"Right," Zoya said, and then she walked around the desk, her hands still up.

The three dark-haired men closed on her fast, spun her around, and pushed her facedown on the desk roughly. They frisked her with surprising skill, pulling off the two knives and throwing them onto the floor. One wrenched an arm behind her back, then reached for the other arm, but she held on to the desk's edge so that he couldn't move it.

They were going to be rough with her, and that meant she was going to be rough right back. It was her defiant nature; it had gotten her into trouble in the past, and if she took the time to be honest with herself now, she would have realized it was going to lead to trouble in the present.

But she held the desk firmly. *Fuck these guys.*

Another man began frisking her waistband, reaching under her crotch, squeezing, and then working his way down her left leg.

The .38 was on her right ankle, and she knew it would be detected within seconds.

Zoya struggled against the three men.

"Stop resisting!" one man said, clearly with an Israeli accent.

"Calm down and I will!" she screamed back. "What the fuck is wrong with you?"

In answer, one of the men punched her in the kidneys, and her gloved hand came loose from the desk.

These boys didn't fuck around, but neither did Zakharova.

The man had finished frisking her left leg, and then he rose back up and started working his way down her right.

Without thinking about what she was doing, she retaliated for the kidney punch. She used her left heel to find her way between the feet of the man frisking her leg. She wasn't sure if this was the one who'd hit her, but she didn't care. With all her might she shot her foot up behind her, between the man's legs, and she heel-kicked him in the testicles.

She knew from the feel and the sound that she had scored a bull's-eye, and the groan she heard next, along with the sound of a body impacting with the floor, only served to confirm this.

Another punch to her kidneys brought a loud grunt out of her mouth, and she felt momentarily frozen in agony.

Behind her she heard the man called Fox say, "She's not to be harmed! Damn you! She's not to be harmed!"

With both hands behind her now she felt zip ties cinching on her wrists.

. . .

Court had reached for his rifle bag and brought it closer to him, but he did not unzip it. He kept Brewer updated on what was going on across the street, but it was hard to do so. Every fiber in his being told him he had to get over there and help her.

"Are you fucking listening, Brewer? They are beating the living shit out of her."

"Sounds like she's getting her own licks in."

"Defensively, only. Let me engage."

"Stand fast. Let it play, Violator. Do *not* engage."

"*Fuck* that. What if they kill her?"

"They aren't going to kill her. They are just taking her into their custody. For all we know they are the police. Or else she could be working with them, and they just haven't ID'd her yet. She sure *as hell* isn't working for us. Don't worry about Anthem; get photos of the others in the room."

But Court didn't grab his camera. He kept one hand on the binos, while the other hand reached for the zipper on his rifle bag and began to slowly open it while he held the binos to his eyes.

. . .

Zoya was pulled to her feet by her hair and shoulders; the two Israeli security men next to her strong-armed her around, and as soon as she faced the open, well-lit room, she saw the man she'd dropped with the kick to the junk trying to struggle back to his feet. He looked at her with eyes that told her he was not going to let her attack on his manhood go.

In Russian, she said, "Fox, tell that one to back off!"

Fox said, "He does not work for me directly, Zoya. I am trying." He switched to English. "Ari . . . let it go."

"Fuck this bitch!" Ari said. "She donkey-kicked me in the nuts!"

He spun his rifle behind his back, balled his fists, and started moving towards her. Zoya tried to pull away from the two men holding her arms but was not strong enough to free herself.

As the man closed, Fox shouted, "Ari! Don't you—"

Zoya used the men grasping her tight as leverage, and she brought both legs into the air, then executed a mighty front kick, slamming her instep into the Israeli's already wounded balls, and dropping him a second time.

He fell to his knees, then went fetal on his side.

Fox couldn't help but laugh at this. "I told you, Ari. The woman before you is legendary for not putting up with anyone's shit. She's more man than you!"

One of the Israelis holding her laughed, while the other just smiled while he punched her in the side of the head, in an attempt to get her to stop her resistance.

. . .

Court bit the inside of his cheek, then spoke softly. "Suzanne, she's not going down without a fight. It's about to get serious over there. I can stop this if you just—"

"Violator, listen to me. Don't do something you will regret."

"I've been doing something I regret since the day I started taking orders from you."

"Sit right there and report! That . . . is . . . an . . . *order*! If you—"

Court closed his eyes and tapped his earpiece, disconnecting the call. He lowered the binos, then yanked the short-barreled rifle with the laser-aiming device out of the bag.

Being a team player had been fun while it lasted, but it was time to go off mission.

CHAPTER 30

Ari pulled himself to his feet for the second time, using a fallen chair in front of the desk for balance. Upon standing he shouted back to Fox. "More man than me? Let's see what she's *really* got on the inside."

He drew a black-bladed knife from his belt, then rushed the two steps forward towards the woman again being held by his two colleagues.

As Fox shouted "No!" Ari thrust the weapon at Zoya's abdomen.

But the blade never connected with its target.

The Israeli security man was shot through the right side of his head, his medulla oblongata destroyed by a subsonic Winchester .300 Blackout round, and this instantly ceased transfer of motor and sensory neurons to his body. He tumbled to his left and dropped like a sack of bricks, as blood splattered all the way to the paneled wall fifteen feet away. The two Israelis flanking Zoya let go of her and spun to the now-broken window. As they raised their weapons they immediately fell backwards in the room, one after the other, both shot through the head.

Zoya launched herself backwards over the desk, difficult to do with her hands zip-tied behind her back, but she kicked her feet over her head and did a reverse somersault and fell down onto the floor awkwardly, out of sight of the window and the two men still alive in the room with her.

She heard Fox and the big man running through the room towards the door, then taking off up the hall for the stairs.

She crawled around to the far side of the desk, away from the window and the sniper, and grabbed one of her knives lying there where it had been tossed by her attackers. Using it, she cut her zip ties from behind. The dead Israeli named Ari was on the floor just feet away, but his rifle was to his right, and in view of the window where the shots came from, so she didn't dare go for it. Instead she tucked back down behind the desk to think.

Zoya found herself so utterly confused right now. A sniper had killed the men holding her, of this she was certain. But what was completely unclear was *why*. Zoya knew she didn't have a single friend, or even an ally, on planet Earth at the moment.

Why had someone helped her?

Just then, a laser pointer marked a spot in red on the paneling to her right. Zoya ducked down quickly, thinking gunfire would surely follow. There was no shooting. The light shook back and forth, as if to get her attention, and flicked on and off several times. It then very slowly began panning to the left along the wall.

Zoya cocked her head in puzzlement.

This mysterious sniper just kept getting weirder.

The light continued panning, past the blood-splattered wall, until it finally stopped on a painting halfway across the room. It then traced up the side of the frame, stopped, and began blinking on and off again, then drawing a circle around a small area.

And then it hit her. Somehow Zoya knew this was where the safe was hidden, and the sniper wanted her to find it.

Who? Why?

She stood slowly from behind the desk, facing the window, looking at an ornate Edwardian-style office building across the street. After a moment she caught a quick flash of red as the laser panned back over to the wall near her. She couldn't see the origin of the beam but could tell it was just slightly higher than her position, perhaps on the roof.

The red dot moved back to the painting and remained there.

Zoya walked over to her Walther on the floor, reholstered it, then moved across the office, her eyes still on the window, her mind still not completely certain that this shooter wasn't going to target her, as well. But when she arrived at the painting the laser moved away again, far to the left, and remained in position there, totally stationary near the door to the office.

She realized the sniper had propped his weapon on something and was leaving his laser designator on to show her he was not pointing the gun her way.

This went a long way towards giving her the comfort to turn her back to the window, and when she did, she felt around behind the picture frame and found the latch. She swung the painting back on its hinges, revealing the safe.

She looked back over her shoulder, out the window.

• • •

Court watched from in his dark hide under the painter's tarp, only fifty yards away. His gun was stabilized on his backpack so he didn't even have to touch it, and he held the ten-power binos to his eyes so he could watch Zoya more closely. The lights were on in the office, so he left the night vision function off.

She turned around and looked back over her shoulder at the window. Through the magnification Court felt like he was right in front of her face. He saw the sweat on her brow, her dark eyes peering hard into the night, and then he saw her soft lips as her mouth moved.

Thank you, she seemed to say, and then she turned back to the safe, pulling out a set of earphones from her hip bag as she did so.

Court's heart was already banging against his rib cage. First seeing her, then engaging the men the instant before they killed her, and now her show of gratitude about what he'd just done, it was almost more than his cardiovascular system could handle.

As he processed his emotions, he felt his earpiece vibrate. He watched Zoya's back as she worked on the combination, and he tapped the device. "Go for Violator."

"Sitrep." There was unmistakable rage in Brewer's voice.

"Zoya's safe. Three attackers are down and dead. Two more escaped."

"What the *hell* happened?"

Court sat up now, turned off the laser on the rifle next to him, hefted it, and folded it up. As he slid it back into his case, he said, "Would you believe spontaneous combustion?"

His handler was furious, as Court had expected. "You engaged the men trying to detain a rogue asset? She was a loose end, not one of us! Whose side are you on?"

"That's yet to be determined. I'm a good company man, but I couldn't watch them kill her."

It was quiet for a moment, and then Brewer said, "Of course not. I understand, Courtland. I'm sorry."

Court knew she was only being conciliatory as some sort of a manipulation tactic. She *never* called him by his real name, and her faux empathy wasn't very well pulled off, because virtually nobody had called him Courtland since his mom died.

Brewer switched back to business mode, just as Court expected. "Now . . . can you get over there and into that safe?"

"I don't have to get into the safe. Zoya is working on it right now, and it looks like she knows what she's doing."

Brewer's softening tone disappeared in an instant. "How the hell does that help us? She's not working for Langley."

"I'm going to ask her for it when she gets out of there."

"You planning on getting a room at the Hyatt to get reacquainted first?"

Court just sighed. "Violator out." He tapped his earpiece and put it in his pocket.

Whatever happened for the rest of the night, he sure as shit didn't want it happening with Suzanne Brewer yapping into his ear.

. . .

Zoya Zakharova took four minutes to get through the steel door, but once she did she found herself in what looked like a medium-sized bank vault. It was ten feet wide and fourteen feet deep, with shelves and drawers all up and down the walls, and a table in the middle of the room.

On the table she saw money bound and stacked like it was newspaper, euros and dollars, mostly; jewelry in glass containers, a row of watches that looked like they each must have cost more than what Zoya made in a year back when she had steady work.

She saw file cabinets and contracts stacked one upon the other in the unlocked drawers, bearer bonds, and satchels full of travel documents and passports.

It was a mother lode of supplies and loot for either an intelligence organization or an organized crime firm of some sort; Zoya could not determine which.

Looking around, unsure what to make of it all, she began scanning the locking mechanisms used on a single horizontal panel built into the wall. Most of the cabinets were unlocked or didn't even have doors on them. Obviously Cassidy considered the vault door itself the only necessary deterrent for all this loot and compromising material. But the panel on the far wall—Zoya assumed it covered a pull-out drawer—had been secured with a heavy key lock, and this she found interesting. It seemed whatever was inside, Cassidy wanted to keep it even more secure than the rest of the items in the vault. She stepped up to the panel immediately and took the lock-picking tools she'd procured from Gorik Shulga's SVR equipment cache.

She began working, and opened the large metal drawer in under a minute. Inside she found one item only. It was an iPad, the newest model, along with a charger.

Perplexed, she put the device inside her shirt and the charger in her hip bag, and then she headed back out of the vault, grabbing a thick wrapped stack of twenty-pound notes on the way.

. . .

Five minutes later she had descended the outside of the building and was just dropping down to street level when a pair of black four-doors skidded through the intersection, turning her way. She tried to dive into a darkened area, but this was Earl's Court, and the street lighting was good. She turned and ran as fast as she could, unsure who was after her, but under the assumption that Fox and his big goon had called for support, and she just happened to be unlucky enough to time her escape to coincide perfectly with the arrival of the reinforcements.

She was on foot, she hadn't brought a car or a motorcycle, but she was able to duck down a side street, then turn into a narrow alleyway, at the end of which she saw a sizable wall.

She sprinted towards it.

One of the sedans turned into the alleyway behind her.

As she approached the fourteen-foot-high wall ahead, her brain worked through the geometry and physics involved with climbing it. She told herself the corners would be key; she could pick a side, launch up, and use a foot against the building next to the wall, then the wall itself, and alternate back and forth, harnessing the momentum generated in her run along with the momentum generated by her legs during the pushoff of the climb.

This basically meant she would be running up the corner, and she knew she couldn't do it for long before the momentum stored and generated equaled less than the force of gravity pulling her back to Earth, and at that point she would fall.

She hoped by then she'd be close enough to the top to grab hold.

The sedan behind her had her pinned in. It stopped and she heard car doors open. The driver put his high beams right on her.

Zoya leapt into the air. Right foot on the building, shoving up and high, left foot on the wall, hands slapping both surfaces for balance and a tiny bit more help with her climb. Back and forth, three steps on each side in all, and then she extended her arms over her head, grabbed the six-inch ledge at the top of the wall, and heaved herself up with her strong arms, shoulders, and back.

She had just started to fling herself over onto the other side and away from her attackers when she saw the second sedan parked there, the men from it just now getting out of their vehicle.

Der'mo!

She launched to her feet and began moving across the narrow ledge no wider than a balance beam.

Guns were raised in her position on both sides, but as she ran she heard no gunfire, only Fox's voice, speaking Russian. "Zoya? Your father would like a word."

Instantly she stopped. She turned towards the side of the alley from where Fox's echoing voice addressed her. She gasped out a reply. "What . . . what did you say?"

"Your father. He sends his love. He asked me to bring you to him. I apologize about the men back there. They had been asked not to harm you, but you frankly sent one of them over the edge. Your father will be furious with them, and me, when he finds out what happened."

"He's . . . *here*? In London?"

"Indeed."

Her heart pounded, both from the effect of adrenaline still and from the man's words.

"You are lying," she finally forced herself to say.

Zoya stood in the gunsights of at least six weapons, still and stationary, her arms by her sides and her chest heaving from exertion from the run and the climb and the crazy stress of all this.

Fox added, "Who is your friend? The sniper?"

Zoya recovered from the news she just heard. "He's watching us right now. I give a signal and—"

Fox laughed. "We are two blocks away, down in an alley. We saw no force of men around the building, so you likely just had one comrade with you in this, and he has lost his line of sight."

She did not reply to this.

"Come. Let's go see the general. You'll have a nice chat."

She didn't trust Fox, but she didn't see many other options.

"All right," she said. "I'm coming down."

"Toss your weapon."

She still had the .38 in the ankle holster; it was hidden under her black pants, and the Israelis hadn't found it during their rough shakedown. So she pulled the Walther and dropped it onto the cobblestones below her.

"Very well," said Fox. "I'd ask if you needed help climbing down, but from what I just witnessed, you should have no problems."

Zoya sat down on the top of the wall, spun around and hung from it, then dropped the rest of the way. She'd just begun to turn around when the sound of a car's engine and squealing tires entered the alleyway behind Fox and his car.

The headlights of a green Volvo spun into view, and the vehicle raced forward at speed, clearly having every intention of slamming into the four-door parked there.

All the men standing next to the car, Fox included, spun their weapons towards the threat.

Zoya turned to her left and saw a window into a darkened room, just fifteen feet from her, and she ran for it.

Racing towards the window, she knew if it was anything more than a single-pane plate she'd probably not be able to just dive through it as though she were in an old Western film. Ideally she'd put a bullet hole or two in the glass to weaken it, then crash through, but she didn't want to stop to draw from her ankle holster.

She kept running, praying she'd get lucky.

But luck wasn't with her. Zoya saw, as she neared the window at a full sprint, that it was clearly double-pane energy-efficient glass.

But she was committed to the leap now, so she tried to generate as much power from her legs as possible. She was sure that even if she did break the glass, she'd probably also break a collarbone in the process.

Der'mo, she thought again as she went airborne.

But an instant before she made contact with the window, gunfire erupted to her right, and two rounds struck the pane in front of her, not two feet away, and by the bullets damaging the integral strength of the glass she was able to dive through easily in a shower of shards, landing and sliding along the floor inside the building.

CHAPTER 31

Court fired the shots at the window from the driver's side of his car to help Zoya get out of the kill zone, but now he bailed out into the alley with his rifle, and scurried behind the vehicle.

As soon as he rolled behind the car, he began taking fire.

The Volvo he'd taken from the young CIA officer was instantly perforated with dozens of holes. Steam spewed from the hood and glass shattered in the windows.

Court was on his knees now in the alley behind the car, trying to make himself as small as an engine block, and as concealed as he could be. He was screwed out here as long as he was stuck in this location, and he needed his own way out. He dumped an entire magazine from the .300 Blackout in a "spray and pray" fashion over the hood of the car, shot through and above the roof, then dropped the rifle and pulled his Glock 19. He spun and fired into a darkened window on his right, the same building Zoya had just escaped into. He reached over the Volvo again, this time with the handgun, and fired a dozen or so rounds, hoping to get these assholes to look for some temporary cover.

He rose to his feet and ran for the broken windowpane, diving through it, chased along by gunfire. He landed hard and awkwardly on a school desk, flipping it and himself over several times before coming to a stop.

He rose in the darkened room and fired back through the two windows into the alley, emptying his weapon into a man who appeared there with a submachine gun.

Court reloaded his last mag and fired another eight rounds through all the windows in the room, back towards the alleyway, trying to buy himself some time.

With only a half magazine in his hot pistol, he spun around and began running.

Looking at the layout and the size of the desks in the classroom, Court could tell he was running through a primary school. He bounded out into the hall, his gun ahead of him. He had no idea if the men from the alley would pursue him in here, but he wanted to get as much space as possible between himself and them as quickly as possible.

He slowed to listen for the sounds of other footfalls, hoping to track Zoya, but his ears were shot for the time being and he heard nothing. He started running again, searching for some sort of an exit on the far side of the building.

Within moments, however, he heard the shouted voices of men behind him. The surviving goons from the alley were clearly pouring through the windows. He had a few seconds on them, no more, so he decided this large and dark school might afford him a decent place to hide if he just looked for one.

Turning down a narrow corridor darker than the main halls of the school, he found a door, barely visible until he was just feet away. He turned the latch and was pleased to find it unlocked, so he entered the perfectly darkened room, shut and locked the door, and listened till the racing footsteps of at least four men passed by up the main hall.

. . .

Jon Hines virtually never left his boss's side, but as Fox watched his surviving men climb through the windows in pursuit of Zoya and her unknown accomplice, he turned to his big bodyguard. "I want you in there, too."

"Sir, I watch over *you*."

Fox snapped now, "If one of our guys hurts or kills Zoya, Mars will have me killed. Believe me, you preventing that will be the best protection you've ever given me."

Hines zipped up his light leather jacket to obscure his white shirt, then walked over to one of the broken windows. He stepped easily inside and began moving through a series of dark rooms and hallways.

He could hear the other men running and banging their way through doors, and he could tell almost immediately they weren't clearing every room of this building; instead they seemed to assume the fleeing pair had just shot out an exit onto the street. But Hines himself took his time, moved with silent footfalls, and thought about what he might do if half a dozen gunmen were on his heels as he ran through this building.

He stopped suddenly. What would he do? He'd find a place in this darkened warren to wait for the danger to pass.

He stepped over to a stairwell, moved into complete blackness there, then leaned back against the wall. He was one man; he could not search the multistory school alone, but he could listen for the moment Zoya and her friend decided the coast was clear, and that was when he would pounce.

Hines had a pistol, but he left it in its shoulder holster. Hand-to-hand fighting was more than just his forte; it was his singular passion, so he was determined to get close enough to the male rescuer of Mars's crazy daughter to snap the man in two. His senses were acute due to some adrenaline, but he wasn't amped up about the thrill and the danger. Hines had killed many times, yet he'd never been seriously hurt in a hand-to-hand fight, and since his confidence was born out of success, he had no doubts about his prospects tonight.

He'd kill the man with Zoya, and he'd scoop up that little Russian bitch and carry her back to Fox so he could take her home to Daddy.

• • •

Court stood in the darkened room, waiting perfectly still for a full minute, the only sound his measured but heavy breath. But even after that minute, there wasn't enough faint light for him to get his bearings. It was clear there were no windows in the room, so he decided to turn on a light.

He felt along the wall for the light switch. As he put his hand on it and started to flip it, another hand slammed down on his, pinning it to the wall.

At the same time he heard the hammer of a pistol being pulled back, just a foot from his head.

Court froze. His left hand was free, but his pistol was on the right side of his body. He could go for it and draw it faster than most anyone on Earth, but not faster than it would take for that hammer behind him to slam forward and ignite a bullet in the gun that was certainly pointed at the back of his head.

He remained perfectly still.

The hand wore a glove, and it clasped around Court's fingers, then used them to flip on the overhead.

A fluorescent bulb flickered on after a few seconds. Court continued looking towards the wall, even when the gloved hand let go, slid down his body, reached into his right waistband, and drew his pistol out of his pants.

He heard soft footsteps moving backwards several feet in the room.

And then, speaking English, he heard the voice that had been on his mind unceasingly for the past four months.

"Turn around slowly or I blow off your head."

Court did so. He knew it was Zoya the instant he'd felt her hand on his, so there was no surprise on his face. Only uncertainty. A *lot* of uncertainty. He didn't know what she was doing, who she was working for, or why the fuck she was here.

Zoya's face, in contrast, showed the astonishment she clearly felt. She was nearly ten feet away now, a stainless steel revolver held on Court's chest, and she peered over the top of the weapon, almost uncomprehendingly.

Court thought she looked exhausted to the point of being ill; sweat beads covered her cheeks and forehead and her hair was soaked. She wore no makeup, and there were dark circles under her eyes, clearly from protracted lack of sleep. Her chest rose and fell noticeably from the exertion of the past minutes.

But she was still the most beautiful woman he'd ever laid eyes on.

It occurred to Court that he'd been under the hot tarp for so long that his hair was probably pretty ridiculous-looking right now. It also occurred to him that he'd never once thought about such things in the middle of an operation.

Zoya looked at him for another five seconds, still not speaking.

He broke the ice with the absolute best opening line he could think of. "Hi."

She lowered the pistol slowly and looked at him a little cockeyed, as if she were still trying to size him up and figure out what the hell he was doing here. Finally she said, "The sniper? The laser? The safe?"

Court nodded. "Yeah. Me." And then, "You okay?"

She slipped the weapon in her waistband, still not taking her suspicious eyes from him, and then she began moving closer. Court kept his hands away from his body, unsure if he was going to get frisked or punched, but unwilling to make any sudden moves to startle her.

She moved faster as she closed, reached out with a hand, and put it behind his neck, and instantly his defenses fired. From this position Court knew that someone, even a smaller woman, could hoist herself up and behind a larger man, get her arms around his neck, and put him into a blood choke that would turn his lights out in seconds.

But instead her hand behind his neck pulled him hard forward; she did not leap up and behind him, but she brought his face to hers and kissed him hard, pushing him up against the door.

Moments earlier he had been running for his life and dodging bullets, and now he was being kissed. After the brief shock he was actively involved in the action now—with the woman he'd thought about thousands of times since the first day they met.

They hugged silently for a moment, and then she broke free and took a step back. "We have to get out of here," she said.

"We're okay for now. They'll run right through this building and back out onto the street. They'll be looking for us on foot." He added, "We need to talk."

Zoya nodded. She put her back to the wall next to him and slid down to the floor, still looking his way in disbelief.

He did the same, leaning against the wall as he sat.

She said, "Brewer sent you after me?"

"No. She didn't have a clue you were here."

Zoya eyed him. "Until?"

"Until I saw you in Cassidy's office. I told her you were here, asked her what the hell was going on."

Zoya wiped sweat from her forehead with the back of her arm, an expression of frustration on her face. Court saw that she thought he'd done the wrong thing by telling Brewer she was even here. "And what did she tell you about me?"

"That you've been in the wind for a couple of days. That's really all I know. Some Mexicans tried to kill or capture you . . . but nobody knows why." He snapped his fingers. "Oh, yeah. There's a leak at the Agency, exposing Hanley's sub rosa ops, and you and I are totally fucked."

Zoya just shook her head and looked at the floor, taking it all in again.

Court said, "It's really great to see you, though."

She smiled at the floor, looked up to him, and leaned forward while sitting. They kissed again, hard. "You, too," she finally said as she pulled back.

But soon she broke away, stood, put her hands on her hips, and began pacing the room.

He said, "I think you need to tell me what's going on."

Zoya stopped. "Why? So you can tell Suzanne? If you do that there will be a team of your cohorts from CIA here on top of me in an hour."

"And that would be bad . . . *why*?"

"I'm here for answers. I haven't gotten them yet. I'm not going back to the States."

"Zoya, you need to realize I'm the only friend you have right now. I'll help you if I can, but you *have* to talk to me."

"Why were you watching Cassidy's office?"

"I was on a transport flight to the States the other night. We landed at an airport in the UK. There was a prisoner on board, unrelated to anything I was doing, a Dutch banker with intelligence about the CIA leak. A group of shooters showed up and took him, I went after them, and in doing all that I found out that a guy named Terry Cassidy in London was a middleman for the whole op."

She nodded, kept pacing. Court leaned back against the wall. "That's my story. Let's hear yours."

"What I'm doing doesn't have anything to do with a leak at CIA." She made a face. "As far as I know."

"What *are* you doing?"

Zoya hesitated, then said, "Not here. Not now. I'll talk to you but let's get somewhere secure. I have a flat in Soho. It's a piece of shit, but—"

"I have a place in West Kensington. Twenty minutes on foot, less if we find a taxi. It's not too bad."

She thought it over.

Court said, "Or we could just say 'fuck it' and get a room at the Hyatt." It was a joke, a reference to what Brewer had said, but Zoya didn't get it.

"Bad tradecraft," she replied. "We need to go somewhere we don't need papers. Your place is good."

"Right."

In moments they were both listening to the door, and soon afterward they were moving through the primary school, looking for an exit.

They walked through the building in the darkness, their eyes wide and their ears open to detect any sort of movement around them.

They neither heard nor saw anything, but they were not alone.

CHAPTER 32

Passing a stairwell on the right, Court eyed the deeper darkness there but detected no man-sized, man-shaped threats. He kept walking and turned his eyes forward towards the door up the hall, thinking he heard a noise on the other side.

They moved forward until the door one hundred feet ahead burst open, flashlights whipping around on the other side, and just then, out of the darkness of the stairwell to their right a huge form reached out, grabbing Court by his right shoulder and yanking him sideways, spinning him to his right and pulling him closer.

Court found himself inside the dark stairwell facing a massive human who loomed nearly a foot above him. Court drew his gun halfway, but a close-in glancing punch to his jaw stunned him and had him stumbling back in the stairwell, slamming into the wall to the right of the doorway.

His gun clanked to the floor but with his heel he kicked it back through the doorway towards Zoya, who was behind him in the hallway. She had her own pistol, but the only weapon he'd seen on her was a revolver, and it couldn't have had more than five or six live rounds in it. His own weapon was only half-full, but he knew she'd need all the ammo she could get.

Court brought his arms up to protect himself from another cracking blow, but even though he blocked it the punch knocked him back into the wall again. More punches rained down into his arms and shoulders and onto his head. He covered defensively and rode them out, all the while expecting Zoya to help him by engaging this beast with her weapon.

But instead he heard her shout, "Contact front!" as she opened fire on the door at the end of the hall.

Court sidestepped a punch from the big man, already recognizing him to be a boxer, and then ducked below a right hook. But when he rose back up again and attempted to fire out a jab of his own to the man's face, his attacker's longer reach got to him first, and Court took another blow, this time to his left eye.

His head snapped back and he was racked with pain all the way across his face.

It was too dark to see much about the man beating him soundly, and he didn't have time to check what Zoya was up against; all he could do was flail ineffective punches at a boxer who was obviously both incredibly powerful and skilled.

The gunfire continued behind him; it sounded like Zoya had emptied the revolver and opened up with another pistol. He assumed she'd grabbed his Glock, because she kept up a steady rate of fire. He knew he only had a partial mag in the weapon, and he started to shout this out to her so that she would be aware, but a fist whizzed by in a left hook, forcing him to snap his head back and out of the way and focus fully on the next salvo of raining fists.

Court knew he had to let Zoya deal with the gunmen down the hall because he wasn't just in a fistfight. He was in a battle for his very life.

A punch to his midsection connected when the man closed quickly on him, and this doubled Court over. He anticipated the uppercut that came next, so he shifted to his left and took the inevitable pounding fist in his right shoulder, then charged forward, wrapping his arms around the man's midsection, driving him back towards the stairs with all the power he could generate. Court had been involved in dozens of hand-to-hand fights in his life. He knew he was using enough force to bowl the man over, but just as Court drove the man to the tipping point, the powerful giant reached back with his left foot and braced it against the stairs.

The big man did not fall. Instead he pounded down on Court's head, neck, and shoulders with his elbows until Court let go. Court then caught a vicious right cross to the jaw, staggered back to the wall, and slid to the cement floor in a daze.

He saw brilliant specks of light in the air all around him, but in the middle of them all the huge man tightened and raised his big fists, then approached with a gait that told Court he was moving in for the kill.

"Z! Shoot this motherfucker! *Now!*"

• • •

Zoya Zakharova had been firing the Glock up the hall, hoping Court's pistol was full, because she didn't have a backup magazine for it. She'd emptied the .38 she got from Kravchenko's aircraft, and now with Court's gun she began the slow but steady fire necessary to keep her attackers back with their heads down. She could see from the glow around their weapon lights that they were the same men who had chased her into the building from the alleyway, and there were at least four or five. All she could do was lie prone to make herself a small silhouette, and fire each time she saw a target, to keep them from engaging her. She was certain she'd injured at least one of their number; the others were holding back on the other side of the open metal door and around the corner farther beyond it.

She glanced to her right into the darkened stairwell and saw Court take a lightning-fast right cross from the colossal attacker sending him back against the wall like a rag doll. Court slid to the ground and then called out through what sounded like a swollen mouth, "Z! Shoot this motherfucker! *Now!*"

She'd assumed Court could handle a hand-to-hand encounter, even with a much larger man, but all she'd witnessed in the quick glances she'd had time to steal was him *taking* blows, not delivering them.

She fired two more rounds at the door, then swung the Glock to her right towards the stairwell. She sighted on the chest of the man looming over Court and pulled the trigger.

Nothing happened. She looked at the weapon in her hands and saw that the slide was locked open on an empty magazine.

And she had no more ammunition.

Court had fallen sideways onto his left hip. She could tell he was beaten; his arms weren't up to defend the blows that would come any moment. He crept back on his elbows out of the doorway and into the hall. By doing this he put himself in the line of fire from the men up the hall, but Zoya realized he was trying to get the hell away from the man currently beating him to death.

Zoya began to stand. Her plan was to attack the massive form head-on, try to knock him back into the stairwell to both get herself out of the line of fire up the hall and buy Court some time to get up and get moving himself.

But before she could do so, the doors opened at the other end of the hallway. High-lumen weapon lights shone up the entire space, illuminating Zoya and the men in the doorway beyond.

"Metropolitan Police!" came the repeated shouts of at least a half dozen men. "Get down!"

Zoya heard Court groan out, "Fuckin' *finally!*"

The big man had entered the hallway and knelt over his crawling victim, and he held his fist perfectly still now above his head as he turned to look at the police. After a second, he lowered his hand, turned, and disappeared into the stairwell. Zoya heard him running up the stairs.

The police shouted for him to stop, but no one fired, so Zoya shot out of the hall and into the stairwell herself, but instead of taking the stairs, she found an unlocked door to the courtyard of the building, and she raced through it.

. . .

Court was racked with pain, but he knew he'd have to move now, because this was his one opportunity to stay out of police custody. He saw that these cops weren't shooting, so he climbed to his feet while the men closed on him. He, too, took off into the stairwell, wincing and grunting with each movement.

He found a door that led to an emergency exit to the building. Court shot through the door, setting off the alarm. He could only hope Zoya had gotten away, as well.

. . .

Ten minutes later Court staggered along the sidewalk, pain in his face, his shoulders, his ribs, his abdomen; all of it encumbering his movement.

It felt like he'd been tossed down a flight of stairs, only to crawl back up to get tossed down again.

A white Mini Cooper pulled up beside him and stopped. He looked inside and was relieved to find Zoya behind the wheel.

For myriad reasons. He was glad she was alive, was free of the police, had come back for him, and he retained the operational focus to be pleased that the person who had infiltrated Cassidy's safe, Court's objective for the evening, was back within his field of view.

As quickly as he could he moved to the passenger side. He grunted and groaned with fresh pain as he sat down, and she immediately began driving off again.

After a few seconds he coughed out, "Nice ride."

She looked at him. "It's stolen. Please do your best not to bleed all over the upholstery."

He put his hand to his nose and felt the blood there. It had worked its way around his mouth and onto his chin. He wiped it off, then gave her directions to his flat.

As they drove, Court put his earpiece back in his ear and placed a call to Brewer. She answered it after several rings.

Court said, "Violator here. Did I wake you?"

Brewer said, "I'm home. I have to pack for a trip."

"Odd time for a vacation."

"This is work. Heading to London soon."

"Cool, you're going to come over and be my door kicker?"

"Obviously not. I'm going for the conference."

"What conference?"

Brewer laughed. "What conference? The annual Five Eyes symposium in Scotland. How can you possibly not know about it?"

Court wiped a fresh drop of blood off his upper lip. "I'm not the kind of employee who gets invited to that sort of shindig. I figure the people who do go drink champagne and pat one another on the back while they send guys like me downrange, first on shitty missions, and then to fix their fuckups."

"You are such the martyr, Violator," Brewer said, and Court knew she had a point. He *was* just bitching because he was annoyed at getting the shit kicked out of him.

But he said, "How the hell are you going to catch the leak at CIA if you're over here having tea and crumpets?"

"We are working on it."

"So you keep saying."

"What about Anthem?"

Court looked to the brunette behind the wheel of the Mini Cooper. "I have her, here with me now."

"*What?* Jesus, Violator, you could have led with that one. What did she find in the safe?"

Court glanced over at her. He hadn't even thought to ask. "Working on it. We've been a little busy."

"*Working* on it? Just reach over and grab her by the neck and shake her till it falls out."

"That's not my style, Brewer."

"Your style is to shoot them and then scrounge through their body, but I'm not lucky enough to get that out of you tonight." When she received no reply to this she said, "Put her on."

Court pulled out his phone and activated the speaker function, moving the call to the phone itself and off the earpiece. He looked to Zoya and said, "It's for you."

Zoya sighed a little; for a moment Court didn't think she would even speak, but then she said, "Hello, Suzanne."

Brewer's clipped tone stressed Court out even when she wasn't talking to him. "Why did you break out of the safe house?"

"Because, for some strange reason, it didn't feel like a very safe house."

"Bullshit. I've seen the videos, and I talked to William Fields. You were already free of holding when the attack started. You knew it was coming."

"I did not."

"Then . . . why did you run?"

"I remembered some unfinished business I needed to attend to."

"Really? *That's* your story?"

"It's hard to explain." Court watched as she thought for a moment. He looked for signs of deception on her face, and he thought he saw a slight twitch that made him feel what she was about to say was not the whole truth. "In the pictures of my father's death you showed me, there was a man standing there. He lives in London. I wanted to come talk to him."

"You are saying an English solicitor was in Dagestan when your father—"

"I'm not talking about Cassidy. I'm talking about Vladimir Belyakov. You know him?"

Brewer hesitated. "Yes. He wasn't identified in that photo by DIA. I would remember. He's now a billionaire over there in London."

"He was standing right there. I knew him back then, recognized him easily. I came over here, I talked to him, and he led me to Terry Cassidy."

"For what purpose?"

Zoya paused a long moment, then took the phone from Court's hand. She hung up the call and handed it back.

"Sorry," she said as she drove.

Court shrugged. "Don't be. I do that to her all the time."

"When we get to your place, when we have you patched up, I will tell you what I know. You can tell Brewer, I don't care. But I want you to hear this first."

CHAPTER 33

Lucas Renfro stood up from the table full of congressmen and aides at the Capitol Grille and shook some hands, waved to others around the restaurant, then headed towards the exit. He was alone, with no protective detail, because even though he was a CIA deputy director, he was in Support and not in Operations, so it was decided he didn't need the extra security.

This was fine with him. If he did have a couple of Joes on his shoulder it would have been that much harder for him to sneak off to see his mistress tonight before returning to his home in Falls Church.

He could have done it, of this he was sure. He could have ordered the men to wait out in the car while he went up to the apartment he'd rented for their clandestine liaisons, and he could have banged her for hours. His protection detail would not have said a word, because they wouldn't be there to report marital infidelity; they would be there to keep him alive.

But it was a moot point, because he had no security team, just a mistress, and he had an itching need to see her tonight before going home to his wife.

He'd met the congressmen and staffers during happy hour and then they'd enjoyed a quick bite, so it was only seven fifteen in the evening now. He made his way through the packed restaurant, heading for the door, and he did not notice the fit man with the beard in the blue blazer who stood from the bar and began following him.

Renfro's car was parked in the private lot just north of the restaurant, and as he walked along in the early throes of dusk he sent a text to Trina to tell her he'd meet her at the apartment in thirty minutes but could only stay a short while. Trina would be there; she could be relied upon to do what Renfro told her to.

She'd left her husband years ago for him, and he'd not left his wife. She belonged to him now, as far as she was concerned.

As he turned into the parking lot he looked back over his left shoulder. A man walked behind him, not fifty feet back, making no sound as he did so. Renfro thought nothing of it, but he knew to keep an eye out and made note of the man's clothing and general appearance. Forties, fit, with blond hair, a blue blazer, and facial hair. Renfro continued on till he arrived at his Lexus sedan, and he climbed behind the wheel.

Pulling out of the garage, he saw the man who had been right behind him climbing into a black Chevy Suburban.

As he drove through evening D.C. traffic he called his wife and told her he was leaving drinks and heading to dinner with a couple of colleagues. She was used to his late nights with the boys, and she told him to have fun.

Then he called Trina and told her he'd be at their rendezvous apartment in Woodley Park in twenty minutes.

Traffic was slow, but he turned up towards Columbia Heights in a bid to get out of the heaviest congestion. He rode along, thinking about the fun he would have tonight before returning home, and he looked into his rearview again. He saw what appeared to be the same black Suburban that he'd last seen ten minutes earlier in Capitol Hill.

Or could it be a *different* Suburban?

The SUV was right behind him now, and it pulled closer, just twenty or thirty feet back. At a stoplight Renfro focused on the driver of the vehicle, and he saw that it was almost definitely the same man who had been behind him during the walk to the parking lot.

Renfro kept looking into his rearview, not certain yet that this guy was tailing him, but his suspicions grew each and every minute as the Suburban followed his turns. He tried to remember long-ago-forgotten tradecraft about how to deal with a nearly overt tail like this, but all he could remember to do was to not panic.

He wasn't panicking, but he was growing more nervous by the moment.

The Suburban looked like a government vehicle, but there was no way for Renfro to know for sure. His mind filled, thinking about those who might be tailing, and slowly a dull feeling of panic did begin welling inside him.

He grabbed his phone, thinking he would call Agency security, but he immediately put it down. They'd have questions for him. Why was he in this part of town, and where was he heading? For what purpose, would he think, might someone be following him?

He'd need a story, and he didn't trust himself to make up something on the fly that would suffice.

Quickly he got the idea to stop at a nearby mall, do a little shopping, and see if the tail would dismount and begin a foot follow. He told himself this would accomplish two things; first, he would be able to see the number and disposition of the tail, instead of just the headlights of a single vehicle behind him. This might tip him off as to whether they were government or private. And second, he'd buy something for his wife here, and establish his bona fides for being in this part of town right now.

He pulled into DC USA, the largest retail space in the entire District, and he parked in the garage. It was eight p.m. now; the mall was by no means empty but it appeared to be a slower night, and he had no problems getting a parking space within a minute's walk of one of the entrances.

As he climbed out of his Lexus and began walking through the evening, he looked around as nonchalantly as possible for the black truck. He saw no evidence of it and began to wonder if he'd imagined the entire affair. This was cutting into his already precious time with Trina, and that pissed him off, but he told himself to stick with his game plan here and go buy his wife some stupid present.

He started in jewelry stores, but within fifteen minutes of arriving he stood in a Bed Bath & Beyond, looking over a set of wineglasses. She didn't really need them, but they were nice, and he decided they would suit his objective.

As he turned towards the front of the store he found himself face-to-face with the man in the blazer. He wore dark sunglasses, strange for indoors when the light outside was low, and he stood next to an end cap selling handheld vacuum cleaners.

His hair was short and his beard was trim around his face, but waxed into a dramatic point on the end of his chin. His sideburns were striking, as well.

And he was clearly looking right at Renfro.

"Good evening," said the deputy director of Support for the CIA.

The big man said nothing. He was a soldier, or used to be, Renfro could tell. Up close his craggy, weather-worn appearance made him seem a little older, early fifties, perhaps, but even through the suit Renfro could tell the man was in chiseled good shape.

He chilled Renfro the way he stood there so brazenly.

After a few seconds Renfro said, "Do I know you?"

The man behind the sunglasses did not make a sound.

Renfro smiled now, though he was terrified, and said, "A little late in the day for those aviators, don't you think?"

The man made no reply.

Renfro's smile drifted off as he turned away and looked around the store. A woman in her thirties stood not far from him, and he thought he caught her looking away just as he eyed her.

She's part of the surveillance team, and there's more out there! There wouldn't just be the two of them, he told himself.

For the next five minutes he wandered the Bed Bath & Beyond—he didn't take the box of stemware with him—and during his stroll he sighted four other people who, he determined, were part of the follow.

Twice he looked back at the man in the shades, and both times the man stared back his way, though each time he held some random item he'd pulled off a shelf.

Renfro was certain he was being followed by a coordinated team of professionals. Other than the one overt man in the aviators, the rest seemed like extremely slick government surveillance operators.

They could be either CIA or FBI. Jurisdictionally speaking, it would make more sense for it to be the latter, but he had good reasons for suspecting it might be the former.

If someone in the CIA was having him tailed, he knew exactly why, and he knew he was in deep trouble. He hurried out into the mall, back to his car, and drove off. Not towards Trina in his secret apartment, but instead home to his wife. It would be an hour's drive in this traffic, and he knew his mind would race during each and every minute of it.

. . .

Zack Hightower smiled as he walked calmly back to his truck. His job was done for the day; he'd head home and get some rest so he could start back tomorrow morning refreshed and ready to go.

His smile wasn't due to the sleep that was soon to come; it was, instead, for the success he'd had this evening, on his first full day of the tail.

From DDS Lucas Renfro's actions tonight, Zack knew in his bones this dude had a good reason to fear a government tail, and it had been so much more fun to lean on someone with fear already built into his life than the two others earlier in the day, who seemed to have nothing to hide.

And it had been clear to Hightower that Renfro was worried about everyone around him: the MILF looking at pie pans, the eggheaded doofus who sat in the massage chair, the well-dressed gay couple who argued playfully over the purchase of an espresso machine.

Renfro thought they were all watching him, because Renfro was wired tight, scared shitless, and guilty as hell.

Zack was sure of it. And he couldn't wait to get back on the man tomorrow and turn up the heat.

. . .

Feodor Zakharov, aka David Mars, didn't sleep much at the most relaxed of times, but in the past few weeks, as the "D-Day" of his plot loomed, he spent more and more of his overnight hours researching, checking contacts, and poring over satellite images and Five Eyes personnel files and every other thing he could think of to better arm himself, for both offensive and defensive measures.

Defensively, he knew his operation had been kept tight, but some force out of his control had intervened, and now he could take nothing for granted.

Offensively, he knew from his career there was always some new piece of intelligence to learn that could help him with his mission: in this case the efficacy of the attack.

Tonight he read through a guest list hacked from one of the hotels that would be housing spillover attendees to the conference, and he worked to match names up to Five Eyes agencies and determine the best time of day to stage the attack for maximum damage.

When his encrypted line rang, he snatched it up. It was Fox with all the details of the events at Terry Cassidy's office and the school a few blocks away. Mars closed his eyes as he listened, at once furious with his men and worried about Zoya's well-being, but he responded in a measured tone.

"Unfortunate, Mr. Fox."

"Yes, sir. We could not anticipate the sniper who—"

Mars got another call. He switched lines without telling Fox. "David Mars. Who's calling?"

The reply was delivered in a frantic tone. "It's me. It's Barnacle."

Mars shut his eyes. *Mr. CIA again.* For a trained intelligence agent this man was jumpy and reckless. He'd all but outlived his worth, although Mars had one final use for the American, so he'd have to placate him now.

"How can I help you?"

"They're on to me. I'm being tailed."

Mars cocked his head. "You're sure of it?"

"I've been with the Agency for decades."

"You are in Support. You aren't exactly George Smiley."

The comment hung in the air for a moment. "I've worked the other end. I've been to the Farm. Obviously I can tell when there's overt surveillance on me."

"Overt?"

"Well . . . a lead tail who is making himself seen. I might have seen others who were low profile."

Mars said, "You'll be here in no time. You'll be fine."

"You don't think CIA would tail me in London? They *will*. They'll pick me up, too, if they have enough evidence."

"What evidence can they possibly have?"

"The fucking banker talked, obviously!"

In response to the American's tone, Mars said, "Barnacle," in a low and threatening voice.

"Sorry. It's just that—"

Mars interrupted. "The banker didn't know your identity. Whatever they have, it's not from Dirk Visser. If you are, in fact, being tailed, it's simply because you are in the small cluster of those who had advance knowledge of all the operations that were compromised. This is nothing more than an attempt to panic you."

"Well . . . if you're wrong, I'm fucked."

"Very true, mate. So . . . let's just assume I'm right, because I am. Go on about your life for a couple more days, because your life is about to change for the better."

Mars hung up the phone and began dialing Fox back for more information. He wasn't worried about Barnacle. If the CIA did ferret out the proof that Mars's man in the Agency was, in fact, the mole, Barnacle did not have much information about Mars beyond the sound of his voice.

Mars had other issues that were of much more concern. First and foremost was Dr. Won's progress on the weapon for the attack in Scotland, days away, but a close second was the fact that he'd learned that his beloved daughter was back from the dead, running around with guns and knives, with an unknown agenda. He worried about what she was up to, and who was pulling her strings, and this made it difficult to focus on anything else.

CHAPTER 34

On the way to Court's flat Zoya pulled up in front of an all-night market next to the Baron's Court Tube station. She went in and bought several small bags of supplies, including food, a bottle of cheap vodka, a six-pack of beer, three large bags of ice, and some lemons.

She returned in under five minutes and they drove around the corner, leaving the car near the station to throw off the police, and they continued the rest of the way on foot, with Court's arm over Zoya's shoulder and his staggering further impeding their progress.

Zoya helped Court descend the iron stairs, and then she took the keys from him to open the door. The West Kensington basement flat was dark until Zoya flipped on a couple of lamps, and then she immediately went to the bathroom to dump all the ice she'd bought into the tub. She closed the stopper and turned on the cold water. She went to the kitchen, looked in the freezer, and found some ice trays, and these she threw into the tub without cracking the cubes out of them.

While this was going on Court sat in the darkened den, holding a cold bottle of beer to his face. His lips were swollen, blood still drained from his nostrils, his left eye was puffed closed, and his jaw, chin, and left cheekbone were gray from bruising.

"Ready," Zoya announced from the bathroom.

Court stepped in; she helped him take off his shirt, and he could barely raise his arms to do so, and then she knelt and untied his shoes. He unbuttoned his pants and let them fall to the floor, sat on the edge of the tub, and slowly and painfully removed his socks.

He wore boxer briefs; his abdomen and ribs were splotched with purple and gray bruising, and he still kept the cold beer to his face, alternating between his mouth, his jaw, and his left eye.

He started to get into the ice bath, but Zoya said, "You're leaving your underwear on?"

Court winced as he lifted a leg and then winced again when he plunged his foot into the water. "I'm shy," he joked.

"You weren't shy in Thailand."

Still wincing from the cold and the pain he said, "Nobody's shy in Thailand. Can you give me a hand? If I try to squat down on my own my ribs and back are going to retaliate."

She helped him down, and within moments he was covered in ice water. It took only seconds to slow the bruising and swelling and a little more time to begin to numb his pain. He lowered farther, sinking his face up to his nose in the ice bath and cooling the pain in his mouth and jaw.

Zoya now unzipped the black athletic hoodie she'd been wearing and let it fall to the floor. She wore a white T-shirt underneath, and as she sat down on the cold bathroom floor she untied her black climbing shoes and kicked them off.

She opened the bottle of vodka, reached into the tub between Court's knees, and grabbed a few cubes of ice. She dropped them into a plastic cup she'd brought from the kitchen, poured the clear alcohol in, and swished it around.

Court was still trying to adjust to the cold, and he did not speak, but Zoya eventually broke the silence.

She said, "So . . . that big guy in the stairwell. Why didn't you fight back?"

Court lifted his mouth out of the water but kept his lower jaw submerged. He turned to her, shivering now, and his eyes narrowed. "That, back there, *was* me fighting back."

"Did you even hit him?"

Court looked down to his hands on the sides of the tub. They shook with the cold. "My fists are the only part of my body that don't hurt, so . . . I guess not. Certainly not in any way that he seemed to notice."

She drank the shot of vodka, leaving the ice in the glass. Matter-of-factly, she said, "He kicked your ass."

"He had a lucky punch or two."

"Or twenty."

Court chuckled and it hurt his split lip to do so, so he sank it back down beneath the ice.

. . .

Thirty minutes later Court was dressed in dark blue pants and a fresh undershirt, and he'd given Zoya a pair of gray warm-up pants and a black T-shirt to wear.

They sat on the sofa in the darkened living room, cups of iced vodka with lemon positioned on the coffee table in front of them, and the bottle alongside. Zoya grabbed her drink, bumped it against Court's on the table, and drank the entire contents down, spitting the twist back into the glass.

Court tried to lean forward to get his own drink, but the pain in his ribs was too severe. Zoya handed it to him and asked, "You don't think anything's broken, do you?"

Court shook his head. "I'm just bruised. Doesn't hurt to breathe, just to move my torso."

Zoya nodded, then got back to business. "Were you on a private contract when this started or are you working with the Agency?"

"Agency. Sort of. I hadn't actually been assigned to anything."

"So did you enlist in this op, or did you volunteer?"

Court replied, "I was sort of 'voluntold.'"

Zoya said, "Brewer can be persuasive."

"That's one word for it."

"She's a bitch."

"I didn't say that."

"I did." Zoya nodded. "Yes, she's a bitch, but she's good at her job."

"She's run me around the world like her little puppet, so I guess I can't disagree with you there."

Court switched the subject off himself, a skill he'd developed by necessity in his work in denied ops. "Let's talk about you. All I know is what
Brewer told me. You were at a safe house in Virginia, and you beat feet out
of there ten seconds before a crew of *sicarios* wiped out the place."

She nodded faintly in the dark. "I got lucky. I've been working on a
puzzle, somewhere in the back of my mind, maybe unconsciously, for a
long time, and I got a new piece from Brewer. Once I had that piece, I knew
I had to come to London to solve the puzzle.

"It just so happened to be on the same night the Mexicans came in
shooting. Fortunate for me, but of course, if I had been *really* lucky I would
have left twenty minutes earlier."

Court said, "Tell me about the puzzle, and this guy Belyakov."

Zoya hesitated; he could tell she had reservations about what she was
going to say. Finally she nodded a little in the low light. "Belyakov was in
the Army. As was my father. My father ran the Aquarium. Do you know
what that is?"

"The headquarters of GRU, military intelligence. It's at Kodinka Airfield, in Moscow."

Her eyes narrowed. "You know my country well."

"Just the shitty parts of it," Court replied. "Spies, soldiers, criminals, Kalashnikovs, that kind of stuff." He smiled a little. "I haven't been to the ballet." He already knew the answer to his next question, but he didn't want to
let on that he knew. "So you are saying your father was head of GRU?"

Zoya nodded. "Yes."

"You told me both of your parents were dead."

"Yes, I did tell you that."

The comment hung in the room till Zoya poured both herself and
Court another drink. Court thought she was on her third already, but she
did not seem muddled by it at all.

"Russians," he said aloud, marveling about the Russian skill of hard
drinking.

"What's that?" Zoya asked as she handed Court his drink.

Court replied with, "Tell me about your mom."

She recoiled a little in surprise at the question, then looked out the
window into the tiny and darkened high-walled courtyard of the base-

ment. "My *mom*? Well . . . she was born here, in London. Her parents were UK citizens."

Court sipped his vodka with a nod. "How did a lady from London end up with a Russian GRU officer as a husband?"

"When she was seven the family moved to Southern California so her mom, my grandmother, could teach acting at UCLA. My mom was raised there, went to school at UCLA in the eighties; she got a degree in speech pathology and became a dialect coach in Hollywood for a short time. Partly because her mom had worked on that sort of thing with her her entire life, and partly because she considered herself half British and half American." She chuckled and rolled her eyes a little. "My mom was also a raging socialist. She moved to the USSR to study in the late eighties. She'd picked up a degree in English as a second language, and she was very open and supportive helping students at Moscow State University learn the language of the capitalists. The KGB heard about her—her skills and her political leanings saw to that—and they recognized an opportunity. Soon she was working with GRU and KGB soldiers and spies, teaching them not just English but how to pass as either Americans or Brits."

Court raised an eyebrow. "So . . . treason against the U.S., right?"

Zoya shrugged. "Pretty much. My dad was a major in the GRU, so they sent him to the classes Mom was teaching. He already spoke fluent English, he was her star pupil, and she got the GRU to spring for private classes for him. She made him better and better at various English dialects, virtually a native.

"He asked her out on a date and they got married a year later. My dad was a real charmer. By then the Union had collapsed, but the government in Moscow kept paying my mom for her training. Russia needed spies just like the USSR did."

Court sat quietly, letting her talk and trying not to think about the throbbing in his jaw.

"Mom got pregnant, they had Feo Feodorovich—my brother—and two years later they had me," Zoya said. "Eventually, my dad was sent to London undercover as a military attaché at the Russian embassy, and in his free time he would do what he could to learn to assimilate as an Englishman. He ran operations while there, but I don't know anything about that.

"Next my father was transferred to D.C., and he remained under cover.

He'd been rising through the ranks at GRU. He was a colonel in D.C., and I imagine he was very good at his job.

"I went to American schools and spoke English better than Russian, my mom said, which annoyed my dad but made my mom proud. I returned to Russia when I was six; I lived in Moscow till I was fifteen, but all the while my mom kept teaching me languages and dialects from around the world, and my father taught me tradecraft."

"You told me once your mother died when you were very young."

Zoya shrugged. "A lie. I'd just met you, wasn't ready to reveal how I had the ability to 'turn' American at will. This is the first time I've told anyone."

"You don't have to lie to me."

She looked at him a long time, took a sip of vodka, and said, "I know. I trust you. I'm sorry."

She continued. "My brother was interested in medicine from a young age, so they knew he'd be a doctor. I wasn't as smart, so I was going to go into the family business, I guess."

"Your own father was grooming you for life as a spy?"

She looked off a moment, considering the question. After a sip of vodka she said, "It's all my dad knew. The focus of his life. That, and my brother and me. It was a way for me and my dad to connect." She shrugged. "Anyway, it was fun. I learned rock climbing and judo . . . In Russia it's a little different, it's called Systema. Dad taught me how to service dead drops and shoot guns and interrogate and run agents, and I was sent to the best gymnastics school still around in the nineties. My dad's connections didn't hurt . . . I was training with Olympic gymnasts even though I wasn't nearly as talented."

"I bet you were pretty damn good."

She smiled at this. "When I was eighteen I moved back to America, to LA, and went to UCLA. Just like my mom, and hers before her. I wasn't operational, had no association with Russian intel other than via my father, but I decided to try to build a cover, to live life as an American. I told everyone my name was Zoë; it was close enough to Zoya. I was obsessed with assimilation, the family talent. I became Zoë Zimmerman. Got fake IDs, credit cards in my American name, and I pulled it off. Other than my Visa, my passport, and my college transcripts, everything I had in LA had Zoë's name on it."

Court laughed at this; it hurt his rib cage to do so. Zoya laughed, as well, thinking about herself fifteen years earlier.

Court said, "The things you're doing now . . . you've been in training for them since the day you were born."

"That's true."

"So . . . by the time you were in college you knew you were going to be a spook?"

She shook her head with conviction. "No way. It had nothing to do with a future career. Sure, my dad wanted me to join SVR after college; he didn't want me in GRU because he had a thing against women in the military. But I planned on charting my own path."

"Why?"

"That's the easiest question you've asked. I grew up in Moscow in the nineties; I saw what a horrible place my country had become. Impoverished and crime ridden, corrupt and desperate. I envied Westerners I saw on TV. Their food, their safety, the stability of their government and their economy. Their money. When I was a little girl I watched *Friends* on TV and I wanted to wear clothes like that, to have a beautiful apartment like that, to sit around and talk to my friends all day and drink coffee. That's what I thought America would be. It sounds superficial, but it became fundamental after years of seeing people starving in the streets or shooting one another over bread."

She said, "I didn't want to spy on Americans. I wanted to *be* American."

"But something happened," Court said, finishing his second drink.

Zoya poured him another, and added lukewarm vodka to her own.

Four drinks in a half hour, Court said to himself.

"Yes, something happened. I got a call in my dorm room in the middle of the night. It was my brother. My mother had been hit by a car on her way to meet friends for lunch in Tverskaya District. She was dead." Zoya stared off into space.

Court poured another splash of vodka for them both this time. His sore body allowed the movement, albeit with some discomfort.

"I went home for the funeral, of course. My father was inconsolable. We all were, I guess. But he told me, in a whisper, that British agents killed my mom to stop her from doing her work against the West. He was obsessed with it. Of course the official accident report indicated no foul play, but he changed when she died. Became more radical. More focused on his work.

"I returned to California a few days later, and then, within a few months, I got another call. This time in the middle of the day. It was my brother again."

"What did he tell you?"

"That he had stage four cancer, and days to live."

Court shook his head in disbelief. "Christ. Had he been sick for long?"

"Not at all. Never anything more than a head cold in his life. I rushed home, but my flight was delayed. By the time I'd arrived, he'd died and I'd missed the funeral. I never got to say good-bye."

Court felt for her. She was speaking dispassionately enough, there were no tears about these terrible events, but he knew her emotions had to have been high, even in the retelling.

He said, "And then . . . your dad."

She gulped vodka now. "Another damn phone call. This time it was Uncle Vladi . . . I mean Vladimir Belyakov. He was crying. He told me my father had been killed on the front lines in Dagestan. I believed him, but I did not understand. Never made any sense that he would be there, a GRU general. He should have been behind a desk at the Aquarium in Moscow."

He thought over his next question, considered shelving it for a few minutes, but he went for it. "But I don't understand what any of this has to do with why you busted out of the safe house and ran to England."

Zoya drank the contents of her plastic cup, and, with eyes only now becoming bleary, she leaned closer to him. "Court, three days ago Suzanne showed me some photos. From them I realized my father did not, in fact, die in Dagestan."

He hadn't seen this coming. "Oh, shit."

She explained about the discolorations she saw on his neck, and what she knew them to mean. Then she leaned forward on the sofa in the dim light. "When I figured that out, I knew I had to come here to see Vladi, because he was with my dad when he was supposedly killed. If his story was an obvious lie, I was sure he knew the truth."

"You . . . you had no suspicions till the other night?"

Zoya seemed to think this over. "Just a feeling in the back of my mind.

I can't say why. I mean, when I was told he'd died, it was done very convincingly. The government left me with no doubts at all. The war was going on in Dagestan, a lot of men were dying across Russia. But I still did not understand, and it always bothered me.

"When I graduated from UCLA three years later, I knew what I had to do." She shrugged. "Maybe it had been inevitable all along. I immediately went in for training at SVR. It was tough. I'm sure you remember that time of your life, too."

Court nodded. "Every damn day." But then he turned incredulous. "If he's really alive, you are saying he's been hiding out for . . . for *how* long, exactly?"

"Fourteen years. With his skills he could be anywhere. The Russian government didn't do this to him so he could retire. They did it because he's on some sort of a mission. He's in some sort of deep cover. *Has* to be."

"How deep can he be? He's a Russian who looks exactly like the former head of GRU."

Zoya responded, "And how many people know what the GRU head looked like fourteen years ago? And as for him being Russian . . . he's like me, that doesn't matter. We are a family of chameleons, trained by the government as infiltrators. He can integrate. He can blend. He can be whoever he wants to be, wherever he wants to be."

"Even in America or in the UK?" Court asked.

She nodded. "That's right. My mother helped create a network of sleepers, men and women who could infiltrate the West, not as Russians, but as locals. She was only involved with the language and customs aspect of their training; the sleepers worked with forgers, weapons experts, tradecraft instructors . . . I don't know how much went into it. My dad was an early graduate of her training, and I met a guy tonight who, I'm sure, *must* have been one of her students."

"Who?"

"Calls himself Fox, speaks with a refined British accent. Oxford, all the way. But he switched into Russian effortlessly to talk to me, and he was a native Russian speaker. I have the training to tell. I'm sure he is a sleeper Russian national, and his presence here only convinces me more that my father is close."

"He's here? In London?"

"According to Fox, he is."

Court thought a moment. He didn't want to drink any more; the last thing he needed was a headache on top of his myriad other complaints, so he just sat in the low light. Finally he said, "So . . . what if your father *is* still alive? What is it you hope to accomplish by confronting him? Just to ask him why he disappeared? Just to see what he's been up to?"

Zoya shook her head. "No. Court, I have to find out about my mother and my brother. Maybe they are alive, or maybe they *are* dead but the stories I got weren't real, just like his story wasn't real."

This confused Court. "You said Feodor told you himself he had cancer."

Zoya swirled the vodka around in her cup. She stared at it as she said, "You know one way to get very intense, very fast-moving cancer?"

Court looked her over for several seconds. His incredulity remained. "Are you talking about radiation?"

"That's right. Polonium-210. That's right out of the FSB and GRU playbook. Used rarely, but used. I never saw any of my family's bodies, and that always bothered me." She looked up at him. "I have to know what happened to them all."

"So, you are convinced your dad is alive, and that indicates to you that either your brother was murdered or he's still alive. Ditto your mom?"

She grabbed the vodka bottle now, started to bring it to her mouth, but Court reached for it, took it from her hand. He was surprised that she made no protest. He saw how tired she looked, imagined the effects of the alcohol having even more impact on her brain than normal, but she was passive, not combative.

She said, "You wouldn't understand. My father was a master of deception. Truly ingenious. He could pull off some sort of a plan like this."

"A plan like *what*?"

"Honestly I have no idea. But he thought my mom was killed by the British, and he went crazy. If he faked his own death, I know it wasn't to live his life in retirement. He was at the top of the intelligence community when this happened, remember. GRU is larger than SVR, more powerful. A man like my father wouldn't run away from that unless his destination was even more important to him."

Now Court furrowed his brow. "How does all this with you tie in with the hunt for the mole at Langley?"

"I have no idea. Maybe it doesn't. But . . ." She rose, stepped over to her dirty clothes piled in the corner, and picked up her pack. From it she removed a small iPad and held it up to him. "But we might find answers in here."

"You got that from Cassidy's safe?"

"Yes."

"Well then, let's get cracking. I'll call Brewer."

Zoya put the iPad on the coffee table, then sat down close to Court. "In a while." She kissed him. "Brewer can wait a while, can't she?"

Court nodded slowly. "Zoë, Brewer can wait all damn night." And he kissed her back, secretly hoping she didn't put her hands anywhere near his rib cage.

CHAPTER 35

ONE MONTH EARLIER

The Airbus A145 business helicopter carrying six passengers flew through the center of a valley, a cold blue river a few hundred feet below the aircraft's belly and high green peaks a thousand feet tall on both sides. Loch Moy was just ahead, and their ultimate destination not far beyond.

They were just miles southeast of the city of Inverness, due east of Loch Ness, but they could see nothing of either from here because of the brutal but beautiful terrain.

The flight through the Highlands was beyond picturesque, but Mars wasn't looking out the window. He was looking at Janice Won.

She was dividing her attention between the terrain, the movement of the clouds in the sky, and a laptop in front of her with current weather conditions and the forecast and a map of the area.

Mars smiled, telling himself that he had chosen his weapon well.

He'd made Won believe that by going rogue, defying her orders from North Korea, she could deal a crushing blow to her nation's enemies, a feat that would certainly be rewarded upon her triumphant return. He convinced her there would be no comebacks on her nation, and he knew she would be thinking that it would be Russia and some strange Englishman who would be seen as the actual perpetrators.

But that was not, in fact, Mars's plan. No, he intended for North Korea to take the fall for this completely, and in so doing protect Russia from any blame.

Janice Won wasn't just his weapon; she was also his decoy, his nation's "get out of jail free" card.

Won looked up at him and spoke into her headset. "How far to the castle?"

Mars pointed in the direction they were flying. "Castle Enrick is on the banks of Loch Ness. Not far."

Won adjusted her microphone and then moved over to sit next to David Mars. She brought her laptop with her and turned it to him.

"I've been running numbers on the potential effects of the attack as we've planned it so far."

"Prognosticating the damage? What have you determined?"

"While working in Sweden I learned that in the West there exists no environmental warning system to alert a population that it's under attack with a plague weapon, and no widely available and rapid tests. If the delivery of the aerosol is covert, a population would only know it had been subjected to a biological attack with plague when patients began flooding into hospitals and clinics, by which time it would be too late for many of them."

Mars knew this from Won already. Impatiently, he said, "Numbers of casualties?"

"As you know, with primary infection, the patient's course becomes irreversible approximately eight hours after infection if not given a large dose of antibiotics, which then must be administered daily for ten days or so. Secondary pneumonic plague results from metastatic spreading by the primary population. It is not quite as deadly, but if we successfully mask our attack so that the primaries remain unaware they've been exposed to the bacteria, allowing them to return to their offices and embassies, it will delay treatment for those who pick it up secondarily. If we manage this, we can expect roughly forty to sixty percent mortality in the secondary population."

Mars was satisfied with this, but said, "Tertiary plague? What's the mortality?"

Won shook her head. "The West will know what has happened by day ten or so when all four hundred attendees of the conference suddenly die. By the time the secondaries infect the tertiaries, most everyone will be given massive quantities of antibiotics, and the majority of the tertiaries should survive except for the very old, the very young, or the very infirm. Say five percent mortality, no more. But this is an exponential formula, meaning each population, primary, secondary, and tertiary, will be successively larger, so five percent mortality of the tertiary population will still be orders of magnitude larger than the total mortality of the primary field."

Won straightened her back with pride. "This weapon of ours will cut a swath of destruction deep in the intelligence community of the West, but the destruction will be carried out in the first ten days. After the second week, many more will die, but there will be few new victims."

"Total estimation of losses to the Five Eyes?"

"I've looked at the known staffing at embassies, intelligence agencies, and military and law enforcement facilities where the conference attendees work. My rough calculation is that in addition to virtually all of the first four hundred infected, another four to five thousand secondaries will die."

He was astonished, even though the plan had been his. He did not have Won's resources to determine the outcome, and was just assuming the number would have been closer to one thousand.

In his excitement he reached out and squeezed Won on the forearm. She looked down at his grasp as if he had placed a tarantula on her skin.

Mars slipped his hand off quickly.

"Five *thousand*," Mars said.

Won relaxed a little but kept looking at her arm. "Four to five thousand, to be precise. Plus the original four hundred. Devastating to Western intelligence," she added.

"Quite," said Mars. "It will take generations for them to recover."

Won closed her laptop, then turned to Mars. "My disease *will* work. If your plan works, together we will take out a sizable portion of the world intelligence community arrayed against my nation. Arrayed against Russia."

"Yes," Mars said.

Now Won's eyes narrowed and she looked at the bearded older man seated next to her. "But not arrayed against you."

The sixty-two-year-old cocked his head. "What do you mean by that?"

"Mr. Mars, I still find it difficult to trust you, because I do not understand your motivations. I *must* know why you are doing this."

She was pressing him and, as much as it annoyed him, again he did have to concede that her demands were reasonable. He said, "Because I want to literally destroy the U.S. and UK intelligence services."

"I will ask you one more time . . . *Why?*"

Mars heaved his chest and exhaled slowly. "I want to destroy these organizations, because, Ms. Won, my wife, my son, and my daughter were all killed by the Five Eyes."

Janice Won put a hand to her mouth and held it there for some time.

Mars added, "Clear now, isn't it?"

She nodded slowly, and when she removed her hand she took a moment, seemingly to clear her thoughts of all but the science of the operation.

"Tell me about the crop duster we will use."

Mars was glad that matter was dealt with. He himself went back to the operational issues at hand. "It will take off from a makeshift airfield, twenty-two miles west of the castle. I've looked at previous Five Eyes conferences, and the security preparations don't include no-fly zones. There will be security in helicopters that might run our aircraft out of the area, but we should be able to get one good pass over the castle before that happens."

Won said, "We will only need one pass. There will be four canisters to the weapon; with the nozzles completely open, the bacteria will fire from each canister in twelve seconds. It will release more than enough spores to do maximum damage." She turned to Mars now. "Of course, your pilot will have to be very good."

"Would you like to meet him?"

She cocked her head in surprise at this, and Mars flipped a switch on his radio to speak with the crew of his helicopter.

• • •

Thirty minutes later they landed. Won had been blindfolded, for operational security, Mars had explained, but now she followed Mars, Fox, and

Hines out of the aircraft and over to a small shack. Several men stood around outside; Won could see no weapons, but they all had light Windbreakers on, and she took them to be a security force.

They obviously belonged to Fox or Mars, because they made no effort to stop the new arrivals as they approached the shack.

On the top of a hill several hundred yards away Won could just make out a rectangular gothic stone church with a cemetery in front of it. From this distance the church appeared to her to be dilapidated and shuttered.

They did not head for the church; instead they walked through a field till they came upon a bright yellow crop duster parked next to a dilapidated wooden shack. Alongside the shack were drums that contained fuel, fertilizer, and engine oil, but this was no real airport property. Won saw no obvious runway, although the ground was flat here and the grass was only a few inches high.

They stepped into the shack, and although it was a cool breezy day, inside she found a small man in his fifties wearing a black tank top and shorts.

She could tell the man was Korean before he opened his mouth, and this surprised her.

No names were exchanged, but everyone shook hands. Mars said, "He doesn't speak English. Only Korean, so you can feel free to ask him whatever you like."

"Where are you from?" Won asked.

The man smiled a little. "Seoul. Yourself?"

Won looked to Mars, ignoring the man. "What is this?"

"This, Dr. Won, is a mercenary pilot. He will do what he says, without question. And since he's South Korean, his presence here will not affect your nation in any way."

She turned back to him. "You can fly a crop duster?"

"I flew big C-130s for the air force. I can *definitely* fly a crop duster."

"Why are you here?"

"I was brought in for the job."

Won was confused. She looked to Mars. "Why is he already in the area?"

Mars said, "He is establishing his cover. I have a team of men here protecting him, watching out for anyone watching him and such, and he is going out every day to spray back the bracken and heather. I have secured a contract for him to operate in the area near the eastern shores of Loch Ness. By the day of the attack, his bright yellow agricultural aircraft will be known by everyone in the area, and no one will bat an eyelash when he comes over flying low and slow."

Won looked to the pilot now. In Korean she said, "You understand your mission?"

"Yes," the pilot said. They all walked out to the bright yellow single-engine aircraft, and the pilot walked Won around it. "In the belly of the plane is the tank; it's called the hopper. A wind-driven pump sends the liquid to this horizontal pipe with spray nozzles, here on the belly of the aircraft. It's called a boom. All I have to do is flick a switch in the cockpit, and a thin spray of liquid will come out of the boom. By the time it reaches the target, it will be undetectable except for a very fine mist."

After hearing the translation, Mars said, "How fine a mist?"

Won fielded this question directly. "We are working on the weapon itself now. Four small canisters, each the size of a home fire extinguisher, strapped together. Hoses all leading to one nozzle, although each canister also has its own shutoff capability for safety in transport. The material is atomized; it is not invisible but very nearly."

Mars exchanged a glance with Fox but said nothing.

The pilot resumed speaking to Won. "I'll drop herbicide from the first hopper until I get close enough to bank over the castle, make a pass overhead, open the second hopper, and distribute the material there. Then I will return here and leave the country by boat long before anyone knows any attack took place."

Won said, "A slow pass. A *very* slow and careful pass."

"As long as no one is shooting at me, I can fly as slow as forty knots."

Won translated this for Mars, who looked to the man and replied in English. "No one will be shooting at you, old boy. We are going to create a diversion so that the last thing anyone is worrying about will be a bloody crop duster flying over the castle."

"A diversion?" Won knew nothing about this.

Mars waved a hand and said, "Let's see more of this aircraft."

After another walk around the yellow Air Tractor AT-602 and more words of assurance from the pilot about his mission, the visitors to the airfield walked back to the waiting helicopter.

Won addressed Mars before they were too close to the rotors to be heard. "I checked the weather conditions for next month. It should be moderate and breezy. If the pilot is good, and if he's able to get close enough without raising suspicions, then I believe we have a good chance for success."

Mars nodded but did not reply.

The North Korean virologist said, "You mentioned something back there about a diversion. What does that mean?"

"Doctor, that will not concern you. By the time all this happens you will be safely out of the country, as promised."

"But if this operation fails we have to—"

Mars interrupted. "We will all see that it doesn't. Trust me, my diversionary tactic will take our shared adversaries by complete surprise. Now . . . shall we head on to Castle Enrick? I'd like to make it in time for dinner. I hear the restaurant is top flight."

Janice Won boarded the helicopter, but Mars held Fox back. They turned away and spoke close into each other's ears. "Your thoughts?" Mars asked.

"Despite what Won and the pilot say, this is far from a sure thing. What if the wind is too high, if it's raining, if the aircraft is shot down?"

Mars had come to the same conclusion. "Nothing will be left to chance. The other option is the only option now."

"So we don't use the Air Tractor and the pilot?"

"Certainly we use them. Won asked me about the diversion. I wonder what she would think if she knew that she and her plan were, in fact, the diversion, and the real play will succeed when theirs fails. Now go blindfold her before takeoff."

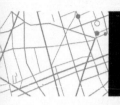

CHAPTER 36

Matt Hanley gave Suzanne Brewer the morning off so she could get her affairs in order for the trip to London, but he was energized enough about the mole hunt that he connected directly with Zack Hightower via text as soon as he got to work, asking his contract agent to let him know if he found out anything.

An hour later, just after nine a.m., Hightower texted back, asking for a meet.

Brewer was supposed to be his buffer between himself and his Poison Apple assets, but he realized there was nothing more important than the mission Hightower was working, so he consented.

They met in the parking lot of a Dunkin' Donuts in McLean, less than ten minutes from CIA HQ. Hanley rolled without his security, driving a borrowed Toyota Land Cruiser from the motor pool, and he pulled up under a thick oak tree growing near the edge of the lot.

He saw Hightower step out of a black Suburban, and Hanley scanned him head to toe as he began walking over. The big Texan climbed in next to Hanley, then adjusted the passenger-side mirror and the rearview mirror without asking. These two men had worked together for many years in some incredibly dangerous locations, and they had conducted clandestine meetings like this for much of that time. Both men knew their roles. Hanley would watch the front; Hightower would watch their six.

"Thanks for meeting me, boss."

"No problem, Hightower, but let's don't make it a habit."

"Yes, sir."

"You said you had information."

With a nod Hightower said, "The traitor has been preliminarily identified, sir."

"How did you come to this conclusion?"

"By his reaction to my pressure."

"Of course. Who is it?"

"My assessment is that the mole in the Agency is Deputy Director Lucas Renfro, sir."

Hanley nodded slowly. Brewer had told Hightower that Hanley suspected Renfro, and there was apparently some sort of a beef between the two of them, but the DDO showed no outward reaction to the confirmation of his suspicions.

"How sure are you?"

"Pretty sure. If you let me do a black bag job on his place, I could be more certain."

Hanley blew out a sigh. "Can you pull that off?"

Zack just looked at Hanley, then said, "It's *me*, Matt."

"And he's a deputy director, Zack."

"Which means Agency security will know all there is to know about his home protection measures, his passwords, everything I need to slip in and have a look around. You get me that intel, and I'll make entry and search for incriminating information. I'll place bugs, too, if you want."

"You've got him scared?"

"Yes, sir. Last night I tailed him through a mall and he freaked. This morning I bumpered him on his way to breakfast near the Capitol. He looked terrified, checked me out every fifteen seconds, but he didn't pick up his phone and call it in as near as I can tell."

"Well, I can say he did *not* contact Agency security last night about your pressure. I would have heard about it." Hanley bobbed his head from side to side. "That's a pretty good indication he's got something to hide."

Zack was totally sold now. "Get me the details on his place, let me go in there. I'll look for anything suspicious, and if I don't find anything, I'll make it clear someone has been in there looking around. Put a little more terror in him. Maybe send him over the edge."

Hanley nodded. "All right. But he'll be back and forth between Capitol Hill and meetings around the District today, budget hearings. He won't be at HQ. I want you bumpering him during the day today, and then you can make entry when he goes to London tomorrow."

"London?"

"The Five Eyes conference. Virtually everybody on the seventh floor is going."

Zack had a blank look on his face.

"You don't know about it?"

"No, sir. My invite must have got lost in the mail. Well, I'll try to wrap this up before everyone jets off to their little powwow."

Hightower shook Hanley's hand, then reached for the door handle, but stopped. Facing the deputy director of Operations once more, he said, "Sir, since I've got your ear for a moment, can I speak with you about my code name?"

Matt Hanley fired up the Land Cruiser. "No, you cannot, Romantic. Those are randomly assigned. You get what you get. Luck of the draw."

Hightower nodded, then reached again for the door handle. Turning back, he said, "Night Train?"

Hanley cocked his head. "I'm not tracking."

"Night Train. Gotta admit, sir, it's a hell of a code name, and it kind of fits me, don't you think?"

Hanley leaned across Hightower now and opened the door for him. "I *don't* think, Zack. Not about shit like that. Get out of here, and get me something actionable on Renfro."

"Sir," Zack said, compliantly, and he headed back to his Suburban.

• • •

Lucas Renfro sat in a booth at the Monocle Restaurant, a couple blocks north of the U.S. Capitol. It was early afternoon; he'd lingered over a boring lunch with his staff and peers from other U.S. intel agencies, checking his phone every few minutes for a text or call from Trina, his mistress, and trying not to worry about the people following him.

This was impossible. Between each nod in response to a colleague's comment, before and after every sip of his Bordeaux blend, each bite of his flatiron steak or piece of his crusty bread, he looked over the room, searched out through the front window, glanced into the eyes of the men and women seated with him. Was the guy in the aviators watching him? Were his colleagues aware of the surveillance on him?

The tail had been on him today already. He'd left his home at seven a.m., and the concern of the previous evening kicked off again in seconds, when the black Suburban began rolling behind him just as he left his neighborhood.

The same bearded man behind the wheel.

He didn't try to shake the tail. He knew this guy was Agency, and *of course* he knew why he was being tailed by Agency assets. He had a secret to hide, and now, it appeared, the secret was out.

With lunch ended, Renfro shook some hands and headed out the door, going back to the Capitol building for another three hours of hearings.

He'd made it most of the way, still checking for messages from his mistress and scanning for Mr. Aviators, when a woman's voice called out from just behind him.

"Deputy Director Renfro?"

He stopped on the sidewalk, turned around, and saw Suzanne Brewer. He knew her from staff meetings and such but had no real relationship, working or otherwise, with her. Marty Wheeler, Renfro's deputy, knew her much better. Still, Renfro was well aware that she had been an absolute rising star at the Agency for the past fifteen years, until she recently and inexplicably switched over to Ops to work under Matt Hanley.

He'd last seen her at the safe house in Great Falls a few nights earlier, the evening of the attack on the facility there.

Renfro didn't know Brewer's actual job under Hanley, but he was aware that she was the point person for a code-word program called Poison Apple.

Operations was a career builder for an exec, for sure, but the black ops Brewer was assigned to, Renfro could tell by her near disappearance from meetings, weren't going to do a thing to propel her ascent towards the seventh floor.

Before he said anything he stopped thinking about her and began thinking about himself again. *What did she want? Was this the next step in the process arrayed against him? Would she take him into custody, deliver him to a safe house, and have CIA men, Hanley's men, rough him up?*

He put on the most composed face he could muster and said, "Suzanne. Don't see much of you on Capitol Hill these days."

"No, sir. Actually, I'm here to see you. Do you have a moment to talk?"

Renfro glanced around for others, men in suits with earpieces who would whisk him away, and when he saw none, he looked back to the attractive woman in the blue blazer and slacks. "Have you been sent?" He meant by Hanley, but Suzanne would know this.

"No, sir, and I truly hope you don't mention our conversation to my deputy director."

Renfro raised an eyebrow. "You have me intrigued, then. There's a bench by the Reflecting Pool. A few tourists will be milling around, but if we keep our voices down, we should be fine."

They walked in near silence for a few minutes, then sat down at a quiet bench in front of the water. Tourists were indeed present, but they were all taking pictures closer to the Reflecting Pool and well out of earshot.

Renfro scanned the area over and over, looking for more surveillance. Finally he said, "We both have to get on a plane for London tomorrow. I imagine you have as much work to do as I do, if not more. So cut to the chase."

"I have important information for you. Information of a personal nature."

A personal nature. He'd calmed himself during the walk, but now his terror returned anew. He swiveled his head back and forth, and he looked back over his shoulder.

Brewer noted this, clearly, because she said, "You needn't concern yourself with the man who's been tailing you. He's one of mine. I called him off thirty minutes ago so we could speak in private."

Renfro's graying eyebrows furrowed, an authentic facial gesture, because he was seriously confused. "I'm being tailed by one of Matt Hanley's assets?"

Brewer nodded.

"But . . . *why*?"

Brewer said, "First. I'm no saint. I want to help you, but I want something in return."

Renfro leaned closer. "What would that be?"

"I want away from Hanley, away from Ops."

He shrugged, confused about the lowball request. "Of course you can come and work for me. You'd be a hell of a catch. Everyone on seven knows your talents."

Brewer shook her head. "Hanley would not allow that at this point and, frankly, he holds more sway with the director than you do."

Renfro made an annoyed face at this, but Suzanne Brewer just waved a hand in the air, as if the fact were obvious.

"You want away from Hanley, you want my help, but you say I can't hire you."

She replied, "Not as long as Hanley's in his position."

Renfro slowly began to understand what was happening. "You think you have some way to get Matt fired?"

"I would like him to resign. That would suit me very well. You might be able to aid in this."

"Five minutes ago I said I was intrigued. Now I am positively riveted."

* * *

Brewer told Renfro about Hanley's suspicions that he was the mole, and Renfro looked at once stunned and angry. If he was the traitor, Brewer determined, he was a damn good actor. She explained to him how Hanley had had four people tailed by a contract agent, Renfro himself included, although the deputy director of Operations had no authority whatsoever to move pieces on the chessboard like that here on U.S. soil.

Renfro took it all in, then said, "If this is true, I could nail his nuts to the wall by talking to the right person in that building over there," he said, pointing to the U.S. Capitol looming on the other side of the reflecting pool.

"The information can't come from me, but I can give you the identity of the asset, and you can easily connect the dots back to Hanley." She hesitated. "Of course, if you *are* the traitor, you will just be bringing more attention to yourself by screaming to a senator that the head of Ops is having you tailed."

"If you really thought I was the traitor," Renfro said, "I doubt you would be associating with me at all."

"That is correct. I don't believe it to be you."

Now Renfro scooted himself to where he was almost shoulder-to-shoulder with the younger woman.

"Tell me about Poison Apple?"

Brewer was taken aback. "No, sir. That I *can't* do."

"You can conspire against the DDO, but you can't give me information on one of his programs?"

"That is correct, and you know why, sir. I can scheme against Matt all day long to try to better my position at the Agency. You can tell him, and he can fire me or demote me or send me off to La Paz if he wants, but that's all he can do. But if I pass intel on a code-word operation, even to you, I will go to prison."

She shook her head again. "I'm not going to prison, Deputy Director."

He nodded. "I understand. But if you are running this asset you mention, I am going to operate under the suspicion that he is involved with the program you manage."

Brewer knew Renfro would put these pieces together on his own. She hadn't mentioned Poison Apple, refused to give out information about it, but she could, and would, give him a man's name. That Renfro would deduce this was a Poison Apple asset was a given, and Suzanne Brewer was fine with that.

"Look into the record of a man named Zachary Paul Hightower. He is fifty, a former SEAL DevGru operator, former Ground Branch paramilitary. He is the man Hanley has on your tail in violation of federal law. From what I can deduce, this asset's association with the DDO goes back fifteen years or more."

Renfro didn't know this name, but that was no surprise, because he didn't work directly with the "sled dogs" who did the actual physical operational work for CIA. "Excellent," he said. "I'll look into him."

He stood, and Brewer followed him to her feet. They shook hands and Renfro asked, "Can you keep him off me while I work? I'd like to have this dealt with before I leave the country tomorrow."

Brewer said, "Ordinarily, yes, but Hanley is in direct contact with the asset. If I pull Hightower off the assignment for much time at all, Hanley will know something's going on."

Renfro conceded this point. "Fine, keep him on me till I get Hanley's future with the Agency sorted out. And when I do, you will be able to write your own ticket." He smiled. "At that point, perhaps my relationship with the director will begin to impress you."

. . .

Renfro walked back to his car, his hands and armpits dripping sweat. There was a lot to process about what he'd just learned.

First, he told himself that he believed Brewer really did want to parlay her warning into some sort of improved situation for herself in Agency HQ; he had no sense this was all some sort of act to garner information or to deliver a subtle threat.

He'd forgo the hearings this afternoon; he could get out of them, and instead he would head to the office to begin digging into this man Hightower. After that he was determined to head back into D.C. to see Trina. Tomorrow he would leave for the UK; he'd have to pack and fulfill family obligations first, and sneaking out would be nigh on impossible then.

He felt better now than he did before speaking to Brewer, immeasurably so. But his fears about the secret he'd been keeping at the Agency remained, and he still couldn't shed himself of the terror that his world was crashing down around him.

As he climbed into his car he spoke aloud. "If I'm going down, that prick Hanley is going down with me."

CHAPTER 37

The three Range Rovers rolled through a cool afternoon in the Scottish Highlands, traveling the twenty miles between the parking lot where the helicopter landed and the passengers climbed into the SUVs and Castle Enrick, the site of the upcoming Five Eyes intelligence conference. The castle appeared over a rise, and Janice Won gasped at its majesty. It was an immense fortification, ringed with an ancient wall and perched on a hillside overlooking Loch Ness.

The structure was off-white in color, not the brown stone of many castles, and its size did not give it an ominous appearance at all. It was imposing, but welcoming, with flags waving in the breeze and ornate landscaping along the drive up to the gate.

The vehicles rolled through the gate of the curtain wall around the entire facility, its parapets still intact, the crenellations maintained, as if archers were standing by even now to protect the castle hotel from marauding invaders.

There were several buildings inside the walls, but the keep was the largest, strongest, and most well-protected part of the entire fortification, and it was also the location of the majority of the conference. They parked in a small lot here, then entered through the gatehouse, walking under the iron portcullis held up by thick rope.

The original castle had been built in 1269, but it had been a simple tower keep at first, and only over the next century was it built up into the massive complex it was today. A great hall, an entry hall, and larger living quarters were added. In the 1800s bathrooms and electricity and improved ventilation were put in, and in the 1970s the family that owned the property turned it into a luxury hotel and conference center.

After they dropped their bags in their rooms, Mars, Fox, and Won met back in the entry hall. Jon Hines did not make this trip. Even though he virtually never let his protectee out of his sight, Mars thought the six-foot-nine-inch behemoth to be too striking a presence in the middle of a covert intelligence mission.

They didn't come here to be remembered.

Together they walked the grounds for over an hour. The three did their best to envision the intelligence summit that was soon to take place, to picture where the guests would be housed, seated for dinner and for meetings. They strolled through the gardens, looked out past the wall down on Loch Ness, lying out before them in beautiful turquoise, just at the bottom of a sheer cliff one hundred feet high.

It became obvious to Won that David Mars knew his way around this property.

"You've been here before?" Won asked.

Mars replied, "Oh yes. Twice already in the past three months. It's a marvelous place for a holiday, even if it didn't have value to me in other ways."

Won was particularly interested in the air itself, the breeze drifting in from the water, the movement in the manicured trees around the property. At one point she turned to Mars. "We will check the conditions the day of, but if it is like this, then the pilot will have to make a low pass, flying just east of the castle, over the grounds but not over the building itself."

Mars nodded, but he didn't appear to be paying close attention.

Back inside they dined on venison and grouse in a dining room off the great hall. Won did not touch her wine, but Fox and Mars indulged in an easygoing and relaxed manner.

Both men were operational, but they also both knew how to operate in cover. Mars had been a spy in one capacity or another all his adult life, after

all, and Fox was a Russian intelligence agent who'd infiltrated Russia's no-
torious Solntsevskaya Bratva, so they were both exceedingly good at this.

Won was a trained intelligence asset, but the tradecraft she'd learned
in the DPRK did not encompass dining out in the center of an intelligence
target. No, she'd learned dead drops, countersurveillance, resistance to
interrogation, and the like. The hard skills of a spy.

They retired to their rooms after dinner, but just twenty minutes later
Mars and Fox stepped out in the hall and went downstairs.

They walked into a main hall, exchanging pleasantries with other
guests and employees of the castle alike.

Moving on to the east wing of the large building, they kept an eye out
for cameras or castle security; then, when the coast was clear, they slipped
into an employee-access-only stairwell off the great hall. They descended
two flights into increasing darkness and ended up on the bottom floor,
engulfed in pitch black.

Fox turned on a flashlight and they saw that they were in the stone
basement, a several-hundred-meter-long warren of halls and rooms. The
castle dungeon had been here once, as well as catacombs to house the dead
in the walls, a place to keep wine and dry goods, even an armory and a
furniture and blacksmith's shop, but now it was mostly used for storage for
the hotel and conference center.

It was musty down here, the smell of water evident.

They walked along, passing under archways above which massive iron
gates hung, held up by cordage as thick as Won's arm.

The men knew where they were going, in general, but it was such a
maze that Mars referred to a map. He'd studied everything ever recorded
about this building, going back to sixteenth-century writings that described the original keep.

After ten minutes behind flashlights' beams, they arrived at a long
room full of stored banquet tables, stepped into a square stone room just
past an archway with a gate above it, and arrived at their final destination.

As soon as the Five Eyes conference was announced for Castle Enrick,
Mars had begun studying the location, reading over every single reference
to the castle to find a way to disrupt the meeting. In his studies on the facility, Mars read that a tunnel had been dug during the construction of the
keep by a wealthy owner who wanted the option of a quick escape in case

of attack. The tunnel, one old tome revealed, traveled at a forty-five-degree angle through the dirt and rock that led from the subterranean level of the main keep down to the water's edge, providing clandestine and quick access to Loch Ness. Those residing in the castle could, in the event of siege, escape down the stairs in the old tunnel to waiting boats at the bottom of the cliff, some 150 yards away.

The stairwell tunnel had been mentioned in passing in a few other writings as late as the eighteenth century, but later maps and media contained no reference to the shaft. It seemed clear that the passage itself had been closed off, probably sometime in the 1800s.

This gave Mars an idea. He knew he had one chance to catch the Five Eyes leadership together, one chance to bring Dr. Won and her creation into his fight, and he'd believed from the beginning that there was too much riding on this to trust the entire mission to a single crop duster, flying in unpredictable weather, slipping past any security monitoring the skies and dousing the castle with plague spores.

He needed a secondary option, so he sent a team of Russian Bratva members who were also construction foremen and engineers to Loch Ness, not to the castle itself, but to the waterline below the cliff. There, under cover of darkness, they moved through the trees along the bank, inland no more than twenty meters, where the cliff face began.

It took the team of eight men over three hours to find a door-sized portion of the cliff that didn't fit the color or texture of the rest of the rock. It had instead been added; stone and mortar. Chipping away at this, as quietly as possible, two men labored an entire arduous day, but when they were through they found a rusted iron door, two feet wide and four feet high.

The rest of the team returned the second night, and with an acetylene torch they cut the door from its hinges, and a flashlight was shined inside.

Broken steps went up at a forty-five-degree angle, just as had been described in the ancient book Mars read. The pathway was not completely clear. There had been numerous cave-ins over the centuries, but the Russians secretly returned three times over the next month and a half, cleaning out the debris, dumping it in the loch, and fortifying the walls and ceiling of the passage.

Finally Roger Fox himself arrived, and he was the first to climb to the top. Here he found an old iron door, identical to the one hidden at the base of the cliff. He did not dare try to open it; he merely determined that the acetylene torch would do the trick.

But no one knew what lay on the other side of the door. Could it be a brick wall, private quarters that could be filled with armed security during the Five Eyes meeting, or something else that would ruin any opportunity for a stealthy ingress to the conference?

The small room where Fox and Mars now stood was lined with leaning folding chairs. And on the far side, behind a stack of chairs, sat a four-foot-high steel door at ground level.

GPS told them this was the access point to the long-forgotten tunnel.

An old, rusty lock built into the door looked daunting, but Fox assured Mars a torch would make short work of it.

Fox added, "Certainly the security people for the conference will know about this passage."

Mars nodded. "It is a fair assumption you're right. Just an inspection of the basement could reveal this easily enough." He looked over the door a moment. "There will be security posted down here, I shouldn't think more than one or two men. Perhaps the sleepers we will have planted inside the security force here will be able to volunteer for this work."

Mars added, "It is also possible security will do something to block the door, so we'll have to tell our friends to bring some explosives for that eventuality."

Fox said, "It continues to worry me that our infiltration team and their equipment won't arrive until the day before the operation."

The two men turned to return to the stairwell. "Men like that . . . you can't just put them in Scotland, leave them be for long, without them drawing attention to themselves. They are professionals; they will be here when we want them here, and it's better that way than trying to hide them away somewhere till the time is right."

As they began ascending the stairwell, flipping off the flashlight, Fox said, "And what of Dr. Won? Does she have any suspicions?"

"I think she is focused on the fermentation process. She has it in her head that her crop duster will take care of the matter, and she is reveling in the fact that an Englishman tied to Russia will be blamed for it all."

Fox climbed the stairs, a low chuckle in the back of his throat.

CHAPTER 38

Court woke in pain, the injuries from the night before clawing their way back into his conscious mind. His back still hurt, though he didn't remember why, as did his jaw and his ribs on both his left and right sides. These blows he had no trouble recalling. But his eye felt okay, he could see through it, and the bruises all over his shoulders and neck weren't bothering him much anymore, at least while he lay here still.

He turned his head and saw Zoya facing him, but her dark disheveled hair hid her face. He couldn't allow this; he brushed her hair back behind her ear. She stirred a little, and he just looked at her.

Court still had all his clothes on, and she wore a T-shirt and panties. They'd had moments of intimacy before they fell asleep, but nothing physical beyond a few kisses, because Court was just simply beaten too badly to move. He cursed the big boxer who'd put him in this state, because there was nothing more in the world he wanted to do right now than to roll over to the Russian woman and wake her up with his touch.

But that would involve physical labor that required muscles he could not employ right now to save his life, so instead he slowly and painfully rolled in the other direction, out of the bed, and lumbered for the shower.

While the hot water did nothing at all for his ribs, it did loosen his back some, indicating that he was dealing with pulled muscles more than bruising back there, and with this new mobility he slowly changed into jeans and a threadbare gray and black Fulham FC Soccer T-shirt he'd bought at a used clothing store when he arrived in the city the day before.

He brewed instant coffee in the kitchen, restarting the process when he realized he'd forgotten to double his usual portion of coffee and water to account for his guest.

Court didn't have a lot of sleepovers.

When his coffee was done he sat down slowly and laboriously on the sofa, pulled the iPad to him, and reached for his backpack. Rummaging through it for a while, he retrieved a cable. Unsure exactly how to proceed, he put in his earpiece and placed a call to the one number in his phone.

Fifteen seconds later a sleepy voice answered. "Brewer."

"It's me."

She cleared her throat. "Haven't heard from you for six hours."

"I count the minutes between our chats, as well."

Brewer ignored the sarcasm and fired back with her own. "Anthem hung up on me last night. It's seven a.m. in London. I'm assuming she's still with you, and you two shared a lovely night."

Court touched his aching ribs absentmindedly. "It was a hell of a party."

"What did she tell you about—"

Court interrupted. "I have a new-model iPad here that she took from Terry Cassidy's safe. Can you get into it remotely?"

"Of course. You still have the phone we gave you?"

"Affirmative."

"That's odd," she said with sarcasm. "It hasn't been transmitting since it was handed to you."

"I disabled it and tossed it in a Faraday cage. It will take me a minute to put it back together."

"When you do, plug in the iPad and follow directions on the screen. It will upload to me, and you'll be able to see what I see simultaneously on the device."

"Roger."

Court pulled the lead-lined bag designed to hide the phone's signal, known as a Faraday cage, out of his backpack and put the phone back together. While he worked on this Zoya entered the living room wearing her black climbing pants and the gray T-shirt Court gave her the night before. They smiled at each other as she passed him to head towards the coffee, rubbing the sleep from her eyes.

She said, "Nobody has woken me up with fresh coffee in a very long time."

Court shrugged. "It's just instant," and then immediately regretted saying that. "But good instant." It wasn't much of a recovery, but Court wasn't much of a Casanova.

She poured a cup and took a sip. "Better than at the safe house." She sat next to him, and together they waited for over twenty minutes while Brewer and her night-shift technical team cracked into the iPad. Eventually, however, Court and Zoya had access to all the files.

There wasn't much on the device out of the ordinary, but an Excel contact list had its own icon. Brewer opened this and began scrolling through, while the two in the basement flat in London looked on.

Brewer found a list of names of offshore corporations, along with country of registry, nominating agent, and other related material for each one. Brewer chose one of the companies, began clicking through links on the screen, and pulled up new windows of information. Court and Zoya watched while she did so. Finally, Brewer clicked a link, and the screen showed a name. Yuri Kuznetzov.

Court had moved Brewer to the speakerphone, so Zoya spoke to her aloud. "I know who this is. He's from the mafia, runs the London Brigade of the Solntsevskaya Bratva, the largest organized crime group in Russia. He lives here. He's Vory. I guess you know what that is."

"Yeah," Court said. "A made man."

Brewer replied over the speaker. "If he is the owner of this offshore account and it was set up correctly, there would be no reason to ever see his name. That's why criminals use offshores."

Court said, "Cassidy is the middleman. I bet he's established the ownership, and is keeping these files on his clients as a safeguard, in case he needs to use them."

"Against the Russian mob?" Brewer asked.

"Why not?" Zoya answered.

Brewer clicked through more links. There were phone numbers, billing records, and other pieces of information attached. They found twenty-one names of individuals who owned the more than eighty offshores, and while the list was not long, the names did immediately tip all three of them off about something. Most of the names were Russian, most of the addresses were here in the UK—London and its environs specifically—and Court and Brewer recognized a few of the names instantly.

Zoya knew most all of them, including her father's colleague and confidant from GRU, Vladimir Belyakov.

Zoya said, "We already knew Belyakov was associated with Cassidy. I say we just start searching for information about these other Russian actors, see who is just some rich asshole and who is some rich asshole with GRU or SVR ties. Those could be the guys who used Cassidy to hire that local crew for the Ternhill operation."

All three agreed. Brewer said, "I'm leaving town later today, but I'll run checks first and get back with you."

Court said, "I know someone here I can talk to about this; he's as dialed in to the fabric of criminals and spooks as one can possibly be."

"And who is that?" Brewer asked.

"An old friend. I'll leave it there. Get some rest, Brewer. Go through that list when you get up."

He hung up the phone, then looked to Zoya. "You want to come with me?"

She shook her head. "No, I'm sorry. I can't."

"You have someplace to be?"

"Yes. I'll meet you back here later."

She seemed distracted to Court now, but he got the impression he wasn't going to get an answer from her as to her plans, and he did not press. She kissed him, gently touched the bruising on his jaw, then rose and went into the bedroom to change. Court lay back on the couch, trying to muster the energy to get out the door himself.

. . .

Court left the flat thirty minutes later, walking stiffly but feeling somewhat better than he thought he had a right to, considering the beating he'd taken the night before. He had a man he needed to see, though he wasn't sure where he'd find him. He'd spend the morning mining this old colleague's known locations, using social engineering to get the man's acquaintances to pass on information unwittingly, and then he would home in on his target, just like he always did.

. . .

Zoya Zakharova departed shortly after Court. She moved up the street with catlike precision and attention, because she was uninjured, unlike Court, and also because she had a plan now, a direction. Her father was here, in town; this she could feel. She knew he was looking for her, and this could only be because of her conversation with Belyakov.

Her plan was simple, though its success was far from assured. She'd go back to Belyakov's house, and she would ask him to invite her father over for tea.

. . .

Zack Hightower knelt between two garbage cans placed between two nearly identical McMansions across the street from Lucas Renfro's larger gated property. It was two a.m., the street was as quiet as could be, and the CIA contractor's threat assessment was that he could cross the street and get over the small fence and into the man's home without being detected.

Renfro was home right now; this Hightower knew because he'd followed him here six hours earlier. He'd seen the man's wife leave with luggage just after, he watched lights go on and off for a couple of hours, and then it all went dark.

The security cameras at the deputy director of Support's house weren't working tonight; this Zack saw when he used his laptop and the Wi-Fi password provided by Hanley to log into the system. He found it fortuitous that the security system was on the fritz: more evidence that the time was now to make his breach.

He also had all the details of the house, the keypad lock on the back door, and the alarm code, so he could simply punch it in and access the house.

It didn't get any easier, Zack told himself.

The only thing holding him back was the fact that he knew Hanley and Brewer wouldn't want him breaching the home at night while Renfro was there. That wasn't the original plan, and neither Brewer nor Hanley knew Hightower was right here, right now. Theoretically, at least, this was obviously a higher-threat operation than penetrating during the day while the man was at work. But Renfro didn't have a dog, his kids were grown, and Hightower had all the details to get into the house. He knew where Renfro hid his pistol, and he knew Renfro's wife had already left to visit family.

Matt Hanley had told Hightower that he wanted him to put the fear of God in this man. What better way to do so than by showing up at two a.m. at the foot of his bed in a ski mask?

Zack rose from his prone position and started to leave his hide. Just then, a single muffled gunshot cracked in the night. Zack saw a flash behind curtains in a second-story window of Renfro's house.

He knelt back down between the cans as dogs began barking.

Softly he said, "Uh-oh."

He pulled out his phone, selected a contact, and put it through his earpiece. A few seconds later a tired voice said, "Brewer."

"It's Romantic. We've got a problem. I am not one hundred percent certain, but there is a decent chance Renfro just capped himself."

Brewer woke up fully an instant later. "*Capped?* As in shot?"

"Affirmative. I heard a single handgun round pop off and saw a flash in his bedroom window."

"Wait. Where *are* you?"

Zack breathed out slowly. He was going to get yelled at. "Outside his house."

"At two in the morning?" When Zack did not respond, she said, "You were intending to breach, weren't you?"

"I'd been thinking about it," Zack admitted, ready for the fallout.

But no fallout came. "How do you know he wasn't murdered?"

"Nobody coming or going since I got here. No other noises."

"He's married. Kids are away at college but what about—"

"Watched his wife leave. I checked; she was booked on a 9:30 p.m. flight from Reagan to Boston. Probably going to see their kid at Harvard."

"Did he see you tonight? Did that cause him to shoot himself?"

Zack looked down at the phone with confusion. "Suzanne, I'd like nothing more than to think I have the power to make the bad guys kill themselves rather than face me, but there is no way he knew I was here."

"Must have been your bumpering, and the shame of being outed as a traitor."

"Yeah," Zack said, still looking at the quiet house across the street. "In the end the fucker folded up like a cheap suitcase."

"What's your exposure now?"

"Somebody is going to call in that gunshot, and this looks like one of the neighborhoods where the police will come running when they do. I need to exfil."

Brewer thought it over and agreed. "Get the hell out of there." She then added, "If Renfro *was* the mole, and if he *did*, in fact, kill himself . . . well then, I guess this is a suitable outcome."

Zack thought his control officer seemed a little unsure, but he couldn't imagine why. "You kidding? It's an *outstanding* outcome, other than the fact that he deprived me of the pleasure of helping him out with that." He reached up to turn off his earpiece and said, "Okay, I'm exfilling the AO at this time. I'm out."

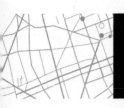

CHAPTER 39

Matt Hanley and Suzanne Brewer arrived at the home of Lucas Renfro at three fifteen a.m. There were no police cars out front, no ambulances in the drive. Apparently, no alarm had been raised by anyone in the neighborhood, because now, an hour after Romantic's report about the gunshot, the street remained utterly quiet.

Hanley punched in the keypad code at a side door, then disabled the alarm with the same codes he'd given Hightower, and they entered the large residence.

Hanley was armed; he'd pulled his holstered .45 from his side table before leaving his house in Woodley Park, and now he held it at the low ready.

Brewer did not have a gun. She had been trained on them, but she wasn't a shooter, and she thought Hanley looked ridiculous right now with his weapon: overweight, hair still slightly askew from his bed, wearing a raincoat though there wasn't a hint of precipitation.

His weapon out in front of him like a jackass.

She knew he'd been a Green Beret, twenty-five years ago or so now, but he didn't look to her like he'd used the weapon for anything more than a prop to make himself look tough since he'd left the Army, and she was not impressed.

Brewer walked behind Hanley as he stalked through the house, clearing from room to room. Finally they made it upstairs, worked their way through the bedrooms and bathrooms down a hall, and entered the master bedroom.

Suzanne flipped on the overhead light, then gasped.

Lucas Renfro lay with his feet on the floor at the foot of the bed and his torso back over the covers. Blood splattered the sheets, the pillows, and the headboard, and the man's eyes were open in death.

A black steel revolver lay on his crotch, both his left and right hands positioned next to it.

Neither Hanley nor Brewer bothered to check for a pulse. A significant portion of his brain was exposed.

Hanley turned away to check the bathroom and the closet for threats.

Brewer just stood there. Her face made of stone. She hid it well, but she was immediately devastated by Renfro's death. Not because she was sad or sickened, but because it negatively affected her own prospects. Just the previous afternoon she'd let Renfro into her confidence, trying to orchestrate Hanley's fall from grace. And now Renfro, her only way out of this morass of black ops and dirty work, had been taken from her.

She recovered somewhat, knowing she had to show Hanley she was focused on the matter at hand, not on her own rise through the Agency ranks. "You think Renfro knew Romantic was outside and about to come in?" It was the only thing that made sense to her.

Hanley returned. Said nothing, just kept looking at the dead man, the blood, and the rest of the room.

Brewer added, "I would say it's safe to assume that Palumbo, Karlsson, and Wheeler are off the hook. I honestly didn't think there was any way Renfro would be the mole, but I don't see how there could be any other explanation for this."

Hanley knelt down, looked at the man's feet. He wore no shoes or socks.

Brewer watched her boss while he stood back up and walked around the room, slowly and silently.

She said, "I told Romantic, all things considered, this isn't a bad outcome to this situation." Hanley did not reply, just kept scanning. "I mean, no trial, no discovery process that could jeopardize operations, no publicity to this other than a few easy-to-deal-with articles about a CIA exec committing suicide. This is much more controllable than Renfro trying to make a run for it or having his day in court."

She wasn't feeling her words, just bolstering her cover. The last thing she wanted Hanley to suspect was that she'd had a clandestine meeting with Renfro, the man she now felt sure was a turncoat against the Agency and the United States.

But Hanley made no reply.

Brewer stared at him as he leaned over the body. She said, "I don't understand, Matt. I thought you'd be pumping your fists in the air. You hated Renfro, you said yourself he was a threat to Poison Apple, and he was obviously the traitor who has been getting Operations and Support officers killed."

Finally Hanley turned to her. "So . . . what you're saying, Suzanne, is that you're buying all this?"

Brewer did not understand. She walked to the foot of the bed and stood next to Hanley, shoulder-to-shoulder, looking over the body. "*Buying* it? You don't think he shot himself? It looks pretty plain that he did. Hell, Matt, Romantic had eyes on the house. He didn't see anyone coming or going after the wife left town."

A dubious look came over Hanley's face. "This looks stage-managed to me."

Brewer laughed a little. "I guess you've seen more suicides than I have."

Hanley walked around the room again, picking items off shelves and tables, looking them over, putting them back down. "No, not really. But I've sure as hell positioned bodies to make it look like a suicide a few times, and there's something seriously wrong with this scene."

"For instance?"

He turned back to the body and pointed. "Placement of the hands, for starters. How do you blow your head off, flop back onto the bed, and have both your hands fall into your lap with the firearm on top? It looks unnatural to me. Too convenient to pass my smell test."

"Perhaps he held the gun with both hands. You can tell by the exit wound that he shot himself through the mouth. That would be awkward to do with one hand, I imagine."

Hanley nodded, paused, then said, "An alternative theory is that the killer didn't know if Renfro was right-handed or left-handed, so he hedged his bets and put the pistol in close proximity to both hands. I bet we find gunpowder residue on both, as well, but only because they strong-armed him to put his hands up to his face when they shot him."

Brewer shook her head in astonishment. "Matt, if someone wants a CIA deputy director killed, you can be sure that someone would use professional killers. If professionals came in here intending to make it look like suicide, how would they not know if he was right- or left-handed?"

Hanley had an answer to this, as well. "What if proxies were used, just like in the UK and just like in Great Falls? What if someone hired the best asset they could find in a pinch, rushed them over here after Zack spent the last two days leaning on Renfro, and what if the shooter didn't have the prep time or the expertise to find out which hand was the target's dominant one?"

"A lot of 'what ifs,' in my opinion, sir."

Hanley stood there silently, but he shook his head. "This is a bullshit crime scene, Suzanne. I can just feel it."

"Sir, I don't see anything that—"

He interrupted. "Give me a pen."

Brewer made a face, pulled a pen from her purse, and handed it to Hanley. He leaned over the bed, over the body, and slid the pen between the man's bloody lips.

"Why don't you just go ahead and keep that, Matt?"

Hanley pushed the man's mouth open and looked inside. "Gun went into the mouth, right?"

"Pretty obviously. No entry visible. Exit through the crown of the head."

Hanley said, "Why is there a hole through his tongue?"

Brewer didn't get it. "Meaning?"

"You know where your own tongue is; if you are going to stick a gun in your mouth, you are going to put the barrel above your tongue, not under it. Why would you pin your tongue to the roof of your mouth?"

"I . . . I don't—"

"Whoever jammed the pistol in Renfro's mouth here shoved the tongue up accidentally before squeezing the trigger."

Brewer thought this over. "But who would murder him? Presumably the intelligence product he'd been handing out was valuable to the perpetrators."

Hanley sat down on the chaise across from the bed, still looking at the body. "The only reason I can think of that his murder was made to look like suicide is if someone wanted to throw us off the scent of the real traitor."

Brewer cocked her head. With a dubious voice, she said, "So not only did Renfro not kill himself, but he's also not the mole?"

Hanley shrugged. "I don't know. Maybe not."

"Dammit," she said. "You were the one who insisted it *was* him."

Hanley shrugged. "Maybe I just wanted it to be him."

"Why? Why did you hate him so much?"

Another shrug from the big man's shoulders. "He rubbed me the wrong way."

Brewer didn't press. She said, "Well, I guess if the compromises stop, we'll know Renfro was the right guy."

"Perhaps," Hanley said, then stood back up. "Tell Romantic that he needs to keep pressing the others. Another round with the two still in the States till they head over to the Five Eyes conference, then we send Romantic over with them. There he can turn up the heat on Karlsson."

Matt Hanley left through the door, his shoulders slumped. Brewer could tell he was devastated that he no longer believed that Renfro was the culprit. She took one last look at the body of the deputy director of Support, then followed her boss back down the stairs and out into the quiet morning.

• • •

Court Gentry sat in a first-floor window above Savile Row, watching over the front door of Norton & Sons Tailors, just across the street. He'd only positioned himself here seconds earlier, after entering the building through an unlocked door and running up a staircase as quickly but as quietly as possible, passing a room full of tailors huddled over their workbenches. The first floor was dark and empty of people, filled instead with huge rolls of fine fabrics and other supplies.

Before he even had a chance to take stock of his personal security here in the large, dimly lit storage area, across the street a black four-door Mercedes S-Class limousine slowed and stopped in front of Norton.

Court knelt down and backed away a bit from the window, even though he doubted he would be seen from here because of the reflection from the sun on the outside of the window glass.

He'd been following this Mercedes on a rented bicycle from the owner's Mayfair apartment through streets so congested the bike had a hard time keeping back from the slow-moving car. Once he saw they were approaching Savile Row, however, he began moving up a parallel street as fast as he could pedal, because he had a good idea where his subject was going.

A young man climbed out of the front passenger seat of the S-Class limousine. He rushed around and opened a back door, and a heavyset balding man with messy white hair stepped out. Together the two men headed through the front door of Norton as the driver climbed out and stood by the vehicle, his eyes scanning up and down the quiet street.

From his vantage point Court was able to see the older man shake hands with two young employees inside, and then he headed towards the back, out of view.

Sir Donald Fitzroy had been Court's handler back when the American worked in the private sector as an assassin for hire. Fitz and Gentry worked together for years; the former MI5 operative and security consultant found jobs that virtually no one on Earth could pull off, and then Court went out and pulled them off.

Usually.

Court did his part; some of his ops were so successful and his getaways so clean that people began referring to a mythical Gray Man, an invisible, uber assassin, capable of anything.

It was close, but it wasn't accurate. Court balked at missions that he didn't think stood a good chance of success, he'd begun operations only to back out when something changed in his target's habits or security structure, and he'd even had a few targets he was never able to find.

But even with this, he became arguably the most successful assassin on the planet, either government run or private.

Court hated the moniker first given to him in a media release by Interpol because he hated the attention, but Fitzroy had thought it perfect for marketing purposes. Those few cutouts in the world that knew Fitzroy was running the Gray Man knew exactly whom to call if they were presented with an extremely difficult problem that no one else could solve.

Now Court looked to the driver of the Mercedes. After a grand total of thirty seconds checking for threats, he was now leaning back against the vehicle, eyeing a shapely mom with two daughters in tow as she strolled up the street to his right.

Some security officer, Court thought. Sir Donald was legendary for his poor personal security. He'd been kidnapped, blackmailed, and otherwise threatened, yet after all this he moved through the city with a grand total of one bodyguard and one lazy driver.

"C'mon, Fitz, I'm not saving your ass again," he said to himself, but then he wondered if the paltry protection in light of all the danger Fitzroy had faced in the past meant the man was retired now, and therefore considered himself less of a target.

The woman with the two girls neared the Mercedes, and Court assumed they would pass the scene in front of him, but the woman stepped over to the driver, talked to him a moment, then turned in to Norton & Sons, the girls following behind.

Court looked on, only mildly curious about the new arrivals in his area of operations, but once he recognized that the little girls were clearly twins, he sat up straighter. The second girl through the door paused and looked back, up and down the street, and he lunged for the small binos he'd placed on the windowsill. He brought them to his eyes, and a soft sound came from his throat.

"Claire?"

He wasn't certain how old Claire and Kate Fitzroy were—he thought they must have been ten or eleven by now. They were Fitzroy's granddaughters, children of his deceased son. Court had saved the kids' lives once, plain and simple, but he never thought of it that way. As far as he was concerned, Claire had saved his.

They were so grown now, and he caught himself blinking mist out of his eyes as he watched them.

Elise was the mother, Sir Donald's former daughter-in-law. Court wondered if she had remarried in the years since her and her children's lives had been saved.

Court watched while Fitzroy came out of the back wearing a new bespoke suit, the girls hugging him, telling him stories that he showed great interest in.

After another fifteen minutes the entire group left the tailor; the body-guard held Fitzroy's bags, a dramatic breach in close-protection protocol that caused Court to roll his eyes. The family piled into the Mercedes limo with the guard and driver, and it rolled off up the street. Court was already downstairs on his bike by now, out of sight of the group, who would have been able to easily identify him.

. . .

Fifteen minutes later the Fitzroys sat at an outdoor café just a block from Buckingham Palace, and Court stood across the street in a passing crowd, looking on while the girls ate and Fitzroy and Elise drank wine. It was a beautiful sunny Saturday, the kids were obviously out of school, and it looked like everyone was happy.

Except Court. He just spoke softly to himself, though he was thinking about Sir Donald. "We can't do this in front of the kids, Don. Wrap up lunch and go home."

He softened a bit, thinking about the girls, wondering about their lives now. There was always fallout on any mission, collateral damage. The kids' lives had been ever affected because Fitzroy was the handler of the Gray Man, and Court wished he could somehow make all the pain they'd gone through after losing their father wash away so their lives could be happier.

But wishing was useless. All he could do was get on with his current mission, because he wasn't a therapist, he wasn't a social worker, he wasn't a psychologist.

He was a weapon. He was the one who caused the damage, physical and mental, that someone else would have to clean up.

Court left his position minutes before the check came.

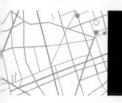

CHAPTER 40

Sir Donald Fitzroy climbed out of the back of his limo and shuffled through the guarded doors of his apartment building. His security man followed him, but only to the lift. The former British spymaster owned the penthouse; the lift could bypass the four floors below it and race directly to the top. Reginald rarely accompanied him up to the penthouse itself, because once Fitzroy was in the lift he was cut off from any threats and deemed safe by his security, and there was a second bodyguard who also served as his butler already waiting for him.

Fitzroy rode the lift in silence, and then it opened in front of a locked door. He put two keys in the two locks, entered, and then double-locked the door behind him. He entered the foyer and dropped his keys on the table, then glanced into his kitchen.

His bodyguard, Lou, wasn't there where Fitzroy expected him to be, making him his first of many drinks for the afternoon. Just minutes ago he'd called ahead and asked for an old-fashioned, and he'd had no doubt in his mind it would be placed in his hand within seconds of walking in the door.

Curious, he stepped into the living room.

Court Gentry sat there in a leather chair, facing Fitzroy, his back to the far wall. "Hello, Fitz."

Fitzroy saw no weapon, but he didn't doubt there was one his old employee could snatch from under his shirt and bring to eye level in a quarter second.

The Englishman did not move a muscle. "You could give an old man a heart attack."

"Sorry to barge in."

"It's all right, lad," the man said. There was concern on his face, still the shock of seeing a man in his house. "What happened to Lou?"

"Who is Lou?"

"My security man."

Court shook his head. "Didn't see him. I *did* run into a bartender, though. Making a drink in the kitchen with his pistol dangling exposed from a shoulder holster. Disarms don't come much easier than that. Not much of a security man, Fitz, but I bet that old-fashioned he was working on would have kicked ass."

"He's not hurt, I pray."

"Zip-tied in the bedroom closet. Spilled a little bourbon on his shirt, but it'll come out."

Fitzroy smiled a little. "Am I free to walk over to the sitting area?"

"It's your house. You should know by now I'm no threat to you."

"Sorry, Court, but when one sees the Gray Man waiting for him in his private quarters, one cannot help but feel a twinge of worry. The world's greatest assassin."

"You know that's just ridiculous hype."

"I know that it's *not*."

"I just need to talk."

"Certainly. Care for a drink? I'll make it myself, since you've given Lou the afternoon off."

Court motioned to the table in front of him. There, previously unnoticed by Fitzroy, stood two shots of Jura eighteen-year-old Scotch whiskey.

"I helped myself," Court said. "Join me."

Fitzroy sat and took a glass. "What the bloody hell happened to your face?"

"I walked into a brick wall."

"How many times?"

Court didn't answer, because when Fitzroy picked up the Waterford crystal highball, Court saw that the man was missing two fingers on his right hand. "How's that doing?"

Fitzroy held it up. "Oh, this little flesh wound? It's nothing. I've cut myself worse whilst shaving."

Court knew Fitzroy had been a hard man in his younger years, working for British intelligence in Northern Ireland. Having a pair of fingers lopped off by Chinese intelligence a few months earlier was more than a flesh wound, but a tough old goat like Fitzroy could handle it better than most, Court knew.

"I knew you couldn't stay away from London long," Court said.

"It's in my blood. Like a disease."

Court adopted an annoyed look. "Three guys, Fitz? You have *three* damn guys in your security detail?"

"Four, actually, but Andy has the flu."

Court closed his eyes in disbelief.

"It no longer matters, lad. I am retired. My network is gone. My contacts are gone. I returned to London a pariah in the community. If you've come to me for work, I've nothing; if you've come to me for intelligence, I've nothing current. I've fuck-all to offer you other than a couch to sleep on and a pot of tea and the scotch in your hand. Of course, if you need some money I could—"

"I don't need money. I need answers. Look, Fitz. You know people."

"I know people who won't talk to me any longer. How does that help you?"

"You know the fabric and the pulse of this city."

Fitzroy drank much of his scotch. Court hadn't yet touched his. "Bollocks, but go on," the Englishman said.

"My question is about organized crime. Both Russian mob here in London, and other groups. Working together in some capacity. Working with the Kremlin, maybe." Court shrugged. "Maybe not."

"What are you on about?"

"There's a mole at the Agency. He, or she, has gotten a lot of Operations people killed. We picked up a man who could help identify the compromise, but four nights ago at Ternhill a group of British gangsters got him away from us. The trail led me to a solicitor here, and from him I acquired a list of mostly Russian oligarchs and mobsters. I need to know how every-thing fits together, because I'm not smart enough to figure it out."

"What do you want from me, then?"

Court pulled out the sheet of paper with the names he'd written down from Cassidy's iPad. "Can you look over this list and tell me where I need to focus my attention?"

Fitzroy made no move to take the list. Instead he said, "So . . . you are doing this at the behest of the CIA?"

"Yes." He paused. "Well . . . sort of."

"Ah, the ambiguity in your relationship with the American govern-ment continues."

"Don't I know it?"

Fitzroy snorted a laugh, took the list, adjusted his glasses, and said, "What are you looking for, specifically?"

"Not sure. Russians who have used the UK underworld in the past, expat Russians with Kremlin ties, as well, maybe. Someone with means."

Fitzroy looked the names over. "Every name here is someone with means."

"Yeah. Oligarchs, crime bosses, a couple of names that sound Western, could be OC."

As Fitzroy read the names again, he said, "More context, boy. I sussed out that you'd be playing this close to the vest, but if you want me to help you . . ."

Court said, "CIA picked up a banker involved with payments to a trai-tor inside the CIA. The banker was snatched back by the opposition and found floating in the Thames. But all that led me here, to a lawyer named Cassidy."

Fitzroy looked up at this. "Terry?"

"Yes. You know him?"

"Youngish bloke, to me, anyway, He's a fixture at my members-only club in Westminster. He's in there all the time."

"Well," Court said, "he's dirty."

"These are his clients?" Fitzroy held up the list.

"Yes, including the head of the local brigade of the Solntsevskaya Bratva."

Fitzroy nodded. "Yes, I see his name here." Fitzroy put the list down.

"These Reds are all known men. I don't see any of them going after MI6 or even Agency blokes, for that matter. Too risky. No . . . the man you need is not on this list."

"Who is he?"

"Bugger if I know. But there's been talk around London for years about a Russian mastermind pulling the puppet strings of both the Bratva and the local OC firms. There are hallmarks of a skilled hand over some of the local criminal organizations' work. Some sort of three-way nexus between the Kremlin and all the Russian criminal organizations, and the billions of dollars expatriated out of Russia."

"Who is the puppet master?" Court asked.

Fitzroy shook his head. "No bloody idea. No one knows. I've heard a code name that's whispered here and there . . . might just be disinformation, exaggerations."

"Tell me his code name."

"*Cherny Volk.*"

Court's eyebrows furrowed. "Black Wolf?"

Fitzroy waved a hand. "Again. Nothing you can hang your hat on at all. But, still, if I had to wager I'd say there is an architect lording over everything going on in Russian circles in the UK these days. I'd also say he is next-level skilled."

"Couldn't he just be running the Bratvas here?"

Fitzroy shook his head. "This Black Wolf, if he exists at all, is not part of the Russian mob himself, that much is assumed. The Solntsevskaya Bratva owns swaths of this town, and swaths of politicians and cops, as well. They own banks here, more property than you can imagine, and they are growing all the time. But they don't have the sophistication that we are seeing in the UK these days that involve Russian interests. Topflight political killings, targeted poisoning, kidnapping, financial and hacking schemes to support the Kremlin.

"Our mastermind has a very careful hand, and an extremely deft touch." Fitzroy added, "That doesn't sound like the Russian mob, now does it? And then the loads of contract killings against Kremlin outsiders that have taken place here. Too many to believe that SVR assassins are causing all the damage. The SVR has its own problems with moles and compromises. They wouldn't be getting away as cleanly as they are." Fitzroy sipped his drink. "*Chernny Volk*, he's the mastermind, if you believe the rumors."

Court said, "What do you suggest I do, Don?"

"Forget all this bollocks and go home." Court said nothing. "But since that is out of the question, you could do this." Fitzroy thought a moment. "Cassidy is at the club every afternoon, usually by four. He takes over one of the small parlors to do business, meets with people there."

"Business with other club members?"

"Yes, you don't get into the Red Lion Club without being a member."

This surprised Court. "You have Russian oligarchs and crime bosses in your club?"

"Heavens, no. We don't let that ilk in. Terry does his deals there with proper Englishmen."

Court didn't suspect that people working with Terry Cassidy were proper anything, Englishmen or not, but he did not say this. Instead he said, "There are just a few people with Western names on his client list."

"Perhaps this list isn't all his clients, just the ones he wants to keep a paper trail on. The corrupt, the criminals, the dangerous ones."

Court asked, "Do you recognize the names of the Westerners? Are they OC?"

Fitzroy looked down again. "Yes, now that you mention it. Most of these blokes are known gangsters of varying degrees. David Mars is a name I don't recognize, although that doesn't mean he's not someone. As I said, I'm out to pasture." He looked up. "What are you planning on doing, lad?"

Court shrugged. "You know, same old thing. Find the bad guy. Kill him."

Fitzroy smiled. "You are a nutter."

"No argument there. Could you get me into your club this afternoon?"

Fitzroy drank the rest of his scotch and then laughed. "You want to beat Cassidy into a confession?"

"Of course not. I could plant some bugs. Do they sweep there?"

"Cassidy does it himself before he starts his meetings." Fitzroy added, "But his detection equipment isn't state-of-the-art. I've seen it. Any device that has a remote shut-off could be deactivated during the sweep and then reactivated to transmit a signal once Cassidy begins his meetings."

"Good," Court said.

"Not so good, actually," Fitz said, and he adopted a pained expression now. "It's just that . . . the Red Lion Club has been there for one hundred fifty years, and I'd much like to know it will be around for another one-fifty."

"Meaning?"

"Meaning . . . when Courtland Gentry walks into a building with an operational intent, often that building and its inhabitants do not fare well. Perhaps you should give the equipment to me, and I'll get it placed in the club."

Court grinned now. "Ho-ly shit. I'm running Sir Donald Fitzroy as a technical asset? I love it."

Fitzroy drained the last of his scotch. "Don't get bloody used to it, lad."

CHAPTER 41

Zoya ran her fingers over the arms of the comfortable wingback chair and picked at a loose thread, but her eyes remained locked on the door in front of her. She fought with her emotions, but this was getting harder and harder the longer she waited.

She sat in the library of Vladi Belyakov's twenty-thousand-square-foot palace just outside Aylesbury, to the west of London, and with each passing minute her trepidation only increased.

Zoya had arrived at Belyakov's Belgravia house three hours earlier and was let in, frisked, and taken to the oligarch in his study. Zoya insisted that Uncle Vladi call her father, and despite the fact that the night before last he'd told her he didn't have a clue regarding what she was talking about, now he just nodded and reached into his pocket for his phone.

He left the room for ten minutes.

After the call, Belyakov put Zoya in a car and drove with her and some security to Barclays London Heliport. They took off and headed west; he told her they were going to his country house.

Zoya assumed everything Belyakov did now was the marching orders her father had given him over the phone. It seemed to her that Belyakov continued to respond to the general like a complete subordinate.

Belyakov told her Feo Zakharov himself would fly out via his Airbus jet helicopter, but for over an hour she was kept here waiting in the library, her heart thundering in her chest the entire time, sweat on the back of her neck and her faint stress hives kept hidden only by the simple black top she wore over black jeans.

She sipped tea but wished she had something stronger, and just when she was about to call across the room to a silent Belyakov and ask for a drink, she heard a helicopter fly over the mansion.

She said nothing about the alcohol now; it was too late for it to make any difference.

. . .

David Mars unfastened his seat belt and climbed out of his helicopter. He marched towards a rear entrance of the private palace, one hundred meters away. Fox was behind him, Hines behind Fox, and three more men, well-trained elite mercenary contractors working for Mars, walked alongside the group, their short-barreled rifles with collapsible stocks hidden under their denim or leather jackets.

As he neared the house, Mars steeled himself to become the person he needed to be in order to face his daughter after fourteen years. This reunion would not be a happy one, he knew, either from her side or from his. He hoped he would find her at least somewhat open to a reconciliation, and he would love nothing more in the world than to have her by his side while he worked on his greatest operation, but he harbored no illusions of this. She was CIA, or helping them at least, and this made her his enemy, unless she could convince him otherwise.

She was half American, this he knew, and this had always bothered him. And how could it not?

David Mars had been born Feodor Ivanovich Zakharov in Minsk, then part of the Soviet Union. His parents were from Moscow, both military officers, and they returned to the capital when he was still young.

He was a smart and physically fit child, enjoyed mountain climbing, chess, and foreign languages. It was a foregone conclusion that he would follow his taciturn father, by now a colonel, into the Army. He graduated from Frunze Military Academy and entered the officers' corps of the Soviet Army. Picked for his able brain and strong body to join the GRU,

Russian military intelligence, he went to Afghanistan shortly after the war began. He interrogated prisoners and supported troops with his intelligence product, paid off goat herders for information about enemy supply lines from Pakistan, and, even though he was not a frontline infantryman, survived over a dozen attacks by Mujahidin fighters during his time there.

By the mideighties he was back in Moscow, learning deep-cover tradecraft, including but not limited to improving his English and his ability to blend into foreign environs.

He met Irene Carson, a young and beautiful language teacher from Los Angeles, and the two married after approval from GRU leadership. They had two children: Feodor and then, two years later, Zoya. After the fall of the Union his entire family was sent to embassies in London and Washington. He was, ostensibly, a military attaché, but with his skills he was able to slip out of opposition coverage of his house, almost at will, and run agents throughout whatever capital he'd been assigned to.

This he and his family did for nearly a decade.

Irene had long since changed her name to Irina, and she and their kids bolstered his cover as a mild-mannered family man, but Irina wasn't an intelligence operative herself.

No, that was Feodor Zakharov's role. Over the years, in fact, he became the GRU's best spy.

Until his next promotion sent him back to Moscow, that is. He was assigned to the Aquarium, GRU's headquarters. He made general, became a deputy to the GRU chief, and when the man retired after a year, the president of Russia himself handpicked Zakharov from a list of candidates to take the reins of Russian military intelligence.

He was young for the job, in his early forties, and he remained ensconced in this position for several years.

And then his wife Irina was run down by a truck that had been stolen from the Red October Chocolate Factory and dumped in the Moskva River after the incident. Inconsolable, he began to look for the culprit.

Evidence came out that the entire sleeper deep-penetration program that she was a trainer for had been compromised to MI6 by a leak at the Kremlin, and while the SVR could never positively conclude that Irina Zakharova had been murdered by British agents, Zakharov's own personal digging into the situation uncovered clues that the compromise at SVR was, in fact, due to a British intelligence operation. These clues sent him on a self-financed private trip to London to slip back into one of his characters using false papers.

To obtain his own private security and foot soldiers in the UK, he reached out to the Solntsevskaya Bratva, the largest of the Russian mafia groups, and he was put in touch with a brigade commander there in London. He built networks of other criminal organizations, local British groups, and transnational satellites operating in London, and soon enough he had men working for him in the Metropolitan Police Force.

He was months into his own investigation of his wife's death at the hands of the British, still living in London, when he had his target. A high-level MI6 operations officer named Wellstone. Zakharov decided to assassinate the man, on the streets of London, in the most dramatic fashion he could imagine.

The operation was under way, but Zakharov shut it down when he learned Feo Feodorovich, his twenty-one-year-old son, was in a hospital in Moscow suffering from advanced-stage leukemia.

Zakharov raced home, but Feo died that very night.

The elder Zakharov blamed the British for his son's death, although no one else knew of any evidence to support this.

Still, his lust for revenge only grew.

After the death of Feo, Feodor Zakharov went to the Kremlin and demanded the opportunity to operate against Britain personally for both the murder of his wife and their involvement in the death of his older child. He himself adopted the plan that was ultimately approved by the president. He was pleasantly surprised that the president agreed to it so easily, but the Kremlin had been looking to send a dedicated intelligence leader into the UK to organize the Bratvas there into a proxy force, to acquire intelligence on the powerful anti-Kremlin dissidents who lived there, to oversee the offshoring of Russian money through and to UK banks, and to conduct targeted killings at the behest of Moscow.

And they recognized that Zakharov was their man. They could always get another GRU chief, but there was no one else with the skill, training, and motivation to do what needed to be done on the ground in the most important foreign location for Russian interests.

Zakharov flew to Dagestan, where war raged against Shariat Jamaat; was declared dead on the battlefield after photographs were taken purporting to show his body; and spent the next two months undergoing cosmetic surgery. He grew the first beard he'd worn since fighting through the Afghan winter of 1983–84, and he darkened his hair several shades, making it almost black.

General Feodor Zakharov turned into David James Mars, a wealthy real estate mogul who'd lived most of his life in the Caribbean, which accounted for the fact that few around town knew much about him. By becoming David Mars, Feodor Zakharov himself became a sleeper, an operative who has not come to the attention of police or security forces.

He slipped into London's elite circles with few questions asked, bolstered by contacts made through front companies run by the SVR around the world, and connections in the UK purchased with Russia's billions funneled into UK banks.

He resumed working with the Solntsevskaya Bratva, whose leadership assigned him to an English-educated Vor named Artyom Primakov. Primakov had been an SVR agent and graduate of the school where Irina Zakharov taught, and he blended into London just as well as Mars.

Zakharov and Primakov, now David Mars and Roger Fox, spent the next several years working for Russian interests across the United Kingdom.

No one in the mafia other than senior leadership and Artyom Primakov knew David Mars was Russian, and neither did any but a very few at the Kremlin. Instead he went by a code name: *Chernny Volk*, Black Wolf.

The money for Mars's operations came from Vladimir Belyakov, the billionaire Russian oligarch who, despite a very public falling-out with the government in Moscow, was in truth a dedicated foot soldier for the Kremlin, a member of the Siloviki, the politically influential elite. The Kremlin eased off the Solntsevskaya Bratva while simultaneously increasing their menace of other mafia groups to further bolster the operation.

David Mars had spent the past several years operating here in London against UK interests and in furtherance of Russian interests, but he had no ties to the Kremlin at all. He was the Russian president's "fire and forget" weapon, sent to cause mayhem, set up with virtually unlimited men and money, and left to his own devices.

He was careful at first, building contacts in intelligence circles, not just in the United Kingdom but with all the Five Eyes nations, paying for dirt on IC personalities, socking it all away so he could initiate his schemes when the moment was right.

This was a time of great Russian expansion into the United Kingdom; secretive banking and property ownership laws saw to this, and London became, quite simply, the oligarch's haven of choice.

And then Zakharov's operational tempo increased when Britain began threatening to strip assets from the Russian kleptocrats who had taken up residence in and around London. The Kremlin let it be known to Mars, through a half dozen cutouts, that it was time the gloves came off.

A month later Mars had an MP killed in West Bromwich. He conducted many other assassinations, often with nerve agents, sometimes with polonium. He killed Russian dissidents on UK soil, he blackmailed bankers and lawyers to ease restrictions on and inquiries into questionable accounts full of Kremlin members' money, and he did it all with no one knowing who he was, or even that he was Russian.

His work had been fulfilling, though he felt he would never do enough damage to the English for what they'd done to his family.

He'd already been planning some sort of intelligence operation against the British at the upcoming Five Eyes conference in Scotland when he learned the news that changed everything. Four months earlier, he learned that his beloved daughter, an SVR operative who was wholly unaware he was alive for operational security purposes, had been killed by American intelligence officers during a mission in Thailand.

Mars was once again inconsolable. But as before, he channeled his rage into action. He had a new foe, a second enemy who had caused him great personal pain.

And soon he knew what he was going to do about it.

The Five Eyes conference would have the elite of all the English-speaking spy agencies in one place at one time, here in the United Kingdom, the nation where Mars and his Bratva minions had operated with impunity for the past dozen years.

He would find a way to kill them all.

He first thought of polonium, but there was no way this would not lead all investigators directly to Moscow's door. A biological attack, on the other hand, could be effectively pulled off, he decided, but only if he used deceptive measures to turn this into a false-flag operation.

He went to an old colleague from the Afghan war who now worked in biological warfare research. He told him he wanted the name of a foreigner who might be persuaded to attack the West, and the man understood exactly what Zakharov wanted.

Zakharov was at first surprised when the name he was given turned out to be that of a female North Korean doctor in Stockholm, but he was also handed access to her FSB file, which detailed both her capabilities and her stated wish to use her knowledge against the West. He learned that she was a North Korean intelligence agent, as well, and she possessed both the knowledge and the temperament to conduct the attack.

He realized by the time he closed the file that this had the potential to be a perfect symbiotic relationship. Zakharov, a warrior consumed with the desire to destroy his target, and Won, a weapon in human form, consumed with the desire to detonate.

He sent Fox to collect her, and he told her enough of his plan to move her to Scotland, where Mars convinced her that North Korea would never take the fall for what was to come.

And at the same time Mars created a paper trail, orders from North Korea, and photographic evidence of Won's movements, and this was all kept safely hidden for the day when he needed to prove to the world that this was not a Russian operation but a North Korean one.

He was just days away from commencing his attack, and all was in place, when Vladi Belyakov met with him at St. James's Park and told him Zoya was alive.

He never wavered a moment after getting this news. She was not dead, but she'd clearly switched sides, working for America, which meant working for the Five Eyes.

He'd rather she'd been killed in Thailand, died a hero, fallen to enemy fire.

He would do what he could for Zoya. He wouldn't have her killed; she was his beautiful daughter, after all. But he would also do what he had to do to keep his operation on track. She was a direct threat to it, the only real potential compromise, and if she got in his way, then this machine he had built and put into effect would not be able to stop in time to keep from running her over.

. . .

Three minutes later Zoya looked on as a bearded man with dark hair entered the room at a fast clip, his eyes wide and searching. Zoya did not recognize the man as her father, but she stood anyway, because he clearly was looking at her.

He smiled; she could see emotion on his face and in his gait, and when he was just a dozen steps away she saw his eyes.

She looked at the right side of his neck. Just above the starched collar of his dress shirt, a single stress hive was pink and splotchy, much like hers were right now, she imagined.

He stopped a few paces from her, but his body language said he wanted to come closer and embrace her. In English he said, "Zoyushka. My little girl. We have so much to discuss. Can your father give you a hug after all this time?"

Despite all her best intentions, Zoya began to cry.

CHAPTER 42

Zoya Zakharova embraced her father. She felt her knees weaken when he kissed the top of her head. But even with her emotions threatening to overtake her, she felt a perfunctory, almost reserved nature to his touch. She'd spent the last few hours anticipating this moment, and it did not hold nearly the tenderness she expected to receive from him.

Soon Zoya and her father sat in wingback chairs in front of each other. Their feet inches apart. Belyakov had removed himself from the room silently, and Zoya wiped her damp eyes, waiting for her father to speak first.

In his faultless British accent, the man calling himself David Mars said, "I am sure you must have a lot of questions for me. Where shall we begin, my darling?"

She wiped her nose. "We'll begin with this question." She switched into Russian. "Do you even speak Russian anymore, Papa, or do you love this cover of yours so much you've forgotten your language?"

Zakharov switched effortlessly into his native tongue. "Of course I do. I am a proud Russian, and that will never change. How about you? You always were more Western than I."

He smiled at her, but even though she hadn't seen her father since she was in her teens, she could still sense a coolness from him that she hadn't expected or prepared herself for.

She next asked the question she'd come all this way to find out. "What happened to Feo? The cancer."

Zakharov nodded solemnly and leaned closer. "You might have heard rumors. I tried to keep it all from you. It was polonium. The Brits had the isotope ready to use in an assassination in Russia. An assassination of me. They wanted to punish the general directing the GRU for our assassination of the GRU defector with polonium the year before in London."

This seemed like madness to her. "How do you know it was the British?"

"I saw the files from SVR and FSB. I am sorry I did not tell you at the funeral."

"You mean *after* the funeral. You had the funeral without me."

"Yes, of course. It was a difficult time, Zoyushka; I did what I was ordered to do, and I did what I thought was best for my young daughter."

Zoya nodded and looked at the parquet floor until her father spoke to her again.

"The British killed your mother, as well, you know."

This she had been told, but she never really knew whether to believe it. She knew her mother had been working with illegals, grooming them to live in England, so she knew it was a possibility, but she never saw any of the evidence herself, and she remained dubious.

Zoya's father said, "After Irina died, after Feodor died, something within me died, as well. I wanted to destroy them, and I was willing to say good-bye to you to do it."

She looked back up to him. "Forever?"

"*Nyet*. I knew there would be a day I would return to my life . . . some life. I would reach out for you again. I have been following you in your career at SVR. That is . . . until *you* 'died' on a boat off the coast of Thailand. When that happened, when the last of my family was killed by Western intelligence, then I decided there was no reason for me to use any half measures. I had to destroy the West. Grandiose, yes, I am just a humble operative trying to effect outcomes, but that is my goal."

Zoya looked down again at the design in the parquet.

"I'm not dead, Papa."

"Flipping to the Americans is worse than a valiant death in the field. You'd be better off gone forever."

Zoya said, "I am still your daughter."

"I know you are. The Americans broke my heart when I heard they killed you, and now you have broken my heart by your actions. I know you were held by the Americans in Virginia, which means I know you were giving them information. You were turned in Thailand?"

Zoya weighed the question a moment. Finally, she said, "I went to them out of necessity."

Zakharov stiffened at this. "What does that mean?"

"I was recalled to Moscow, but I didn't go. I went off mission, and for this an SVR operative tried to kill me. I couldn't go back after that. I would have been killed or imprisoned. I had to run."

The sixty-two-year-old Russian switched into English. "But you didn't have to run to the bloody Americans!"

She shrugged. "Our objectives coincided. They won't always, but they did during that operation."

"I'm sure they sucked every bit of intelligence value out of you in the past four months."

"I haven't hurt my nation with anything I said. I told them about corruption in the Kremlin, in the SVR, things that would only help Russia if they came to light."

Zakharov shook his head. "That's insane. You aren't helping your nation by talking to the West."

"Who do *you* work for?"

Zakharov pumped out his chest. "The *Rodina*." *The motherland.*

Zoya furrowed her brow. "You mean the Kremlin."

"No."

"So what you are doing doesn't have the backing of your government?"

"*My* government? Listen to yourself. Aren't you Russian, too?"

Zoya didn't answer. She said, "What insanity are you involved in here? What is your connection with the Russian mafia and the other organized crime groups in London?"

Zakharov seemed surprised by the question. "Who's been talking to you about such nonsense? Why were you sent?"

"No one sent me. I am here on my own. I snuck away as my safe house was attacked the other night."

Zakharov did not respond to this.

"Do you have any idea who tried to kill me?"

This time Zakharov did reply, in an apologetic tone. "It was me, I'm afraid. Only because I didn't know it was you. You were just some un-known compromise that needed to be eliminated." He added, "I am very glad you survived."

She delivered a cold smile. "How very kind of you, Papa."

"Now, we need to discuss last night. You stole something, I am told, and a cohort of yours killed several men who worked for me."

"In fairness, Papa, I killed one or two of them, too."

"But of course you did. What were you doing in Terry Cassidy's office?"

"I went there to find you. I didn't find you, you found me."

"Something was taken out of his vault."

"I took nothing."

Zakharov shot a hand out; it wrapped around his daughter's neck, and then he pulled her closer. It was fast and threatening, but his touch was not violent. He reached out and unzipped his daughter's jacket, no more than six inches, and then he moved the top of her shirt down a few inches more, until the start of her cleavage.

She said, "What the fuck are you doing?" in English, but she did not pull away or fight him off.

Zakharov looked at his daughter's skin. "Ah, the stress hives." He let go of her now, and she sat back up, putting hair that had fallen into her face behind her ear. He said, "You know, nearly forty years in the intelligence field and I'd never been compromised by my skin condition by anyone but my own daughter."

She said nothing.

"And now I see yours. You are lying. The CIA sent you in to retrieve a computer file from Cassidy's safe. A file he was quite stupidly holding on to." Zakharov smiled. "An indiscretion like that can get a man in Cassidy's position, a man with Cassidy's bedfellows, in a great deal of trouble."

Zoya said, "You're right. I have Terry Cassidy's client list. Uncle Vladi is on it, as well as some very bad men. Offshore account information, a lot of money coming through."

Feodor Zakharov stared his daughter down. "Things are not always as they appear."

Zoya had strengthened in front of her father during the conversation. She sat up straighter. "Or maybe they are exactly as they appear. You came to London under cover to work against the British. Vladi was sent over, too, propped up with oil wealth from the state to fund your operations. You joined up with the goons in the Solntsevskaya Bratva to give you foot soldiers for your ops. Vladi used Terry Cassidy as his money launderer and you used Terry Cassidy as some sort of a middleman to help you acquire non-Russian goons to help you recover a man detained by the CIA."

Zakharov's face reddened. "This is all the theory of your friends in the CIA?"

"I'm here on my own, Papa. I told you. I heard about the attack at Ternhill, I know Cassidy was the man who helped set it up, and I know Belyakov works with him. That indicates to me that you were involved in the attack, and involved with the leak out of the CIA."

"And you have come to plug the CIA's leak. Is that it?"

"I came to find out about you, about Feodor, about Mother. That is all."

Zakharov stood, looming over her. A door opened suddenly and four men entered. Among them was the man who called himself Fox that she'd run into in London the previous night. They'd obviously been just outside, and listening in on the conversation.

Fox said, "Sir . . . it's time."

The older Russian smiled at his daughter. "I am going to need to keep you close to me, Zoya. Just for the next few days. After that you are free to choose. You can stay with me here, or you can return to Russia." He sighed. "You won't be returning to America, not as long as I have blood pumping through my veins."

The men moved closer around her. Unlike the day before in Terry Cassidy's office, however, she made no move to resist.

"What happens in a few days?"

Zakharov only smiled and said, "You will be kept comfortable at all times."

"You are kidnapping your own daughter?"

"I am kidnapping a CIA agent with malicious intent. If that person also happens to be my daughter, then yes, I am kidnapping my daughter. I was sent here to make the hard decisions. I pride myself on my utter mission focus at all times."

He put his hand on her shoulder. It was a gentle touch, but his eyes and his words conveyed a different attitude.

"So, my darling, do not test me."

Zoya felt like a child being admonished. Meekly she asked again, "What is this all about?"

"It's about your mother, your brother, and you. It's about the Five Eyes attacking me . . . personally. And now, my dear, it's about my personal retribution."

"So this operation has no sanction," she said.

Zakharov pulled his shoulders back. "*I* have sanction!" he shouted. "*That's* all that matters. Moscow will benefit, but I take orders from no one."

Zoya couldn't believe it. He was insane. "You're off reservation. A rogue agent."

Zakharov gave his daughter a look of disappointment. "You've met Mr. Fox here. He studied under your mother in Moscow. Very much a Russian, he has infiltrated the fabric of life here in the United Kingdom. He is one of a dozen sleepers still active, after all these years, many working within Scotland Yard, the intelligence services, even at Whitehall."

Fox said, "Your mother was a remarkable woman. Of all my trainers, no one did more to give me the tools to remain alive and operational over here for all these years."

Zakharov said, "He will oversee your care, because I have much to do, both back in London and at our destination. I will see you again very soon, Zoya. We will talk more then about what it is you want out of this life of yours."

"Where is he taking me?"

"Not far, in the scheme of things. You'll see." And with that he turned and walked out of the room. Zoya wanted to call out to him, but she couldn't make a sound.

She didn't know what she'd expected, but what she had just learned was almost too much to process. Whatever he was doing, whatever his plan, it was obviously more important to him than she was.

Fox led Zoya and the men holding on to her arms out the door and back towards the waiting helicopter. As she was getting strapped in, she saw her father's big black helo lifting off from the perfect lawn a hundred meters away, turning on its axis, and then dipping its nose towards London. It disappeared over Vladimir Belyakov's mansion moments later.

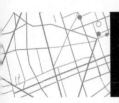

CHAPTER 43

The benefit to Court Gentry of having Sir Donald Fitzroy working for him as a technical asset, even if it was just for a few hours, was that Fitzroy could produce virtually any piece of gear he wanted simply by pulling it out of a drawer somewhere in his home. The man had collected more than a half century's worth of the tools of spycraft, and much of it was still modern enough to employ effectively. Fitz selected a pair of tiny listening devices, both with encrypted wireless connection and remote power switches, and while Court could tell they relied on fifteen-year-old technology, he could also see they'd been well kept and therefore remained good enough for his purposes.

This was all the gear Fitzroy needed to go to his club in Westminster shortly before three p.m., enter the quiet room off the main hall where Cassidy liked to do business, and position the bugs for maximum effect. He hid one on the top of a curio cabinet and out of view and taped the other to the bottom of the table in the center of the small room, on the side where Fitzroy had seen Cassidy sitting when Fitzroy would glance in passing by the open door from time to time.

He left the equipment on the "off" setting, then headed into the men's lounge to order a brandy and read the paper in an overstuffed leather chair.

Terry Cassidy showed up alone just fifteen minutes later and came into the lounge holding his briefcase to say hello to some acquaintances. Fitzroy barely knew the younger man, so he looked at his paper, opened and closed the three remaining fingers on his right hand to combat the phantom pains he felt from the two missing ones, and waited patiently. Soon Cassidy had mingled sufficiently, so he slipped back out into the hall. Fitzroy followed him out with his eyes and saw the forty-something heading towards his usual room, pulling a small transistor-radio-looking device from his case as he walked.

Fitzroy recognized it as a store-bought bug detector, and he breathed a sigh of relief that the solicitor had not upgraded his tech since the last time Fitzroy noticed it.

Cassidy would sweep the room slowly, the walls, furniture, the phone, but the detector wouldn't pick up the equipment that was currently turned off and not signaling or even emitting any electrical current.

Sir Donald headed out the front door, walked across the street, and climbed into his Mercedes. Court Gentry was behind the wheel, dressed as Fitzroy's normal chauffeur, but in his lap he held a micro notebook computer and in his ears he had Bluetooth earpieces ready to receive from the recording devices as soon as they were turned on.

Fitzroy climbed into the back, diagonal from Court, and he said, "They are both placed. He is probably just finishing up sweeping for bugs now."

Court said, "He entered the club alone. Is there anyone in the room with him?"

"Not at present."

Court said, "We'll wait a bit."

"Fine by me. I'm a pensioner, you know. I've no place to be."

Court reached into his pocket and pulled out several over-the-counter pain pills. He took them with a swig of sparkling water.

Fitzroy saw this. "How do you feel?"

"Like I look."

"Good lord."

Court smiled. "I feel like I lost a fight with a steamroller."

The older man in back said, "Most blokes know better than to get into a fight with a steamroller."

Court sipped more water. "This bloke believed his hype for a minute and thought he could take down a monster."

To this Fitzroy laughed. "You'll get him next time, lad, and your hype will continue to grow."

Court didn't want there to be a next time with the big ape, and he certainly didn't want his hype to grow.

He closed his eyes and tried to ignore the pain he was in.

. . .

David Mars was on his way to London, sitting in the back of his helo, when his phone vibrated in his pocket. He patched it through his headset, stopping any intercom transmissions so the pilots couldn't hear his conversation.

"David Mars."

The voice was soft. Unsure. "It's Barnacle."

Mars had been expecting this call. It had been the biggest item on his plate today, until he got the call this morning about his daughter showing up at Belyakov's house requesting to see him.

"I thought I might be hearing from you," he said.

"Did you do it?"

Mars smiled a little. "And by 'it' you mean—"

Now Barnacle all but yelled into the phone. "You know *exactly* what I mean! Did you have Lucas Renfro killed?"

A slight pause. "The Agency was getting too close to our prized possession, you, and we couldn't let them swoop in and prevent you from leaving the country. This will lower the heat in the kettle until you arrive here." He added, "I told you I'd keep you safe."

"Jesus Christ, Mr. Black. You can't just *kill* a deputy director of the CIA."

"Apparently, you can. It's already on the news, man. They say it was an obvious suicide."

"Yeah, well, I hope your assassin was fucking perfect, because I heard Matt Hanley was first on the scene."

"Matthew Hanley, you say?" Mars's supreme confidence remained unfazed by the news that the deputy director of Operations was investigating the case personally. "He'll be pleased they got their leak sorted, and he'll be on his way over to the UK, ready to put this all behind them. He'll believe the suicide story, and he'll not suspect you for a moment."

"I don't want to go to Scotland, now. Too risky. I want you to pick me up in London."

Mars paused a moment. "I very much could use you inside at the Five

Eyes conference. You might hear a thing or two that could earn you a lot of money from me."

"At this point, sir, fuck your money. You told me you had a dacha waiting for me in Russia, and I have enough Bitcoin to cash in and live comfortably. Sure as shit beats living out my days in a supermax prison here in the States."

Mars breathed slowly into the phone for several seconds. "Fair enough, Barnacle. We'll come up with a plan to sneak you away as soon as you arrive in the UK."

. . .

A man sitting alone at a picnic table in a park in McLean, Virginia, heaved his chest and blew out a long sigh of relief, right into the phone he held to his ear. But his relaxation was exasperatingly short-lived, because CIA's assistant deputy director of Support noticed a big black GMC Suburban pulling into a parking space on the far side of a baseball diamond.

He thought the vehicle looked like the exact same one that had tailed him through the streets of D.C., and fresh panic welled inside him.

The door opened and the big blond-haired man in aviators who'd sat across from him at Whole Foods climbed out, stood there, and crossed his arms as he looked on. Marty Wheeler sucked in a terrified gasp. "That's great, Mr. Black, because the same goon who tailed me yesterday is standing next to his truck watching me from about fifty yards away. I don't know if I will even make it to England."

Mars's aristocratic British voice always remained cool. "You'll make it, lad. Means nothing. Renfro's been dead less than eight hours. It takes time to stand down a counterintelligence operation. You'll be on your jet over here soon, right? You won't see the watchers on you for much longer."

"I hope you're right."

"You have a plane to catch, mate. We'll see you once you get to London. I'll have a taxi pick you up, one of ours, with a driver who knows what he's doing. He'll take you to the Peruvian embassy; I have an arrangement with them that they'll shelter people before I get them out of the country."

"You do this sort of thing a lot, do you?"

"Only when required. Just relax, do what you do, the same way you always do it, and everything will be fine. In forty-eight hours you'll be at that dacha we bought for you in Ekaterinburg, and living an easy life."

"Don't try to sell me bullshit, Black. It won't be an easy life."

"It definitely *won't* be if you don't find a way to modulate your tone before the two of us finally meet face-to-face tomorrow."

Wheeler closed his eyes. He needed Mars now. Everything that had led up to today had resulted in this mysterious Englishman being his only lifeline. "I'm sorry, sir."

"Don't trouble yourself. You'll be fine when you get here."

Wheeler hung up, eyed the big man in the aviators again, then stood to head back to his car. It was farther up the lot from the man surveilling him, so he didn't have to walk by him, but still he gave the man an extra-wide berth.

Soon he was in his Nissan and heading towards Ronald Reagan to board a commercial flight to London.

· · ·

Court Gentry and Donald Fitzroy sat patiently in the Mercedes, eyeing the Red Lion Club across the street. They were giving Cassidy enough time to scan the room for bugs and to settle in before flipping on the transmitters.

Soon the Englishman broke the silence. "Let's say Cassidy says something that implicates him in whatever's going on. What are you going to do?"

"Whether or not he says anything, when he leaves here I'm going to grab him by his collar, put a gun in his ribs, take him to a basement somewhere. Then I will start cutting pieces off him till he tells me what I need to know." He turned back to Fitzroy. "I'll wait for him to leave your club. I won't burn the place to the ground."

"I do greatly appreciate your discretion."

Court nodded to his friend and former employer. "Thanks for all this."

"For nothing, lad. Anytime. But allow an old man to offer some advice."

"What's that?"

"You know . . . you *know* you can't do this sort of thing forever, don't you?"

Court touched his still-painful jaw with his fingertips, then looked down to the laptop with the listening software on it. "Depends on your definition of forever. I wake up every morning wondering if today is the day that forever runs out for me. But this is all I know, and I'm pretty good at it, so—"

Fitzroy leaned forward, between the seats. "Let some other poor sod get good at it! You need to get *out* of it! You'll die on this bloody job, and you are smart enough to realize that."

It occurred to Court that Sir Donald had never talked like this back when he was making a commission on Court's operations. But he still felt the old man had genuine affection for him, so he didn't judge. "Yeah, no question I'll die on this job. But there's always some new asshole that needs dealing with, and I have a hard time turning away from that."

Fitzroy nodded. "Well . . . if I can't convince you to stop, perhaps I can remind you to keep your head down."

Court said, "That I can do." He put his fingers on the buttons of the micro notebook. "Okay, let's listen in on this asshole."

Court flipped the transmitter on, but as soon as he looked back up he saw a pair of black Range Rovers pulling up in front of the Red Lion Club. Court's eyebrows furrowed as a three-man security team exited the chase vehicle, and a single young, fit man climbed out of the front passenger seat of the first Rover and opened the back door.

A man in his sixties exited the vehicle; he was heavy with a mostly bald head and an expensive-looking suit. He headed up the steps and through the front door of the Red Lion Club with three of his body men staying close to him the entire time.

Court said, "Is that bald-headed dude a member?"

"No," Fitzroy said. "But I recognize him. That 'bald-headed dude,' as you put it, is on the list you showed me."

"The list of Russians? I thought you said your club didn't let Russian gangsters in."

"Yes, well, this bloke isn't a gangster. That's Vladimir Belyakov, the oligarch. Owns a football club, department stores; hell, he owns as much land as the queen."

Court looked back over his shoulder in astonishment. "Really?"

Fitzroy snickered. "An exaggeration, lad. The point is, he's got the money to walk in any door in this dirty city he wants to walk in. He's not a member of the Red Lion, but I've seen him there a time or two."

Court reached down and turned the volume up on the receiver app on the laptop. Almost immediately he and Fitzroy, who had his own Bluetooth earpiece in, listened to the squeak of a heavy door straining on its hinges, then the sound of the door shutting.

"The room's been swept?" a Russian-accented voice asked.

The response came in British-accented English. "Just did it. Let me pour you some tea."

"I don't want tea. I want to know what happened."

"Dead bodies all over my office. *That's* what happened. The police are swarmin' the bloody place now."

"What might they find as they look around, Terry?"

"My safe was broken into."

"Your safe? What would someone possibly be looking for in your safe?"

Court detected a tone from the Russian that indicated he was aware of more than he was letting on.

Cassidy hesitated. "After I got the call about the gunfight from building security, I managed to get in and take out all the incriminating evidence left behind before the cops arrived."

"All the evidence *left behind*. You are saying there was something missing."

"Yes," Cassidy said, after a moment's delay. "The computer with the client data. It was well protected, but the bloody thing is gone. It's got your name in there, Vladi."

Even through the audio Court could tell that Belyakov already had this information. He seemed completely unfazed when he said, "That is extremely unfortunate for you, because I was a good client, whom you have now forever lost."

Cassidy said, "Wait. I just—"

Belyakov kept talking. "Still, I'm not worried about myself. What does the information prove? That I have offshores? People would think me mad if I didn't, and I can move the money from my foreign banks into new accounts by the end of the day, certainly before anyone can access them and clean me out. So don't worry about me, Terry. I'm not your biggest problem.

"Your *biggest* problem, however, is the other names on the list. I know who some of your other clients are, and they are the types who express their displeasure . . . harshly."

Cassidy did not respond to this. Court imagined the man squirming as he thought about the names from the Russian mob tied to account numbers, all information now in the hands of the CIA.

Belyakov said, "The Bratva will come for you, Terry. You *must* know this."

Apparently, he did not, because he said, "Don't be ridiculous. I am just a solicitor. A middleman. I was robbed, not my bleedin' fault. I just need to get the iPad back and then that will put everything right."

Belyakov laughed loudly over the microphones hidden in the room. "If you didn't keep that file as a security blanket you wouldn't be in this fix, and you wouldn't have the Bratva after you."

"Look," Cassidy said. "You could reach out to your . . . *our* . . . friend."

"For what purpose?"

"He has influence over the Bratva. He can calm them down. And if he can't, he has all the protection I need. You know he could get a dozen guns around me in an hour. The real deal. He has connections in Moscow. Hell, he could probably get Spetsnaz over here to help me."

In the Mercedes outside, Court cocked his head. Behind him, Fitzroy spoke softly. "The mastermind."

Court nodded. *"Cherny Volk."* The Black Wolf.

Belyakov said, "Terry, it will surprise you to learn this, but the person who stole the client list from you last night was none other than our friend's daughter."

In the Mercedes, Court looked up, out the window towards the Red Lion Club. *"What?"* he whispered in amazement.

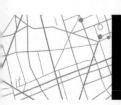

CHAPTER 44

Back inside the tony members-only club, Terry Cassidy said, "*What?* He has a daughter?"

"*Da*, and she's CIA."

The solicitor gasped.

Belyakov added, "I just found out about it myself. *He* just found out she's alive and working with the Agency. I don't understand it all, but I know she is a danger to his work, and to my livelihood."

"Bloody hell," Cassidy said.

"He met with her an hour ago, and now he's holding her prisoner. He recovered the iPad, but there is no way of knowing if the information has already gotten out to CIA. We have to assume it has."

"What are we going to do?"

"You, Terry, are going to do nothing but take a vacation. Somewhere far away. Get lost, it's your only chance to stay alive." Belyakov's voice lowered. "I am Russian. I know what the Bratvas are capable of. You do not want to be here when they decide they are angry with you. There are no half measures in their revenge."

"Yes. Yes, of course, Vladi. You are right. I'll leave today."

"No, you'll leave *now*. Let's exit the club together; I have a security detail outside. You'll ride with us; we'll get you back to your flat, but then you are on your own."

. . .

Court Gentry was a flurry of movement in the driver's seat of the limo. As Fitzroy watched from his seat behind, he saw his former contract assassin take off his chauffeur's cap, pull a Glock pistol from his hip, and then quickly grab a long, black suppressor from a bag next to him and spin it on the threaded barrel.

"Whatever you're planning, lad, I think you need to—"

Court finished screwing on the barrel. "You still know how to drive?"

"Of course I do."

"When I get out, you will get behind the wheel. I want you to floor it in twenty seconds, just race across the street and pick me up right in front of those two Range Rovers. Keep your head down."

"No, Court. We can get to Cassidy at his house, where he doesn't have a gang of Russian bodyguards standing around next to—"

"I'm not going after Cassidy. I'm going after Belyakov."

Court pulled a black mask out of his pack and put it on top of his head like a cap. He did not pull it down over his face, but he readied it to do so.

"Not with six men protecting him, you aren't," Fitzroy pleaded.

"Fuck that, Fitz. Did you hear him? Zoya's dad is the Black Wolf, and he grabbed her. He's a deep-cover asset, former head of GRU. He sounds like a scheming prick, dangerous to Zoya and dangerous to the U.S., and I bet that rich prick who's about to come through those doors can lead me to him."

Court did a press check to make sure his weapon had a round in the chamber, pulling back the slide and touching the casing itself, then dropped the magazine to ensure that it was fully loaded before snapping it back in and holding his gun in his lap.

"Lad." Fitzroy spoke slowly and softly from the back. "I haven't been in anything like this in thirty years. Not sure I'll do you much good."

"If you can turn the steering wheel and punch the gas, you'll do fine."

Court then reached for the door latch, taking a slow settling breath as he did so.

Terry Cassidy and Vladimir Belyakov walked out the front door of the club and descended the steps to the sidewalk. Belyakov motioned for his bodyguards to move on to the Range Rovers while he slowed with Cassidy, taking a moment to speak with the younger Englishman alone. Court observed it all from across the street, where he quietly opened the car door and climbed out, his weapon shielded behind his right leg. He stood on the sidewalk, not forty feet away, watching the two men behind the crowd of security. He started to cross the street, pulled the mask down over his face, and prepared to lift the pistol and shout out in Russian that any one of the four guards or two drivers who drew on him would catch a bullet between their eyes if they moved, but a white cargo van raced by in front of him, causing him to leap back to avoid getting run down.

The van slammed on its brakes, the tires squealed, and Court immediately heard the sound of what seemed to be at least three AK-47s firing fully automatic.

Court yelled to Fitzroy, just now climbing out of the back of the black Mercedes to get behind the wheel.

"Stay low!"

Court began running across the street, shielded by the white van. In just seconds he was at the driver's-side window on the right, and he could see two men in the front of the vehicle. The front passenger fired through his window, directly into Terry Cassidy, who went down in a hail of bullets and smoke, but Belyakov's security men poured from the two vehicles, guns up and out, and they began returning fire.

Court had concealment from the van but little cover; Belyakov's men's pistols could tear through the vehicle's skin with ease and hit him while returning fire at the van.

But Court did not fire on them. Belyakov was on the sidewalk, and if there was a chance the oligarch hadn't yet been shot, Court sure as hell wasn't going to shoot him and lose his one link to Zoya.

Instead Court knew he had to end this gun battle as fast as possible. He put the muzzle of the Glock against the driver's-side window, the driver spun towards the movement, and Court shot him dead between the eyes. A second round went into the back of the neck of the front-seat passenger, and then Court moved around the front of the van, his trigger finger pressing and pressing and the silenced pistol snapping and snapping in his hand. He poured rounds through the windshield at the two men with AKs seated in the back and firing up onto the sidewalk out the side door. He moved backwards in the street as he fired, desperately trying to back away from the ripe target the van made for Belyakov's bodyguards, and hoping against hope that Belyakov's men who were still alive would realize he was helping them engage these targets.

He fired a total of fourteen rounds in the middle of the street into the van before he stopped to check for any remaining threats. Seeing no movement through the spiderwebbed and broken windshield, he pulled a fresh magazine from his waistband, dropped the partially depleted mag onto the street, and hammered the new one up and into place.

The van smoked and hissed, but no more gunfire came from it.

Court spun his reloaded weapon towards the sidewalk now. He couldn't see past the two shot-up Range Rovers, so he moved between them, pistol high, and through his ringing ears he heard screaming, shouting, crying, all from terrified civilians nearby. And he heard sirens approaching from multiple directions.

He came out from between the SUVs and saw Belyakov clearly alive and Cassidy clearly dead. The Russian was on his hands and knees, looking around in a state of shock, and the British solicitor was sprawled on his back in a growing pool of blood, eyes wide and vacant.

Around the sidewalk side of the Rovers, he saw four of the six of Belyakov's detail on the ground, and the other two slumped dead behind the wheels of the Rovers. Two men on the sidewalk looked like they'd died shielding their protectee, their bodies close together in front of where he now knelt, and the other two were sprawled out on the sidewalk behind the two Rovers, one alive, one dead.

The one guard still living looked to Court like he might have some fight left in him. He lay on his side and bled heavily from his stomach, but he still struggled to move closer to the Russian oligarch.

A rifle fell onto the street outside the van on Court's left, and then a wounded attacker stumbled out; he fell to the street, as well, then pushed himself up to his hands and knees and reached for the AK. Just as he wrapped his hand on the sling to drag it closer to him, Court spun to him, calmly lined his pistol up on the front of the man's head, and fired a single round into his brainpan.

The man dropped flat on top of the weapon. Court shot him once more to be sure.

The sounds of sirens grew louder.

Court rushed over to Belyakov, who by now had rolled into a sitting position. He didn't seem to be hurt, but the surviving bodyguard next to him had been gut-shot, and Court could see intestines between his fingers as the wounded man tried to hold them in. Though horrifically injured, the man saw Court and started to lift his pistol up, but Court just reached down and pulled it away from him. He knelt over the wounded man. "I'm taking your protectee, but I'm not with these killers, and you have bigger problems than losing your job right now."

The man spoke with a weak voice. "Med kit. Back of both Rovers."

Court pulled Belyakov to his feet, yanked him out into the street, and threw him into the Mercedes as soon as Fitzroy pulled up. He then opened the rear of the lead Range Rover, pulled out a red backpack with a white cross on it, and threw it to the man on the sidewalk. Court doubted he'd be able to do much for himself, but at least he'd die with some purpose.

Court climbed in after Belyakov and Fitzroy began driving off.

After just a few seconds Court leaned up between the front seats. "Fitz! We aren't going to church! Step on it!"

The older man accelerated, but not much. Court just rolled his eyes and returned his attention to the dazed Russian next to him.

. . .

Sir Donald Fitzroy followed Court's directions back to his safe house in West Kensington, dropped him off, and then, following his former contract employee's wishes, drove off through the rainy afternoon and tried to forget everything that had just happened. He'd get rid of the Mercedes, he'd stay inside his flat for the next week or more, and he'd have his daughter-in-law and grandkids come and keep him company.

This had definitely been a first for the old man. He'd been in hundreds of operations in his lifetime, but being the wheel man during a shootout on a street in Mayfair was a new experience, and one he had no desire to repeat in any fashion.

. . .

Court manhandled Belyakov down the stairs to the basement flat, held him there while he unlocked the door, then pushed him into the house and down onto a kitchen chair. He ripped the cord of a floor fan out of the wall, cut it off where it went into the fan body, and used this to lash the Russian's hands behind him and through the slats of the chairback. The sixty-five-year-old was still in a state of disbelief, looking around him in confusion even now, twenty-five minutes after the shooting stopped.

Court drew a large kitchen knife out of a drawer, then held it as he dragged the chair with a terrified and compliant Russian billionaire in it across the kitchen area and into the small living room. He positioned him in front of the sofa and Court sat down in front of the man, wincing with pain as he did so.

He had suffered no injuries in the shootout, but the effects of yesterday's one-sided fistfight would remain with him for quite some time.

Holding the knife down between his own knees, he leaned close to the heavy Russian. "Okay, boss, I need you to pay attention here, so I can lay down the ground rules. You with me?"

"*Da* . . . yes. Who are you?"

"First rule. I ask the questions."

A slight nod from Belyakov, and then he looked towards the front door.

Court shook his head. "Nobody's coming for you, except to retrieve your body when the smell gives it away."

Belyakov's eyes snapped back to Court. "I can make you a very rich—"

Court cut him off. "Asshole, you know how many dead bodies have said that to me ten seconds before they became dead bodies?"

The Russian had no response to this other than a look of dread.

"Now," Court continued, "as things stand, you are dead. I have no intention of letting you walk out of here with your life."

"What have I done to you?"

"I'm a psychopathic killer, Vlad. I don't need a reason to stick this knife in your neck. I am, however, open to negotiation. I only need a little information from you and, if you give it to me, I won't kill you. If you delay in giving it to me, then I'll hurt you." Court leaned forward. "You *do* believe I am capable of hurting you, do you not?"

Belyakov nodded slightly. "I saw what you did back there. I know you are capable of anything."

"Good. Now. First question. Where is Zoya?"

"Who?" Belyakov asked, giving a reasonable performance.

"And we started off so well," Court said. He lifted the knife, slid it up the inner thigh of the horrified man, and placed it with the tip on Belyakov's genitals. "Here's where the hurting will start."

"*Nyet!* Please!"

"Zakharov's daughter. You told Cassidy he took her. *Where* did he take her?"

Belyakov's eyes remained locked on the steel blade between his legs. "I . . . I don't know what he's doing. Where he's gone. He doesn't tell me things."

"You might be filthy rich, but that lie just cost you one of your most prized jewels."

Court made as to thrust the blade into Belyakov, but the Russian screamed. "*Nyet!* No! No! Okay!"

The knife was retracted a few inches. "You have five seconds."

"Look, sir. Whoever you are working for, I can, I can buy you off that job and—"

Court pushed the knife forward, into the crotch of Belyakov's trousers, and then he made a quick cut through the fabric. Belyakov's manhood, covered by black silk boxers, fell out of the hole. He'd not been cut, and neither had his boxers, but now he was even more exposed to the knife.

Court looked down, then back up at Belyakov. "I *really* don't wanna see your junk, dude. I don't wanna cut it off, either. That's nasty for a bunch of reasons. Just tell me where Zakharov is, and you spare us both a really lousy afternoon."

"I don't know where he is, I swear it."

Court sighed, then shrugged. "Here we go." The knife tip pressed against Belyakov's balls.

"But I know who he's with!"

Again, the knife was retracted a few inches. "Who?"

"Artyom Primakov."

"Means nothing to me."

"Goes by the name Roger Fox. He looks and talks like a proper Englishman, but he's from the Bratva. He's a Vor. He and Feo are working together. Outside London right now, I do know that much."

"That's not going to help me—"

"Two hours ago Fox called me and told me one of his helicopters is grounded for repairs. He asked to use one of mine based in London at Battersea Heliport. I am sure they are in the air by now, but I can give you the tail number. Maybe you can find it."

Court just looked at him with eyes filled with malevolence. This wasn't enough.

Belyakov recognized this, then said, "I can contact someone, find out where the helicopter is now. It's run by a corporation in Wales; they'll be able to track it."

Court nodded slowly. "That would be nice, Vlad. I appreciate it. You just bought your nutsack another ten seconds. Now, who were those gunmen back there at the club? Why did they try to kill you?"

"They were Solntsevskaya assassins. They weren't there to kill me. I haven't crossed the Bratva. They were there to kill Cassidy for losing a list with their names and account information on it. But those gunmen are just poorly trained animals; they would have killed everything on that street to get to Cassidy."

Court said, "Zakharov . . . is he the mastermind?"

"What? What does that mean?"

"He's working with London organized crime to promote Kremlin interests?"

Belyakov's face gave nothing away. "That's absurd. Where did you hear—"

"*Cherny Volk*. Is Feodor Zakharov the Black Wolf?"

Belyakov gazed down again at the knife, a look of utter defeat on his face. Eventually he said, "*Da*."

Court responded with, "I need to know what he looks like now."

Belyakov shook his head. "He doesn't allow himself to be photographed. You'll find him in person before you find a picture of him."

This wasn't what Court wanted to hear, but still he untied Belyakov's hands and handed him a burner phone. He ordered the Russian to find the location of the loaned-out helicopter. It took him less than ten minutes to do so. Immediately Court retied the bindings.

"It flew to Edinburgh. Just arrived."

"Why would Zakharov be going to Scotland?"

"I . . . I have no idea. He owns businesses . . . Perhaps he—"

"Under what name?"

"Name?"

"He doesn't walk around doing business in London calling himself General Feodor Zakharov. What's his alias?"

Belyakov looked even more defeated now. "I . . . I don't know." He didn't even try to sell this lie to the man with the knife.

"Bullshit. Sorry, Ivan, after all that info, you're *still* gonna lose a nut." The knife went down between the Russian's legs; Court pulled the tip of the blade up and slit the boxers wide open. He pressed in farther, then flicked the tip of the blade up an inch.

Belyakov screamed.

Court didn't think he'd done much more than break the skin with the knife, but he also didn't want to look at the man's exposed balls to check.

Belyakov was totally his now. The man shouted, "Mars! David Mars!"

"David Mars," Court repeated. His name was on the list from Cassidy's vault. He asked, "And what is he planning, Vlad?"

"I truly do not know." Court thought that was all he was going to get out of the man, but slowly the terrified prisoner looked up, locking eyes with him. "But whatever it is, it does *not* have Moscow sanction."

"How do you know that?"

"He doesn't get orders from Moscow. He runs anti-Western operations here, keeps things deniable for the boys at the Kremlin. But . . ."

Court cocked his head. "But *what*?"

"But he changed when he thought his daughter had been killed. I know he is planning some sort of retributive strike against the West. His wife, son, and daughter all were killed by England or the U.S. When his daughter showed up I thought he might just call off his plan, but he's bent. The wheels were already in motion, plus he sees his daughter defecting to the Americans to be much worse than death."

Retributive strike. Court said it to himself. *In Scotland.*

Court pulled out his phone. "Your lucky day, Belyakov. You get to keep your life and both your *huevos*."

He left the room as he dialed Brewer's number.

CHAPTER 45

The Bombardier Global 7000 was the largest executive jet in the world; this particular model, owned by the CIA, had seating for twenty, and at present there were fifteen on the aircraft in addition to a crew of four.

Most of the passengers were clustered in captain's chairs and sofas near the front, but Director Fred Capshaw sat alone in one of two small offices in the back of the plane, looking out the window at the Atlantic Ocean forty thousand feet below him.

Matt Hanley appeared in front of the director, Capshaw motioned to the chair opposite him, and the deputy director of Operations took a seat in the tiny room.

Hanley said, "You wanted to talk?"

Capshaw was from Kentucky, and had an accent to match. "I do." Now the older man looked out the window a moment more, seemingly collecting his thoughts. "It was just months ago when your predecessor sat in front of me and I gave him a version of the talk I'm about to give you. As you know, within a couple of weeks, you had replaced him."

"Am I being replaced, sir?"

Capshaw moved around in his chair uncomfortably for a moment, as if trying to find a position that didn't hurt his back. Finally he said, "Matthew, you came into the DDO position like a bull in a china shop. I let things go, because your predecessor ran Operations like it was his own private army. The department needed an enema, and you sure as shit gave it one."

Hanley didn't know if he was supposed to say thank you, so he just nodded.

"But here we are, four or five months after you took the DDO desk, and I am beginning to harbor concerns about your decision-making abilities and your unaccountability."

"I am completely accountable, Mr. Director. Accountable to you."

"I told you on day one, son, that I was going to give you unusual latitude to conduct your work as you see fit. But a horse can take loose reins to mean his rider isn't paying attention."

"I always assume you are paying attention, and you know everything that you need, and want, to know."

"I don't know what's happening in your special programs."

"I could fill you in, sir," Hanley said, and this line was received as he'd expected.

"Don't get cute with me, Matthew. You know I need to be insulated from sub rosa activities. You and I can have a verbal agreement that I've loosened up your sanction, and you can take that to mean, within reason, that I'm okay with you doing what you think is right. But when the light of day finds your dirty work, then it becomes a problem that must be rectified."

"I understand."

Director Capshaw said, "Matt . . . I've given you enough rope to hang yourself with, and it appears that's *exactly* what you're doing right now."

"Sub rosa ops are always difficult, but the potential rewards outweigh the risks. We've got a lot of moving parts, and yes, some problems right now, but I will take care of everything."

Capshaw didn't seem to be listening. He said, "I won't be taking the fall when you go down. I'll cut you away from me to survive."

Hanley nodded at this. He actually appreciated a man who told him hard truths, as opposed to lying to his face. He said, "It won't come to that. I'm rectifying the situation. I have my best people working on it, and I expect to have it all wrapped up before the end of the conference."

Capshaw said, "I am hearing talk that you don't believe Renfro was the traitor." Hanley seemed uneasy, and the director noticed this. "Speak up."

"I don't think he was the traitor, no. I believe his death was staged. He was murdered so that we'd stop looking."

Capshaw heaved a big sigh. "Well, shit. That complicates things even more."

"It does. But it's narrowed down to two men. Both are either in or on their way to the UK. I'll find out who is responsible while they're here, I guarantee it."

The Director of Central Intelligence said, "I'll give you till we return to the States in four days. But no longer. I want all dangles tied off in a ball before we are feet dry in the U.S., or I shutter all your sub rosa activities until you get your house in order. Is that clear, Matt?"

"Absolutely clear. Thank you, sir." Hanley stood up and left the rear of the aircraft.

. . .

Zack Hightower didn't like flying commercial, and he sure as hell didn't like flying economy, but he'd booked his ticket to London at the airport just ninety minutes prior to takeoff, so he had to take what he could get.

He did manage to get a seat far behind Marty Wheeler, who lounged up in first class. Zack wasn't bumpering him at the moment; he didn't want Wheeler to know he was heading to Europe just yet. Brewer had reached out to him before takeoff, telling him his job when he got to the UK was to tail Wheeler until he went to the U.S. embassy, directly from the airport, and then begin his close surveillance of Operations executive Alf Karlsson, already there at the embassy.

Zack was on his computer looking over a London map when a secure message system popped up on the screen. It was Brewer checking in with him. Zack knew she and Hanley were also in the air to London now, a couple hours ahead of him.

Brewer typed, **Wheeler is behaving himself?**

Of course he is, Zack wrote. **Because he's not our guy. Palumbo is clean, too.**

Well, if it's not them, then it's Karlsson, and you'll see him soon enough.

Zack typed back, **I bet it was Renfro. That dude was obviously hiding something big.**

After a time a response came. **Yes. I concur. I'm going to talk with DDO about this again.**

Brewer logged out of the chat, and Zack closed his own computer. He had his orders, and he would obey them. For now it was time to watch a movie and get some sleep.

. . .

Suzanne Brewer moved over to an empty seat next to Matt Hanley, who had just returned from a short meeting with the director in the rear of the aircraft. He was handed a bourbon by a flight attendant, and he sipped it as he noticed Brewer's arrival.

"What's up?"

"I've been messaging Romantic. He feels certain Wheeler is clean. We've also established that Palumbo was not the mole."

Hanley said, "I knew it wasn't Marty. So . . . that leaves Karlsson."

"Well, sir, that is one theory. The other theory is that we had it right all along. It was Renfro."

Hanley shook his head.

"Sir, I have to ask. Why have you suddenly become Renfro's champion? You hated the guy, everybody knows that. Romantic said he was hiding something, he was scared of his own shadow, always looking over his shoulder. What the hell else would Renfro have to hide other than being the traitor?"

Hanley took the glass next to him, then drank down the remains of his bourbon. He leaned forward just a little, although no one was in earshot considering the low volume of their voices. He spoke even softer now. "Marital infidelity."

Brewer cocked her head. "What are you talking about?"

Hanley's big chest filled with air and he let loose a long sigh. "Lucas Renfro was sleeping with a woman at an apartment he owns in Woodley Park. Her name is Katrina Lawrence, it has been going on for some time, and his wife is very much in the dark about it. Renfro was worried he'd been found out, and this is why he was freaked out by Hightower's surveillance of him."

Brewer did not hide her shock. "That's an incredible compromise for a deputy director. How could he pass his periodic lifestyle polygraph if he was having an affair? He would be fired in an instant if that ever came to light."

"Narcissists don't poly well. He probably thought nothing of it."

She cocked her head. "How the hell do you know about this affair?"

"I've known it for a very long time, actually. Katrina Lawrence . . . is my ex-wife."

Brewer was gobsmacked. "You knew Renfro was screwing your wife, and you didn't do anything about it?"

"Ex-wife," he repeated, then shrugged. "We've been divorced for years." He shrugged again. "Renfro broke up the marriage."

She just stared at him, astonished he'd never confronted the man about sleeping with his wife.

Hanley understood the reason for her expression. "It's the spook in me, Suzanne. I wanted to hold this bit of intelligence in my pocket till I needed to leverage it against him. I could have called his wife and told her whenever I felt like it, I could have told the director, but I wanted to save my big reveal for the moment it could do me the most good, or Renfro the most damage. Even getting him fired was setting my sights too low. I wanted to destroy him personally, professionally, psychologically."

Brewer sat back in her cabin chair a little. "Well . . . just because he was committing adultery, that does not mean he wasn't *also* a traitor."

Hanley said, "Very true, Suzanne, but there were enough clues at his crime scene to tell me he had help with his death. I did not do it, much as I would have liked. Removing me as the prime suspect, my conclusion is someone killed him because they wanted . . . they *needed* to implicate him in the treason. Perhaps to throw us off the scent."

"So . . . then, who did it? Romantic insists Palumbo and Wheeler are clean."

"He hasn't evaluated Karlsson yet."

Brewer smiled. "Romantic's on a flight right now. Will be in London a couple hours after we land."

Hanley nodded. "This is exactly why you are in the position I have you in." He reached for his iPad and began thumbing through some work.

Brewer started to stand, but Hanley took her by the arm gently and she leaned down to him.

"Suzanne, Romantic and Violator are weapons free, as of right now. If

Anthem is recovered alive, she is now officially a Poison Apple asset, and she is weapons free, as well. I want them to find the traitor, with Romantic tracking the potentials while Violator works the problem from the other side, tracking Belyakov and his Russian mob connection."

"Yes, sir," she said, wanting to put up some sort of a fight, but knowing resistance was futile at this point.

Hanley added, "MI5 and MI6 are both operating under the assumption they have a mole, same as we are. Therefore, Poison Apple will not be supported by local assets in the United Kingdom. The two of them . . . the three of them, if Anthem shows up, are going to have to find a way to do this themselves."

Hanley looked towards the rear. Walt Jenner and his seven other operators sat close to one another in the low light. Many slept; a few watched movies on tablet computers.

"Scratch that," Hanley said. "I've got a Ground Branch team available to assist them in an in extremis situation. Let Violator know that."

Brewer closed her eyes, unconcerned that her boss would see how much she fundamentally disagreed with what she was being ordered to oversee. CIA assassins and paramilitaries running willy-nilly and without local approval across the United Kingdom, targeting Russian mafia and sleeper agents, a CIA mole, and God knew whatever else was involved.

This entire shit show was about to blow up even more, Suzanne Brewer could just feel it, and she hated her life.

Then her phone rang, and everything suddenly got so much worse.

"Brewer?"

It was Violator. "Zakharov is alive, he is in play, and I think he's going to attack the Five Eyes conference."

"*What?*"

"I don't know how, but he's in Scotland, and he's planning some sort of retributive strike against the UK and America for what they did to his family."

"What the hell did we do to his family?"

Court explained everything that he knew, then finished by saying, "You have to get them to call off that conference."

"You don't just *call off* the Five Eyes symposium. I will let Hanley know about this new threat, see what he wants to do."

"We don't even know what the threat is, Suzanne. How do you protect against that?"

"Guns, gates, and guys," she replied flatly. "Trust me, that castle in the Highlands will be the safest place to be on Earth for the next few days."

• • •

The knock at the door to Court's basement apartment came at seven in the evening, a half hour after Court had been promised by Brewer that someone would arrive to watch over Belyakov.

He looked through the peephole, then unlocked the door and opened it. The same young bearded redhead from whom he'd taken the Volvo and the equipment the day before stood there, and he gave Court a surprised look.

"You?" he said.

"Me. What's up, Red?"

"It's Jason, actually. What happened to your face?"

Court didn't answer. Instead he said, "November, Delta, Zulu, fourteen, Golf, Whiskey." He crossed his fingers, then lifted them up by his face. "Your turn, kiddo. I'm rootin' for you."

Jason laughed at this despite himself. "I've been practicing. Oscar, Oscar, Kilo, seven, eight, India, X-ray."

"You rock," Court said with a tired and pained smile.

To this Jason just said, "I heard you shot up my Volvo."

Court stepped aside so Jason could enter and said, "Dude, I was crouched down behind it when the bullets started hitting it."

"The thing this afternoon in Mayfair is all over the news. Was that you, as well?"

"I don't kill and tell."

Jason continued up a hall towards the main room, but Court took him by the arm and stopped him in the darkened hallway. "The subject is Vladimir Belyakov. You know him?"

"Know *of* him, sure. *Damn.* Really?"

"He's going to need some new pants before you take him out of here. We don't need him charged with indecent exposure."

"Damn," Jason said again.

"I want a gun in your hand at all times. The location is secure, and he's tied to a chair and not going anywhere. But remain vigilant. He knows things that people will do anything to keep quiet."

"I . . . I don't have a gun."

Court sighed. CIA case officers didn't normally carry firearms.

"Take mine. I've got a spare." He unstrapped the Glock 43 from his ankle and handed it to the young man.

Jason took the weapon and said, "We can't work with the Brits for some reason, so it will take two hours for a cleanup team and an extraction team to show up. I'll watch him carefully till then. When the cavalry arrives, we'll get him out of here and the safe house sanitized."

"Good man."

Court hefted his backpack off the floor and slung it over his shoulder, groaning in pain with the movement. "Thanks, Red. I've got to run."

The young CIA case officer followed Court to the door and locked it behind him when he left, then drew the Glock from its holster. He headed back up the hall to begin his shift babysitting one of the richest men in London.

. . .

Zack landed at London Heathrow at nine in the morning, shuffled off the aircraft with the rest of the passengers back in steerage, and made his way towards passport control. Since Wheeler was traveling under a diplomatic passport, he made it through much faster than Hightower, who had documents supporting his civilian cover.

When he finally got through, Zack began jogging through the airport, scanning in all directions, knowing he couldn't lose Wheeler, not because there was still any chance that he was the mole, but because his orders from Brewer were not to lose him, and Zack was a man who prided himself on always following his orders to the best of his abilities.

Soon, however, Zack realized he needn't have worried about misplacing the dapper fifty-one-year-old assistant deputy director. While Zack just had a satchel over his shoulder with another set of clothes and a few odds and ends, Wheeler stood waiting for his checked bag with virtually everyone else from the rest of the flight.

Zack rushed on through the airport, went outside, and then, after a few more minutes of jogging, found his way to the vehicle Brewer had waiting in the short-term lot for him. It was a boring four-door Kia, which didn't exactly thrill the former SEAL Team 6 man, but he climbed behind the wheel and dropped the visor to catch the key fob that fell down.

Minutes later he was back in the arrivals area in front of the international terminal. He pulled in as if he were picking someone up. Wheeler appeared ahead of him, climbing into a black cab, and Zack followed him through the scrum of vehicles trying to get off airport property.

He thought about his job to come. For some weird reason Hanley wouldn't admit that Renfro was the traitor, even though that seemed obvious to Hightower. So Zack would be stuck following this innocent bore to the embassy, and then following some other innocent bore around London before he headed up to Scotland for the conference where, no doubt, Zack would be tasked with following both Wheeler and Karlsson around some more.

Zack followed Wheeler's taxi, hanging back, not bumpering. The thrill of all this was long gone now that the man he was certain was responsible for the treason was dead in the morgue.

This was a boring gig, nowhere as exciting as what he'd hoped for.

He figured that wherever Court Gentry was these days, *that* was where the real action would be going down, and this pissed him off.

Zack followed the taxi to the east, approaching greater London. He stayed far back, not that he was worried about the cabbie noticing he had a tail, but simply because it was more work to do a close-in follow, and he already knew the assistant deputy director was heading to the embassy, so he had no real fear of losing him outright. He hung a dozen car lengths off his objective vehicle, trying not to lose him in the sea of other black cabs out there, but didn't stress too much about it.

In morning traffic it was over an hour's transit from Heathrow into the city, but when Zack began driving along the Thames on Great West Road he knew he was getting closer. The U.S. embassy was on the south side of the river, and he fully expected to be following the taxi across the Battersea Bridge, but the cab bypassed the turn and continued along the northern bank of the Thames.

This seemed odd to Zack, but still, he didn't stress. The cabbie would know the way better than he.

And then the taxi made a left on Oakley Street, turning to the north and away from the embassy, and now Zack was thoroughly confused.

He started to call Brewer, just to let her know that he'd be delayed getting to the embassy because the suit he was tailing was diverting, probably heading to Harrods for pink socks or some shit, but just before he tapped his phone, the taxi made a quick right turn on Kings Road. This was followed by another right on Chelsea Manor, and now Zack was pulling up tighter to the taxi, worrying he would lose Wheeler with all the oddball maneuvers his cabbie was making.

Another right turn on Cheyne Walk, and then a jog to the left to put him on the Chelsea Embankment, and for a moment Zack wondered if the cabbie was heading to Battersea Bridge to cross the Thames, because he was now traveling back to the west.

But this theory didn't stand ten seconds of time. Wheeler's cab turned right again, back on Oakley.

They'd just driven in a large square.

Zack knew a few things in life, for sure, and one of them was that London cabbies do *not* get lost.

And that meant only one thing to him.

Is Wheeler running an SDR?

And then another thought occurred to him. It would have to be one hell of a weird conversation in that vehicle ahead for Wheeler to ask the cabbie to make an unnecessary series of turns and double-backs.

The only thing that made sense was that the cabbie was the one doing the SDR, and Wheeler was just along for the ride.

As the taxi made another right, Zack reached for his phone.

CHAPTER 46

David Mars took his phone from his pocket and answered it while stepping out of Dr. Won's laboratory. He stood on a third-floor stone balcony, looking down at the University of Edinburgh. It was a rainy day in Edinburgh, but for the moment the precipitation was light enough for Mars to stand here and remain dry.

"Hello?"

"Black? It's Barnacle."

"Excellent, mate. You're in London?"

"Yes, yes I am. But . . ."

"But what?"

"The driver you had pick me up is doing an SDR, and we've detected a definite tail."

This was distressing to Mars, but not overly so. "That's unfortunate."

"No shit, it's unfortunate. If they get the idea I'm not going to the embassy, they might make the reasonable assumption that I'm running, which will lead them to the assumption that I'm the one they're looking for."

"Don't worry, Barnacle. We won't let that happen. You're almost free and clear. That cabbie works for the Solntsevskaya Bratva, and he'd get his bloody throat slit if he doesn't get you to the destination in one piece."

"That's it? *That's* the only assurance you have I won't get picked up in the next ten minutes? Look, Black. Don't forget how much you don't want me to fall into the hands of your enemy."

"Go carefully, Barnacle. I don't want you harmed or held, but I also do not take well to threats."

"Just . . . *please*, get me out of here. I don't want to go directly to the Peruvian embassy; I don't have any manpower to stop a snatch team if they come for me."

"You soon will. I'll send a team to meet you; we'll get you out of that cab and better protected. Just tell your driver to keep driving, and give me a few minutes to arrange something."

"Rush them, *please*."

David Mars hung up, then called out to Fox, who was in the hallway outside the third-floor lab, talking on his phone. He hung up and rushed in to Mars to see what he needed.

"Sir?"

"Barnacle is compromised down in London. Need some of your boys to bring him in. As quick as you can assemble them."

"On it," he said, as he pulled his phone out again. "I'll have them contact the driver and meet somewhere near the Peruvian embassy, but not too close by."

• • •

Zack Hightower was having a difficult time convincing Suzanne Brewer that he now believed Wheeler was up to something. She challenged him on this over the phone, insisted the cabbie must have been looking for some address, and told Zack to calm down the more animated he got.

But Hightower could not be swayed. "They are just driving around in circles now. They know they have a tail, and they aren't trying to shake me, so they're obviously trying to stall. That makes me worry."

"Worry about what?"

"About the possibility they are planning something."

Now the cab drove north up West Carriage Drive, through the center of Hyde Park and Kensington Gardens, and Zack tried to think ahead several steps in his adversary's plan. He didn't know where he was going, but driving the one road that led through the middle of the park seemed like a bad idea from the perspective of someone who was being tailed.

But then he realized what his adversary's game was. Right in front of him the taxi rounded a turn and stopped in the road, right next to a maroon passenger van, which itself slammed on its brakes.

Marty Wheeler leapt out of the taxi and into the open side door of the van, which immediately launched forward, whipping past Zack at speed. He could see that the van was full of at least four more men in addition to the American CIA exec.

Zack pulled a hard U-turn, bumping up onto the grass alongside Carriage Walk Lane to do so.

Zack spoke to Brewer through his earpiece mic. "Subject has changed vics, and now is heading south, surrounded by muscle."

Brewer just muttered, "Unreal."

"I need you to tell me what you want me to do here. He's making a definite, overt run for it now, and he's got four Slavic-looking knuckleheads surrounding him."

Brewer said, "Look, Romantic, you might just have to handle this yourself."

"Lady, I just got off an international flight. I don't even have a damn gun!" Zack said.

"Yes, you do," Brewer interrupted. "There should be a weapon with extra magazines in the glove box."

Zack checked quickly, pulled out a Smith and Wesson M&P .40, a forty-caliber pistol in a retention holster, then checked to make certain it was loaded with one hand while he drove with the other. He said, "Got it. Orders?"

"If Wheeler switched vehicles and has security, then there is a reasonable chance he is guilty of being the mole. Do you concur with that assessment?"

"Sorry, lady, went to state college. It was more about baseball and coeds and less about learning what 'concurring with assessments' means. But if you're asking me if this motherfucker who's surrounded himself with Russian shitheads and is desperately trying to lose anyone tailing him is guilty as hell, well then, my answer is *abso-fucking-lutely* I concur."

Zack read off the street names he passed, and when the van turned to the left he told Brewer they were heading into Knightsbridge.

Brewer took a moment to respond. "I'm driving myself to the embassy now, but I'm looking at the map on my phone, trying to figure out where they are going. That part of Knightsbridge has a lot of embassies." After a moment she said, "Shit. The Peruvian embassy. Their government is tight with the Russians and decidedly anti-American at the moment. They'll carry Moscow's water for them."

"How far from where I am?" He gave her the intersection he passed.

"Five minutes, with traffic. You don't have much time to stop this."

"Stop this? No chance you can get *any* backup on the way to me, is there?"

"I really need you to handle this alone, Romantic."

Zack then asked, "Wait. You're in London. You're in your car, and you're near the embassy. That's less than ten minutes from me. Why don't you get your butt over here?"

"Wait a second, Romantic. I . . . I am not trained for—"

"I need a car to help me tail, box, and extract Wheeler. My vic is blown to the oppo."

She hesitated. After a moment she said, "Okay, I'm not a field operative, but I'm in Whitehall, less than five minutes away from you, in fact. I can head that way, but only to help with the tail. I *don't* have a weapon in my car."

"C'mon, then. I'm going to break off this tail and go up a side street. Haul ass to the Peruvian embassy. If I can get in front of them I can be waiting for them when they get there."

"Good."

"Rules of engagement?" Zack asked.

Brewer said, "Listen up, Romantic. I don't want them taking him someplace we can't reach him. I am giving you authority to detain Assistant Deputy Director Marty Wheeler at this time."

"I'm not gonna ask who gave you the authority to give *me* the authority to do that, but I *am* gonna ask you what I'm supposed to do when the Russians protecting him express their displeasure in my actions."

Brewer replied with, "Only escalate if absolutely necessary. But meet force with equal force." And then she added, "You have lethal authorization."

Zack waited no time before giving his response. "Hot diggity damn, Susie! I love it when you talk sexy. Call me when you are a couple minutes out." And then he touched his earpiece, ending the call.

. . .

In the passenger van, Marty Wheeler looked down at his shaking hands. He'd so hoped to just slip away, to be a quiet problem for the CIA, the assistant deputy director who one day disappeared in Europe. He'd fantasized about living in luxury in Russia, watching American satellite TV shows about his own disappearance and presumed death.

He'd been looking forward to it since Mr. Black reached out to him months earlier.

But it wasn't going to happen now; that was obvious. The CIA knew he was the one they'd been looking for; the murder of Deputy Director Renfro had not caused the heat to be turned down on Wheeler, and now the only thing he could do would be to overtly run to the other side, get spirited out of the potential clutches of the Americans, and be whisked off to Russia, where he'd always have to watch his back, worrying about the CIA knowing exactly where to go to settle an old score.

He'd still have the money he made selling secrets to the Chinese, the Iranians, and the enigmatic Englishman who seemed to be laser focused on protecting the interests of a group of Russian oligarchs, as well as a long-dead general whose name had popped up in a CIA printout just days ago and who had seemed to precipitate this entire affair.

He hadn't a clue what a dead general named Zakharov had to do with all this shit, and he wondered if he'd ever know.

Wheeler first decided to sell secrets to the highest bidder just days after he was moved out of Operations and into Support and then bypassed for the deputy director position there. Matt Hanley, the new deputy director of Operations, had been his friend and his superior officer in Fifth Special Forces Group. They'd served together in Grenada, in Panama, in the Gulf. Wheeler appealed to Hanley to intervene to save him from the move into Support, because even though it was a promotion, leaving Operations would be a career-ender for a guy like Wheeler. He was an Ops man, always would be, and Support was no place for Ops men.

But Hanley refused to intervene. The director wanted the move, and Hanley was playing ball to curry favor for his own reasons.

Immediately, however, Wheeler found out more about those reasons. It became clear in just weeks that Hanley was setting up his own off-book operations, all with the director's tacit blessing. Wheeler was constantly getting calls from Hanley asking for aircraft, safe houses, offshore dummy corps, and the like, always with a wink and a nod to check it out with the director if he had any doubts. It seemed clear enough early on to the new assistant deputy director of Support that Hanley had moved Wheeler over to Support to have his own inside man there who could make things happen without any red tape.

Wheeler did as his old friend and superior asked, but inside he fumed.

Meanwhile his asshole boss, the former congressional staffer and lazy prick Lucas Renfro, treated him less like a second-in-command and more like a petty underling. Wheeler thought seriously about the private sector, but every time he got the feeling it was time to leave the Agency, his anger at what he saw as his mistreatment by his superiors left him with a desire for vengeance.

He knew things, he knew *a lot* of things, and the one place he knew he could pass information to others with little fear of being caught was in the sub rosa realm. Matt Hanley, like his predecessor, was going full tilt now on secret ops. Wheeler didn't know details of the programs themselves, but as a Support executive he was privy to transportation needs, safe house security, and other elements of these off-book initiatives, and passing this intel off to parties who would pay handsomely for it had seemed like a good idea at the time.

His first sale was to Chinese intelligence, letting them know that a CIA aircraft would be landing in Hong Kong as part of a code-word operation. The Chicoms paid handsomely for this, so Wheeler then sold info to Iran, as well.

After a potential deal with Russian intelligence fell through, Mr. Black appeared from nowhere, told Wheeler everything he wanted and how much he would pay for it, and Wheeler obliged.

And now he was racing for his freedom through London, hoping like hell he could make it into the Peruvian embassy, from where he'd be snuck out, delivered to some out-of-the-way airport, and flown to Russia, or Peru, or . . . at this point just *anywhere* where no agency in the Five Eyes could lay hands on him.

It was all such a fucking mess.

He looked up from his shaking hands as they turned onto Sloane Street. He'd checked the map himself on the plane the night before, and he knew the Peruvian embassy was just up ahead on the left. He tried to look out the front windshield to see it, but instead he saw an oncoming gray four-door, its driver-side door open, veer out of its lane and into the lane right in front of the racing van.

• • •

The Russian driver stomped on his brakes, but the sedan slammed grille first into the van at speed, sending the van's driver forward, his head pounding the steering wheel and rendering him unconscious.

The front seat passenger had not been belted in, and his face hit the windshield, squirting blood from his nose across the inside of the glass.

In the back of the van Wheeler was thrown forward but his restraints sent him banging back into his headrest, simultaneously both saving and dazing him.

But the remaining two Russians were unscathed. Seat belts were unfastened, guns came out of jackets, the sliding door was opened, and the first man leapt out onto the two-laned street in a cloud of smoke and steam from the damaged engines of both vehicles.

While one of the Bratva men trained his weapon on the gray vehicle that was crumpled into the front of the van, the second man reached back in, unfastened Marty Wheeler's seat belt, and pulled him out by the collar.

• • •

Zack Hightower climbed to his hands and knees, just twenty-five yards up the road from where the crash happened. He'd taken a shortcut through a parking lot to get there first and floored it, then angled his Kia at the approaching van. He opened his door and rolled out onto the street, banging virtually his entire body into the asphalt as his momentum carried him forward.

He was still rolling forward as his vehicle scored a direct hit with the oncoming van twenty-five yards away.

But rolling along the street had been no big win for Zack Hightower. His knees and elbows and back screamed in pain, and it took him longer than he would have liked to recover enough to stand upright, pull the Smith and Wesson out from the retention holster under his torn blazer, and raise it towards the car crash.

Brewer had instructed him to meet force with equal force, and he intended to do that, more or less. But Zack had no interest in a fair fight, so when he saw the first man step out of the steam, his pistol leveled at the car Zack had just exited, the American went lethal, firing twice into the man before he even looked up the street.

A woman standing on the sidewalk near Zack screamed, and this sent his gun spinning in her direction, but only until he saw that she was no threat, and then his attention, along with his pistol's barrel, shifted back to the wreck. He advanced on it, weapon high, and then he saw two men close together, moving out from the smoke and steam.

He recognized Marty Wheeler and took the other man for an armed extraction asset, so he shifted aim off the CIA man and onto the unknown individual.

A pistol jutted from the man's hand, and for Zack that was more than enough justification to go weapons free. He shot the man twice, once winging him on the left side of his head and once in his upper chest, knocking him back from Wheeler a few steps, but somehow the man did not drop.

The gunman raised his weapon towards Zack, who fired again and again, finally spinning him down to the pavement with a half dozen .40 caliber rounds in him.

And then Marty Wheeler began to sprint off.

"Shit!" Zack said, because he fucking *hated* to run.

CHAPTER 47

Suzanne Brewer had last heard from Romantic three minutes earlier, telling her he was going to attempt to cut off Wheeler's access to the Peruvian embassy on Sloane Street. She didn't know exactly what he meant by this, but she drove along Knightsbridge Road, planning on seeing her asset holding Wheeler and the others at gunpoint, and she thought about driving up on that crazy scene, right here in the heart of London.

Brewer asked herself what the hell she was doing here. She was not a field asset, and the only reason she'd told Romantic she would come to his aid was that she knew he would tell Hanley if she *didn't* come. She didn't know what she could do to help; she was unarmed and only knew her way because she'd punched Romantic's location into Google Maps while she drove.

But here she was, barreling into danger in a blacker-than-black operation that would do *nothing* to advance her career, even if she somehow managed to save the *fucking* queen in the process.

Her phone rang and she answered it, expecting it to be her asset, but instead it was Matt Hanley.

"I'm at the embassy, meeting with conference security officials, giving them vague and useless information about a new threat we've identified. Can't tell them about Mars because of their leak, and I need you here to—"

Brewer interrupted. "Sir . . . the mole is Wheeler. He's been picked up by some kind of security crew here in London and they seem to be making their way towards the Peruvian embassy in Knightsbridge. Romantic is in pursuit with orders to stop the vehicle by any means necessary, and I am going to the location to assist."

Hanley did not reply.

"Sir, did you—"

"I've known Marty Wheeler since the Army. Thirty *fucking* years, Suzanne."

"The evidence is pretty clear, Matt. Romantic says Wheeler ran an SDR before switching vehicles, loading up with some fighting-age Slavic-looking men."

"Not Marty."

"Matt . . . the asset is seconds away from attempting a stop on the vehicle."

After another delay, Hanley said, "*Dammit!* Okay. All right. If Zack gets him, tell him *not* to bring him here to the embassy."

"Sir?"

"We need to interrogate him outside the official chain of custody. I'll call you back with an address, somewhere out of the way."

Brewer closed her eyes a moment in deep irritation. "Matt, you can't interrogate a senior executive of the CIA off book."

"Who the hell says I can't? Certainly not the director. He'd want me to get this sorted out as quickly and as quietly as possible."

Brewer just said, "Yes, sir," told him she would be standing by for the location of the safe house, and then disconnected the call. After she did this she screamed in the car. "Shit!"

She hated the position she'd been put in working for Hanley, and told herself that once she plugged the leak named Marty Wheeler, she would begin putting all her efforts into finding a way out of this morass before she ended up dead or in prison.

• • •

Hightower ran in his Western roper boots, finally catching up to Wheeler as he tried to cross Knightsbridge Road, but was forced to stop because the traffic was too heavy. The big blond American with the beard and sideburns reached out and grabbed the thin white-haired man by the neck, then pulled him along the sidewalk.

Zack sucked in a few breaths before speaking, then said, "Not a big fan of runnin', Martin, gotta be honest with ya."

He kept his hand on his prisoner's neck, tight in back, pushing him onward quickly now.

Wheeler himself was wheezing from the forty-five-second sprint. "What . . . what do you want?"

"To shoot you in the motherfucking heart for making me chase your ass, but I'd probably just get in trouble. So instead, you and I are gonna go to the embassy. The U.S. one, not the Peruvian one."

"I don't know what you are talking—"

"Save it for someone who wants to hear your whiny spiel about how this is all some kind of an honest mix-up. I'm not in the mood, asshole."

Police cars raced by, paying no attention to the two men on the sidewalk.

Zack's earpiece beeped and he answered it. A minute later Brewer picked them both up in her Ford Taurus. Zack shoved Wheeler into the back. Climbing in next to him, he resumed his rough hold on the back of the man's neck.

Wheeler said, "Suzanne! You know I didn't—"

Zack elbowed Wheeler hard in the mouth, then leaned forward to talk to Brewer. "To the embassy?"

She started driving off, and she shook her head. "I just spoke with Hanley. We are taking him to Wimbledon."

"For tennis?" Zack asked. "What the fuck?"

"No, not for tennis. It's the name of a neighborhood to the southwest of London."

"Why are we going there?"

"We are to deliver ADD Wheeler to an agency black site we have established in a warehouse."

Wheeler snorted. "C'mon, Suzanne. Who do you think you are dealing with here? I'm a Support exec. I know *all* the black sites, and we sure as hell don't have one in London."

"We didn't until we snatched you, Mr. Assistant Deputy Director. But Hanley knows a place, and says it will work fine for his purposes."

Zack smiled now and looked at Wheeler, who was clearly uneased by what Brewer had just told him. "You hear that, Mr. Assistant Deputy

Director? Sure you did, and you know *exactly* what that means. You aren't getting the aboveboard treatment. Nope, you're about to go down the rabbit hole. From this moment on, *anything* can happen to you, and *nobody* will know unless and until Hanley decides to put you in the system."

Wheeler looked at Zack, then made a pained expression. Zack smiled at the man's discomfort, but he quickly realized what was happening. He grabbed the man's head and turned it forward, just as Marty Wheeler vomited, covering himself with bile and partially digested coffee and croissant from his in-flight breakfast.

Suzanne Brewer looked back at the scene and shook her head. She just could not understand how her career, her life, had fallen so *fucking* far, so *fucking* fast.

. . .

For the first several hours after her father left her in Belyakov's mansion, Zoya Zakharova waited under relaxed guard. She was given ample food and drink but told nothing, not until Fox entered and informed her that the helicopter that was going to take her to her destination would be arriving shortly. Eventually it landed, and Zoya was walked to the large black aircraft, surrounded by Fox, the big blond-haired man she had heard referred to as Hines, and a pair of Russian security men with high-quality gear and weapons.

No one told her where they were going, but she could see the setting sun to her left, so she realized the helo was heading north.

They flew into a gray evening, the clouds forming around them. Soon she could see nothing of the terrain below.

After several hours the helo slowed and descended under the clouds.

She'd tried to calculate how long they were in the air, and she thought back to her knowledge of the map of the United Kingdom. They must have gone all the way up to Scotland, of this she was relatively certain, but since she'd seen little in the way of mountains or even severely hilly terrain before landing she doubted they could have gone north of Edinburgh or Glasgow, both in Scotland's southern third.

No one had laid a hand on her, nor had she attempted to resist at all. There were a couple of times she thought she might be able to make a break for it, right before they boarded the helo and right when they climbed out, but both times she realized someone would just catch up to her and, anyway, she knew that being close to her father and his operation was the best play for her right now. She wasn't worried about being killed, but she was *very* worried about whatever scheme her dad was working on, so she decided to stick around to see what she could learn.

The helipad was adjacent to a two-story industrial building; from the looks of it Zoya imagined it had something to do with the oil and gas industry, and as she walked through the rainy night behind Fox and in front of Hines, she saw a sign above the building that said "Edinburgh Pipeline Supplies, Limited."

Soon she was shepherded into a car, and they headed off. Just when Zoya was about to ask where they were going, a question she knew would not be answered, Fox leaned over to her. "Sorry, Ms. Zakharova, but I can't let you see our destination." And with that he put a blindfold over her eyes.

"I'm not going to tie you up, but don't take it off, or big Jon here will get annoyed with you." She could feel Fox lean closer, and his breath was in her ear now. "You don't want that. I would *love* to watch it, but your father would be mad at me, so let's all just behave."

She sighed, sat back, and crossed her arms in front of her.

Zoya suspected it was nearly midnight when they entered a city. This she could tell by the sounds and light that filtered through her mask, and the increasing number of starts and stops on the steeply graded roads. Soon they slowed, made a ninety-degree turn, and began heading down a decline. From the echoes and even more bright light than before filtering through the mask, it registered in her brain that they had entered an underground parking garage, obviously somewhere in Edinburgh.

When the vehicle came to a stop, her blindfold was removed, and she was led out of the backseat. She indeed did find herself in a garage, and she followed the entourage through a door and up several flights of stairs.

Almost immediately she could tell she was in some sort of medical facility or research laboratory. She was led down a cavernous hall past a few open doors, and then Fox asked her to enter the last room on the right. She did so, immediately saw the little cot and the bottles of water and the blankets, and realized this was to be her quarters. She turned around to face the Russian.

"You're locking me in here?"

"Yes, but I'll have food brought to you. There's no en suite, I'm afraid, this is a converted office, but there is a bathroom just back up the hall. Knock on your door and one of my men will escort you."

"Where is my father?"

"He will be arriving in the morning. Until then, let me know if there is anything I can do to make you more comfortable."

She looked up at the British man named Jon Hines who always shadowed Fox, the man who had beaten Court so badly some twenty-four hours earlier.

The man smiled at her. "How's your friend feeling?"

Zoya replied, "Never better. You know, if I'd had one more bullet in my gun last night, you'd be dead."

The giant just grinned at her. "If I'd had three more bleedin' seconds last night I'd have snapped both your skinny necks."

Zoya looked to Fox now. "How tough are you when he isn't by your side?"

To this Fox laughed. "I would not know. He's *always* by my side."

Fox and Hines turned and left the room, the door clicked shut, and then Zoya heard a lock being engaged.

She sat down in the windowless room that, she couldn't help but notice, was set up much the same way as her room at the CIA safe house back in Virginia. There was significance to this, she decided, something to do with the fact that both sides saw her as both a potential asset and a potential threat, but she was too tired to think it over right now. Instead she lay back on the hard little cot and closed her eyes.

The door opened once when a Russian mob goon wearing a scowl delivered her a bowl of stew and a bottle of white wine. She ate every bite of the stew and drank all the wine, and soon the same man came to retrieve it. Zoya looked around the room a moment and saw the camera that had shown him she was finished.

This group of Russian mafia men seemed to run their holding cell just like the CIA did.

Soon she just lay back down on her cot and wondered if Court was doing any better than she was right now.

CHAPTER 48

Marty Wheeler had been lashed to a chair in an empty white room, his shirt and pants had been removed, and the bearded man with sideburns who had captured him squatted against the wall in front of him, giving him constant stink eye when he wasn't picking at his badly scraped elbow.

Marty was hungry, Marty was cold, Marty was tired, but he was hopeful, as well. Hopeful the British voice over the phone, the man who had paid him for his intelligence product, was right now working on some sort of plan to get him out of this mess.

But hope faltered as he thought it through. He'd already given him the information about Ternhill, the information about Poison Apple and Matt Hanley and Lucas Renfro. The Englishman didn't really need Wheeler any longer, and this pierced his heart like a dagger.

As an asset, Barnacle was spent. No one would be coming for him and he knew it now.

The man with the sideburns took a call. He talked quietly for a few moments, said "Yes, sir," a half dozen times, and once glanced malevolently towards Wheeler. Soon the door opened behind Wheeler; he didn't even try to look back over his shoulder to see who it was, because his bindings were too tight to turn his head more than a few inches.

He heard the voice of his old friend Matt Hanley. But it didn't relax him now. No, it terrified him.

"Romantic, I need you to give me some time with the guest."

"Yes, sir." The big man stood and passed by Hanley as he stepped around in front of Wheeler, and soon the bound man heard the door clicking shut behind him.

Wheeler thought Hanley would take the chair, but instead he stood just feet in front of his old comrade and friend.

"Why, Marty? Why the *fuck*?"

"It's all a mistake, Matt. You know me. You know I—"

"Don't embarrass yourself. We've got all we need on you."

Wheeler deflated slowly, then said, "Wish I had an exciting story for you. But it's just the same old tired thing, I guess. Passed over for a promotion, pissed off and vengeful, ready to burn some shit down and get paid for it on my way out." He made another effort to shrug, gave off a hint of a smile. "Nothing you and me both haven't heard a hundred times."

Hanley's thick neck reddened.

"I guess now you're going to beat a confession out of me. Or get that junkyard dog of yours who's been following me for days to do it."

Hanley shook his head. "A confession? No. Not necessary. I want to know what Zakharov is planning, though. Any chance you could fill me in on his endgame?"

"Zakharov?" Wheeler was confused. "The dead GRU chief? What are you talking about?"

"You didn't know Zakharov was the one who paid you for the intelligence on Dirk Visser?"

Wheeler said nothing.

"He goes by an alias. Maybe that would help. David Mars."

The bound man shook his head. "Don't know him."

"Englishman, or appears to be, anyway."

Wheeler cocked his head now. "You said he was the GRU general. How is he English?"

"Zakharov is a trained linguist. He's also a murderer. And you helped him."

Marty looked at the floor a long time. Then said, "Okay. Okay. I knew my contact as Mr. Black. But that's all I know. Never met him, didn't know he was Russian." He looked around the room. "I want to speak to whoever is in charge here."

"Save it, Marty. It won't help you."

With more fear in his voice, Wheeler said, "I don't know anything. I just don't."

"Then what the fuck do I need you around for?"

Marty Wheeler realized what Hanley was saying. "Wait . . . I *do* know things. My extraction. I was supposed to hook up with the Solntsevskaya Bratva here in London, get a ride to the Peruvian embassy, and hang out there until I was shipped off to the port to take a freighter to Russia."

"But none of that happened, so that's pretty fucking irrelevant, isn't it?"

Wheeler looked down.

Hanley said, "You know *something*, Marty."

He shook his head. "I don't know shit. He didn't involve me—"

Hanley interrupted. "I'm not talking about Zakharov. I'm talking about what you know about the Agency."

"What . . . what do you mean?"

"You've seen some faces a guy like you isn't supposed to see. You know some things a guy with morals like yours shouldn't be allowed to know. You aren't making a case for why I should keep you around."

The bound man looked uncomprehendingly at the DDO. "Because . . . because you'll go to prison if you make it to where I'm *not* around. *Jesus*, Matt. Power has gone to your head."

"You got a lot of good men dead, Marty. And you standing trial . . . that would be a mess for the nation."

Wheeler thought he understood. With a crack in his voice he said, "You're going to get your asset to kill me, Matt? Is that it?"

"Of course not."

Wheeler breathed a sigh of relief.

"I'm going to do it myself."

Hanley drew a Glock 23 pistol from inside his coat. Held it up. "Standard issue. Nothing fancy. A gun a guy like you might happen to get hold of somehow."

"We're friends, Matt."

"Which makes it harder, no question, but it also makes me more pissed off at you, so in some sense I guess it will make it easier. I'd let you know after . . . but . . ."

"Suicide? You actually think anyone will believe I shot myself?"

Hanley shrugged. "Your people staged Renfro's body. I saw right through it. I think I've got the skills to make it look like it was death by your own hand. Let's find out."

"You're *fucking* crazy, Matt. You're worse than the last guy in your position. All your off-book shooters blasting their way across the first world. Washington, London, Paris, Hong Kong. It's *fucking* nuts, man."

Matt knelt down next to Wheeler. "I don't do a damn thing the director doesn't let me do."

"Tell that shit to someone else. I was Ops before I was Support, you remember, don't you? The director doesn't have a clue what you're up to. He just told you he didn't want to know, so you've taken that as carte blanche to do whatever the fuck you want to do."

Hanley moved closer to Wheeler now, his face inches from the seated and bound man. "Well, I gotta tell you, Marty. I know that's not true because I do a whole lot of shit I don't want to do." He lifted the gun in his left hand. "But this . . . this I very much want to do."

Hanley shoved the barrel of the gun up under Wheeler's chin.

"Fuck you!" Wheeler shouted.

The gun went click and Wheeler screamed falsetto.

Slowly Hanley stood back up and holstered his weapon. Tears filled Wheeler's eyes now, but through them he was able to see his old friend look at someone or something behind Wheeler's chair.

Addressing the person who was obviously now standing there, Hanley spoke slowly, emphatically. "To within an *inch* of his life. You copy?"

The bearded asset who'd been squatting in front of Wheeler minutes before responded, demonstrating that he had not, in fact, left the room. "Solid copy, sir."

Deputy Director of Operations Matt Hanley walked past the assistant deputy director of Support without another word or glance, and then the asset appeared. He'd put on a pair of contractor gloves, and he turned to face the man strapped to the chair.

"Matt! God, Matt! No! Please no!"

Hanley shut the door on the way out, but this did little to drown out the screams.

. . .

Zoya Zakharova awoke with the loud click of the lock being disengaged from the heavy wooden door to her cell.

She rubbed her eyes, and they cleared to reveal her father standing in the doorway. She sat up while he grabbed a chair and walked over to her with it. Behind him he left the door open. She could see no one out in the hall. It was a show, she was certain, a means to convey to her that she was not a prisoner here, although she didn't believe that for an instant.

"My darling Zoyushka. How are they treating you?"

"Don't call me that."

Zakharov frowned. "I understand why you are angry. I have taken your liberty, just like your friends in America did." He looked around the little room. "Was it much like this over there?"

"It was better."

He acted like he didn't hear her. "I imagine it was very much like this. And then they would have subjected you to the daily debriefings. They took away your clocks, they came at all hours at first to confuse you, to catch you off guard, to destroy your daily rhythm. And then . . . when you gave them things they wanted and needed, they gave you more little prizes. What was it you wanted from them? Some exercise? You are looking very fit. Yes . . . I'm sure they let you work out to your heart's content. Some information? Certainly. You asked to see the file on my death, and they rewarded you by showing it to you."

Zoya said nothing.

"It's the standard playbook, all intelligence agencies do it."

Now Zoya said, "Do they? Please, Papa, tell me more about what it's like to work for an intelligence agency, because your dumb daughter would have no idea about any of that."

Zakharov smiled; Zoya thought she saw a flash of pride on his face, but he hid it well with his words. "Of course you do. I am just emphasizing the fact that you were played by the Americans."

"Then why am I here? No one sent me. If they had, do you think they would have left me alone to be kidnapped by you?"

"You were not alone. Your friend who assisted you two nights ago. The one they tell me Jon beat into a bloody pulp. Are you telling me he wasn't sent along with you to find me?"

"That's *exactly* what I'm telling you. He was over here pursuing something that happened to a CIA jet in the UK; I don't know the specifics, but I'm sure you do. His investigation led him to Terry Cassidy's office. I was there at the same time."

"And he just spontaneously decided to save you and then team up with some stranger?"

Zoya bit her lip, then glanced away. "He . . . he and I . . . we know one another."

Zakharov eyed his daughter. "Well . . . that is interesting. My little girl is in a relationship with a CIA officer."

"He's not a CIA officer, and we are not in a relationship."

Zakharov leaned back in his chair. "Zoya, we were a family of chameleons. You, me, even Feo, though his real love was the sciences. But your mother . . . she was the best."

Zoya nodded. "Yes. She was."

"We could change ourselves, adapt to different places, languages, cultures. Fit into different legends. We could make ourselves what we needed to be in order to help the *Rodina*. But ideas, beliefs. I *never* changed these. Feo and your mother *never* switched sides.

"So help me understand what happened to you."

Zoya responded with, "What are you doing here? I've put together on my own that you are working with both the Kremlin and the Solntsevskaya Bratva; you've been conducting targeted killings, mostly to support the aims of Russian oligarchs, Siloviki. Uncle Vladi is helping you with money, because the Kremlin has anointed him a billionaire, and they would have only done this for operational purposes.

"So, what is it all about?"

"It's about supporting my country."

"Interesting. I thought it was about revenge."

He smiled now. "Tell me about Poison Apple."

Zoya's brow furrowed. "I don't know what you are talking about."

Zakharov regarded his daughter for a long time. "Either you have learned to completely mask your microexpressions, or you are telling the truth. I find it curious you don't know the name of the CIA program you are a part of, darling. If you really don't know, then your new masters are keeping something from you. What else might they be keeping?"

"How do *you* know about this?"

Zakharov said, "I am an intelligence officer. I have a mole in the CIA."

"Not high enough to tell you about me."

The bearded man raised an eyebrow. "Touché. But that doesn't help your case, it only tells me you are a prized possession of the enemy."

Zoya looked down at the floor. Finally she said, "What else could I have done but what I did? I just needed to get away from SVR. The Americans grabbed me in Thailand and brought me back to the States. I wasn't a prisoner; after the debriefs they told me I could come and go as I pleased, but if I chose to stay, they had work for me. Combating terrorists, proliferation, things of that nature. Not against Russia. I told them I'd stay with them as long as I agreed on the missions, and they told me they were fine with that."

"That is impossibly naïve, daughter."

"No, it's not. There is another asset there who has the same relationship."

"Then he is Poison Apple, as well."

Zoya shrugged. She had never heard the code name. "It was either work with the U.S. or head back to Europe where, sooner or later, SVR would find me and assassinate me. I know exactly what happens to disgraced operatives. I wouldn't have a chance."

Zakharov stood, dragged his chair a little closer, and sat back down. He put his hand on her knee, and she did not pull away. "But now you are back among family, my darling."

"Lucky me. My only family is a father who kills people."

"You are a daughter who kills people."

"Not innocents. I don't know what you are doing here in Scotland, but I'm no fool. You are preparing something. Some retribution for Mom and Feo and . . . and for what you see as my betrayal."

Zakharov put his hands on his own knees now. "You always were perceptive."

"You have gone mad," she said softly.

"Zoya, darling, many great men were called mad in their time. But on such individuals of singularity and conviction, the world turns."

She looked away again, and Zakharov stood. "I have work to do. But someday soon we will talk again."

"What are you doing in Scotland?" she asked again.

He ignored the question. "Part of me wants to make you disappear. Can you even imagine the shame I will feel the moment I report your . . . reemergence? It is a black cloud on my otherwise perfect record as a patriot of my nation."

"Then why don't you just let me go?"

Zakharov shook his head. "You will be escorted back to Russia, delivered to your leaders at SVR. They will figure out what to do with you. I will speak to some people, old friends to whom I don't like owing favors, but I will make certain they do not end your life. You are still my daughter, even though you have disgraced me."

. . .

Fox was standing just out of view in the hall next to the open door when Zakharov stepped out and closed it behind him, then locked it. He began walking away, and Fox trailed him.

"Fox, contact SVR in London. Tell them we will deliver Zoya to them. I want you and Hines to do it personally."

"Yes, sir, but I'm sure they'd be happy to come get her."

"Do it yourself. Stress to them that if anything happens to her, either here or in Moscow, there will be consequences for them."

The elevator door at the far end of the hall opened, and Janice Won appeared in her lab coat. She stepped out and waited for Mars to come closer, then said, "It is complete. The bacteria is fully weaponized, combined with the aerosol, and placed in the four canisters that will be loaded onto the aircraft."

"Very well," Mars said, but she clearly noted a distracted look on his face.

"When will the weapon be delivered to the staging area?"

"I'll take it up to the Highlands right now." He looked to Fox, who just nodded and pulled out his phone, ready to order men to transfer the biological weapon into the trunk of the Mercedes waiting downstairs. "Are you ready to come with me? I want you to oversee the loading of the goods on the aircraft before we get you out of the area."

"I need two or three more hours here to remove any trace of activity from the building."

Mars nodded. "Very well. I'll leave you a half dozen men for security, with orders to bring you up to the Highlands the moment you're finished."

Won said now, "I *am* finished with my two lab assistants. They won't be able to help me further, so, if you had some sort of a plan for them . . ."

Her voice trailed off and Mars glanced again at Fox, who was still on the phone to one of the Bratva men somewhere in the building. He just looked up to Hines and gave him a quick nod, and the big Englishman turned and began heading for the elevator to take him down to the first-floor laboratory where the technicians worked, far away from the weaponization lab on the third floor. He'd break the two women's necks, and he wouldn't even remove his suit coat to do it.

Mars started for the elevator to catch it along with Hines, but when he moved Janice Won was able to see down to the end of the hall. Two men sat in chairs outside a closed door.

"What's going on? Why are there guards at that door? Who is being kept in there?"

Mars sighed. "My daughter, actually."

Won screeched her reply. "The CIA agent?"

Mars entered the opening elevator, then turned and faced her. "Don't worry about her. She knows nothing, and she will be leaving us shortly."

As the doors closed, Mars thought about Zoya and wondered if he was condemning her by sending her back to Moscow. He hoped not, but his utter conviction to his cause determined his decision.

He realized now that even though this would not be the outcome he wanted for her, he possessed sufficient conviction to, potentially, anyhow, send his daughter to her death.

And it filled him with a sudden and unexpected feeling of strength.

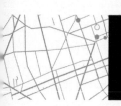

CHAPTER 49

The lunch crowd was full of tourists at the Ensign Ewart, a pub in a seventeenth-century building just a hundred yards or so from the front gates of Edinburgh Castle. The street out front was even more packed than the pub, so when an average man of average height with average hair and a short beard stepped through the door, not a single person looked his way. He continued on to the back, followed a sign through a narrow door, and entered the men's room.

Once he was out of view of others in the privacy of the locked bathroom, Court Gentry reached out to the wall to steady himself before moving slowly to the urinal. He'd been popping over-the-counter pain pills since the previous morning, but he still felt like he'd been put in an industrial dryer that had been left on overnight. He hurt like hell, and the past twenty minutes of uphill walking had done his battered body no great favor.

The Ensign Ewart billed itself as the highest pub in Edinburgh, as it was perched on the tallest hill in the city. Court did not know this until he heard a waitress mentioning it to a table as he passed, and had he known beforehand he would have gone elsewhere. He'd picked this central location off the map, figuring it would be as good a place as any for him to stage himself while waiting for more intel from Brewer about just where he was going in the city, but as he left the cheap hotel where he'd spent the morning hours, Court quickly began to regret his decision. There weren't many European cities Court had never operated in during his career, both with CIA and as a private operator. But this was his first visit to Edinburgh and, when he'd looked at a map on the drive up the evening before, he'd neglected to consider that his map was not topographical. Edinburgh was a city in the hills, however, so the trek had included multiple staircases, a steep climb up a cobblestone street, and a lot more effort than he'd wanted to put in just to find a place to wait for a phone call.

He had acquired a motorcycle late the evening before, but it was ten minutes' walk from him, a walk that required climbing over one hundred steps in a narrow alleyway, called a "close" here in Scotland.

Court made it to the urinal and unzipped his fly; even this hurt his ribs to accomplish, and he wondered what possible good he could do if he had to go into some defended location and rescue Zoya today.

As he pissed, he thought about the day to come, and both hoped for and feared the nugget of intelligence that would lead him on into action. He also fought the urge to look down for as long as he could, but eventually, this challenge became too great for him.

His gaze lowered, into the bowl of the urinal.

He closed his eyes tight. Fuck. A day and a half after he'd had the shit kicked out of him by the huge boxer, and he was still pissing blood.

His earpiece vibrated, and he touched it, not even bothering to stop pissing.

"What's up?" he said in a tired voice.

"Violator?" He could tell Brewer couldn't tell if it was him.

He replied in a bored tone. "Iden to follow. Whiskey, Oscar, Tango, Lima, Mike."

"Okay. It's you. Are you operational?"

She wasn't asking him if he was feeling all right; she was asking if he could do his job.

"I'm just peachy," he replied, glancing down again at the pinkish urine.

Brewer's voice filled his left ear now. "We've got a facial recog analysis hit up there in Edinburgh. I've had a team looking at security and traffic cams for the past eight hours. We finally found who we're looking for."

"Zoya?"

"Artyom Primakov aka Roger Fox."

"The made man for the Russian mob that Belyakov mentioned?"

"That's right. He was picked up on a camera near the University of Edinburgh. Riding in a black passenger van that turned into an underground garage below a building that used to house a science lab. I have an address." She added, "He was not alone."

"How many with him?" Court asked as he zipped up his fly and sat back against the sink.

"It was hard to tell inside the van from the images. We think there were a total of five. Two in the front and three in the back."

"Was Zoya in the car?"

Brewer paused.

"Was . . . Zoya . . . with . . . him?"

"Anthem was there, yes. Along with a man who looked like he had to have been at least six foot six."

"Bigger. Much bigger," Court mumbled.

"He came up on facial recog, too, because of a stint he did in prison for murder. His name is Jon Hines, he's English. You know him?"

"Only socially." Court then asked, "What about Zoya's father?"

"We aren't sure what he looks like, but there was no one of his age in that vehicle. We ran a wide search of cameras around that location and we just snagged a hit from about an hour ago. A large Mercedes pulled into the same garage. A man in the back of the vehicle might have been General Zakharov."

"Might have been?"

"This man wore a beard, but he seemed to be the right age and general build. No photo of Zakharov has been taken in fifteen years, so we can't be certain."

"What do *you* think?" Court asked.

"I think we can assume it's him."

"Are they all still in the building?"

"We are monitoring all the cams in the area and believe so, but there is only one way to know for sure."

"I'm gonna take a guess. You need me to just be-bop in there and find out."

Brewer sighed. Court knew the woman hated him, but he couldn't help being a smartass to her considering her constant superior attitude.

She said, "Look, the British have a mole, too, so the fewer who know what we're doing, the better.

"But I am able to offer you some help if you can wait. We are en route to Inverness right now and will fly right over Edinburgh. We can stop off there, get to you, and help hit the science lab."

Court laughed. "Oh, great. You and Matt Hanley are going to come in with guns up and save the day?"

"No, Violator. That's not what I'm proposing. Matt has Jenner's Ground Branch team working as his security, and they are on board the aircraft. Eight operators. The best. If you can wait two hours, we'll drop off Jenner's boys, and you all can make entry on the building."

Court said, "The enemy gets a vote, Brewer. If I think they are about to leave, I'm going to have to go in whether or not Jenner and his pipe hitters show up in time."

"I understand. There is another singleton asset who just arrived in Edinburgh, along with a case officer. I sent them up last night to help in the hunt for Zakharov. I can send them to you."

"The CO. Is he a shooter?"

He heard her typing for a moment. "Well . . . of course he's been through the Farm, but . . . that's about it." The Farm was the CIA's officer training program at Camp Peary. A former Ground Branch Special Activities Division paramilitary officer like Gentry considered the firearms instruction at the Farm to be just step one of one hundred to becoming proficient in shooting and close-quarters battle tactics.

But Court knew he was nowhere near one hundred percent himself. "I'll take the asset, and I'll take the CO as a driver, just in case we've got to move in before Jenner gets here." He next asked, "What are my orders, specifically?"

"Your orders are to kill Feodor Zakharov."

The possibility that he himself would be tasked with killing Zoya's father had somehow not occurred to him. He'd been looking for a missing prisoner, who'd turned up dead, and then his mission morphed into trying to save Zoya. Now he was being sent to kill her dad. It put a lump in his throat, but he said, "Understood."

"Violator?" Brewer added. "I need you to understand something. Zakharov is the primary objective. Killing or capturing Primakov is the secondary objective."

When she said nothing else Court said, "But?"

"But *nothing*. There is *no* tertiary objective."

"Meaning?"

"Meaning Anthem is not, I repeat, *not*, mission critical. Accomplish your primary and secondary, and then get the hell out of there."

The lump in his throat was replaced by anger welling deep within him. "Anthem is an asset, same as me. My life isn't more important."

Brewer hesitated a long moment. Court wondered if she was trying to calculate whether the life of *either* of her assets was important to her.

"How grateful is she going to be if you kill her father and then try to save her?"

"It's not about gratitude."

"My point is, we don't know if she is in league with General Zakharov. Making contact with her might just put your mission in jeopardy. You need to consider her a hostile until you learn otherwise, and I don't know how you are possibly going to learn otherwise while hitting that building alone."

He didn't argue the point, because it would just waste time. Instead he said, "I don't even know what this guy looks like."

"I'm sending you three images. One is Primakov; another is a photograph of General Zakharov back when he was the GRU head. The third is the image taken of the man in the Mercedes who I think could be Zakharov."

Court replied, "Get me the images, the address to their location, and the iden codes on the two who will be joining me."

"You don't need iden codes; you will recognize both of the men coming to assist you." She gave him the address; he typed it into his GPS and saw that it would take less than ten minutes on his motorcycle, once he got down the hill to retrieve it, to get there.

"Roger, I'm en route," Court said, and then he hung up. He was ready to continue on with his mission. *His* mission, not Brewer's, because despite his clear orders from her, there was no way he was going into that building without making every effort to leave with Zoya.

. . .

Seconds later Court was out of the men's room, faking a normal walk and a placid face so as not to draw any attention to himself from the dozens of patrons in the pub. On his way out the door he stopped and looked to the bar. It was midday, and he was operational, carrying a firearm in a capital city in the United Kingdom. Under most any circumstances he wouldn't consider drinking now, but he needed to be able to move, and he told himself the good effects of the alcohol would, in this instance, anyway, outweigh the bad.

He ordered a double scotch; the bartender reached for a menu containing descriptions of the dozen they had to offer and he started to mention his favorites, but Court just said, "Dude, I don't give a shit. Something strong, wet, and cheap."

The bartender raised an eyebrow, reached down into the well in front of him, and drew out a bottle. He poured a double into a glass, took the pound notes, and turned away before Court shot the entire contents in two gulps.

It tasted to Court like singed horsehair, and the bartender apparently was aware it was awful because Court caught him grinning.

The American put the glass down with a nod, then headed for the door.

CHAPTER 50

Thirty men arrived in Scotland in three black Zodiac boats that had been disgorged from a freighter in the North Sea. They'd landed on an Uplands coastline at three-ten a.m., exactly on schedule, and then they carried all their gear, one hundred forty pounds of kit to a man, across barren landscape, moving slowly but surely, boots sinking into the blanket bogs and thighs straining with the climbs up and down rolling hills.

By ten a.m. they had been hiking nearly seven hours and had not seen one other human being during all that time. Their route had been carefully chosen to keep them away from meddlesome locals, so by the time they neared their rally point, they knew they'd infiltrated the United Kingdom undetected.

They were all Russian, with hard faces and tattoos and body armor on their chests and backs, poorly concealed under oversized raincoats. There were rifles hidden in their oversized packs, Kalashnikovs mostly, though some other weapons were represented.

These men worked for David Mars now, but they bore little resemblance to the other armed men Mars had utilized here in the UK. No, those had been mafia shooters and hired security, dangerous and skilled enough, but they weren't cut from the same cloth as the formidable new arrivals at all.

At the rally point they climbed into a pair of sixteen-passenger vans with all but the driver's seat removed and sat in back on their gear for the two-hour drive to their destination. They left the highway for a road, left the road for a gravel track, and left the track for a muddy field with a few other tread marks directing the way. Here they ascended a hill and parked at the stone fence around a cemetery in front of a formidable-looking stone church.

A high-end executive helicopter caught the men's eyes in a nearby field, but there were, at first, no signs of life around.

. . .

David Mars himself stood in the doorway to the old gothic church on the far side of the cemetery. He'd only just arrived from Edinburgh via helo, and he watched the men as they climbed out of the vehicles, moving silently through the gray, wet afternoon, hefting impossibly large rucks, and then heading up in his direction.

All thirty entered the sanctuary and began placing equipment in the few old pews lying around the shuttered house of worship, taking off their coats and adjusting the equipment on their bodies.

Mars just looked on while a Bratva foot soldier, part of his protection detail, stepped up to one of the men as he unslung his rifle and propped it against the wall.

The Bratva man said, "Nice rifle. Who are you guys with?"

The big gunman in the body armor did not look his way. "Fuck off."

The mafia gunman sniffed and turned away. Mars heard him mumbling. "Fucking Spetsnaz. Think they're such hot shit."

. . .

The thirty men who arrived at the dilapidated church were not, in fact, Spetsnaz, Russian special forces. But they all had been. These were former GRU, military Spetsnaz, as opposed to foreign or domestic intelligence special forces. They worked for the same organization that General Feodor Zakharov once ran, but they had no clue they were working for him now.

Mars surveyed many of the former special forces men as they assembled, but soon they dispersed. Some moved to the higher church windows or out in the terrain around the castle, performing 360-degree security for the others while they readied equipment and prepared their living space.

Mars had definite reservations about using former Russian military in his attack, but his reverence for the skills of these men outweighed his misgivings.

This event could not, in any way, lead back to the Kremlin. But the UK was full of Russians, and more specifically Russian mafia, so Mars had decided that infiltrating non-mafia mercenaries with advanced training would be an acceptable risk, especially if he ensured that the hiring of these troops was done carefully.

First, even though they were mercenaries, Mars knew these men would not leave a fallen comrade behind. There would be no evidence of Russian "Little Green Men" operating in Scotland on the day of the attack.

And second, he'd had Terry Cassidy set up a shell corporation, and one of Belyakov's bankers in Cyprus set up a numbered account that was attached to the firm. The lawyer, following Mars's instructions, left a few misleading bread crumbs in the paperwork of the shell corporation, should it ever fall under scrutiny. A company that had been sanctioned for doing business in the past in North Korea was tangentially linked to the shell via joint holdings in the shipping industry, and this allowed Mars to breathe a little easier.

His highly skilled mercs weren't just here to bolster his attack on the conference, an attack that was initially designed as a feint while the real danger fell from above. They were here to bolster the false-flag operation that would keep Zakharov's precious *Rodina* safe from retribution when American and British spies started dropping dead from lung conditions all around the world at the same time.

Some men took positions outside, around the church; a few of them moved out into the cemetery and found a place to hide themselves in tall grasses around the tombstones there. They set up their weapons to defend the location. A sniper climbed the bell turret and broke out a section of stained-glass window so he could see the approach from the little road.

Mars's real force was here now. He knew they'd all been taking a specific regimen of antibiotics for days, rendering them virtually immune to the *Yersinia pestis* they would deliver into the belly of the meeting of Western intelligence officials. They'd continue taking the Cefalexin during and after the operation, as well.

With these men here and in place, Mars began thinking of the next stage. Janice Won was still needed, but not for her scientific expertise. No, she had one more night to live. Only in death would she truly serve her final purpose.

. . .

Zack Hightower had spent much of the morning in the back of a U.S. Army UH-60 helicopter that was being flown up to Inverness, Scotland, to assist with security for the Five Eyes conference. With him was the young, red-bearded case officer named Jason, who looked nervously out the open door of the helo for much of the flight, while Zack, in contrast, lay on the hard deck and slept with his head on his backpack.

The UH-60 wasn't taking the two CIA men all the way to the Scottish Highlands; instead it was to drop them in Edinburgh before getting back in the air and again heading north.

Brewer wanted Romantic there in case Gentry found himself in need of support while tracking Zakharov and Primakov, and she wanted the case officer loaned out to her to work to establish the safe house and assist the assets with driving and anything else they needed.

The helo dropped the two of them off just behind a secluded farmhouse run by the CIA, then departed while the two Americans approached the building. It was a ranch-style property with a large, detached garage and an empty barn. Before going inside, Zack checked the garage and found two black Range Rovers waiting there. They were dusty but appeared to be well maintained.

Inside, the safe house was simple, but expansive, with a large living area and five bedrooms off a hall towards the back.

Zack had only been in the house for twenty minutes when Brewer called him. "We have an in extremis situation there in Edinburgh and need your help."

"Where and what?"

"Violator is outside a building on Lauriston Place, in the city proper. I need you there to assist in case he needs to make entry. Take Jason with you to drive. Violator might be able to wait on a team from Ground Branch, but if he suspects the occupants are planning on moving, his orders are to penetrate the building to capture Zakharov."

"Who the hell is Zakharov?"

Brewer realized Hightower knew nothing about what was going on in the UK. She filled him in quickly, telling him that the entire Five Eyes conference seemed to be imperiled by this former GRU general and his scheme. She ended with, "Hurry, because if you don't get there in the next few minutes, Violator might have to make entry on the opposition location without any backup."

"No sweat. I've saved his ass before, I can do it again."

Zack went into a back bedroom and opened a safe in the closet there, using a code Jason gave him. From it he pulled a suppressed HK VP9 pistol with a silencer and a collapsed-stock SIG MPX submachine gun. Ammunition had been preloaded, so he took a fistful of magazines for the subgun and two extra for the pistol and headed for the garage of the safe house.

Jason grabbed a Glock 17 and an extra magazine, and Zack warned him not to point it at anything he didn't intend to destroy.

As Jason slipped it into his waistband he said, "I've been through the Farm."

"Big fuckin' deal, kiddo. Watch your trigger and muzzle discipline, or I'll shoot you myself."

Jason said nothing.

When Jason launched one of the Range Rovers out of the dusty garage at speed, Zack, in the front passenger seat, connected again to Brewer, who was now flying over northern England. "I'm moving," he said. "I have one unsuppressed submachine gun and one suppressed pistol. Jason has a sidearm. I sure as hell hope Sierra Six has his own weapon, because I ain't sharing."

Brewer said, "It's Violator we're talking about. He's *always* got a weapon. Jenner's team is still seventy mikes out. You can get there in twenty-five. Your job is to support Violator and capture or kill the primary target personality, but if Violator goes off mission in *any* respect, you need to bypass him by any means necessary and get the job done."

Zack held on to the dashboard as the SUV bounced over the rough terrain. "And I take it you suspect that is a possibility?"

"There is a prisoner there. Zakharov's daughter. Violator might try to recover her at the expense of the operation."

"Here we go again," Zack groaned. This wouldn't be the first time he and Court Gentry had operated at cross purposes.

CHAPTER 51

Court sat on a rooftop, five feet back from the edge, and rubbed his eyes. He wasn't sleepy, really. He'd gotten a few hours on the train ride up from London the evening before. No, his eyes were blurry because he'd drunk another scotch on his way to Lauriston Place, pulling his motorbike over outside the pub and not even bothering to lock it up, because he was in and out of the establishment with a drink in him in well under a minute.

He could tell the alcohol was having some effect on his overall pain level. Things still hurt; most things on his body still hurt, but he was able to move around more freely now, which had been his aim.

He looked out over the street towards the target location now. It seemed like the tenth building he'd had to conduct overwatch on in the past seventy-two hours, but he was too hazy to count them all. The location appeared abandoned, just a four-story brick structure with shuttered windows and no hint of light or movement behind them. He found this odd here on the edge of the campus of the University of Edinburgh. Classes were out for the summer, mostly, but there were still quite a few students and tourists around, and the street below Court was a bustling thoroughfare all but gridlocked with double-decker buses, taxis, and private vehicles.

It wasn't even one p.m., so Court worried he might have to hit this location during daylight with civilians potentially in the line of fire.

Whatever the hell was going on in there, he hoped it at least continued till nightfall.

Brewer called and told him the assets en route were twenty minutes out. He told her to notify them to park in a lot a quarter mile down the hill, just at the base of a long outdoor staircase that ran down a narrow close. He then instructed her to tell the driver to stay with the vehicle and vector the asset to his position.

Two men entering the large quiet building across the street would be suboptimal, Court told himself, so he still hoped the Ground Branch team en route had time to make it into the area before he had to act.

No sooner did he think this, however, than he saw a Mercedes roll out of the garage under the building. Looking through his binoculars quickly, he registered a pair of wide-chested tough-looking men in the front seat, and in the backseat was an older bearded man in a suit. Court recognized him as the man who might or might not have been Zoya's father.

Either way, he was Court's target.

Court had a motorcycle; he could get down to street level and catch the black Mercedes in traffic. But he didn't move from his hide. Filled with indecision, he just glanced back and forth between the building and the luxury sedan as it moved slowly in bumper-to-bumper traffic.

Zoya was *not* in that vehicle, of this he was certain. This meant she was likely still inside the building across the street.

The decision should have been a hard one for him to make, but in the end, it wasn't.

He would *not* be leaving. His mission, right now anyway, was Zoya, Brewer's orders be damned. But it also occurred to him that with the departure of some of the players from the scene, he had no way of knowing if others inside would be leaving soon, as well. He didn't want to run the risk of seeing Zoya rolling out of there in the back of a truck full of Russian gangsters.

He decided to enter the building and find her.

There was a mantra his principal trainer at CIA, a man he only knew as Maurice, used to drill into him time and again. "Finesse, not force."

Court was a master at both, but he didn't imagine the odds would be in his favor if he kicked in the front door of that building across the street with guns blazing.

Finesse was his only shot at this.

Normally he would have contacted Brewer, but he realized there was nothing she could do for him now but complain about his decision to let Zakharov escape. No, recovering Zoya wasn't one of his assigned tasks, so the last thing he wanted to do right now was update Brewer on his plan to bail on the mission to attempt to achieve a non-mission-critical objective.

She would disallow it, he told himself, and he would do it anyhow, so why trouble her with a phone call?

Court would go it alone. He'd been going it alone for a long time, after all.

. . .

Minutes later he stood at street level, alongside the target building, just steps away from the down ramp to the underground garage. Brewer had tried to call him, but he hadn't answered, so she'd texted him that his backup was ten minutes out. He thought about waiting, but he didn't know who she would be sending, and didn't know what she had told the other asset about Zoya.

The last thing he wanted was some asshole coming in here and breaking up his rescue mission because it didn't look anything like what Brewer told him his job was.

He took the ramp down to the parking garage. *Finesse, not force,* he reminded himself.

At the bottom of the garage was a barricade to prevent cars from entering, but Court simply stepped around it and moved deeper under the building. He found a door to a stairwell, picked it in seconds, then slipped inside silently.

Almost immediately he detected a presence one floor above him on the stairs. A shuffling of footsteps. He drew his 9-millimeter and screwed on the Gemtech silencer, then began moving slowly upwards.

. . .

Zoya Zakharova knew she was being sent back to Russia the second her door opened and she saw the men. Fox was there, as was Hines, but they had been joined by four tattooed, rough-looking, square-jawed types, armed with HK MP5K short-barreled, folded-stock submachine guns. She had not been tied or blindfolded, but there was still no way for her to escape at present. Fox spoke to her in Russian and told her to come out into the hall.

She was led towards the elevator, while Fox and Hines walked silently behind her and the gunmen. The rhythmic echoes of footsteps in the big university building's hallways reverberated, and the elevator down loomed closer with every step.

She wondered if there was anything she could have said to her father that would have prevented him from shipping her back to Russia where, despite his assurances, she knew she faced certain death. She could have begged him, pleaded for a chance to work with him, but her pride prevented it.

She was going to die in a gulag or be assassinated walking to the grocery if she didn't find a way to get away from these men before she was handed over to SVR.

As the group approached the elevator, it surprised everyone when it dinged to indicate a car arriving on the floor. The armed men stopped and looked back to Fox, and Fox immediately reached for his radio to see who was coming.

The doors began to open, and everyone reached for their weapons. Hines moved in front of Fox, pushing the smaller man back.

"The girl," Fox said, and the Englishman grabbed Zoya by her shirt and yanked her onto her heels and back behind him, as well.

As the door opened, the carnage was immediately apparent. Two dead men were lying one on top of the other on the floor of the car. Blood splattered the walls and drenched the carpet below them.

Zoya recognized both men as Bratva soldiers who had been guarding the stairwell and the elevator when she'd arrived.

"What the fuck?" one of the Bratva men said, his MP5K up at his shoulder and scanning left and right. The men around him did the same. No one advanced on the elevator, and soon the door closed again.

Fox brought the radio to his mouth and ordered all the men still alive in the building to be on the lookout. He sent three of the five men who had been guarding Janice Won downstairs to immediately head to the rear stairwell to meet this group on the top floor. They would descend the rest of the way together, all the way down to the parking garage.

Zoya complied in silence, but inside she was telling herself two things.

One, she needed to find an opportunity in this moment of chaos to get away.

And two, Court had come for her.

. . .

Court had made his way to the second floor after killing the two guards and dumping them in the elevator, then pushing the button for the top floor and leaping out. He didn't know who would find them, but he did know that once they were found it would create a moment of chaos that he wanted to exploit.

And he didn't have to wait long for an opportunity. When the frantic radio call came over the walkie-talkie he'd taken from a dead guard, he understood enough of the Russian to recognize that the principals, whoever they were, would be descending from the top floor via a staircase at the back of the building. Court raced through a hallway past one laboratory after another, his Glock's silencer shifting left to right to cover all the angles as he moved.

Two men came out of a doorway on Court's right. He fired one round into each man's head, then shifted aim to a third figure, moving just behind them. At first he thought he was looking at a child but quickly realized it was an Asian woman in her thirties or forties, her black hair tied severely back, and her tiny frame covered in a white lab coat.

She held no weapon, just stared at Court with uncomprehending eyes.

"You're interesting," Court said. "You're coming with," and he pulled her into the well-lit hallway, past the two dead bodies, and he shoved her up against the wall.

He began running his free hand all over her body while he pressed the suppressor to the back of her head.

"English?" he asked while frisking her. He pulled a phone from her back pocket and slipped it into his. He left no inch of her body untouched, taking no chances that she might have a gun or a blade stashed somewhere.

Her body began to shake uncontrollably and for an instant he thought she was having a seizure from panic.

But when she didn't answer him he repeated himself. "English?"

He put his hand in the crotch of her slacks, and pressed up, almost lifting her off the ground in the process of searching her. She shut her eyes tight and slammed her forehead against the wall. "Stop it!"

"Cool," he said. "You *do* speak English, which means you and I can have a chitchat. Where's the Russian woman being held?" He knelt and felt over her quivering legs.

She didn't answer him, even when he stood back up and spun her around to face him. Her pupils were all but dilated now. She looked to Court like someone with a preternatural fear of sharks finding herself surrounded by great whites in an ink black ocean.

He realized his hand was wrapped around her throat, but he was just holding her in place, not clamping down. He detected some sort of aversion to touch, but just as he was about to use this to get her to talk, the elevator fifty feet down the hall dinged, and Court immediately dropped to the floor amid the two dead guards he'd shot a minute earlier. The woman stared down at him in shock and confusion and Court said, "Raise your hands."

"What?"

He twitched the pistol in his right hand so she'd notice it. "I said, raise your hands." She did so.

"You say a single word, and I shoot you first." He lay flat, his legs draped across the bodies there, his right arm outstretched with his pistol in it pointing at the elevator, his captive standing above him.

· · ·

Janice Won was frozen in fright, fighting waves of nausea she'd never felt in her life, but she did manage to turn her head towards the elevator. Two Russian mafia men carrying rifles came out; one went to the left wall of the hallway, the other to the right. They saw her immediately and held her at gunpoint. They both knew the scientist and were aware she spoke Russian, so one called out to her. "What happened?"

Won did not reply at first. Below her she heard the man whisper.

"Byt ostorozhen. Ya gavaryu paruskie." Be careful. I speak Russian.

The crazed gunman played dead at her feet, and she knew if she made any utterance of this fact, *any* gesture to the two security men, then he would shoot her just as he'd shot the two others with her.

She called to the Russians. "A man shot these three, then went up the stairs."

Both men rose, lowered their guns, and began running forward towards the stairs behind where Won stood.

They made it less than ten feet before Court sat up suddenly and shot them both twice in the chest. The two men fell dead, still thirty feet from where Won stood.

Won saw the gunman struggle to get back up to his feet, as if he had a problem with his back and shoulder. But soon he was with her, turning her roughly up the hallway, away from the rear stairs.

. . .

Zoya Zakharova descended the rear stairs surrounded by muscular men. She was behind Fox and Hines and in front of five Bratva foot soldiers now, all moving at speed to get the hell out of there.

The circular stairwell was open in the middle, and glancing down she could see all the way to the ground floor, some fifty feet down. She knew there would be more Russians down in the parking garage waiting for them in vehicles, and although her chances for escape now were not good, they would only get worse once she had more men around her to deal with.

She slowed her descent, a man pushed her from behind, and she stopped on the stairs, spun around, and grabbed his arm. As she yanked him forward and off balance, he stumbled into Hines, who was only able to keep from falling by grabbing the railing.

This was Zoya's chance. She put her own hand on the railing, kicked her legs over the side, and then spun back around to face the staircase as she let go, falling straight down.

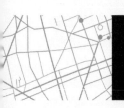

CHAPTER 52

She dropped one entire flight before landing on the balls of her feet right on the outer edge of a step, collapsing her body to absorb as much of the shock as possible while also lowering the momentum of her fall. And then, before her body absorbed all the impact, she let her feet slide from the step. Her hands slammed on the railing and again on the step below to try to break her fall a little more, and then she dropped another story.

This time she used her hands to grab onto the railing at the third floor, repeating the maneuver with her feet that had her just catching the edge of the stairs to slow herself. Still, her arms were wrenched nearly out of her shoulder sockets when her feet slipped off and she dangled there.

Above her she heard men racing down the circular stairs. They had been instructed by her father not to kill her, but that didn't mean one of them wouldn't go off mission and try to put a bullet in her during the heat of the chase.

She slid her hands down the vertical bars of the railing and then quickly swung her legs in and dropped on the stairs. She found herself on the second-story landing, so she opened the door and started to run up a tiled hallway.

She made it all of thirty feet before the door opened behind her, a voice shouted for her to stop, and a pistol cracked.

Zoya ducked lower and kept running, but as she passed an open doorway she ran right into a hand that reached out, grabbed her by the left arm, and swung her inside.

Zoya spun back around to face her attacker, balled a fist and drew it back, then let it fly.

Court Gentry caught Zoya's small but powerful fist in his hand, wincing with the pain of the impact. "Hey! It's me! How many of them?"

The echoing footsteps of men running up the hall was cacophonous now.

"Five, I think."

"Your dad has a fucking army."

"You got another gun?"

"Negative," he said, then spun out into the hall and fired four times with his suppressed Glock 19, sending two men to the tile with wounds to their legs, and three more diving into other laboratories and offices.

Hines and Fox were nowhere in sight.

Zoya turned back around and saw that she was in a lab of some sort. A large fermentation tank took up the center of the room. She stepped to the side to look for another exit, and when she did so she saw a small Asian woman in a lab coat sitting on the floor.

"Who are you?" Zoya asked.

The woman did not answer; she appeared to be in shock.

Court leaned out the doorway with his gun up, looking for fresh targets. While doing so he spoke back to Zoya. "She's with them, I think. You haven't seen her before?"

"Been locked in a room since I got here. Who is she?"

"Hell if I know."

Court turned and hefted the small Asian woman up by her left arm, then slung her around towards Zoya, who then all but caught the lady before she fell to the ground. Court said, "We're sure as hell going to keep her till we find out. I can hold these guys off if you can get her out a window and down to street level. There is a driver outside; get her to the car!"

"What kind of car?" Zoya asked as she began running for the window, pulling the woman along with her.

"Forgot to ask."

"*What?*" Zoya shouted.

"Just get her away from here! I'll find you on the street a few blocks east."

Zoya moved close to him and put her hand on his back. "Are you okay?"

He just nodded, looking up the hallway again for threats. A hand reached around a door frame pointing a pistol; Court fired at it and missed, and the gun and the arm behind it retracted quickly.

Zoya squeezed Court's shoulder, then turned to the woman in the white coat. "You're with me, bitch." She pushed her towards an old plate glass window. Picking up a rolling chair, she threw it at the glass, shattering it, then kicked at the loose shards to make a hole safe to exit through.

Behind her Court fired his pistol till it locked open, then changed mags and fired a fresh round.

. . .

Zack Hightower accessed the building through a ground-floor window and found himself moving through a hallway. He arrived at a stairwell and began ascending, heard firing coming from the second floor, but took his time clearing his way up the stairs, worried about anyone above him.

He encountered no hostiles, so when he arrived at the door he knelt down on the floor, lifted his submachine gun, and reached up for the latch.

As soon as he opened the door he saw a man lying a third of the way up the hall, and he was bleeding out, trying and failing to hold his life's blood inside his leg. Another blood smear went across the tile and disappeared into an open doorway just thirty feet in front of Zack on the right. Gunfire boomed from this room; some of it fully automatic, and there were either two or three people shooting from this position. Quickly, however, Zack realized the fire wasn't directed his way. Another room, twenty feet up the hall from the first and on the opposite side, had slow, controlled pistol fire emanating from it.

He understood the tactical situation quickly. A group of two or three men with automatic weapons and seemingly plenty of ammo were shooting at a single man with a pistol, who was clearly trying to conserve his.

In addition to the tactical situation, Zack correctly assessed the composition of the two forces. He pointed his gun at the door on the right and shouted to the man firing from the door farther on his left.

"Six? Six? Do you copy?"

The pistol fire stopped. "Who's asking?"

"Who else calls you 'Six,' dumbass?" Court's call sign on Hightower's Ground Branch team had been Sierra Six. It was virtually the only way Hightower ever referred to Court Gentry.

An MP5K reached out from the door on the right and pointed in Zack's direction. He fired a four-round burst at it, striking the brick wall inches from the door frame and forcing the weapon back into cover.

"Turn on your fucking comms!" Zack had been trying to communicate with Gentry since he'd arrived on scene, but he'd received no response. He figured it a safe bet he'd simply turned off his earpiece to get Brewer out of his head.

While he waited he looked out again in the hall, and saw the man with the leg wound lying still.

After a few seconds a reply came through Zack's earpiece in Court's voice. "Whose side are you on in this one, Zack?"

Hightower kept the holographic weapon sight of his MPX centered on the doorway to the right, but he shook his head with a little laugh. "That hurts my feelings, bro! Mommy sent me in here to help you achieve your objective. How many dudes you up against?"

"Three on your right, first door. One is wounded. I think the guy on the floor in the hall is down, but dead-check him to be sure. I don't have an angle, and I don't have the ammo."

Without responding, Hightower shifted his subgun to the left, and shot the man with the leg wound once in the top of the head.

"Dead check complete," Hightower said. "He's even deader now."

Court said, "We're still missing Primakov and Hines. They might be in the building, so watch your six."

Zack didn't know who the hell Hines was, but Primakov was the second name on the target list Brewer had given him.

"What about Zakharov?"

"No joy. He's not here. I've recovered one hostage and one enemy; they're outside the building, getting off the X now."

Again one of the Russians reached out with his pistol and fired, sight unseen, towards Zack's position in the stairwell. Zack ducked tight against the wall and then fired a burst of rounds of his own in response.

"Roger," Zack said. He had a feeling Court was saying he'd saved

Zakharov's daughter. He was certain Brewer would be displeased when she learned of this, especially because Court had failed to achieve the primary objective.

Zack said, "What do you need to do to get out of here?"

"You have any frags?"

"Negative."

"Smoke?"

"Negative."

"Bangers?" Bangers were flash bang grenades.

"That's a negative."

"The fuck kind of rescue is this?"

Zack shouted now. "The one you don't bitch about, because I can keep their heads down while you bounce! Now, what are you going to do?"

Court said, "Best bet is the window here in the room with me. It's already broken out. I can shimmy down to ground level, but it's gonna take some time. There's a doorway on the far side of this room that I think will get me to the front stairwell by the elevator. But with the angle these assholes have on me there's no way I can make it across the room without getting hit."

"No sweat. I'll keep them right where they are. You bug out, then I'll exfil down these stairs."

After changing magazines, Hightower said, "Move!"

"Moving!" Court shouted.

Zack dumped round after round at the doorway with the Russians behind it. He didn't expect to get an angle on anyone in there unless they popped out from cover like idiots, but he knew he could keep their heads down for the next thirty seconds or so, and keep them right where they were hiding for even longer, giving Court a good chance to get away.

. . .

Court ran for the laboratory window Zoya had exited from two minutes earlier, but as he neared the doorway on his right he looked through it. This led to an open office, and on the far side of that was another doorway. From the layout of the building he'd noted so far, he thought it likely the front staircase and the elevator would be through that door. The stairs would lead him straight down to the underground parking garage, where he hoped to catch Fox before he made his escape.

He ran with his Glock out in front of him, then neared the shut door, but just as he got there, it flew open and Fox came bursting out at a sprint. Ten feet behind him Hines ran down the circular stairs.

Fox was as surprised to see Court as Court was to see him, but Hines just charged forward like a bull from a dozen feet away.

Court saw Fox's silver semiautomatic pistol rising towards him, so he raised his weapon to shoot him but the big man went airborne, diving on him lightning fast. Court tried to shift aim to the threat more dangerous than a pistol, but Hines collided with him, slamming Court against the wall as if he'd been hit by a truck.

Court's weapon flipped out of his hand and clanged down the circular stairs. With the wind knocked out of him, he fell to the ground, and Hines fell on top of him.

Court now knew better than to fight the big man head-on, so he wrapped his arms and legs tight around him, attempting to use his knowledge of judo and Krav Maga against the pure boxer.

Fox tried to aim at Court, but Court shifted his body to position it behind the brick wall that was Hines's torso.

The Englishman shouted to his protectee as he wrestled on the ground. "I got this wanker sorted. Get to the car!"

Fox ran down the stairs with the gun still in his hand.

Hines struggled to get an arm free now; Court head-butted him in the forehead, but the man made no reaction to it at all apart from head-butting him back.

Court tried to shout out for Zack, but his earpiece had fallen out with the collision. Hightower was one hundred feet away and separated by multiple walls now, so there would be no way for him to know what was going on.

Court squeezed the big man tight while preparing to deliver another head butt, but by brute strength Hines was able to get an arm out of Court's clutches, then use it to push off on the floor and roll over. He made a complete revolution and slammed his six-foot-nine-inch frame up against Court, pinning him to the wall of the stairwell.

Court's battered ribs hurt anew.

He reached for the folding knife in his pocket, but just as he drew it Hines punched Court's hand, and the unopened knife went flying, through the doorway and twenty-five feet across the lab, banging against a plate glass window there and dropping to the floor.

A punch to Court's jaw stunned him, but when Hines made it up to his knees Court finally managed to land a blow of his own, a hard left jab into Hines's nose that knocked him onto his back on the landing between the two floors.

But the huge man quickly got up, and Court used pure adrenaline to mask the pain in his body enough to push himself back on the tile to make some room to do the same.

Hines touched his hand to his nose and looked down at the blood there. He shouted, "Is that all you got?"

Court spit a mouthful of blood. "No!" He leapt up to a crouch, lunged forward, slipped under a right hook, and came back up to deliver a spear hand to Hines's throat, but before it landed he was caught by a left jab that knocked him back down. He hit hard on his back; the wind that was only just returning to his lungs seemed to disappear again.

Hines laughed now, a wild look on his bloody face.

Court used the wall to pull himself yet again to his feet, understanding that Hines was toying with him now. He moved forward and threw blows at the Englishman, but this was an act of futility. Hines had ten inches of reach on Court, and the skill to keep his opponent from closing the distance.

Finally Court got under an incoming punch, shoved forward, and slammed Hines into the wall. He could hear the man groan in real pain now, and he followed with a kick to his knee. He connected, but Hines barely reacted, instead sending a chop onto the side of Court's already bruised and battered neck, causing him to fall back to the ground in agony.

Court rolled onto his side, then slowly started climbing back to his knees. He moved much slower now than the last time he got up.

Hines shouted above him, "How 'bout now? Is *that* all you got?"

"Not quite," Court mumbled, then spit more blood and added softly, "but we're gettin' there."

Hines grabbed Court by his shoulders when he stood, yanked him back around, and put him in a headlock from behind. As he did so he spoke into Court's ear. "You're a goer, aren't ya? I like your heart, mate. But a job's a job, and it's time to snap your *fuckin'* neck!"

Court's right leg kicked up, back, and then down, trying to strike the inside of the boxer's knee to buckle and break the joint, but he wasn't able to find either of the man's legs. Hines was so tall that he was able to keep Court in a headlock without exposing his body to Court's counterstrikes.

Court wrestled halfway out of the headlock when Hines tried to shake him like a rag doll to snap his neck, and then Court kicked his feet out in front of him, walked them up the wall, shoved off with all his might, and drove the boxer back, knocking him to the floor at the edge of the stairs.

They both lay flat and still for a moment. Hines was wounded. Court was worse. Slowly, Court rolled to his side. He saw that Hines was moving slower now, too, but the Englishman used the railing to pull himself to his feet and was the first to stand. Amid true pain and fatigue that Court didn't see in his first encounter with the man, Hines stood fully erect and balled his fists. Blood drained from a cut on his left eyebrow as well as the continuing trickle out of his nose.

Still, Hines grinned through the blood. "That! Is *that* all you got?"

Court climbed to his knees, then up to his feet. He crouched, looking like he was going to charge yet again, but through gasps for air he said, "Yep. That's it," and then he turned to his left and began running out of the stairwell and into the lab with a plate glass window just twenty feet away.

Diving out the window would subject him to a fall of fifteen feet or so, but at the moment he thought it his most prudent course of action. His energy was quickly depleting, and that meant Hines was seconds away from making good on his promise to break Court's neck.

Court dove headfirst through the glass; it exploded around him easily, causing him less immediate pain than any of the blows he'd received from Hines the past few days. But he was now sailing through the air, windmilling his arms and legs, trying to keep from falling headfirst.

He kept his eyes closed for a moment because of all the shattered glass in the air around him, but after he'd fallen a few feet he opened them just in time to see the hood of a small burgundy hatchback directly under him. He tightened into a ball, shifted to his left side, and slammed into the hood, crumpling it down to the engine. The wind was knocked out of him yet again, and he felt something crack in his left hand when it banged hard against the windshield.

He screamed in fresh pain, then slid off the car and onto the concrete surface of a parking lot at the back of the building.

Worried about Hines or someone else grabbing a gun and shooting him from a window, he pulled himself up the car and back to his feet, held his injured hand across his chest, and ran away, running poorly, but running for his life, nonetheless.

CHAPTER 53

Court made it around the side of the building towards the street out front, where he saw an armed man running in his direction. The man wore a beard, sideburns, and a short haircut, and it wasn't until he smiled that Court realized it was Zack. He was pleased to see that his former team leader was uninjured and carried a submachine gun slung around his neck.

Zack said, "I've got a car across the street and down the stairs!"

The two of them ran through the traffic and made it to the other side, and here Court chanced a look back and saw three men rushing out of the building. One of the three was Hines. They were all armed, and they clearly saw where their prey had gone because they dashed out into the congested street to cross it.

Court and Zack entered the narrow close and began descending a series of over 150 stairs. Above them gunfire kicked off the stonework of the building on their right, and then it pounded to their left.

Court shouted at Zack as he moved. "Get your driver out of his fucking vehicle and tell him to point a gun up this staircase. We need suppressive fire over our heads!"

Zack did this, and in seconds Court could see a figure coming into view at the bottom of the stairs, still some fifty yards away. The man drew a handgun, and then he raised it.

As Court descended as fast as his legs would take him, it looked to him as if the pistol in the distance was pointed right between his eyes.

"Can this fucker shoot?" Court yelled to Zack, who was just a few feet behind on his left, trying himself to get his SIG pointed behind him to squeeze off a few rounds without slowing.

"Wouldn't count on it," he said as he gave up, realizing he had to concentrate fully on the steps at this speed.

"Great," muttered Court.

Just then the man below opened fire.

The first round struck the stairs eight feet below where Court and Zack raced; they both slowed and crouched but continued their descent, now as worried about the supposed confederate trying to help them.

"Zack!" Court yelled, admonishing his former team leader, as if there were something he could do to improve the red-bearded man's aim.

The man fired again, and this time he hit the wall eight feet above and to the right of Court's head. Bits of stone rained down on him as he ran on.

He looked back up to the man and realized it was Jason, the young case officer he'd met in London.

Now the man just forty yards down the staircase fired a controlled but constant string of fire. Court heard rounds zipping over his head, and he was satisfied Jason was starting to get the hang of it.

All the fire from behind stopped immediately as the pursuers scrambled for any sort of cover in the narrow close.

At twenty yards Zack shouted out to Jason. "Get in the car!"

The case officer ran off to his left, out of view, and as Court himself approached the turn he shouted, "I hope you backed it in!"

He turned the corner, slowed, and saw the nose of a Land Rover pointed right at him, facing a long, straight stretch of road.

"Good job, kid," he wheezed to himself, completely out of breath now.

Zack and Court climbed into the Land Rover, Zack taking the front passenger seat, and, as Jason stomped on the gas, Hightower began reloading his MPX.

Right in front of them two men with Kalashnikovs barreled down the stairs on the left and out into the street. They turned, saw the onrushing SUV, and made to raise their weapons.

Zack was still reloading; Court had no gun in the backseat.

Zack said, "Run 'em down, Jason!"

The CIA officer started to swerve to miss the men, an automatic movement, but Zack grabbed the wheel and shifted it back to the left. Jason recovered quickly and, at fifty miles an hour and accelerating, he slammed into both men in the street, crumpling the hood of the Land Rover and spiderwebbing the windshield as an AK slammed into it.

But the airbags did not deploy.

Zack slapped Jason on the back roughly. "Atta boy! And you even thought to disable the air bags, too! Damn fine work for a rookie, kid!"

Court caught a glance at Jason through the rearview mirror. The kid looked like he was about to have a heart attack. Court reached up and squeezed the young man's shoulder. "Relax, Red. Just breathe and drive. We're good."

Court directed him to the east, and seconds later he saw Zoya and the Asian woman moving purposefully up the street amid a crowd panicking about all the gunfire emanating from just a couple of blocks away. "Stop!"

Jason stomped on the brake pedal, the Land Rover squealed to a halt, and Court opened the back door.

Zoya pushed the woman forward, right in front of astonished passersby. The white SUV squealed again as the driver floored it.

Zoya grabbed a roll of electrician's tape in the door of the SUV, then spent several seconds binding the woman's hands behind her back. She put more tape all the way around her head, covering her mouth and hair at the neckline.

Then, with wild eyes and in a rushed and fluid motion, she grabbed Court by the back of the neck. She pushed him back against the side door, put her entire body on him, and kissed him deeply.

Court's fight-or-flight reflexes spun in confusion, but within a few seconds, he kissed her back, aware simultaneously that the adrenaline coursing through his body now was having a nearly complete painkilling effect on all his injuries of the past forty-eight hours.

That's not going to last long, he told himself.

When she finally pulled off him she said, "Thank you." He saw his own blood streaked on her face.

In the front passenger seat Zack's head was craned all the way towards the action in the back. He said, "So . . . yeah . . . I was there, too. So . . ."

Zoya glanced his way quickly. "Thank you, sir," she said, then turned her attention back to the man next to her.

Zack muttered to himself as he turned back around to the front.

"You're welcome. Not exactly the same as what he got but . . . you're welcome."

When Zoya pulled back away after kissing Court again, he looked down at his left hand. The back of it was a deep purple, and it was swollen at the wrist.

"Shit," he said. "This is broken."

"Shooting hand?" Zack asked.

"Negative."

"Don't need it. Carry on," he replied matter-of-factly.

Jason directed Zoya to a medical kit in the back of the Rover; from it she pulled a chemical cold compress that she activated by breaking a capsule inside a plastic bag. Almost instantly the eight-inch-by-six-inch compress whitened with frost. She put it on the back of Court's hand, then began wrapping it with an ACE bandage.

Looking him over, she said, "I see you met your big friend again."

"I did."

"How did it go this time?"

"How do I look?"

"Not good."

"Then you have your answer."

She adjusted the compress. "Well, you got at least one solid hit in."

Court realized she assumed he'd broken a bone in his hand while hitting Hines. He sighed and laid his head back on the headrest. "This happened when I punched out a totally innocent windshield."

They drove back to the safe house in near silence as everyone worked on fighting the effects of adrenaline and the onset of exhaustion. Even Jason was too amped up to talk.

CHAPTER 54

Jason pulled the Land Rover into the detached garage of the farm west of Edinburgh, then helped Gentry out of the back. Court's body was besieged with pain; even walking was difficult, and he warned them it was going to take him some time. Jason then took the prisoner out of the vehicle and guided her by the arm to the house, and Zoya rushed forward to get another ice bath prepped for Court.

This left Zack to get under Court's right arm and help him walk up the long drive.

As they moved slowly, Zack looked at Court, regarding his black eye, cut nose, and fat lip, and the purple-gray discoloration along his jawline.

"I just want you to know I respect your ability to maintain your cover identity as a punching bag."

"Thanks," Court said through gritted teeth. Then, "This dude was unreal, Zack."

"A *human* did that to you? I thought you'd lost a fight with a trash compactor."

"Superhuman. Like nothing I've ever faced."

Zack spit on the gravel. "Whatever. I'll kick his ass for you next time we see him."

Court ignored the bluster.

After a few more steps Hightower said, "That's Zakharov's daughter? She doesn't sound Russian."

Court shuffled along slowly with Zack's help. "She's got a thing with accents."

"She's hot. Tell me she's with us."

"She's with us." Court glanced to Zack. "I think."

"Brewer said your mission was the dad. He's cooking up something nasty. Saving the chick was just personal."

"She's good, man. We needed to get her back. I did the right thing."

"Maybe we'll get some downtime tonight. You're beat to shit, so the only two dudes here able to give her any attention are me and that goofy-looking case officer. I like my chances." He laughed to himself as they neared the front porch. "Never did a Russian. Wonder if she smells like caviar or borscht."

Court pulled up, causing Zack to stop.

"What?" Hightower said. When Court did not respond, Zack's jaw dropped. "Wait. Six . . . you hittin' that?"

Court didn't answer, just closed his eyes as the pain came in waves.

"You're hittin' the fuckin' Russian chick. You *are*, aren't you?"

"Zack. No. I'm not."

Hightower laughed, then started pulling on Court again, helping him with each step. "You are *totally* bangin' Marina Oswald. Hot damn, good for you. Honestly didn't know you liked girls."

Court's body told him he'd be pissing blood for a week now, but despite himself he laughed.

They made it into the house. Zoya shepherded Court to the bathroom, where she'd already filled the tub with two bags of ice from the freezer and turned it on cold. Jason secured the mystery woman with metal cuffs around a bedpost in a back bedroom, and now he pulled security at the front window with a Benelli shotgun and his Glock.

Zoya helped Court out of his clothes, stripping him down to his underwear as he'd done himself in London.

Zack stood in the doorway, looking on. "I always go commando, personally."

Zoya glanced over her shoulder with annoyance. "Who's this charmer, Court?"

She helped Court into the bathtub, slower than last time. As he sat down, he said, "Zack, Zoya. Zoya, Zack."

Zack said, "So . . . what? You're Agency?"

She looked to Court, who shrugged back as if to say to her, *Fielding that question is your problem.*

"More or less."

Zack turned to Court. "Your kinda girl, Six."

She added, "And Feodor Zakharov is my father."

"Yeah, that I heard. You're an American spook with a GRU general for a dad? How the hell does that happen?"

"I'm Russian. Former SVR."

"Ho-ly shit. So . . . you gonna play the sweet-girl-from-Nebraska act till we let our guard down so you can knife us in the back?"

"I'm on your side."

"Yeah, so was Marty Wheeler."

Court said, "Who the hell is Marty Wheeler?"

Zack laughed. "While you two have been vacationing over here, I was back in the States on a mole hunt. Tracked the assistant DDS to London, ID'd him as the mole, and bagged and tagged him for ole Matt Hanley."

Court said, "Never heard of him."

"Yeah, well, Wheeler almost got your ass killed more than once." He turned to Zoya. "So, in light of recent events, I'm not in a super trusting mood at the moment."

Court said, "She's with us, Zack. End of discussion."

But Hightower kept at the woman. "I'm gonna keep my eyes on you, sister." He looked her up and down. "I mean, I would even if I didn't suspect you were an asset for the oppo, but now that I have my doubts, you're *really* gonna get watched over."

Zoya wasn't interested in this conversation at all. "Do what you have to do, but stay out of my way."

Zack raised an eyebrow at Court, who just shrugged.

Jason leaned into the bathroom and looked down at the bruised and broken asset in the ice bath. "Sir, you need some painkillers?"

Court thought about it. "What you got?"

"Everything from Tylenol to morphine."

"Something in the middle would be nice."

Jason retrieved the medical bag from the closet off the living room and began going through it. "Twenty milligrams of hydrocodone? Looking at all those contusions, I don't think it will do more than take the edge off; it won't get you too high."

Court winced with the cold engulfing him now. "Ten milligrams."

"Suit yourself," Jason said, and he pulled out a pill.

Court swallowed it with a beer Zack brought from the fridge, then winced again as he put the beer down next to the tub. He looked back to Jason and said, "Let's make it fifteen."

The young man broke a tablet in half and Court drank it down with another swig of beer.

He held up his hand; the compress was still on it, but he was able to see the swelling around it. He dropped it back into the ice water.

Zoya turned to the two Americans. "Guys. He's going to need fifteen minutes in the ice. Is somebody going to call Brewer in the meantime?"

Zack took the hint and headed towards the back of the farmhouse. He leaned into the back bedroom to snap a digital image of the shackled woman lying on the bed, then stepped into the living room and made the call, sending the image to Brewer in the process to see if she could ID her.

Brewer told Zack she'd just landed in Edinburgh and would call him back, and then Zack returned as Zoya helped Court change into jeans and a T-shirt she'd found in a guest bedroom closet in the safe house. All three of them then went into the living room, Zoya passed around beer, and they opened the cans.

Jason stood by the window looking out, gun on his hip.

Court was feeling the hydrocodone take effect, improving both his pain level and his mood. "What's your dad up to, Zoya?"

"I still don't know," she admitted. "He had a group of Russian mob with him and whoever the hell that lady in the lab coat is. He admitted to me he was about to make his play, but he didn't tell me what it was."

Court said, "Belyakov told me it's some sort of retributive strike. Totally unsanctioned. I think it might be related to the Five Eyes conference here."

Zoya sat up straighter. "The Five Eyes annual meeting is here in the UK? *Now?*"

"In Scotland even," Court said. "Everybody senior at Langley will be there, but that's just the tip of the iceberg. Intel and counterintel sections of FBI, DIA, NSA, all there. Plus the Brits, Aussies, New Zealanders, and Canadian intelligence and counterintelligence."

"Where is it?"

"Near Loch Ness. They've rented out some swanky castle for the venue."

Zoya stood and paced animatedly. "That's it. That's *got* to be it. They have to cancel it."

Court said, "They won't cancel it, and Hanley won't pass intel to the Brits unless we have enough to wrap the whole thing up. Zack might have caught our mole, but the Brits think they have one, or more than one. We need to know what the plan is. Bomb it? Security will be insane. It would be tough to get in deep enough to do enough damage."

Zack fielded a call back from Brewer, going into a back room to do so. When he returned he said, "Look alive, kids. Brass is inbound."

Court immediately started pulling himself up to his feet, but Zoya didn't understand. "What does that mean?"

"Brewer is ten minutes out," Zack explained.

• • •

Suzanne Brewer arrived in a rented BMW 3 Series; behind the wheel was Chris Travers, one of the Ground Branch men from Walt Jenner's team. Hanley had sent him along for her security, while Hanley and the seven other Special Activities Division operators got back in the air and flew on to Inverness, the closest airport to Castle Enrick.

Travers parked in the driveway and walked up the hill to the house, where they were met at the front door by Jason. In the living room Brewer saw the three assets and immediately noted Violator's bruised face and the ice pack on his left hand.

She made no mention of it, but Travers said, "Damn, Violator. I'd hate to see the other guy."

Court shrugged. "Me, too. Two ass kickings was enough for me."

Travers laughed at this.

Brewer looked at Jason, then jerked her thumb at the front door. The young case officer left compliantly.

Now Brewer looked at Zoya like a teacher regarding a misbehaving student. "I have a lot of questions for you," Brewer said. "You were in captivity for a day. Did you learn anything during that time that could help us determine what's going on?"

Zoya nodded. "David Mars is my father, General Feodor Zakharov. He is working against the West because he thinks MI6 killed my mom and my brother, and he thought the CIA had killed me."

"So, did they?"

Zoya blinked. "I'm sitting right here."

Brewer said, "I'm talking about your mother and your brother, obviously."

"I don't know, but I have my doubts. My dad moved to London under an assumed name and started operating in Russia's interests. All part of Russia's strategy of indirect warfare. But I think he's been plotting his personal revenge all this time, too. He's not working for GRU, not working for the Kremlin, per se. He was probably sent over here by the president and his billionaire cronies, but whatever he's doing right now, it's his own plan, no one else's. He's an independent puppeteer carrying all this out on foreign soil.

"Maybe the British really did drive him to this, but you know the Kremlin and its schemes. Perhaps they were the ones who killed Feo and Mom, to stoke his fury, to place him like a ticking bomb in the middle of their adversary."

Brewer said, "Well, the woman you are holding here has already provided us with one clue. We easily matched her photograph. Her name is Janice Won. She is a virologist. Until about four months ago she was working for the European Center for Disease Prevention in Stockholm. She's from South Korea. I've sent a message to Seoul station to try to get more information about her."

"What did she do in Stockholm?"

"She is an expert on the weaponization of pneumonic plague."

Court muttered, "Well, shit."

"Yeah," Brewer said. "We have people looking into her, trying to figure out her link to Zakharov."

Zoya said, "My father has the contacts to get whoever he wants. And he has the motivation. He is convinced the British killed his wife and son, and he's positive you guys turned me from a valiant and loyal Russian spook to a dirty American operative. My father is a man of utter conviction. As long as he believes all that, he will attack, and nothing will stop him but a bullet to the brain."

"You're playin' my tune, sister," Zack said, and Zoya just gave him an "eat shit" look.

Zoya then turned to Brewer. "Now *I* have a question for *you*. What is Poison Apple?"

Neither Zack nor Court had any idea what she was talking about, but to their surprise Brewer said, "Where did you hear about that?"

"From my father. He doesn't know what it is, either."

Brewer looked to Travers. "I need you to leave the room, please."

"Ma'am, I'm TS/SCI, with a full scope poly. I don't have to leave *any* room." He was telling her he had the highest security clearance.

She didn't blink. "I said, I need you to leave the room."

Travers pushed himself off the wall. "Yes, ma'am." He stepped out the front door and closed it behind him.

Brewer looked back to the three in front of her. "I assume Wheeler got the name of the program somehow and passed it on without knowledge of its scope or sanction."

Court tightened a fresh cold pack on the back of his left hand and said, "What is it?"

Brewer said, "It . . . is you. You three make up an initiative that has been code named Poison Apple. It is approved by the director himself, and it is run by me, with the DDO determining the operations."

Court said, "So . . . what? We're Matt Hanley's private assassins?"

He expected pushback from Brewer, but she said, "That's exactly what you are. That and spooks, surveillance artists, whatever he needs done that's blacker than black. Look, I don't like it, so don't bitch about it to me."

Court replied, "I'm not bitching. Matt makes good decisions. He's a good man."

Zoya turned to him. "I've seen 'good men' attain power and abuse it."

Court waved his functioning hand in the air. "I've known Hanley for over a decade. I trust him."

Zack said, "The Russkie has a point, Six. Matt did order me to kill you once."

Court turned to Hightower. "You ordered your team to kill me, too. By that logic I shouldn't trust you, either."

"Dude, I'm all you got." He looked at Zoya. "Not her. She's trouble. I can feel it."

To Zoya, Brewer said, "I'm going to talk to Matt. He has people he can call on in the British IC. Men who know where the bodies are buried. He just might be able to get someone to tell him what happened to your mom and your brother."

Zoya said, "I'd appreciate that, Suzanne."

Court said, "What are we going to do about the Korean?"

Brewer said, "Frankly, I don't want to know what you do with her, but whatever it is . . . I need you to do it quickly." She stood.

Implicit in her comment was that she wanted the three off-book assets to get information from Janice Won, and she had no desire to know the particulars of how they were going to go about it.

Zoya said, "Now that we know this might involve a bioweapon, *please* tell me Five Eyes leadership is smart enough to call off the conference now."

Brewer shook her head. "It would make the Five Eyes look impotent if it got out there was some threat to the annual conference that presented itself the day before it began and they shut the whole thing down. These are intelligence agencies; they would be admitting they had poor intelligence. They'll increase security, I'm sure, but the show will go on." She pointed to the back room where Won was chained up. "What we *need* are answers."

She headed for the door now. "I'll be outside. Get her talking."

When Brewer left the room the three Poison Apple assets stood together. Zoya looked to Court. "You want to do 'good cop, bad cop'?"

Court shook his head, then pointed at himself. "Bad cop." He pointed at Zoya now. "Worse cop." Then he turned and motioned to Zack. "Psycho cop."

Hightower and Zoya answered as one. "Got it." And they sat down in the living room to go over their plan.

CHAPTER 55

Castle Enrick was stunningly beautiful, and Matthew Hanley assumed that when the sun rose the next morning he would find the Highlands to be equally breathtaking. He and his entourage of assistants and Ground Branch security men were led to a suite of guest rooms, and along the way Hanley stopped a dozen times to greet cohorts from other agencies already here for the three-day conference.

Hanley had made a call while on the aircraft to Inverness and secured a meeting with one of the most senior and well-connected people in the UK's Secret Intelligence Service. Sir Robert Holly was the number one man in the operational pecking order at Vauxhall Cross, the name given to the SIS's headquarters. Holly had been a friend to the United States on many occasions, and while he wouldn't say a thing he wasn't allowed to say to any of the other Five Eyes organizations, Hanley had found him utterly candid and trustworthy in his actions before.

They had reserved a small drawing room to speak in, and the counter-surveillance technicians were just finishing their sweep for bugs as Hanley stepped inside. Walt Jenner and Art Greer stood outside, while the rest of the GB unit walked the grounds to meet with the various security officials working the conference to coordinate movements.

Sir Robert Holly was a handsome man well into his seventies, perfectly dressed even late in the evening, and in possession of a blond toupee that fooled no one. The men shook hands, pleasantries were exchanged, and a vetted member of the castle staff brought tea for them both. Hanley had no use for tea, but the Englishman poured himself a cup from the service and sipped it immediately.

"Right. So, you said this was time sensitive."

"Very much so. It involves a potential threat to this conference."

"Good lord," Holly said. "Sounds like you need to talk to our security folks. Not my department, but maybe I should take the opportunity to slip off to do some fishing? Hear the rivers around here are full of perch and brown trout. Might be safer on a stream somewhere."

Hanley smiled at this. "We are working to get a handle on the situation. I need to talk to *you*, not security. I need information about an MI6 operation about fifteen years ago."

The Englishman cocked his head. "Well, then. The past is definitely my department. Go on."

"It's regarding an assassination."

Holly sat back in his chair. "Iraq?"

Hanley shook his head. "Moscow."

The intelligence chief said, "I don't believe I have any information relating to that."

Hanley did not back down. "The victim was the son of the GRU chief at the time, General Zakharov."

Holly made a face, leaned forward, took his teacup, and held it to his mouth. "His son?"

"Yes, Robert."

Before Holly took a sip he said, "Who's telling you we killed that boy?"

"His father."

Holly almost spilled his tea as he chuckled. "Langley is quite behind the curve on that one, old boy. General Zakharov is long dead."

Hanley shook his head. "We aren't the ones behind the curve at the moment. Zakharov has been in London for over a decade, Robert. Operating under the alias David Mars."

"You're completely mental."

"Sorry. It's true."

"My God!" He then spoke softly. "The Black Wolf."

"He says you killed his wife and then killed his son." Hanley did not mention Zoya and her defection to the United States. He was here to get information, not give it.

Holly sipped tea in silence for nearly a minute. Hanley was rushed, but he knew his colleague would be weighing all the pros and cons about talking to the Americans about this subject. Finally he said, "Do I have your assurance that what I am about to say does not leave this room in any official capacity?"

"You have my word."

Holly nodded. "Well . . . we bloody well *did* kill the wife. She was creating sleepers, long-term penetration agents, SVR assets to come into the UK to operate against us. A linguist, a native of England, she was good at her craft and we saw no other way to stop her. Had a proxy from Belarus run her down on a Moscow street. Problem solved." The erudite man gave a halfhearted shrug about the killing. He wasn't conflicted about it at all.

Hanley nodded. He felt certain he would have given that kill order himself if he'd been in a position to do so. "What about the kid?"

Holly shook his head. "We didn't kill the boy. He died by accidentally exposing himself to polonium-226."

"How the *hell* did he do that?"

"We kept it all hidden; there was too much riding on Russian-British relations at the time to reveal our findings publicly. But our investigation concluded that young Zakharov was ferrying the isotope into the UK for his father. We didn't know General Zakharov was already here at the time, only sussed that out later. This was before Dagestan, mind you. He was mad about his wife's death and came up with his own plan to get revenge. His plan was to kill top intelligence officials with the polonium, and at the time he knew we had assets in the Kremlin. He didn't have sanction, but he did have men and women in the intelligence services who owed him. He got the polonium and had it stabilized and processed for travel but couldn't acquire someone who could get into and out of the UK without the chance they would be identified as GRU. So he used his own son, under doctored papers; had him come to London. Poor sod had no idea what he was doing. The bloody polonium was in a chocolate bar, wrapped in foil made out of some material that prevented it from leaking out. The candy was given to the boy by a friend of the general, obviously an agent of the GRU, ostensibly as a gift for his old friend in the UK. The poor lad got hungry on the plane, I guess, ate some of the bar, and was sick within hours. Dead within days."

Hanley shook his head at the absurdity of it.

Holly said, "Not long after that Zakharov turned up dead in Dagestan. We have the photos of his body."

Hanley shook his head. "Doctored. We have multisource confirmation."

"What sort of confirmation? What sources?"

"Sorry," Hanley said.

Holly let it go. "If the father is alive, I am sure he knows it wasn't a British op at all, it was his own Russian op that went wobbly because they didn't use a bloody trained courier to get the radioactive isotope into the British Isles. It was a tragedy for the young lad, no question, but I can tell you all of us in MI6 were bloody pleased that that bomb detonated prematurely, in a manner of speaking."

Hanley sat up, his hands on his knees. "Well . . . now it seems Zakharov is working with a Korean expert in weaponized plagues."

Holly blinked hard. "That fishing trip is looking more and more enticing. Fancy going with me? Now?"

The understated English humor wasn't lost on Hanley, but he was already thinking about his next steps. He just looked off a moment.

Holly said, "What can we do? This is our country. Not yours."

"The penetration into the CIA, the one that got all those guys killed at Ternhill, was not some drunk in the mail room, some dead-ender mid-level case officer who just wanted a houseboat. It was an assistant deputy director. If you have been penetrated, as well, the last thing I want to do is share intel with the UK."

"I understand. We'll ferret out the tout, sooner or later. For now, do what you have to do."

They both stood and shook hands.

Hanley said, "I appreciate the intel. Whenever you need something from us, you just shout."

"Oh, I've a bloody list, Matthew. Trust me. I'll come knocking for my own information, but first do go out and save the bloody day."

• • •

David Mars sat at a table in the kitchen of the old Highlands church at the top of the hill, within sight of the little airfield down in a valley hundreds of yards away. He stared across the table at Roger Fox. Fox and Hines had just arrived from Edinburgh, and although Fox had passed on the news of what happened at the laboratory to Mars while en route, he was now getting the third degree from the former GRU general in person.

Fox said, "Of course, it is very possible your daughter and Dr. Won were killed during the attack or during their escape. It was a fluid situation and we do not know—"

Mars barked back. "I have people in the Edinburgh police. No reports of any female dead or injured at the scene."

Behind Mars, a pair of elite Russian mercenaries loomed ominously, Kalashnikovs hanging off their shoulders and their eyes on Hines, the only real threat in the room if the altercation between Fox and Mars got any more heated. Mars was the man paying their wage. They'd kill for him, and they'd kill to keep him alive.

Fox said, "This was not the outcome we wanted, David, but we can use it to our advantage."

Mars looked out the window towards the bottom of the hill. Slowly he nodded. "Won didn't know the plan. She only knew what we told her. The fact that they have her in custody is problematic, but it won't alter our mission. If she talks, the Brits will just put Tornados in the air and shoot down a plane we never put much stock in to begin with."

Fox said, "Yes, and if she talks, then all the security men will be looking towards the sky, won't they? When the Five Eyes shoots down the crop duster it will think it repelled a potentially devastating attack, and the four hundred occupants of the castle will have no idea they only have days to live."

Mars said, "There is one problem, though. Won has been here."

"I had her blindfolded the last twenty minutes of the flight here, and she was blindfolded almost all the way to Castle Enrick. We drove an extra hour so she couldn't judge distance. She can tell them about an old church on a hill, perhaps, but . . . this is Scotland, there are thousands and it could be anywhere in the Highlands."

Mars said, "Inform the team leader of the mercenaries that they need to be even more vigilant. I'll check with my sources in MI5 and MI6, see if they are getting anything out of Won."

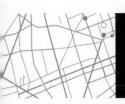

CHAPTER 56

Suzanne Brewer called the safe house near Edinburgh, just seconds before Court planned on beginning his grilling of the woman shackled in the bedroom, with the news that no one in South Korea had ever heard of Janice Won. At this point it was obvious to all that the woman in their custody was a DPRK asset.

Court knew she would be trained to handle interrogation, but he knew they had to get *something* out of her.

He moved towards the back of the house, his body feeling much better with the opioids deadening a portion of his pain. He entered the bedroom alone, facing the woman. He could tell how upset she had been when he frisked her, and it told him she was uncomfortable with touch in general. To capitalize on this discomfort he leaned close to her face, into her ear, his beard scratching her cheek.

"Comfortable?"

She said nothing.

"You and I are going to have a little talk. If you don't give me what I want, you're going to be taken away to a black site and interrogated more forcefully. I think we'd both like to avoid that, if possible."

She had no reaction at all to this, so he steeled himself for some frustration. She'd be a tough nut to crack. Perhaps it would go all the way to

Zack before she opened her mouth, and he caught himself almost feeling sorry for her for a fleeting instant.

. . .

As expected, Court's role as "bad cop" in the interrogation of Dr. Janice Won yielded no results at all, not a single word out of her mouth. He stepped through the door and tagged up with Zoya.

Court had told Zoya that he'd heard Won speaking Russian to the Bratva soldiers, so when Zoya entered the room she did so impersonating an SVR officer. In shouted Russian, she told Won that Russia did not sanction any of this, which she felt certain was true, and Zakharov's plan all along had been to frame her as the mastermind of the entire scheme, which she also assumed to be accurate.

Zoya could see the enemy agent's mind thinking through everything she was being told, the first hint before someone cracks.

Still, Won gave up nothing. Zoya had seen this level of fanaticism before, both in Chechnya and the Middle East. Won would gladly kill herself right now if she had any means to do so.

She wasn't going to say a word.

And then came Hightower.

He entered the room with a toolbox taken from the garage, nonchalantly opened it, and began putting various tools on the nightstand next to the bed where the North Korean was shackled. A hammer, a saw, a hand drill, a vise grip. They were all rusty. He took his time doing this, never once speaking or glancing over to the woman while he "prepared."

Finally, he turned her way and stood over her. "I don't want to hurt you," he said, and then after a few seconds he started laughing. "Who am I kidding? I *totally* want to hurt you."

Janice Won blinked.

He turned serious in a heartbeat. "But I'm not supposed to. Rules. I'm sure you've got some of those where you come from, right? How many bugs you can eat on holidays so you get some protein, how many prisoners you can do your biological testing on. Everybody's got a boss, and every boss has rules. You and me? We're no different."

He sat on the bed next to her, then leaned forward. "Except for the fact my boss tells me I have to get you to talk, and my boss made me promise to never tell her what I did to *make* you talk. So, I guess we can say that what happens in this room, stays in this room, Janice. Are you picking up what I'm putting down?"

He saw a little tremble, a quickening of her heartbeat evident in the veins of her throat.

Zack picked up the saw. Smiled. "My coworkers usually don't let me anywhere near an interrogation. I had a couple of . . . unfortunate experiences. But it's your lucky day, honey, because we've got the place all to ourselves."

He rolled up the sleeves of his denim shirt. "What do you say we get to know one another."

. . .

Zoya and Court sat out on the front porch with Travers and Jason. Brewer paced the darkness twenty yards away talking into her phone, although no one knew who she was talking to.

A woman's scream came from the house, followed by the authoritative shouts of a former Navy SEAL and CIA paramilitary, followed by a long moment of silence. This was repeated over and over, but no one outside commented on it at all.

Finally Zoya reached over and put her hand on Court's back gingerly. "How are you feeling?"

"Better than her. Not much, maybe, but some."

She looked down at his hand. The ice was off it, for now, but he'd get another icing in a few minutes. She said, "You know you can't operate with one hand, don't you? Whatever happens next, you'll need to stay out of it."

There was no way that was happening, Court knew, but now wasn't the time to argue. He just said, "What about you? At some point, someone has to stop your father. I think *you* need to stay out of it. Don't you?"

Zoya looked off into space. "Suzanne says no one knows what this mole told my father. And we don't know what contacts he has in UK intel. But we know he doesn't know details of Poison Apple. That means it will probably have to be one of the three of us who takes him down."

Court looked to Travers, sitting next to him. "Hey, Chris. Earmuffs."

Travers rolled his eyes. "Dude. Full scope poly."

Court said, "Please?"

Travers put his hands over his ears with a sigh and walked off into the dark, out of earshot.

Jason just sat there. Court eyed him a few seconds. Then said, "Really, kid? You think you're cleared for any of this?"

"No, sir," he replied, and he walked off into the night, as well.

"Sorry," Zoya said. "I shouldn't have said Poison Apple."

Court shrugged. "Hell, the only reason we know about it is because the enemy told us; we didn't get it from our own side."

"The enemy," Zoya repeated. Then said, "My father."

"I'm sorry."

"Why? You are right."

More screaming came from the house.

Court said, "Yes, it will have to be one of us most likely that kills him. But it should *not* be you."

The argument died there, and Court had the feeling he'd won. They talked for a few minutes more before Zack came out, covered in sweat. He was animated, amped up, his eyes searching. "Where's Brewer? Get me Brewer!"

Suzanne Brewer came walking out of the dark, disconnecting her call in the process. "What did you get?"

Zack said, "Eight liters of pneumonic plague, weaponized in four aerosol delivery canisters, each the size of a commercial fire extinguisher. The target is Castle Enrick, but she does *not* know the time of the attack. She said total casualties of a successful attack like this were upwards of five thousand dead, most all of them IC members and their families."

Brewer closed her eyes. "Oh my God. Means of attack?"

"Would you believe a *motherfucking* crop duster?"

Brewer smiled a little now and opened her eyes. "Not anymore, it's not. We'll put twenty helos and fast movers around that castle and blast anything bigger than a duck out of the fucking sky."

Brewer had spent years in CIA working on threats to Agency personnel and facilities; she was more in her element now than she was running sub rosa assets, by far.

Zack said, "Zakharov and his mob bozos have a staging area up in the Highlands. She doesn't know where, although she was there a few weeks back. Within about three to four hours of the castle. I think we've just got to go look for it. There is a bright yellow crop duster, away from any airfield. She said there was an old church and a graveyard."

Brewer bit her lip. "Might take some time, but I'll get people on that now."

Zoya turned to Zack. "You got all that out of her in thirty minutes? I didn't get a damn thing."

"Lady, 'Psycho Cop' was the role I was born to play."

Brewer walked off, and Court asked, "What's the prisoner's condition?"

Zack said, "I was ready to get nasty, but I put my hand on her knee as I was moving around. She acted like I was made of lava."

Court had noticed the same thing. "She apparently doesn't like to be touched. At all."

Zack shrugged. "There's not a scratch on that woman's body, but she's *not* gonna be okay. All the scars I gave her are on the inside. They ain't never going to heal, but I may have just saved five thousand assholes by fucking her up for life." He shrugged again. "And I can live with that."

• • •

Jason gave Janice Won a shot of an anesthetic that would have her out cold until a CIA team could arrive from Edinburgh to collect her, and soon after a U.S. Army helicopter landed out of the darkness, picked all the Americans and Zoya up from the safe house, and flew them north to the Highlands.

Court knew there was no way he and the other two assets of Poison Apple were going to get to go to the castle itself, so he was surprised when it came into view on a cliff above Loch Ness.

They overflew the massive white building, and as they came in for a landing Brewer revealed that Court had been correct in his assumption. She spoke into her headset's microphone. "You three aren't getting on the premises. Five Eyes security is too tight. We'll put you up in a safe house we have in Inverness, ten minutes out. Jason is cleared to go to the Five Eyes conference; he was coming anyway as a gopher for Matt, so he'll leave with me. I want you rested but ready to move as soon as we find out where Zakharov is staging for the attack."

Brewer and Jason climbed out of the helo, and it took off again immediately. Twenty minutes later it dropped Zack, Court, and Zoya off on a street north of the city of Inverness. They walked for twenty minutes before finding a cab, which took them to their safe house on Fairfield Road, just west of the River Ness.

The accommodations were a simple two-story building on a residential street. Court and Zoya ended up upstairs in a room together, and even though Zack had the apartment downstairs all to himself, he almost immediately came upstairs and opened bottles of beer he found in the refrigerator for all three.

Zoya asked Zack if he'd found any vodka around the house, and he told her he hadn't; at this time of the night it was the beer or nothing.

Zoya took a long swig, then said, "So . . . you two worked together, I take it?"

Court said, "Zack and I have a little history together. Some of it is good."

"And the rest?"

"He tried to kill me," Court said, matter-of-factly. And then added, "Twice."

"And you shot me," Zack replied. "Once."

"So far," Court said.

Court finished his beer and went to the bathroom to take a shower. His aches and pains were unabating, and he thought a painkiller and a hot shower would do him good.

When he was gone, Zack and Zoya drank beer in silence, till Zack said, "Good ole Court. Hell of a guy. But you know there's no future, don't you?"

Zoya pretended to look disinterested. "Why do you say that?"

"Dude has issues. He will never get off the hamster wheel. He lives for the righteous grind of fighting for what he believes in. He'll keep kicking in doors, halo jumping onto targets, and smoking the worst of the worst till that day his number comes up. Might be tomorrow, might be next week, might be ten years." He chugged beer, then shook his head. "Nah. It won't be ten years."

"And you? You're planning on quitting all this to work in a hardware store so you can raise a family?"

"No, lady, I love the work almost as much as Six does. But I don't have this chip on my shoulder about fighting all evil, everywhere, all the time. I punch in, do what my country tells me to do, then punch out." He smiled at her, raised an eyebrow. "I'd be home for the wife and kids, should that be something you're into."

Zoya kept looking at the big man with the beard. Finally she said, "You're hitting on me? Sorry, it kind of seems that way, but I can't tell for sure."

"I'm just sayin'. A woman needs a man."

"That's in the Bible, isn't it?"

"Actually I picked it up from a porno."

Zoya shook her head in disbelief. "Court needs better friends. I'm not as good a person as he is. I know that without question, but I wouldn't hurt him. I would be there for him, just like he's been there for me."

Zack shrugged. "I'm *always* there for him."

"When the assignment you're on calls for you to be?"

"The rules of the job, sister. If Six is my partner, we'll take down armies. If Six is my target, then I'll put a bullet in his eye."

"Always there for him," she said dryly.

"Life's a bitch, girl."

Court stepped back into the living room to grab his phone, then looked them both over when they went quiet.

Zoya said, "We were just talking about you."

"God, I wish you wouldn't."

. . .

Zack overstayed his welcome but finally took the hint to go down to his room, and Zoya pulled out a medical kit and opened it, preparing to put fresh bandages on Court's hand when he got out of the shower.

He sat next to her and placed his arm gingerly on the kitchen table.

Court said, "I need a trigger finger and a thumb to wrap around a grip if I have to shoot left-handed. Otherwise, immobilize the hand."

Zoya said, "That's crazy."

"Just do it. Please."

She complied with his wishes, using a splint from the medical kit, wrapping him, then taping everything securely. As she worked on this Court glanced at the medical equipment. It was a robust collection of medicines, wound care supplies, even heavy tranquilizers and drugs to counter poisons or drug overdoses.

Hardly a normal first-aid kit you'd find in a typical residential home.

Court said, "I wish someday you and I could do something normal."

Zoya continued wrapping his hand with tape. "Like what?"

"I don't know. What do normal people do? Catch a movie, I guess."

Zoya laughed. "We're *in* a movie, Court. Just not the kind I want to be in."

Soon his hand was mummified save for his fingers and his thumb.

He opened and closed it, wincing while he did so. She saw his discomfort. "You can't tape the pain away."

"I know."

"What's recoil from a rifle going to feel like?" she asked.

"It's going to suck." He looked up at her. "This is all going to suck."

"Not all of it," she said, and she stood and took his hand. He followed her into the bedroom.

"Did the shower make you feel better?"

"I'm a new man," he said as she began to undress.

Brewer had specifically ordered them to rest, but this was another order Zoya and Court decided to ignore. They made love passionately; difficult for Court with a broken hand, but he was motivated, and he found a way.

• • •

When it was over, Zoya joked with him. "Did I hurt you?"

Court laughed, and then his phone buzzed on the table next to him. He started to reach for it with his splinted left hand but then caught himself and reached out with his right.

"Yeah?"

Suzanne Brewer said, "I need to talk to Anthem."

Confused by this, Court said, "You have a target?"

"No. Still working on that. Anthem."

Court handed the phone across the bed. Zoya listened quietly for several minutes. Asked a few questions that didn't tell Court anything about the matter being discussed. She thanked Brewer, then hung up the phone and sat up. The light from the lamp at her bedside table showed him the tears in her eyes.

"My father tricked my brother into helping him with a nonsanctioned intelligence operation. My brother was accidentally radiated with polonium-226 in the process. He died because of my father."

Christ, Court thought. *What does one say to that?* "I'm very sorry. What about your mother?"

Zoya shrugged. "Assassinated by the British. I understand their reasoning."

"That's a harsh thing to say."

"She worked for a foreign intelligence force and her work was designed to directly damage the interests of the United Kingdom. That was her job, and she died for it. The British who ordered her death were doing their jobs, as well." She shook her head. "No, it's my brother's death I can't accept. He wasn't part of this world.

"My brother wasn't like me. Wasn't like my dad or my mom. He was like you."

Court was surprised by this. "What do you mean?"

"He was . . . innocent."

"You see me differently than I see myself."

Zoya wiped tears away. "That says more about me than about you. You don't know you're the last good guy around."

Court most definitely did not know that, but he dropped it for a more important matter. "This information doesn't change anything. If your father is found, Zack and I are going to go take care of him. Not you."

"I want to be the one to kill my father. For Feo."

Court shook his head. "No. That *can't* happen. You'll spend your whole life regretting it."

"If you think that, then you don't know me as well as I give you credit for."

"I think you don't know yourself as well as you give yourself credit for. You are furious now, rightly so, and you want revenge for your brother. But you will be damaged if you go through with it. Trust me."

"This is because I am a woman, you are a man, and you think it's your job to protect me."

"No, you don't need me to protect you. It's because I know what it will feel like if you do it."

"Did you kill *your* father?"

Court shook his head. "No . . . but I've done less, and have been damaged by my actions. I'm just trying to save you from that."

Zoya gave a half nod. "Okay, you're right." She leaned over and kissed him.

Court sensed she was just trying to end the conversation.

He said, "Going alone after your father will either get you killed or mess you up for life. Just stay here tomorrow. It will be taken care of, and we'll never have to talk about it."

Zoya's reply was firm. "I said 'fine.'"

Court knew to drop it immediately.

They staged a firearm on each of their nightstands, then turned out the lights. Exhausted and under the effects of the hydrocodone, Court fell asleep quickly, but not Zoya.

Zoya stayed awake for hours.

CHAPTER 57

Just after dawn Zoya woke Court with a freshly brewed cup of coffee, kissed him, and told him she was going to take a shower. Court climbed up, out of bed, and sipped coffee as he walked into the living room. Standing there in his underwear, he looked out the window at the placid residential street below.

This would be a nice place to live, he thought. *Here, with Zoya. This house, this city, this country.*

This life.

He was still hurting, and he'd be hurting for a while; the throb in his left hand commanded his attention, though it wasn't the only ache in his body. But all in all he was better. He realized the sex had cleared his mind and made him the happiest he'd been in a long time.

He thought about taking a pain pill to make him looser and more ambulatory but decided against it.

Zoya had done wonders for him physically and mentally.

He checked his phone and saw a text from Zack saying he was going to go scout a location for the helicopter to pick them up that wouldn't draw too much attention. He said he'd be a couple of hours but would be reachable at all times.

As the shower began running in the bathroom, Court took a moment to look over a map of the area on the coffee table here in the safe house. He found Castle Enrick, not too far away at all, and then looked around it at the undeveloped countryside. That church with an airstrip they were searching for could be anywhere, but he was sure the Five Eyes would have a lot of people looking for it now, and he hoped they'd get a hit.

After a few minutes the sound of the running water made him realize how much it would help his beaten body if he climbed into the shower with Zoya. He felt a wave of exhaustion hit him, rather suddenly, and he thought the water just might reenergize him. He finished his coffee and stepped into the bathroom, and immediately he could tell the shower window was open to the cool morning, because the room was only partially steamed up, though the vapor was growing.

"You're too little to hog all the hot water," he said, and he walked towards the curtain to open it. But he stopped when he noticed something on his left.

There, on the medicine cabinet mirror, someone had written something with their finger that the slowly rising steam was just now starting to reveal.

The first words he made out quickly. *I love you.* He smiled at this, reached for the shower curtain, and then read the second line of the smeared note.

And I am so, so sorry.

Court cocked his head and pulled open the curtain. Water pounded down into the empty bathtub. The window there was open, and it was just wide enough for Zoya to squeeze through.

Court turned for the door, but the movement made him dizzy suddenly. He put his hand on the wall, continued moving forward, and then stumbled. He made it out into the little hall off the living room, used the walls to keep him up for a few more feet, then fell down onto the floor behind the sofa there.

What . . . is . . . happening?

And then it hit him. He'd seen inside the medical kit here in the safe house when Zoya patched up his hand. It was full of prescription pain meds, but he'd also noticed a small liquid vial of M99, an animal tranquilizer the CIA had altered to make safe for humans. It ensured two to six hours of hard sleep to whoever took it and was even used as a nonlethal weapon as well as a tranquilizer for darts.

Court realized Zoya had drugged him so he couldn't stop her from going after her father.

He wanted to be angry, to shout, and he wanted to pull his phone to call Zack or Brewer, but his eyes shuddered and closed before any of this happened, and he put his face down on the wooden floor and fell unconscious.

. . .

Zoya raced west through the morning in a stolen minivan she picked out of a driveway four blocks away from the safe house. She'd only walked that far because she needed to find something she could boost easily with the tools that had been left in the upstairs apartment closet for use by CIA officers working there, and was thankful enough to spot a Toyota Sienna van old enough to be an easy mark. She was in it and driving in three minutes, and not one of the neighbors already up this morning had seen or heard a thing.

All night long she thought about it; sleep eluded her because of the stress and strain, but eventually she'd become convinced there was only one possible solution.

She'd told herself she had to do it. From the moment Court fell asleep Zoya knew she had to be prepared to find a way to get out of there and go for her father on her own. She couldn't let Zack or Court kill him; she *needed* to be the one to do it herself. But not until after confronting him about the death of her brother.

While Court slept Zoya took his phone, put earphones in, and turned off the ringer. The hope had been that Brewer would call with the location of her father's staging area for the air attack of Castle Enrick.

And her plan had worked. At five thirty a.m., just as the first rays of dawn hit, Brewer called and asked to speak to Violator, but Zoya told her he was too drugged to talk. Reluctantly Brewer explained that a high-flying Royal Navy jet had spotted an abandoned church on a hill twenty-two miles west of Loch Ness. A few hundred yards away, the figure of a small aircraft could just be made out from its concealment under a tarp and some brush.

Another overflight with thermal imaging confirmed a half dozen or so men in defensive positions in a graveyard in front of the church.

Zoya wrote the coordinates down and was told the Ground Branch team at Castle Enrick was being mustered to attack the location, but that Romantic was already out scouting a location for the helo to land. Violator would wait for a call from Romantic, then meet him at the pickup point for the helicopter to join the raid on the church.

Brewer informed Anthem, in clear and unambiguous terms, that she was disallowed from leaving the safe house, because of the personal nature of the opposition.

The men would take care of things without her.

She deleted the evidence that Suzanne had called from Court's phone, and she made coffee. While it brewed she went back into the bedroom and stood over Court, watching him sleep. Even in the low light she could see the discoloration on his face from the beating he'd taken. His hand, bandaged to the wrist save for his thumb and fingers, lay on the bed to his left.

She had felt sickened by what she was about to do, but at that moment her anger and need for revenge were even stronger than her love.

She felt like the worst person in the world for this, but she also felt committed to her task.

There would be no stopping her. She was, after all, her father's daughter.

She put a few drops of the M99 tranquilizer in Court's coffee, then positioned her clothes and a few other items in the bathroom. She kissed his bruised and tired face, handed him his coffee, and then lied, claiming Suzanne Brewer had not called.

After that she went into the bathroom and turned on the shower.

She thought he'd be down at least three hours with the tranquilizer, and according to the GPS on her phone it was only forty minutes to her father's staging area.

She pushed down on the pedal of the Sienna now and increased her speed, determination and shame coexisting in her consciousness.

. . .

Forty-five minutes later, Zoya stood at the bottom of the hill below the church, her arms outstretched to show that she was unarmed. Although it was raining, breezy, and in the upper fifties, she had taken off her raincoat and even her gray sweater to reveal a black sports bra, showing the men who would inevitably have her under riflescope that she was unarmed.

Slowly she began walking up the rain-soaked hill, her sweater held in one hand.

A pair of men in ski masks appeared out of the tall grasses in the un-kempt cemetery in front of the church and ordered her forward in Russian. At the low stone wall they commanded her to drop to her knees and then lie flat on a patch of pasture trimmed short by a flock of sheep grazing on the hill. She complied, they stepped over the wall, and she was searched. She was pulled to her feet and walked towards the entrance to the sanctu-ary, and she put her sweater on as she did so.

Zoya noted the gear and stature of the men walking alongside her. Immediately she could tell these were *not* Bratva gunmen from Moscow's Solntsevo neighborhood, nor were they like the other security forces she'd seen around Fox and her father. No . . . these guys were not in military uniforms, but they sure as hell looked like the Spetsnaz men she'd worked with in the past.

Looking up into the church windows she saw a pair of snipers, also in ski masks. Again, their positioning, the gear she could see, their profes-sional demeanor: it all told her there was a sizable force here protecting her father's operation that the Americans knew nothing about.

This suddenly terrified her. She knew a raid on this location would be coming, perhaps within a couple of hours. Ten or so American operators, even highly skilled ones, would not be able to take this place from a pla-toon of Spetsnaz men with high ground and fortified positions without suffering devastating losses.

. . .

Feodor Zakharov sat at the small wooden table in the church canteen. He looked on at his daughter as she was brought in and placed in a chair in front of him. He had a cup of tea for himself but offered his daughter noth-ing even though she shivered in her wet clothes. He ordered Fox and Hines to give them the room, but he allowed two mercenaries to stay. They leaned against an empty bookshelf behind Zoya, providing security in case she tried something stupid.

Finally he relented in his hard stare, then asked one of the men to grab a towel from the kitchen, and when he returned Zakharov handed it over to his daughter himself. She began toweling off her face and hair without thanking him for the gesture.

His voice was low. Soft but intimidating. "My little Zoyushka. I was so pleased you escaped the laboratory with your life. But it was foolish of you to come here."

"And you are a fool for *being* here. Did you not think you would be found when the Americans captured Dr. Won? You're working with the DPRK? Was that to reflect responsibility on them when this was over?"

"That's exactly what it was. Your mind works in the strategic realm as well as the tactical realm. That makes me proud. All the years of instruction I gave you." He didn't seem proud. He sounded as if he was about to have her shot.

Zoya glared at him, and her face reddened. Under her shirt her stress hives positively glowed.

"Why did you come, Zoya?" Zakharov asked.

"I am here, Father, to provide you with the intelligence you need to make a reasonable decision."

"Go on."

"They will be here soon, and they will end your operation, destroy your plans."

Zakharov seemed completely unfazed by this, which confused his daughter.

"And even if you do make it out of here, do you really think there's any way in hell you are going to get a crop duster within half a mile of Castle Enrick? Won talked. They've already put snipers on the roof. They've already got helos in the air circling for ten miles. Attack jets ready to swoop down from twenty thousand feet. You're done."

"So you came to ask me to just go quietly off into the sunset? To concede defeat and forget it?"

She didn't answer. Instead she said, "I learned something else last night. You lied to me. The British didn't kill Feodor, Father. You did, by your foolishness."

General Zakharov made no reaction to the charge.

"Am I wrong?"

The big bearded man sat there quietly for several more seconds. Finally he said, "Feo was the fool, Zoya. Not me. I invited him to the UK during a short break from his studies. I had doubts he'd come at all; our relationship had been . . . fractured for some time. But he agreed. A colleague of mine gave him a small case of chocolate bars, a gift for me. You know, and Feo knew, that I've always loved Alenka chocolate. Better than this Cadbury shit the English seem to be addicted to. The case was all packaged up neatly, and my colleague told him to be sure I received the entire box. But you know Feo. He held a grudge against me, did little passive-aggressive things to spite me all the time."

Zoya said, "He held a grudge because you were hard on him. You tried to turn him into something he was not. The only thing that kept Feo from running away, or slitting your throat in your sleep, was that I came along; you saw that you could train me, you could turn me into what you wanted Feo to be. You were just as hard on me; the difference was that I had the drive, the desire, that he did not possess. That was not his fault.

"You hated that you didn't have the son who would honor you by following in your footsteps, so you settled for your daughter."

Zakharov looked out the window at the misty morning. "You simplify twenty years of our family."

"It wasn't simple," she said. "But . . . Feo. You should have left him out of this life. He wasn't like us. He wasn't evil."

"Evil? You think we are evil?"

Zoya nodded softly and looked at the floor. "It's in our blood, Papa. You . . . Mother . . . me." She looked back up at him. "But *this*. What you are doing here. It's wrong, it's for the wrong reasons, and it won't even succeed. Please, let's leave together. We can leave the country somehow, go wherever you want. Even back to Russia. I'll give up my life if I can stop you from doing this."

Zakharov looked at his watch, and Zoya noted the action. He said, "You're absolutely right, I should have left Feo out of all this. Because he was unskilled when it came to the simple task of bringing me my polonium. He came to see me at my house in Knightsbridge and, when I asked for the chocolate, he handed me a handful of loose bars. He told me he ate one of them on the plane. There were ten bars, and four were secretly marked to indicate that they contained the isotope inside the triple-wrapped lead foil. He ate one of the four."

Zoya's face reddened more and tears filled her eyes. She had loved her brother more than life itself, and she still did.

"So," Zakharov said with a wave of his hand. "Feodor Feodorovich was more than just incompetent, he was bloody unlucky."

"He was *untrained*."

Zakharov shouted, his first show of real anger. "What bloody training do you need to carry a fucking box of chocolates on a fucking airplane?"

Zoya looked at her hands a moment, then back at her father, her face suddenly a guise of malevolence. Without warning she lunged at him, over the table, her hands grasping for his throat. The two mercenaries behind her were slow to react because her action came without warning, but they finally dove onto her and tackled her off the table and to the wooden floor, pressing her hundred-forty-pound frame hard under the weight of two two-hundred-pound men, each covered in thirty-five pounds of guns and body armor and gear.

Fox and Hines rushed into the room now. The Englishman grabbed Zoya by her hair and yanked her up and away from the two Russian mercs, her feet leaving the ground. As he shoved her hard against the kitchen counter, she reached for a butcher knife in a block there, but a gunshot froze her as well as everyone else in the room.

Zoya looked back over her shoulder. He father stood by the table with a small Makarov pistol in his hand. He had fired into the ceiling, and now he pointed the weapon at his daughter.

"It doesn't have to end like this. But if you don't stand down, it *will* end. For you. Right here, right now."

He looked to Hines, who stepped up to the brunette, and he grabbed her by the back of the neck.

Zakharov said, "British Intelligence forced my hand when they killed your mother. Do I regret using my son in my operation to exact revenge? Of course I do. Every day of my life. But I am not to blame for his death. It was the British who put me in England with retaliation on my mind . . . *they* are the culprits, and today, *finally*, they will pay for what they've done. The entire Five Eyes will pay."

Zoya snorted an angry laugh. "The sky above the castle is a no-fly zone. Your crop duster will be obliterated."

Still Zoya realized her father seemed unconcerned about this. He said, "We will be leaving soon, before your friends arrive. I've lost visibility about what the Americans are doing—my man on the inside of the CIA has been captured—but my contacts in British law enforcement and the police will alert me the moment any movement to conduct an operation against me has begun."

Zoya suddenly realized her father had miscalculated. Hanley was using one team from Ground Branch and two Poison Apple assets. As far as she knew he was not in contact with British or Scottish authorities at all about the attack he had planned, so there was no way her father's contacts could warn him when it was on the way.

She didn't reveal any of this. Instead she just repeated herself. "Your plane will never make it to its target."

When she said this her father holstered his gun under his jacket and turned for the door. "It doesn't have to, darling. If you think we told Dr. Won the full scope and breadth of our plan, then you underestimate your father's intelligence. She designed and built the weapon, but I alone wrote the plan for my retributive strike."

Zoya's heart sank. He had something else in mind, not the crop duster. The Americans knew of no other plot against Castle Enrick. If she didn't find a way to warn them, she worried they would think the danger was over when the plane went down.

CHAPTER 58

Court Gentry's eyes opened slowly, and he found himself staring at the back of a shit-brown sofa. It took a moment more to remember his last thoughts before he went out, and even before he had a clear idea of where he was and what had happened, his body began reminding him about his myriad pains, located from head to toe. His left hand was the worst; it throbbed and hurt like a small car was driving over it, back and forth, over and over.

He then realized why he'd awakened just now. A banging on the front door seemed to shake the entire building. Court's first inclination was to get back to the bedroom and grab his pistol, but he'd just made it up onto his forearms when the front door came crashing in, fifteen feet away.

Zack Hightower flew into the living room behind it. He'd slammed his shoulder against the door to smash it, which gave Court the impression he'd been knocking for some time before going to such extremes.

Hightower looked around the room and finally saw Court, still on the floor, still bleary-eyed and disoriented.

The jarring sound of Hightower's voice penetrated through the cobwebs in Court's brain. "What the hell you doing, you lazy fuck?"

Court's words were garbled from the drugs. "What . . . what are *you* doing?"

"Coming to get you two. Brewer's been ringing your phone off the hook for an hour. Where's Marina?"

"Who?"

"Oswald. Where's the Russian? In the shower?" The water still ran in the bathroom down the hall. "Fuckin' women."

Court was still coming to. "She's, she's gone. She . . . I guess she drugged me. She's going after her dad."

Zack approached, knelt down closer. "How the hell did you let her drug you?"

Court did not answer; instead he struggled to sit up without touching his left hand against anything, and Zack saw his predicament. "I got you." He pulled Court to his feet. His knees were wobbly. "What did she dose you with?"

"M99, I think."

"Cold-blooded bitch. I told you that you had to watch her."

"I'll be all right. In a minute." He grabbed Zack's arm and pulled it up, then looked at the watch on Zack's wrist. "Eight a.m. She's been gone over an hour."

Zack said, "'Bout a forty-minute drive time from here to Zakharov's lair. If she went straight there, she's on scene now."

"Shit," Court said.

Zack snorted. "Face it, Six. Your girlfriend's got daddy issues."

"She went to kill her father."

"Bro, what did I just say? Langley's now hiring fucking Russian spooks who want to kill their dads, who themselves are bent on killing thousands. Who in the *fuck* is driving this clown car of an intelligence agency, anyway?"

Court rubbed his eyes with his good hand. "What now?"

Zack sighed. Annoyed. "More dipshittery from Brewer. She's sending a car to pick us up to take us to the Ground Branch helo. Jenner is assembling his team at a staging area close by for the hit on the airstrip and the church, and Brewer wants us to ride along."

"Ride along on their hit?" Court looked at his hand.

Zack said, "Between you and me, sometimes I wonder if Suzanne doesn't really love us."

Court smiled weakly, then headed to the bathroom to take a cold shower to wake himself up.

. . .

Thirty minutes later Court and Zack stood in a steady cool rain in an open field next to two helicopters. One was a UH-60 Blackhawk, possibly the same one he'd flown there in the night before. The other, however, looked similar to a Blackhawk, but it had special design features that indicated to Court it was something new, elite, and highly classified.

He was pretty sure he was looking at one of the newer models of Direct Action Penetrators, souped-up Blackhawks that supposedly gave off the radar cross section of a bird and flew faster, longer, and much more quietly than a regular helo.

Outside the helos, the seven junior men of Walt Jenner's team worked on assembling gear, while Brewer alternatively talked on her phone and then spoke to Jenner, who was standing over a map lying on a large black Pelican case. To Court, Jenner seemed to have a lot of questions for the senior CIA officer, and the bearded paramilitary team leader clearly wasn't pleased with the answers he was getting.

There was a heavy mist in the air in addition to the rain; visibility was no more than one hundred yards. Court wondered about flying in this soup but told himself the pilots of the high-tech bird could probably fly it upside down and backwards through conditions worse than this.

He and Zack had been out of the conversation; no one had spoken to them since they'd arrived, and other than a nod between Gentry and Chris Travers, the only man on the team Court knew personally, there had been no recognition by the Ground Branch team of the two new assets.

Finally Zack cleared his throat. "Suzanne? What's our role here?"

Walt Jenner held a hand up. "Hightower, we haven't figured out what *our* role is yet. We'll get to you."

To Jenner, Brewer said, "*Your* role is exactly what I said it was. You will assault the staging area for the impending attack on Castle Enrick. You will capture or kill all hostiles and, if possible, destroy the agricultural aircraft on the ground."

"In broad daylight? You don't know how many men are there, what training they have. I'm not going to hit that target till I have a better idea of—"

Zack spit on the wet ground and muttered loud enough to be heard. "Here we go. Everybody wants to be a gangsta till it's time to do gangsta shit."

Jenner pointed at Hightower. "Fuck you, Dad. Shouldn't you be somewhere playing golf?"

Some of the men laughed at this, but Court was fixated on something else. "Hey, Brewer. Were you planning on mentioning the fact that there is an Agency asset at the target location?"

Suzanne Brewer gave a half shrug, then spoke to the entire group. "Violator is correct. A female asset, thirty-three years old, hair dark brown, eyes green. You are the same team that exfiltrated her out of Thailand a few months ago, so you should recognize her. She is now an asset of ours, code name Anthem, but her current status is unknown. You have to consider her potentially hostile at this time."

Court said, "Bullshit. She went there to kill her dad, same as us."

All the men on Jenner's team turned to Court, unsure if they'd heard him correctly.

Brewer said, "Yes, as Violator said, she is the daughter of General Zakharov, the mastermind of this entire plot."

"Yeah," Court said. "But—"

Jenner broke in. "But nothing. We treat her as unknown. Disarm her, restrain her, but we won't kill her unless she poses an imminent threat."

Court could live with this, and he let it go.

The argument between Brewer and Jenner about the sensibility of a daylight attack against an unknown force resumed, but the other Ground Branch men continued to kit up as if they knew they would inevitably be going into action, no matter how much their team leader protested to the suit in charge.

Court took Hightower over closer to the map, and they looked at it together. Then they stepped away, into the misty field, out of earshot of the others.

Court asked, "What do you think about the tactical equation?" He deferred to almost no one on close-quarters battle tactics, but Zack Hightower had been his team leader in the Goon Squad, and if there was one person with more knowledge than Court on team tactics, it was Hightower.

Zack looked up at the rain. "What do I think about the tactical equation? The tactical equation is a big fat bag of dicks. Jenner's absolutely right about that."

"Are you going to tell Brewer what you think?"

Zack shrugged. "Nah. We got this. These are Mafia goons. It's not like we're up against Spetsnaz."

Court didn't know who, in fact, was there at Zakharov's staging location, but Zack had a point. So far all the foot soldiers in this operation they'd encountered had been London-based Russian mob gangsters. Dangerous, to be sure, but no match for Special Activities Division paramilitaries.

Still, he didn't mask his concern.

Zack saw Court's reticence and slapped him on the shoulder. "Go big or go home, bro."

"I can go home? Cool."

"It's a figure of speech, Six. You're in this shit till the end."

"Well, then, I guess I'll just get on the helicopter and fly into certain death."

"*That's* the spirit!"

They stepped back into the group of men in time for them to hear Brewer say, "Violator and Romantic will be folded into your team and assault alongside you."

Jenner replied, "I'd be willing to take Hightower along for the ride, as long as he remembers to let the younger guys take the lead." He looked to Court. "But I don't trust Gentry. He tends to do his own thing, and that shit won't fly on my team. Plus . . . look at him. He's a wreck. I don't need a wounded man watching my back."

Court didn't say anything, but Hightower stood up for him. "Six is solid. He was my door kicker for years."

Jenner just rolled his eyes. "And then he fucking *shot* you, Zack!"

"Dude, it's cool. We hugged it out. Didn't we, Six?"

Jenner just pointed to Court with a gloved finger. "That goofy head case is *not* riding on my team."

Brewer wasn't officially in charge of the Ground Branch team, but she had cards to play to exert her authority. She said, "Jenner . . . I'll call Matt Hanley, right now. There isn't *anyone* at the Agency that has more respect for Violator than Hanley does." She looked off a moment into the mist. "Believe me, I deal with the unfortunate fallout of that fact every damn day." Looking back his way, she said, "You really think he's going to take your side?"

Jenner held firm. "Call him."

Brewer did call Hanley, and five minutes later Court was kitting up with Hightower and the rest of Jenner's team. He was on the mission, broken hand and all.

Jenner strapped himself into his body armor while he stood next to Gentry. He was pissed, but compliant, because there was no way to go against the wishes of the deputy director of Operations. He said, "Okay, Violator. Listen up. I want you squared away. I want you where I can see you at all times. In fact, you take the Number One."

The Number One was the first through the door after a breach. It was the most dangerous position in the flow.

"What was that about having the younger guys take the lead?" Court retorted.

Jenner said, "Everybody says you're such hot shit, I wanna see your ass in action."

Zack leaned forward to Jenner now. "Hey, boss. Why don't you slap a GoPro on your helmet? You're gonna want to film this shit once Sierra Six starts doing his thing."

Jenner just rolled his eyes and fastened the cummerbund of his body armor tightly around him.

Court took an HK416 short-barreled rifle offered to him by one of the Ground Branch men, slung it across his chest, and yanked the sling strap tight. The rifle cinched up to his body, pointing down. He worried about the recoil his left hand would endure wielding the weapon, but the .223 caliber wasn't particularly powerful, so he told himself he could manage the pain. He climbed aboard the high-tech-looking helicopter, keeping his mummified hand close to his chest so he didn't bang it on anything while finding a seat amid the equipment there.

Chris Travers boarded behind him. He extended a gloved hand. "Hey, brother. How you getting on?"

Court took it with his own gloved hand. "Older every day. How you doing, Travers?"

He shrugged. "This shit beats a real job."

Court looked at Jenner, still by the makeshift map table, who looked back at him disapprovingly. "Your boss doesn't like me. You might want to keep your distance for your own good."

"Walt doesn't know your softer side." He laughed. "Dude. What in the hell happened to you? You look like you fell off the back of a bus and got ran over by a shit wagon."

Other team members climbed aboard around them now. Court said, "Chris, promise me one thing. You see a big monster dude, anywhere around the target, six foot nine or so, you shoot his ass from standoff distance. I'm not smart enough to stay out of his reach."

"Six-nine? Yeah, I can hit that at a mile and a half."

"You better *hope* you're a mile and a half away when you see him. That guy is fucking scary."

Travers swiveled his head to Court. "You mean something scares the Gray Man?"

"*Everything* scares me. That's why I'm still here."

Zack climbed in and slapped Travers on the back. "Christopher! Ready to rock 'n' roll?"

"Yeah, boss."

Brewer stepped up to the helo now, but she did not climb in.

Zack of course knew she wasn't going along into combat, but he extended a gloved hand to help her aboard anyway, just to be sarcastic.

She ignored it. "I've got to get back to Castle Enrick. Destroy that aircraft so I don't regret that decision."

Hightower said, "Yes, ma'am. We'll save all those unappreciative suits at your fancy party. No sweat. Enjoy the champagne and finger sandwiches."

She turned away and climbed into the other helo.

Zack turned to Court now and shouted over the sound of the turbines spooling up. "You know what the worst part of this shit is?"

"What's that?"

"If we all die, nobody's going to even notice I got killed. Everybody will be like 'Oh shit, the Gray Man got fragged by some Russkies in Scotland.' Nobody's going to remember ole Zack getting popped."

"Watch my back. Keep me alive. Problem solved, Romantic."

"Night Train."

Court cocked his head. "What's that?"

"Night Train. My new code name. What do you think of that?"

"When did it change?"

"It hasn't, officially, but Matt is thinking it over."

"Good luck with that, Romantic," Court said. He looked down at his aching left hand, the tight wrappings on it, and he thought about Zoya.

CHAPTER 59

As the Ground Branch team augmented with the two Poison Apple assets flew towards their target, there was an important piece of intelligence that they were missing.

Jenner and his team fully expected to encounter a sizable force of Russian Bratva gangster shooters, but they had no idea the target location also contained thirty GRU Spetsnaz-trained mercenaries.

There was an incredible force multiplier effect involved in dealing with a cohesive unit of men as opposed to a group of thugs of the same number. Thirty special operators who'd trained together and had fought together in the past posed a formidable, perhaps insurmountable, obstacle to the success of the CIA paramilitary mission here.

But without this knowledge the Direct Action Penetrator touched down behind a grove of trees two kilometers from the church and the airfield, ensuring that no one at the target location could hear it. Ten men leapt out and began moving up towards their destination through light rain and heavy mist.

Court was near the back at this stage; he wouldn't take the front until they arrived at the door to the church. For now he just jogged along through the heavy vapor, holding his slung rifle up with one hand. Trudging their way through short grass, he and the others came upon a flock of sheep. They moved through the animals, guns high in front of them.

Court ran along with Hightower, Greer, Stapleton, Lorenzi, McClane, Jenner, Travers, a guy Court thought he heard someone call Partridge, and some other asshole Court didn't know at all.

They made their way higher on the hill, saw the graveyard through the heavy mist in front of them, and dispersed left and right.

Lorenzi and McClane were the two snipers on the team, and once they crested the rise of the hill, they dropped down behind a low stone wall, took up positions, and looked through their 416s' scopes, scanning the stained-glass windows of the church, just forty yards away.

As Zack, Court, and the rest of the team crouched and moved through the tombstones, they slowed and took knees when they heard their headsets come alive.

Lorenzi said, "Four has a target. Top left window. Armed with an AK."

McClane came over the net next. "Seven has eyes on one combatant in the top right window. He's got a Dragunov. Did I miss some intel giving us a heads-up that the Russian mafia had snipers with sniper rifles on this op?"

Court waited to hear Jenner give the order for the snipers to engage, but before he spoke the booms of gunfire from the church sent Court, Zack, and all six Ground Branch men in the cemetery diving behind tombstones.

A pair of masked men rose from behind grave markers, not more than forty feet away from Court, and they raked the Ground Branch team with automatic fire. Partridge went down before firing a shot, and the team member Court didn't know spun away, blood ejected from the side of his head, and he fell facedown in the grass.

He was clearly dead.

Court fired back, sending both men back to cover, but the flicker of muzzle flashes came from the front door of the church, and Court dropped flat again, slamming his injured hand on the hard earth as he did so.

Behind Court, both snipers fired. Lorenzi took down his target, then began scanning for a second, while McClane killed the man in the top right window with the Dragunov sniper rifle, but he was himself immediately shot by a second sniper, well hidden in the darkened bell turret window, half shrouded in mist.

Court shouted to Zack. "This is well-coordinated fire! These fuckers know what they're doing all of a sudden."

"So do you! Shut up and shoot somebody!"

"I'm saying, this isn't Russian mob! These are Spetsnaz. Let's flank east through the cemetery, try to divide their fire."

Zack moved over to Court's tombstone, chased by rifle rounds fired from in and around the dilapidated gothic church. He dove in behind Court and actuated his radio. "TL, Nine and Ten request a move to the south to flank target and approach from rear."

"TL, request approved," Jenner shouted back, then said, "Two and Six, see if you can flank to the north."

Jenner was ordering Travers and Greer to break away from the body of the team and begin moving off to the left, shielded by low boulders in the tall whipping grasses of the cemetery. This left only three men in the fight in the graveyard itself, but attacking the structure from multiple directions would inevitably draw fire away from Jenner and the other two here.

Court and Zack moved low through the grasses, out of the cemetery and then along a driveway on the south side of the church. As soon as they made it into the open, fresh gunfire rained down from the church bell turret, kicking up rocks and splashing rainwater into the air.

"Son of a bitch!" Zack said as he ran for concealment behind a parked van. Diving into the mud, he looked back for Six.

Court Gentry appeared in the air, crashed into Zack, and knocked him down. The younger man rolled on the ground, clutching his taped and splinted hand in obvious pain.

Rounds tore into the van, forcing the men to press their bodies and faces lower into the muddy water and gravel.

Zack said, "Dude, you're a bullet magnet!"

"I'm lucky like that." As he rolled up to a knee and shouldered his rifle, he said, "Zakharov snuck some tier ones over here from Russia. Mercs or active duty. Why would he do that, just so they could pull security at his staging area?"

"Figure that shit out later, numbnuts. We're in a *motherfucking* firefight!"

Court rose higher and looked down the hill at the rear of the church.

In the misty distance he saw the yellow Air Tractor begin its takeoff roll. He aimed at it, but before he could fire, bullets slammed into the van and exited right next to his head. A second string of three rounds pierced the vehicle and pounded into the back plate of his body armor.

He fell onto his stomach.

"You hit?" Zack asked between the cracks of his return fire.

"Negative." Court pushed himself up again. "The crop duster is taking off!"

Zack had shifted his rifle to aim it under the van at a side door to the church there. Just as he did so he saw movement, as a man in combat boots came running out.

"Handle it, Six. I've got contact north!" Zack opened fire, ripping into the man's feet and sending him tumbling to the gravel drive. When he hit the ground, Zack fired once more into the masked man's head, killing him.

Court now shouted, "Cover!" and went prone, positioning his broken hand on the vertical of the rifle to steady it. Zack climbed to his feet and began firing around the front of the van. "Covering!"

Court aimed at the tiny yellow aircraft, already gaining speed, as it bounced along the wet grass of the airstrip.

He fired a single round, then another, his hand throbbing anew with each volley. He kept shooting, aiming, trying to judge for the aircraft's increasing speed, the distance, and the bullet drop. The 416 was not a sniper rifle, but Court knew he should be able to hit a damn airplane at six hundred yards or more.

But the mist was heavy, the plane kept rolling away, and it didn't look like he was going to be able to stop it.

He changed magazines with his good hand, flipped his weapon's fire selector switch to fully automatic, and re-aimed at the tiny yellow plane as it took off from the bright green grass.

"C'mon, Gentry," he said to himself, and he pressed the trigger, firing burst after burst as his left hand screamed in agony.

. . .

Four Russian mercenaries in full body armor burst through the rear door of the church in formation, rifles swinging right and left, searching for targets. When they found no threats they waved forward a group of people in the doorway. Fox, then Hines, then Zakharov, along with two Bratva men, all came running out towards three sixteen-passenger vans parked just meters from the door.

Behind them, Zoya appeared, her arms tied behind her back at the elbows, and two Bratva soldiers bracketed her as she was rushed out the back door and towards one of the vans.

Behind this group, a dozen more mercs in masks and the latest tactical equipment brought up the rear, scanning 360 degrees for enemy contact.

Gunfire raged from the roof, from the north, west, and south sides of the church, but here on the eastern side it was clear. The sound of the accelerating Air Tractor carried through the mist from the south, heard intermittently between the nearly incessant shooting.

Zoya watched while her father, Hines, and Fox climbed into a van, wasting no time racing off down the hill, making its own lane in the tall grasses. The other two vehicles revved their engines, their drivers already at the wheel, and Zoya was placed next to one of these while her two minders stepped up to the other. The back door was open, and inside were stacks of scuba tanks and other diving gear, as well as stacked Pelican cases, no doubt holding some other equipment for the unit.

As the men began to shut the back of the van, Zoya found herself unattended for a moment. In that instant, she turned to run back inside the church, but before she could take three steps a hand grabbed her shoulder and spun her around, leading her back to the door of the second white van.

. . .

Chris Travers and Art Greer bounded around the northern side of the church now and saw a white vehicle racing down the hill in the distance. Travers pressed his transmit key on his chest. "Squirters in a white van, heading east at speed."

Jenner called back over the net immediately. "Once we suppress the threat here, we'll bring the helo up and go after it."

Travers and Greer took a few more steps towards the back of the property and saw a second, identical van racing off. Greer raised his rifle at it, but Travers stopped him. "The asset!"

Greer understood. The woman from CIA might be in the vehicle, so they couldn't just rake it with gunfire.

As they finally rounded the back edge of the church they saw a third van, with several people moving around it, including a brunette woman with her arms restrained behind her back.

The men at the van saw the two Americans, and they raised their weapons. Travers and Greer fell flat onto the ground and, from the prone position, expertly picked off all four men without hitting the hostage.

They thought they had all the threats down, but the driver dove out of the vehicle with his short-barreled AK and aimed it at the attackers at the northern side of the building. He fired at them, and then they returned fire. He raced over to a stone wall in the back garden of the church to dive behind it, but Greer took him in the left hip before he got there, spinning him to the ground and wounding him fatally.

Travers changed magazines in a flash, then rose and began running over to the woman, his weapon now pointing back at the church, because gunfire continued booming from inside.

Travers raced up to the woman, shouting over the raging gun battle. "Ma'am, come with me. I'm taking you to cover."

"Cut my arms free," she shouted back.

"I'll do it when we get somewhere safe."

"I can't run like this. Just cut the rope."

Travers realized the folly of standing here in the open arguing, so he pulled his knife off his chest rig and moved behind the attractive woman he'd last seen months earlier near Phuket, Thailand. He cut her free, resheathed his knife, then said, "I want you tight on my back. We're running to the wall of the church. Got it?"

"Got it!" she replied.

Travers began running for the church, twenty yards away. He'd expected to feel the presence of the female CIA asset right on his heels as he ran, but he did not. He slowed a little, concerned he'd gotten ahead of her, and then, when he made it to the stone wall, he spun around and looked back.

The brunette was not behind him at all. Instead she had climbed behind the wheel of the remaining white van. Before his eyes the vehicle lurched forward and took off down the hill, following the tracks of the two before it.

. . .

Zoya Zakharova raced down the hill, trying to catch up with the closest van, now three hundred meters away or so and barely visible in the mist. As she buckled herself in to reduce the thrashing she was taking from the rough terrain, she looked to her left. There, next to her, was a wounded man in the front passenger seat. He was a Bratva soldier, not one of the elite mercenaries who'd shown up, and as she drove on she rifled through his body with her left hand and pulled out a CZ 75 pistol, which she placed on her lap, and a mobile phone, which she examined. When she saw the phone was locked, she used it to smack the wounded man across the face. In Russian she said, "Hey! Unlock this."

The man had been shot through the left arm, and from the blood on his mouth she realized at least one of his lungs had been perforated by bullet fragments.

He turned his head to her slowly but said nothing.

Zoya now snatched up the CZ 75 and thumbed off the safety. Pointing it at him with her left hand she said, "Unlock it!"

Reluctantly, the man did so. Zoya kept one eye out the front windshield and the other on the wounded mafia goon, and when he tapped in his code he handed it back to her.

She reached for it, turned the wheel to avoid a rainwater-filled pothole in the gravel road, then looked over to the man.

He reached out and lunged at the pistol.

Zoya fired three times across her body, knocking the Russian dead into the passenger-side door.

She scrolled through the man's apps. Once she found the navigation app, she checked it to see where she was in relation to Castle Enrick.

She knew she had to hang back so as not to be detected but stay close enough to not lose the entourage racing away from the church. She knew her father. He wouldn't drive these obvious vehicles up to the castle. No, he would switch vehicles, do something to obscure his plan and his approach to his target obliquely.

As she was thinking over her desperate predicament, the yellow Air Tractor flew through the air above her on her right. She looked at it in surprise, then saw that it was trailing both smoke and fire.

As it plunged back to Earth, Zoya was relieved that the plague weapon had been destroyed, but she was still worried. She worried the Americans behind her would think their battle was won, when in truth her father had hinted he had a different type of attack up his sleeve.

She pushed down harder on the gas, increasing her speed, and the dead body slumped over into her lap.

. . .

Court watched as the yellow airplane sputtered and died in the air, then began its death spiral at only four hundred feet.

It hit a field of heather nose down, then exploded in a ball of fire.

Court pumped his fist in the air. To Zack he said, "I shot down an airplane with a rifle!"

Zack snorted. "Dude, get over yourself. It was a crop duster."

Crestfallen, Court said, "It's still a plane, Zack."

"Does this mean we're about to get the bubonic plague or some shit?"

"Pneumonic," Court corrected. "I didn't think it through that far when I started shooting at it."

Zack started moving around the van for the church. "Fuck it, Six. Let's go out in a blaze of glory before I cough up a couple of lungs."

Court followed behind him, and he and Zack entered the church, but only after notifying Jenner of their intentions to do so.

The four able-bodied men of Jenner's team, plus Court and Zack, cleared the church over the next ten minutes, killing three Russians on the ground floor and two more hiding in the tower. They radioed back to Castle Enrick and were informed that the burning crash site would have immediately destroyed all the weaponized bacteria, so they had not been exposed to the plague.

As they looked over all the dead inside and out, the majority of the combatants appeared to be Bratva soldiers, but a few were clearly of a different mold. Their gear was better, more coordinated and uniform, and the men looked more fit, more rugged.

But no less dead.

Jenner called in the Direct Action Penetrator helicopter, and he and his mates began treating the wounded. He had two KIA—McClane and Aaronson—and two more, Partridge and Stapleton, were wounded, stable but out of the fight.

Court asked if anyone had seen Zoya.

Travers said, "I saw her. She took one of the vehicles and headed off in the same direction as the others."

Jenner said, "So she's with them, after all."

Travers countered, "She was bound when I found her. I cut her free."

Again Jenner replied, "And then she ignored your instructions and jumped in a van and drove off with her father."

Court said, "Not *with* her father. *After* her father."

Jenner shrugged. "She hauled ass right behind the rest of them, Gentry. That's all we know."

Court and Zack were tasked with carrying the body of Aaronson—Court didn't learn the man's name till after he died—towards a makeshift landing zone at the bottom of the hill on the airstrip. As they struggled with the dead weight of the operator, Court took a moment to look back to the burning wreckage of the aircraft in the distance.

When they had the body at the LZ, Zack said to Court, "I'm going to call Brewer. You know what she's going to say about Anthem, don't you?"

Court *did* know exactly what Brewer would say, but he defended her to Zack now. "Zoya is on our side."

"Good ole Suzanne's not gonna see that. Zoya drugged you and ran, and then she ran again from Ground Branch. It looks bad for her."

"She's on our side," Court repeated.

Zack said, "You need to stow that sentimental bullshit. If Brewer or Hanley orders me to take her out, then that's what I'll do."

Court squared off in front of the bigger man. "Then you and I are going to have a problem."

"*Again?*"

"It's not me, Zack. It's you."

"Wrong, Six! That hard-on you have for her is making the rest of you soft! And soft makes you dead. Quit your job and you can be as big a pussy as you want for as long as you want; you can get a whole slew of kittens and grow flowers or whatever else it is that makes you whole. But as long as you are in this shit, with me, especially, you will *fucking* man up and do the jobs we are assigned."

"I'm not killing Zoya." His voice lowered. "And neither are you."

"If Brewer tells me to—"

"I'm not saying you won't try. I'm saying you'll die before you do."

The two men stared each other down, but behind them the helicopter landed, drowning out any further conversation.

CHAPTER 60

Suzanne Brewer sat in the living room of Matt Hanley's suite at Castle Enrick. His accommodations were much nicer than hers, but he was DDO so she was not surprised or offended by this. She expected to have his job someday, or she *had* expected it until recently. Now she knew she'd have to extricate herself from the black ops world to have a shot at a higher position and the perks that came along with it.

Together they'd sat on the sofa and listened to Zack Hightower's voice over the sat phone, talking over the rotors of the helo, delivering his after-action report about the attack on the church. Two Ground Branch men killed, two wounded, no sign of Zakharov or Primakov, Mars, or Fox. Anthem was freed, but she immediately fled the area, and her status remained unconfirmed.

None of this was good news.

But there was some good news: very good news. The aircraft presumably carrying the bioweapon crashed shortly after takeoff, burning on impact, so the conference was already in full swing here this morning at the castle, and those few security officials who did know the reasons for the heightened vigilance and increase in sentries had already mentally ratcheted back their threat level, though they kept helicopter gunships in the air in case of any other aircraft flying low and close enough to pose a threat.

When he was finished listening to Hightower's debrief, Hanley said, "I want Violator, you, and any of the Ground Branch men still in the fight here at the castle until we can get a fix on Zakharov." He paused. "Who's left?"

Hightower said, "Jenner, Travers, Lorenzi, and Greer are the only four up, sir."

"Okay. Have the helo land outside the castle walls. Suzanne will acquire security credos for you and Violator. Jenner and his men already have them. We'll set up a command center here on the third floor because this is the U.S. portion of the quarters. And from the command center we'll hunt for Zakharov via satellite, traffic cams, and local police."

Brewer said, "Matt, is it a good idea to bring the assets here?"

"I want all our paramilitary operations officers and singleton assets together, ready to go after Zakharov the moment there is a sighting. We know he's got a large security force with him; he might not have the plague weapon anymore, but he can still cause trouble for the Five Eyes conference. The Ground Branch men are my security detail. We fold Gentry and Hightower into their remaining numbers, and no one will notice." He looked at the phone; Hightower was still on the speaker. "Romantic, I know Gentry is the Gray Man; I need you to develop the power to blend in, as well."

"Like a plant in the corner, sir."

Hightower hung up, and Brewer headed out of Hanley's suite to arrange for the badges for two new close-protection officers for the DDO of CIA's detail.

. . .

Feodor Zakharov stood on the shoreline of an inlet on the western side of Loch Ness, outside one of four black Mercedes cargo vans he and his men had picked up in the underground garage of the Eastgate Shopping Centre in Inverness. The vans were full of equipment: scuba gear, firearms, ammunition, cases of explosives and rolls of det cord, all transferred from the white vans that made it away from the church.

And there was one more item: a large, locked, black plastic Pelican case that sat in the back of one of the Mercedes vans.

Zakharov called Fox over, and he arrived, as always, with Jon Hines at his back. The former general said, "Fox, I have eighteen mercenaries left. And we have a total of four sleepers working for us on the inside of the castle."

Fox said, "And we still have three aerosol canisters of plague, along with all the plastic explosive, detonation cord, the acetylene unit, and ammunition."

Zakharov asked, "What about the cases of syringes loaded with the injectable antibiotics?"

Fox said, "Yes. We have a full course of medicine for thirty men, more than enough." The younger man cocked his head. "What are you planning, sir?"

"The men will penetrate the facility via the thirteenth-century passage; that part is unchanged. They will set the explosives in the subterranean levels, and then they will go upstairs and attack the great hall tonight at eight p.m. when the opening formal dinner is taking place. At that time, everyone will be in one large room. The entire event will become a hostage scene. We will make some demands, release a statement. Meanwhile the canisters will be brought into the room and discreetly released.

"The difficult part of this is the need to hold all the participants, or as many as we can, for eight hours. That renders the plague fatal. Then we leave, claim that our demands have been met. If we do that, then *they* will leave Castle Enrick, return to their offices, and infect thousands of others over the next ten days or so."

"And that's the reason to make this look like a hostage situation?"

"Yes. If the biological agent is detected or seen, or even if there is any presumption it might have been used and not destroyed in the plane crash, then everyone in that building will be quarantined and given antibiotics immediately in local hospitals. Most will live, and no others will be infected back in their respective intelligence facilities around the world."

"So, take the building, hold the attendees hostage, infect them secretly, wait for them to turn into weapons themselves, then let them free."

"That's it. Honestly, I think we can be out in six hours, especially if we detonate the explosives under the building. The ensuing chaos will make it highly unlikely the attendees will be transported and treated correctly in only two hours for the strain Dr. Won created."

Fox said, "I am no military man, you know this. Still, I don't see how eighteen men can take over that building, not even from the inside. There is a company of Scottish military on-site, plus dozens of armed security. The original plan was an attempted covert entry and delivery of the aerosol, and only if our force was detected were they to engage. Taking and holding a massive building with that much security on-site . . . it seems impossible."

"Yes," Mars said, "but the sleepers on-site have informed me that seventy-five percent of the security and one hundred percent of the military will be outside the main building. Due to the classified nature of the items discussed in the conference, even during speeches in the great hall tonight, everyone without the highest level of access to secrets will be outside the keep itself.

"The mercenaries can hold the great hall as long as they get in quietly. And they can stall the response from authorities with good leadership, someone who can control the situation on the inside. Someone who speaks English."

Now Fox understood. "You yourself are going in with the mercenaries."

"*We*, Artyom Alekseyevich. We."

Fox nodded slowly. He'd been sent here as a sleeper by Russia to take orders from Zakharov, and previous to that he'd been a member of the Vory. He was brave, committed, and skilled. Still, he asked, "Do you have a plan to get us out of there?"

"The original exfiltration through the passage is still the plan. We detonate the explosives in the subterranean level, and this will buy us time. They won't find the exit for hours with the destruction we will leave them to pick through.

"But if they do detect the passage entry down at the water while we are in the castle and cut off our escape, we will demand a helicopter. Take the heads of UK, Canadian, American, Australian, and New Zealand intelligence services along with us. That should keep anyone from shooting us down. We can fly to the continent, land in a busy area, and disperse among the crowd before authorities arrive."

"And how will you get into and out of the castle? We will have to cross Loch Ness underwater. I've never heard you mention you were a trained scuba diver."

Zakharov said, "To get out, I will put your reserve air regulator in my mouth, hold on to you for dear life, and hope for the best. Once my plan is enacted successfully, my life is unimportant. But to get into the castle, I have a different idea."

"Which is?"

Zakharov smiled. "I plan on simply driving up to the front gate."

Fox looked at him like he was insane. After a moment he recovered. "Well, we will survive the plague, we have more than enough antibiotics for that. But I *don't* know that we will survive penetrating a well-defended intelligence target like the Five Eyes symposium."

Zakharov said, "If we live, we live. If we die, we die. Either way, if we succeed, we have utterly destroyed the West's intelligence apparatus." Zakharov looked up to Hines now. "How about you, old boy? You up for a wee bit of excitement?"

"I go where Fox goes, sir."

"Good chap." He looked at his watch. "Five hours till we move. Have the men make sure they remain hidden from the air, because as soon as they are sure I did not die in the fighting at the church, all five eyes will be open in search of me."

. . .

Court, Zack, Jenner, and the three other able-bodied men of Jenner's team arrived at Castle Enrick in the early afternoon. They had changed out of their wet, sweat-stained, and bloody clothing from the action at the church and now wore neat clothes: khakis, blazers, leather shoes. Court and Zack dressed themselves with clothing from the rucksacks of the dead and wounded of Ground Branch, and the surviving members of the team in the helo gave them dirty looks for this. As Court sat there on the helo in Aaronson's dark blue suit, he fully understood the looks he was getting. He would have felt the same way if someone on his team had died and a virtual stranger put on his clothes, but there was no way he could walk around the Five Eyes conference dressed like a commando.

His broken hand would draw attention, but when he unwrapped it to test it, he determined there was no way he could allow free movement of the broken bones in it, so he got Travers to reapply the metal brace and a fresh ACE bandage.

After landing they walked to the main gate and were searched by Scottish military and met by Suzanne Brewer, who showed their badges to the security force on duty there to get them checked in. Then she told them to follow her into the castle.

They all went directly to Hanley's third-floor suite.

She told them, "We'll put you right back out as soon as we have some clue as to where to send you. We will, at that time, request support from the United Kingdom. A squadron of paramilitaries from SAS, because clearly you've shown yourselves to be unable to handle Zakharov and his men without assistance."

Jaws flexed in anger, and eyes narrowed in the group of hard men, but no one commented.

Brewer ignored the looks. "For now, blend in, try to look like typical security officers. I hope to have a target for you very soon."

Inside the command center next to Hanley's suite, over a dozen agency analysts pored over computers, checking satellite photos of the area, maps, traffic and security cameras, and the like, all desperate to find a group of men, probably traveling on the roads, probably moving in this direction, and probably carrying weapons. British intelligence was in on it now, after a fashion, with their leadership putting David Mars and his known cohorts in the national crime database and with the suspects involved in the mayhem at the church to the west being identified as an unknown group of military-aged Russian nationals.

Local police were on the lookout now, but there was a lot of area to cover in the Scottish Highlands, and much of it was remote or rural.

Outside the castle, British and Scottish security experts were told to be extra vigilant. A pair of police boats patrolled the waters of the loch, and helicopters flew patterns high above.

• • •

In the late afternoon, Zoya Zakharova stood on the banks of Loch Ness, next to a two-door Nissan she'd stolen in Inverness so she wouldn't be driving a hunted van around.

She gazed up in the sky at the helicopters circling above Castle Enrick on a cliff on the opposite bank, just barely visible through the mist pouring off the water, even now in the afternoon. With binoculars she'd purchased at a store in Inverness she scanned the entire area, left and right.

She noticed two small patrol boats bobbing in the water at the bottom of the cliff, a fifty-caliber machine gun mounted on each one, along with a crew of four.

Zoya wasn't flying blind by being here now. She'd seen the scuba tanks in the back of one of the vans, so she knew this was how her father's unit of commandos was going to infiltrate the conference. She couldn't figure how they would do it, though. There seemed to be no other access up to the castle other than scaling that sheer cliff.

And even if they did scale the cliff, they would be completely exposed to security forces in the parapets of the castle wall overlooking a well-manicured lawn. It would be a shooting gallery for the defenders if the attackers chose that means for their ingression.

No, there had to be some other way into the castle grounds that could be accessed by water.

She was missing something, but she wouldn't find it here, searching from across the loch. Instead she looked again at the map on her phone, trying to find the best place for someone to put a boat in the water nearby. Somewhere out of view of long-range spotters on the security force of the Five Eyes conference, but close enough to access the shore below the cliff.

After a minute thinking about it, she decided that her father's divers would be in plain view of the castle if they tried to sail a boat out into Loch Ness to get closer.

No, the scuba divers would not be diving off a boat. They would enter the water close enough to make their way to the castle directly, without using a boat at all.

It was probably four hundred meters across the water here, an easy swim for fit men in still water.

She looked on her GPS again, and within moments she found the spot. An inlet, just a half mile north of where she stood, was completely obscured by a hill from the castle across the blue water, yet close enough to swim from cover there to the area at the bottom of the cliff.

Zoya was back in her car in seconds, racing to get a vantage point on the inlet.

．．．

As she drove up the road in the blue Nissan, a gray commercial van passed by on her right. She normally wouldn't have paid any attention to an oncoming vehicle, but in the front passenger seat was a blond-haired giant.

She didn't run into many men who were six foot nine, so she identified him instantly. It was the monster who always shadowed Fox, the man who had beaten poor Court so badly.

Twice.

The gray van just drove on to the south, while Zoya drove on to the north.

But not for long. Once the van rounded a turn behind her Zoya slammed on her brakes, turned her little car around, and took off in pursuit.

She didn't know if her father was in the vehicle, but she sure as hell *did* know that these men were part of his crew, so she decided to follow them.

• • •

The tail lasted less than ten minutes before they entered the beautiful little town of Fort Augustus, on the southern bank of Loch Ness, and here Zoya saw the commercial van pull to the side of the road. She herself stopped, pulled out her binoculars, and focused them on the scene just in time to watch her father, wearing a crisp suit and tie, step out of the side of the vehicle.

Alone.

The van drove off, leaving him there.

Zoya couldn't believe her eyes. He was less than fifty meters away, unguarded, and she could walk right up to him, drive right up to him, run him the fuck down if she wanted.

But for a few precious seconds, she froze.

Could she really do it? She had been so certain until this moment. But now, when the fantasy met the reality in front of her, she hesitated.

Slowly she shifted the Nissan into gear, but just then a taxi pulled up next to her father, and he climbed in.

She muttered softly, *"Kagogo cherta?" What the hell?*

She drove off, tailing the taxi.

• • •

General Feodor Zakharov took a deep breath to calm himself as his taxi pulled up to the guard shack in front of Castle Enrick. There were a few cars ahead in the line; each driver and each passenger had their documentation checked out by both Scottish military in full combat uniforms and men and women in civilian attire, no doubt Metropolitan police or even MI5, British domestic intelligence.

The taxi driver looked in the rearview mirror. "I take it you've got your papers to get in 'ere. Been ferrying people back and forth from hotels and B&Bs in Fort Augustus and Inverness to this big government conference, and the blokes here at the gate are all business."

Zakharov was using his David Mars legend. "Don't worry, old boy, I'll zip right in. They'll be quite happy to have me."

They inched their way to the front of the queue, and then a young Scottish soldier looked in on the taxi driver, who said, "Evenin', mate. This gent is here for the conference."

Zakharov rolled his window down, and the soldier reached out a hand. "Papers, sir."

"Listen carefully, lad. Inside that building is a woman named Suzanne Brewer. She's a Yank. I am here to see her, and she will quite like to see me."

"You got papers?"

He pulled out his passport and handed it over. The man looked at it. "No, sir. You need a special pass to get into the conference."

"That passport says 'David Mars.' Be a good lad and go tap that name into your computer, and see what pops up."

The young soldier stepped over to a man in a suit and tie and talked to him a moment while showing him the passport, and then the man looked in on the taxi. After some hesitation, he stepped into the guard shack.

The driver said, "How 'bout you settle the fare and get out here, mate?"

Mars handed the man the fare in cash with a healthy tip, then opened his car door.

He didn't need to stand up, because soldiers rushed him, grabbed him, pushed him onto the ground, and put guns to his back.

Lying there on the drive next to the astonished cabbie looking down on him out his window, Zakharov said, "Suzanne Brewer. CIA. If someone could be so kind as to call her, I'd appreciate it very much indeed."

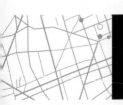

CHAPTER 61

Suzanne Brewer sat at the opening night formal dinner, sipping chardonnay and looking at her phone, held down below the table so as not to make obvious the fact that she was not paying attention to the man speaking. The director of the New Zealand Security Intelligence Service was giving a talk about the benefits of cooperation, and the four hundred guests in attendance were eating salmon or filet and trying to stay awake.

An Englishman with the site security detachment knelt down next to her at the table. "Ms. Brewer, is it?"

"That's right."

"We have a situation at the front gate. Could you come with me, please?"

"I don't have anything to do with security here. You need to find someone who—"

"You've been requested personally, ma'am."

She flashed a glance at Hanley, seated at another table and no less bored, and then she followed the younger man out through the tables and into the hallway.

Once there, he stopped and turned to her. "There is a man we've taken into custody trying to get in to see you. He has no credentials. Only a UK passport."

"What's his name?"

"David Mars. He's showing up on a brand-new watch list that was—"

Brewer spun away and ran back into the banquet hall in the direction of Matt Hanley.

• • •

Court Gentry had slept five hours that afternoon and early evening but finally woke when the meds began to wear off and the pain in his hand began to flare up. He dressed quickly in Aaronson's suit; it was a little big for him but he made it work, struggled mightily to tie his tie with one good hand and just the fingertips of the other, and he put his badge lanyard around his neck. He left his room and went to the lobby in front of the closed doors of the grand hall. A black tie affair was going on inside; he expected that a couple of Ground Branch men would be inside watching over Hanley, and he started to head that way.

"Hey, Six. Have you checked this place out?"

Court turned to find Hightower, also dressed in a suit and tie, coming up the hall from the main doors.

"The castle? No, not really."

"There's an armory, a dungeon down below, three really swanky libraries. It's pretty sweet."

"It's good to be king," Court said, but he didn't really care about the old building. He was more concerned about where Zoya was and what she was doing, but he knew he had to be here, ready to kit up and climb back in the Direct Action Penetrator as soon as there was any sighting of Zakharov.

"How is security?" he asked.

"Just fair, to be honest. The troops outside are the bulk of the protection of this place. Since the meetings in here are all classified, they are minimizing the number of security personnel inside the castle. The UK relies more on gates and cameras than it does on guns, anyway. I've seen maybe twenty armed guards inside the keep itself, but that's about it."

Suzanne Brewer burst out of the ballroom with Matt Hanley, followed by Jenner and Lorenzi. They walked at a fast pace, and Court and Zack fell into step with them when Hanley motioned to them.

As he walked Hanley said, "Zakharov turned himself in at the front gate."

Court said, "Why the hell would he go and do a thing like that?"

Brewer answered, "We have no idea. He's being brought into a makeshift interrogation room on the third floor. I need you two there guarding him, at least till we know what his play is."

• • •

Ten minutes later, Zoya Zakharova pulled her Nissan up to the guard shack. A woman in a Scottish military uniform nodded at her curtly. "Your credentials, ma'am?"

Zoya spoke in her American English accent. "I am here to see Suzanne Brewer."

The woman's brow furrowed. "I don't know who that is, ma'am, but you're not getting in without proper credentials."

Zoya had seen the entire takedown of her father through her binos from two hundred meters away. She noted one of the men who, just ten minutes earlier, had a boot in her father's back.

"Sir," she said, and the man in the suit looked her way. "David Mars. You just met him?"

He stepped over, immediately wary. "Aye."

Zoya shrugged. "The thing is . . . he's my dad."

Unsure, the man reached over and put his hand on the female soldier's shoulder without looking away from the woman behind the wheel. "Take out your weapon, sergeant."

The woman drew her pistol, and Zoya raised her hands.

• • •

Feodor Zakharov had been placed in a small room off the third-floor library and relieved of his suit coat, tie, and shirt, along with his belt, watch, and shoes. Hightower had frisked the man from head to toe, leaving nothing untouched in the process. Through it all the former head of GRU had not spoken a word.

Hanley, along with Lorenzi and Jenner, had gone to the security office on the second floor to meet with officials there to warn them to be wary, and to look at the feeds from the myriad cameras around the castle for any sort of threat.

Now the former Russian general sat in his undershirt and dress pants, hands uncuffed, fingers interlocked and resting on the table. Hightower stood behind him, close enough to take him down if he had to.

Suzanne Brewer entered the room, out of her ball gown and now dressed in business attire. Zakharov smiled charmingly at her, and he spoke with an English accent. "Ah, Ms. Brewer, I presume. Lovely to meet you. I've heard a lot of interesting things. I believe you and I have a mutual acquaintance."

"I assume you are talking about your daughter."

"No, I am talking about Martin Wheeler. He told me about you, about Poison Apple. I told myself you were just the person I needed to speak to here, straightaway."

Brewer was about to reply, about to sit down, but the door opened behind her. Turning to it, she saw Jason.

She followed him back out the door without a word to Zakharov. In the third-floor library, Violator stood with Travers, both men waiting for orders. Brewer gave them both a look of anger for allowing this junior officer to interrupt her interrogation.

"What the hell is it?" she asked Jason.

"Ma'am, it's Anthem. She's out at the front gate. She wants to see you."

She looked at Violator and then back to Jason. "What the *hell* is going on around here?" When no one answered her she said, "Take security with you, go down, and bring her up here. But only under guard. We don't know whose side she's on."

Court wanted to protest, but he didn't know what the hell Zoya's game was, either. Instead he said, "I'll go with him."

Brewer shook her head. "No. You stay right here, Violator. Jason can take Travers."

Brewer went back into the parlor off the library being used as an interrogation facility to continue her interrogation of Zakharov.

• • •

Ten minutes later Zoya Zakharova entered the library, followed by Jason and Chris Travers. Travers had been exceedingly polite during the long walk through the main entry hall, up the stairs, and down the narrow third-floor hallway, but he'd stayed close enough to her to give her the indication that he was something more than just an escort.

Once she entered the library, she looked around for Brewer and her father and instead saw Court standing there alone. This surprised her. She didn't expect to find a black ops contract agent like him inside the Five Eyes conference.

She gave him a nervous look, followed by a little smile. "Are you okay?"

Court replied with, "Your dad's in the next room. This is as close as you get."

She said, "I understand. Brewer is with him?"

"Yes. I guess your plan to kill him went about as well as our plan to hit the church this morning."

Zoya said, "Maybe I didn't kill him, yet, but I bet I've killed more bad guys than you did today."

"In my defense," Court said, "I slept in."

Zoya frowned. "I am really sorry about that. I just—"

"I know. You needed some alone time to kill your dad."

Zoya nodded. "I did."

Court shook his head in disbelief. "If you think anybody is going to let you in there to talk to him, you are out of your mind. Not even me."

Zoya said, "He isn't here to surrender. Something's happening."

Court nodded. "We're all saying the same thing. There is some other game here, isn't there?"

"His men have scuba gear, that much I know."

Jason immediately took off for the war room to let the men there know this new information.

Court said, "But that will just get them to the shore at the bottom of the cliff. If they climb it they'll walk right into a company of Royal Scots Dragoon Guards waiting for them. They have Jackal armored vehicles with machine guns and grenade launchers. Those Russian paras would get chewed up in ten seconds."

Zoya had no answer for this. It seemed like a pretty obvious flaw in her father's plan, but she knew he was far too good not to see it himself.

. . .

The patrol boats out in Loch Ness traveled in a lazy pattern, and the twenty men under the water simply waited for them to churn away from the area they planned to use to land ashore. By the time they did, the divers had all moved to shallow water, and they rose as one in the dark, almost invisible in their thick black wetsuits on the cloudy evening. Each man had a large waterproof pack strapped to his chest and a smaller one on his hip, and each pair of mercs carried a massive heavy Pelican case between them.

The men took cover behind boulders on the narrow shoreline, then moved into the thick brush towards the hidden iron door to the staircase into the castle. After doffing their scuba equipment, two members of the team moved acetylene and oxygen tanks up to the door, attached and fired up the torch, and began working on the hinges. The rest began dressing in dark business suits and dress shoes brought in waterproof bags. This done, they pulled on thin nylon coveralls to keep their suits clean from the climb. Soon the team pulled their short-barreled rifles from their packs and slung the weapons, packing extra magazines and radios into pockets. Each of the men put a headset on, and soon they ran a whispered comms check.

It took the men with acetylene torches five minutes to open the rusty door, and then while those two got dressed it took the rest of the group five minutes more to remove the rock and dirt filling the bottom part of the tiny stairwell to make it appear inaccessible if the iron door had been checked by security.

The passage was less than five feet high and so narrow it was claustrophobic, but eventually the first man on the team began climbing, and the next man followed. Fox entered, with Hines behind him, struggling to fit. The fifth man hefted the Pelican case containing the three canisters full of the weaponized *Yersinia pestis* spores, and the rest carried the other cases of equipment.

Finally the last man pulled the door closed behind him and jammed it back into place on the off chance someone discovered it.

. . .

Two security officials from Scotland Yard stood with flashlights in one of the dozens of darkened basement chambers below Castle Enrick, their beams pointed at a rusty metal door they'd just cleared of stacked boxes of dishes and plastic-wrapped linens. On the other side they could hear movement, an acetylene torch being used on the inside of the sealed door.

The shorter of the two men looked at his watch. "Taking too bloody long."

His partner wiped sweat from his brow and shined his light back over his shoulder, out of this little room and into a main chamber, once used as a common area for the servants' apartments built down here but now used simply as a storage room for old, scratched, and broken banquet tables and chairs.

"We're okay," the man said, but his voice belied his words.

The men were not, in fact, English. One was born in Sevastopol, Ukraine, to Russian parents, and the other in Leningrad, now St. Petersburg. They were Russian agents, infiltrated into the UK fifteen years earlier as part of the sleeper program that Zakharov's wife had been part of. They spoke perfect British English and possessed fully backstopped and rock-solid legends and a decentralized controller in David Mars, their only link with their home nation.

Suddenly the door opened with a painful screeching of iron on stone. A flashlight beam illuminated the two men for a moment, then switched off.

"*Dobry vecher,*" *Good evening,* said the shorter Scotland Yard investigator.

. . .

Roger Fox climbed out of the tiny stairwell third in line, stood up fully, and wiped a small amount of the debris and dirt from his hands. He wore black coveralls and carried a backpack. Behind him, the men with the acetylene tank and the men with guns and heavy packs and cases struggled out of the passage and into the light, and then Hines crawled out on his hands and knees and slowly stood erect.

As more men made it out of the stairwell and into the room, Fox looked over the two cops in the employ of David Mars. He said, "Have you heard anything about someone being taken in at the front gate?"

The men looked at each other. The short one said, "Not a word."

Fox said, "That must mean the Americans have him sequestered to interrogate him. Where would they take him?"

"The Americans have the entire third floor to themselves. If I was gonna take someone for a chat without the rest of the castle knowin' about it, I'd take him up to three."

Fox nodded, then turned to the mercenary team leader. "Okay. Take twelve men to the banquet hall to meet up with the other two sleepers there. I'll take two of your men along with Jon, and these two sleepers. We'll go to the third floor and recover the general. The rest will set up the explosives down here."

All the new arrivals to the basement took off their coveralls, revealing their dark business attire. Their short-barreled weapons were checked one last time in the dim light, and cases were opened. Three men began pulling out several explosives and detonation cord, and with head lamps on they began positioning them around the dungeon level of the castle, while the others headed for the stairs.

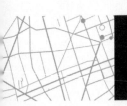

CHAPTER 62

Suzanne Brewer looked at her watch. It was nine p.m. and the banquet was in full swing downstairs. Up here in the makeshift interrogation room she'd spent the last fifteen minutes explaining to Feodor Zakharov that he had no rights, that he would have no contact with the British here, and if the Americans wanted to, they would shove him in a suitcase and take him out of the Five Eyes conference and deliver him to an Agency black site without anyone knowing they had him in custody.

Zakharov seemed positively relaxed about his predicament. He noticed her looking at her watch and said, "Can I bother you for the time? Seems someone nicked my watch."

To this Brewer said, "It's time to tell me why you are here."

"My plan has failed. I see that. I am able to face the facts. There is no sense trying to hide from the long arm of the United States of America. I decided it was best I turn myself in. Throw myself at your mercy."

Brewer just replied with, "Horseshit."

. . .

Thirteen men in suits and ties walked up the wide corridor, not in formation, but grouped closely together. They approached the great hall; the three sets of doors were closed and the murmur of voices and the clanking of plates could be heard over music playing.

There were a pair of UK security men in front of each set of doors. The farthest pair from the approaching Russians watched them coming and immediately reached into pockets, removing red elastic sweat bands. These they both quickly slipped around their right biceps, indicating to the other Russians that they were the sleepers infiltrated into the security services and should therefore not be engaged as hostiles.

When the other two pairs of men pushed off the wall and approached the group to check their badges, the two men with the red bands on their arms pulled silenced pistols from their hiding places inside their coats.

The four security men standing right in front of them never stood a chance. The approaching group of Russians all stepped to one side of the corridor so as not to be downrange of the gunfire, and then the two Russians in back fired their suppressed weapons into the four men, dropping them dead before any of them knew they were in any danger.

The bodies were left where they fell, and the music and crowd noise from the great hall masked the muffled gunshots.

Now the Russians divided into three units, approached the three doors off the main corridor to the great hall, and waited. One of the sleepers looked at his watch and determined the time was right, and then he and his colleague entered the room, leaving the rest outside.

The mercenary leader began counting back slowly from forty-five.

. . .

In the drawing room on the third floor, Zakharov smiled and interrupted Brewer, who'd been getting nothing out of the ex-general. He said, "I would like to make a polite proposal to you, and to all security officials working in the building."

Brewer cocked her head. "I'm listening."

"There is no need for anyone to get hurt. Yes, our original intention involved Dr. Won's biological weapon, but as you know, the aircraft crashed today, no doubt due to the actions of your commandos. So now we enter our plan B, with ambitions less lofty than before. We only wish to make a series of statements to the world press, and then to leave in peace."

Brewer's look of confusion matched her words. "We?"

. . .

Inside the Great Hall, the two Russians with the red bands went in separate directions, along the walls, passing servers and bartenders, all of whom were MI5 employees due to the classified nature of the conversations, and they took positions on opposite sides of the huge, dimly lit room. The men themselves were counting down, and at the ten-second mark, they reached into their coats again, this time pulling out two flash bang grenades each. The only six armed men in the room covering four hundred attendees were separated from one another, but only by twenty meters or so, standing along the wall.

The three double doors off the main corridor burst open, the two sleepers tossed their distraction devices in the direction of the six armed guards, and then they turned away.

. . .

Brewer was confused. "You and who else? What are you talking about?"

Zakharov sat in silence for a moment, then started to speak again. "I am talking about—"

The muffled sounds of explosions and the sudden chatter of gunfire seemed to come from inside the castle and somewhere below the room where Brewer stood.

Zakharov smiled. "I am talking about that. My forces have orders only to return fire to protect themselves. Whatever shooting you hear only happened because your people insisted on violence."

Zack Hightower drew his pistol, stepped forward to the seated man, and jabbed the barrel into the side of his head. "How 'bout I pop this one right now to get the ball rolling and then go down and deal with the others?"

Brewer put a hand up to stop him; the door to the room burst open and Violator entered, his own pistol in his hand.

Brewer said, "Zakharov knows about this. It's some sort of attack."

"Not an attack," Zakharov protested. "Merely a political statement, although as I said, my men will defend themselves if necessary."

. . .

In the banquet hall it was pandemonium. In the initial attack, all six security men were killed, as well as four waiters and three conference attendees from the UK. One Russian mercenary had been shot through the knee; he was now down on the floor applying a tourniquet to his thigh. A second merc took a pistol round in his Kevlar vest, but it did not penetrate.

The Russians who survived the first quick, chaotic gun battle rushed to lock all the doors, and two of them were positioned by the open hallway that gave access to the kitchen, making sure no one came or went via this route.

A number of men and women in formal attire managed to escape through the kitchen before the mercs secured the hall, as well as through the double doors closest to the main entrance to the castle, but only about forty of the nearly four hundred were so lucky. The rest were rounded up and ordered to their seats.

Most of the kitchen staff made it out the back before Russians sealed it off, but a few stayed behind, panic-stricken. These employees were rounded up and brought back into the great hall.

The overhead lights were turned on, and all the 375 or so in the room were ordered to place their hands on the tables or to lie down on the floor. Four armed men climbed onto the stage, their automatic rifles sweeping back and forth over the crowd.

Four of the remaining Russians stepped back into the corridor and took up positions facing the main entrance of the castle.

When a platoon of armed and armored Scottish military came bursting through the front door, fragmentation grenades were hurled at them by the men guarding the corridor, killing three and sending the others back outside to assess the situation more carefully before committing to another frontal assault.

. . .

Zoya Zakharova entered the drawing room where her father was being held, followed by Chris Travers, who immediately grabbed her. Before he could pull her back out, she shouted, "What's going on, Papa?"

General Zakharov turned to see her, and he grimaced. "Zoyushka. I *truly* wish you weren't here among your friends from across the pond right now."

Brewer motioned to Travers to let Anthem go.

Zoya turned to Brewer. "What has he said?"

"Nothing. He's been stalling, waiting for whatever's going on to kick off."

The gunfire continued and seemed to grow closer. Court had moved to Zoya, ready to stop her if she made any moves towards her father. Hightower kept his gun pointed at the former GRU director, and Travers went out to cover the hall with Jason.

Zoya yelled at her father. "You think you can just shoot everyone here?"

"Heavens, no. That's not our game at all."

She thought a moment. "The bioweapon. You brought the bioweapon."

"We lost that in the airplane crash this morning. Now we wish to only make a—"

Zoya stepped forward and shoved his head to the side, exposing his neck. Just like Travers, Court wasn't fast enough to stop her.

She said, "Stress hives. He's lying."

Zakharov was unmoved. "The discoloration doesn't mean one is lying, only that one is under some stress. I should think everyone in this building, myself included, has reason to feel a bit of anxiety at present, don't you?"

She looked up to Brewer. "I don't believe him. He told me at the church that he had a plan that Won didn't know about. He said that before the crop duster went down.

"I don't think the plague was on that aircraft at all."

Brewer just stared back. "Oh shit."

Matt Hanley raced into the parlor now, tailed by Jenner. Zakharov turned his head to look at the new arrivals, but Hightower twisted it back around forward.

Brewer said, "There is a chance the attackers brought Dr. Won's plague with them."

Zakharov said, "No. We only wish to—"

"Shut the fuck up!" Zoya screamed.

Hanley had never met Zoya Zakharova, his third Poison Apple asset, but now was hardly the time for introductions. He simply addressed her. "What do you think?"

"I don't think. I *know* he's lying. He will infect everyone here somehow. He's banking on the fact that we don't figure that out."

"Why on earth would I come myself if I had any intention of releasing the spores?"

Zoya did not even address her father. She spoke to Hanley. "He needs to hold everyone hostage until the effects can't be reversed. He has to do this without anyone knowing they have been infected, so they aren't quarantined, but instead return to their home nations and infect others."

"Good lord, Zoya. The plot you just concocted is much more diabolical than anything I could possibly come up with." Zakharov followed with a snorted laugh.

Just then, a voice called out from up the hallway, audible because the parlor door was open to the library. "I am looking for David Mars! I request you release him now. Downstairs we have nearly four hundred hostages in the great hall, which we have barricaded and wired with explosives. Other explosives have been set around the castle. We will grant you a two-minute grace period, and then, if Mars is not released, we will begin shooting a hostage every minute. The first hostage will be from the United States. The clock begins now."

Gentry raced out into the library, where Jason and Travers now knelt, guns facing the doorway. Whoever was shouting the commands was down the hall to the left, out of view, but the two Americans held their weapons up at the doorway in case anyone tried to enter.

In the parlor Zakharov said, "My men will do exactly as they threaten. You can save a lot of lives by releasing me. In turn, I won't demand you come with me, Deputy Director Hanley, or you, Ms. Brewer. Or even your security people here. They can stay." He turned to his daughter. "I will, however, demand that Zoya come along."

"Not happening," Hanley said.

Zakharov replied, "You are hardly in a position of power. The directors of all five English-speaking intelligence agencies have been taken hostage, and will be shot, one by one, if I am not allowed to walk out this door . . . *with* my daughter. Now."

Zoya said, "I'll go with him." To Hanley she said, "Sir, if you test his mettle, someone downstairs *will* be murdered. My father does not bluff."

Hanley hesitated; the voice down the hall called out that he had less than one minute before the first victim was to be shot in the great hall, and then he turned to Hightower. "Let the prick go." To Zoya he said, "We'll get you back."

Hightower lowered his pistol and took a step back compliantly. The Russian stood, walked over to a sofa where the items that had been taken from him were lying, and put his shirt back on and stepped into his shoes.

He took his coat and tie in his arm, then began walking. Zoya followed her father through the parlor, into the library, and towards the hall. Court had taken a position behind an oak table, and when he saw what was happening he stood up. "You've got to be kidding."

She just looked at him without speaking as she passed.

Court called back over his shoulder. "Matt? Matt, what are you doing?"

Hanley came out with Jenner and Brewer. "Let her go. They hold the cards for now."

Court stood, conflicted and unsure.

Zakharov stopped suddenly, faced Court. He said nothing for a long time, just looked him over. Finally he turned to Zoya. "Your friend, I take it."

Zoya looked down at the floor.

The bearded Russian looked back to Court. "Interesting. In other circumstances, I suppose I could be calling you 'son.'"

Court did not reply. He wanted to lift his pistol and shoot the bastard in the windpipe, but he remained still.

Zakharov stood there silently for several more seconds, staring at Court, before yelling out in Russian. "We're coming out!"

The Russian father and daughter disappeared up the hallway.

No sooner had they gone than Jenner said, "We're armed with pistols. I'm hearing grenades and automatic weapons downstairs. We're not taking down those Russians without a lot more firepower. We've got to get to the security armory on the second floor."

Hanley said, "Where are Greer and Lorenzi?"

"They were on night watch, so they racked out down in their room at the far end of this floor."

Hanley nodded. "I want you to go grab them, then all six of you make for the armory. There might be others up here we can recruit."

Jenner said, "Not leaving you here, boss. You and Ms. Brewer will be safer coming along for the ride."

Hightower said, "Jenner, it's your show, but I suggest we split into two teams to cover all the rooms faster. Violator and I will take Brewer and go right, you and Travers take Hanley and go left. Find Lorenzi and Greer, see if anyone else is hiding up here. We'll meet downstairs in the security office after we've had a look around."

Hanley loosened his tie around his thick neck, looked at Brewer, then said, "Let's go."

. . .

At the turn of the hallway towards the main wing, Zakharov met Fox, Hines, two Russian mercenaries, and two of the four sleepers. Hines took Zoya by the back of her neck and yanked her to him, her feet nearly leaving the floor in the act.

The general looked at his men. "Who has grenades?"

Both the mercenaries immediately pulled a fragmentation grenade.

"Destroy that room. The deputy director of the CIA is in there with friends. Let's unburden him with the task I have for the others. Then follow me down to the hostages."

Pins were pulled, grenades were lobbed, and just as Zoya started to scream a warning, Jon Hines smothered her entire face with the palm of his hand.

Zakharov began heading down the corridor for the main staircase, followed by all the others.

. . .

Jenner was first into the corridor, and he saw a man down the hall throw something towards the entrance to the library behind a muffled scream. He spun, raced back into the room, and turned Hanley away.

"Grenade!" he shouted, and Court grabbed Brewer with his one good hand and yanked her, heaving them both backwards in the air over the side of a large leather-and-wood sofa. They crashed on the ground and Court rolled on top of the woman.

Jason turned to run away, and Travers put himself right behind Jenner, adding more protection to Hanley, as they ran back towards the little parlor used as an interrogation room.

The first grenade went off; shrapnel fired in all directions, hitting Jason in the back and Travers in the upper right leg, just below his butt cheek. Both men went down.

The second grenade wasn't thrown as well as the first; it bounced against the doorway and detonated just in front of it in the hall. Travers took a nick to the back of his head from this blast, then climbed up and trained his weapon on the entrance to the drawing room.

No more grenades came, and soon Jenner, Court, Hanley, and Brewer were standing in the cloud of dust.

"Travers?" Court found him down on the floor, grabbing his upper thigh. There was blood on his leg, on his hands, but he wasn't hemorrhaging. Still, he was obviously in a lot of pain.

Hanley himself checked Jason. "The kid's dead. Son of a bitch."

CHAPTER 63

Feodor Zakharov finished tying his tie as he walked up the main corridor towards the great hall. At his side were Fox, Hines, and two men who had been trained by his wife fifteen years earlier to blend in perfectly in the UK.

Behind them all Zoya Zakharova walked, trailed by two mercenaries holding PP-2000s, 9-millimeter machine pistols with thirty-round magazines. The men knew what they were doing, Zoya realized, because they stayed far enough back from her so there was no way she'd be able to disarm them before they poured bullets into her body.

When Zakharov got to the lobby in front of the great hall, he turned and looked at his daughter. "I would send you out the front door to safety right now if I weren't convinced you'd just find some way to get back in and come up behind me with a stiletto. No, I want to know where you are at all times." He paused. "You might not like what is happening, but you loved your mother and your brother. This is all for them."

Zoya shook her head. "You don't get to use their deaths to justify your madness."

"Zoyushka, I love you, but the one thing I believe in more than you is my cause. I should have killed you when I first found out you'd been flipped by the Americans. But I was weak, and now you are the one person who can threaten my entire plan. You need to watch yourself *very* carefully now. Spend the rest of your life hating me, pursuing me, I'll let you do this." He darkened as he said, "But don't you *fuck* with me right now, or I *will* kill you myself."

. . .

The former general turned and opened the door. Stepping in, he walked directly to the stage, aware of hundreds of terrified eyes tracking him as he did so. After thirty seconds he'd moved through all the tables, and he stepped up to the lectern microphone.

"Ladies and gentlemen, I apologize for the interruption. Unfortunately I am going to have to keep you right where you are for a short time, before my colleagues and I leave you in peace."

He'd seen several bodies on the floor along the walls of the room, and he knew these men and women wouldn't buy the line about peace, but he wanted them as compliant as possible.

He said, "I am going to speak with the military forces arrayed outside, men and women who are most certainly even now preparing to attack this building. I will explain the folly of that decision to them, but perhaps I could have Director Capshaw of the CIA and Director Rutherford of MI6 come with me outside to confirm the hopelessness of the situation.

"After that, we will make a series of statements publicly over the next several hours. Crimes committed by the Five Eyes nations against the innocent and unfortunate of the Third World. Within a few hours my colleagues and I will leave, and you all may resume with your conference." He smiled. "Perhaps with better moral clarity about your mission."

As Zakharov spoke, one of the suited Russian mercenaries stepped behind one of the small service bars that had been placed on the edges of the room and slipped off his backpack. He unzipped it a few inches and put a hand inside.

Closing it around the knob of the tank full of specially modified *Yersinia pestis* spores, held in aerosol, he took a few quick breaths. He'd already injected his antibiotics, he would take more in three hours, and he would have a full IV infusion going into him as soon as they left this place and made it back to the freighter waiting for them off the east coast of Scotland. Still, he knew what he was doing, and he didn't like the fact that he'd have to breathe this shit at all.

Two more mercs did the same thing simultaneously behind other bars.

As the former general spoke, the mercenaries turned the knobs, and a barely audible hiss could just be made out.

Then the men stood back up.

The one who called himself Fox watched them all, making sure they did as they had been instructed. He turned away when he saw all three men guard over their bioweapons as they sprayed invisible death into the air.

. . .

Zoya stood in the back of the room, with Hines's big hand on her shoulder. She watched her father, listened to his words, and paid attention to his every movement.

This wasn't about a statement.

He was stalling for time. She just knew it.

She looked around the room, wondering if the aerosol had already been released into the air. She wondered if she was breathing pneumonic plague spores even now. Just thinking this had the effect of tightening her lungs, shallowing her breathing, making her eyes itch.

Assuming they believed her father's promises, all the men and women around her in the great hall thought they would be free in hours. But these people didn't have hours; they had to get out of here so they could get treatment to stave off the plague.

She had no way of proving her theory about the existence of the bioweapon. She only had absolute confidence in her thinking that nothing else explained the actions of her father. His assertion that there was no way he would have been here himself if he was planning on disseminating the spores rang hollow to her, because she knew her father; she knew he would not leave it to chance that the entire operation would fall apart because he wasn't here, commanding it all, constructing the ruse to keep everyone in their seats and the forces arrayed outside the castle at bay so the plague could root itself inexorably into each and every senior member of the Five Eyes before they could return to their offices and their military installations and cause thousands more deaths.

No, they didn't have time to wait. She had to act, and act soon, to end this thing.

And the only way she thought she had a chance of achieving this was to go after her father.

Just then, Zakharov, Capshaw, and Rutherford passed by on their way towards the door so they could go to the front door to talk to the military officer in charge outside about the dangers of the Scottish Dragoons attacking the castle. As he passed her, her father looked her way, and she saw in his eyes that he was worried about her. Not worried about her safety, but worried that his operation was in danger because of what she suspected about his plan.

He did not slow, he did not speak to her, but in that moment Zoya knew unequivocally that her father would make good on his promise to kill her himself if it was necessary to keep his plan on track.

• • •

Suzanne Brewer walked behind her two assets as they moved quietly through the oratory, but her mind was not silent. She was afraid, yes, but her prevailing thought was unmitigated anger. How was it that one of her own agents, part of a program Brewer did not even endorse and wanted no part in, happened to have a father who seemed poised to kill most of the seventh floor at CIA?

And she wondered if she was already infected with *motherfucking* plague.

Her anger about Anthem switched to anger about Violator and Romantic. Working the sharp end of the spear running these maniacs was destroying her own life, taking her further and further from where she thought she would be at this point in her career. She would never rise higher as long as she was sending smelly bearded men or histrionic former Russian agents down dirty alleyways and into shootouts, shootouts that, despite her secret wishes, they always seemed to find their way back out of.

Her fuming thoughts were disrupted when Violator motioned for her to stay where she was, walking along a set of pews at the front of the room by the ornate pulpit. He and Romantic ventured forward towards a doorway, and she stood back and watched, half hoping they'd get her the fuck out of there and half hoping they would kick a damn tripwire and blow themselves up so she could be done with them.

• • •

Zack and Court went to opposite sides of the large, wide, open doorway that led out of the oratory and into the main corridor on the second floor.

Court, on the right, sighted his weapon down the hall to the left of the doorway, while Zack, on the left, leaned out and aimed his pistol to the right.

Zack immediately saw two men wearing dark suits. He thought they were security guards for the Five Eyes conference, but something didn't seem right about their movements. They were patrolling, in the opposite direction now, but they looked into each doorway, chatting.

They didn't appear nervous enough to have been part of the force that had been overrun here. Nope, these were the bad guys.

Zack whispered to Court. "What you got?"

Court said, "I've got nothing. You?"

Zack replied, "Two assholes with guns. Opposition."

"I win," Court whispered back.

"You win."

They motioned for Brewer to come forward, and she put her hand on Romantic's back. Then all three moved off to the left, Zack in front, then Brewer, then Court, who walked backwards, his handgun aimed at the two men fifty feet on, facing away.

They checked each chamber on this wing of the second floor, but they found no one hiding out. As they reached the end of the corridor, they moved towards the armory to meet the others.

．．．

Travers, Jenner, Lorenzi, and Greer, with Hanley in tow, met Hightower, Gentry, and Brewer at the entrance to the second-floor security office, off a parlor that had been converted into a bar area for hotel guests.

The office was locked and guarded by a pair of terrified young security officers who only opened the door when Jenner looked into the camera and then held his badge up to it.

Once inside, the group of Americans made their way past a bank of security camera monitors and into a back room, already open because the security men had armed themselves when the attack began.

Lorenzi kept watch outside the rooms into the parlor while the rest of the men went to arm themselves with more potent weapons.

While Jenner treated Travers's upper thigh and neck wounds with a medical kit he found in the armory, both Zack and Court picked out SIG

Sauer Rattlers, .300 Blackout rifles with short barrels, folding stocks, and sights with holographic reticles. They loaded the weapons and crammed flashbangs and loaded magazines into their pockets. Zack also strapped a pistol-grip Remington shotgun onto his back.

Jenner and Travers then grabbed M4A1s, short-barreled fully automatic rifles, and all the ammo they could carry.

There were Kevlar vests on a shelf, and all the shooters put them on. They wouldn't stop rifle rounds but could be effective against pistol-caliber ammunition.

Court then passed a Kevlar vest out of the armory to Hanley and another to Brewer. Hanley took off his coat and slipped it on, but Brewer just said, "No thanks. That just makes me look like another gunman, and that's the last thing I want."

"Fine with me," Court replied, and he dropped it on the floor to return to the room to find more ammo for his pistol.

Hanley barked at his subordinate. "Suzanne, put on the damn vest!"

She complied immediately and without comment.

Hanley himself stepped into the office and grabbed a Remington shotgun, loaded it expertly, and carried it back out. Granted, it had been nearly thirty years since he'd left active duty for the CIA, but the shotgun he chose was virtually unchanged from the one he'd fielded back in his Army days.

Once everyone was outfitted, they looked at the bank of camera monitors. An entire row was blacked out. One of the security men said, "They disabled the cams in the great hall and the ones in the lobby outside it. Looking at the others around the castle, we saw a couple of fishy-looking guys dressed like regular security, but they are up on four now. Might be that there aren't too many attackers, so they couldn't hold the entire building. They've got that one room, and access to it locked down, and they have one little patrol to round up people hiding, but the rest of the castle seems clear, for now."

Hanley addressed the six armed men from the U.S. "Anthem says her father would only be here if there was a bigger mission than a hostage taking. She thinks the plague will soon be released on everyone here. I am going to have to trust her judgment on this. We need to take this facility back, and it needs to happen soon."

Brewer said, "Matt, there is something like one hundred Scots Dragoons outside. You think these six men have a better chance of—"

"Yes," he interrupted. "Right at this moment, I do. Zakharov doesn't know these men are Ground Branch and SAD singleton assets; he thinks they're just bodyguards. He probably also thinks he killed us all with those frags they threw into the library. That gives us an advantage. He won't expect an attack to come from inside the building; therefore, an attack *must* come from inside the building."

Jenner said, "You need protection, too, sir."

Hanley pointed out that there were already two Scottish security men here, and it was a secure room. He and Brewer would be fine here watching what monitors were still up and providing intelligence for the counterattack.

Everyone put in radio earpieces and set them to the same channel, and soon the half dozen men, led by Jenner, began moving through the bar and back towards the second-floor corridor.

. . .

They found the east wing staircase barricaded. When Travers managed to get the door open a couple of inches, he looked through the gap and saw wires coiling over the table braced on the inside that seemed to be attached to the door itself.

He turned back to Jenner. "Booby-trapped. Could be explosives."

"Okay, we'll make our way to the first floor via some other route." Looking at Hightower he asked, "Any ideas?"

"I walked around the castle for an hour earlier. Suggest the main staircase. They might have tripwires or something, so keep an eye open, but there are no doors so it probably won't be blocked."

Jenner nodded. "Let's keep it tight, all angles covered. We move as a team."

"Roger," Zack said, and again they set off up the corridor.

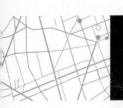

CHAPTER 64

Feodor Zakharov returned to the great hall, along with Rutherford and Capshaw, who both went back to their tables while the Russian stepped over to Fox. Softly, and in Russian, he asked, "Is it done?"

"Finished distribution of the spores five minutes ago, sir."

"Very well." Zakharov looked at his watch. "We start the time now."

Fox nodded.

"You've taken your antibiotics?" Zakharov asked.

"As I was climbing the stairs."

"Good. I will read statements once every other hour on the stage, with an open phone line to the outside, and then I will begin the negotiations for a helicopter. That will take six to eight hours. We will egress via the passageway to the loch as the helicopter lands."

Fox said, "We only have one group of two men searching the castle for more conference attendees hiding out. I suggest we put more roaming patrols out in the building. They will eliminate any threats inside our defenses, and will serve as a tripwire in case those outside enter the building. We have this room covered, and have men to spare."

Zakharov said, "Very well. Send the other sleepers out, and one more two-man patrol from the mercenary force. That's three teams. And get me a handgun. I will help keep the people in here compliant."

. . .

Zoya had been ordered to sit at one of the round tables along with a group of senior intel analysts from New Zealand, near the center of the room full of round tables. The mood around her was somber; those who whispered said they were sure the whole building had been wired to blow, and once this unknown man and his unknown force made their statement, they would set off the bombs.

One of the men surprised Zoya by saying, "Doesn't that guy look a little like General Zakharov, the old GRU chief who died? Chechnya or Dagestan, I think it was."

"Yes, but this fellow is obviously English," a woman replied.

Zoya received several strange looks from her tablemates because no one recognized her, and she wasn't in a ball gown. Instead she wore jeans and a black tracksuit top, no makeup, with her dark hair back in a ponytail.

Everyone seemed to assume she was one of the young MI5 members serving as the castle staff, and they left her alone.

And Zoya did not interact with them at all. No, her focus was on Court, as well as the others up in the room. A pair of grenades had been thrown in, and she heard no shooting after that, but she'd been hustled down here and didn't know if the Russian attacking force had gone into the room to engage any survivors.

She had no way of knowing if Court had made it, and no way of knowing his condition if he *had* managed to survive.

. . .

Jenner sent Court and Zack to check the second floor for stragglers, and now they moved through the wardrobe, a large dressing and storage area for the lady of the castle. It had been converted into a conference room, but it retained antique paintings and furniture around a long oval table.

Matt Hanley came over the men's earpieces suddenly. "Romantic and Violator. Halt."

Both men stopped in their tracks. Said nothing, knowing Hanley would fill them in.

"The room in front of you just had its camera go dark. Could be a technical glitch, or there might be someone in there. Advance with caution."

"Roger."

The two men with the SIG Rattler rifles moved up to the closed door quickly and silently and stepped to either side. After a look from Zack, Court reached over and picked up a brass candlestick from a table next to him and heaved it across the room. It landed on the far side of the conference table with a *clang*.

The door flew open, and flashlight beams streaked across the room.

A voice with an obvious Russian accent spoke English. "I hear you, friend. Come out and join the others."

Zack gave Court a quick hand signal, indicating he thought there were two shooters, judging from the swaying beams, although he was flush with the wall and couldn't tell for sure. He lowered his Rattler on his chest and grabbed the shotgun on his back, bringing it forward.

"Who is there?" the man called. "Who is there?"

Zack Hightower knelt and spun into the doorway, fired a blast, pumped the fore-end of the weapon, and fired again.

"It's America, motherfucker!" Zack blasted three more shells from the shotgun, covering the darkness with steel shot, then spun back to concealment to reload.

Court swung his own body into the doorway now, ready to fire fully automatic, but first he shined his light on the room. Two buckshot-riddled bodies of armed bearded men lay just feet away. He looked to Zack. "You've been waiting your whole life to use that line, haven't you?"

Zack slung his shotgun and again grabbed his rifle. "Haven't been waiting. That's the third time I've pulled it out. I need some new material."

The men moved out.

· · ·

With the fresh gunfire upstairs, Zoya's head popped up with the rest of the room and turned towards the sets of double doors to the main corridor. But while the people around her wondered what was happening, Zoya felt like she knew. There had been at least some survivors in the library where the grenades were thrown, and they were now fighting back. She hoped like hell that Court had been one of the ones who'd made it, although he'd been close to the doorway as she left, and she worried he would have been right in the middle of the blast radius of the grenades.

The fact that some sort of combat had started back up indicated to her that Hanley had listened to her when she asserted they didn't have time to wait, that each hour before getting antibiotics into the bloodstream of the attendees meant another hour closer to death for everyone.

That she'd been listened to and positive action had been taken to fight back filled her with new hope, and made her return her mind to coming up with a way she could be involved in ending all this. She was certain she could be helpful to those trying to retake the castle from the inside, but to do this, she needed to accomplish two difficult things.

First, she needed to gain some intelligence about the force in here they'd be facing. And second, she'd need to find a way to get the hell out of this room.

She looked around; the lights were up so she had no problem scanning the entire area. She counted the armed men around the room, difficult to do without being able to get up and move around. Ultimately, she determined there were either twelve or fourteen, plus Fox and the goon Hines who followed him everywhere.

And her father. She almost didn't count him. Yes, he was a combatant, too, but this wasn't relevant intel for the group outside.

Because, whatever happened, she still planned on killing him herself.

* * *

Feodor Zakharov sat with Fox on the stage at the front of the Great Hall, with Hines standing compliantly behind. He watched Zoya in the center of the room as she looked around. He cursed himself for thinking about his daughter right now. He had to keep his focus on his mission, his life's work, playing out at this very moment. But he could not help but look across the room, gaze at his beautiful daughter, and consider whether to take her out of here and administer antibiotics to her right now.

He was a realist, so for the good of his mission, he knew he absolutely should not. For one, once he gave them to her he'd have to sequester her from the rest of the hostages so she didn't alert everyone. And that meant he'd have to take one of his too-few mercenaries here to guard her in some other part of the castle. It also meant when he and his team slipped out of here, he'd have to bring her along, and the thought of making their get-away with a noncompliant, resourceful, and clever enemy—he had no question but that she was now, and would forever be, his enemy—left him feeling frustrated.

For ten minutes he thought about nothing else, but ultimately he told himself Zoya had put herself in this position by siding with the Americans, he didn't have the manpower to spare in dealing with her, and she could not know that the bacteria had been released on the crowd, or she would undermine the entire operation.

Yes, for the good of this operation, Zoya would have to die. It brought a thick mist over his eyes when he made the decision, but once he did make it, he was resolute through his profound sadness.

. . .

Zoya had the head count of combatants in the room solidified now. There were fourteen, plus Fox and her father and Hines. She'd seen another six or so men leave in pairs, presumably to search the interior of the castle for anyone they'd missed by locking down the great hall.

Now she had to find a way out of here.

She looked to her father. He looked right back at her; he appeared sad, sadder than she ever remembered seeing him.

He was thinking about her; this she knew for certain.

Zoya realized that his remaining softness for her, what little left existed, was her way out of here. The gunmen working for her father in this room would be reluctant to shoot her if she made a run for it, and her father would be reluctant to give them the okay, at least for a moment.

She looked across the room towards the center double doors. These were not locked, but they were guarded by two men with submachine guns on their chests. Making her way around the tables would have taken too long; this she knew by tracking the route she'd have to run. But there was a faster way to the doors. She looked over each table between herself and her goal, and then she moved her hands slightly on the table, covering up a small, thin steak knife. This she slipped under the cuff of her track top, and the elastic there held it firmly in place against her forearm, with the handle across the palm of her hand.

She took a breath to prepare herself and looked back over to her father, and then her heart sank.

He was standing from his chair now, his eyes on her. There was no doubt in her mind he'd seen her take the knife and likely figured out exactly what she was going to do.

Which meant she had to do it now.

Zoya leapt up and onto the big round table, raced across it over dirty dishes and crashing wineglasses, vaulted over the people sitting on the far side, and landed on the floor. She was up onto the second table an instant later, her legs kicking between those seated there.

Screams and shouts erupted from the men and women at the banquet.

Back on the floor now, she vaulted over a seated lady from the Canadian intelligence services and took another two steps across this table, then landed on the floor a third time.

Behind her she heard her father shout into the microphone on the stage. "Kill her!"

The last table she ran around instead of over, knowing her surprise had been lost and her pattern had been established, but she was lightning fast, and the two men at the door had just got their weapons pointed towards her as she executed a diving forward roll. Gunfire cracked, but the rounds had gone above her, and she snapped back up in front of the men, stabbing one through the throat as she used her momentum to crash into the other, knocking him out through the doors. She fell with him and slammed down hard onto the wooden floor, and, as men shouted behind her in the great hall, she got up and made a left and began running for her life up the main corridor.

· · ·

Court and Zack had arrived first at the rectory on the ground floor, the rally point where they'd meet Jenner and his team. Court had just begun looking down the main corridor towards the great hall when he heard screams, shouting, and then shooting from that direction. He went prone in the corridor, expecting to see someone trying to escape, and then the middle doors flew open and two bodies came flying out and slammed onto the ground. The first person up was Zoya, he quickly saw, and she turned in his direction, away from the main exit, and began running up the corridor.

Behind her the man on the floor rolled onto his side and began to aim his subgun at her back.

Court shot him twice in the chest from thirty yards.

Quickly two more men came rushing into the corridor, and both Court and Zack fired at them, killing one outright and sending the other stumbling back into the great hall with wounds to his legs and feet.

Court went up to his knees and moved back into the rectory, keeping his head and his rifle out in the corridor ready to fight off other threats. Zoya saw him ahead; she dove to the ground and landed on her hip, slid on the flooring right past him, and crawled into the room behind him.

Court pulled his Glock 19 pistol and handed it to her. She spun back to her left and aimed up the corridor.

Zack stood behind her. As he also trained his rifle out the doorway and down the corridor he said, "Player three has entered the game."

Jenner and his team arrived seconds later, and Zoya gave them her intelligence through breath labored by her activity of the last minute. "Like thirteen, maybe fifteen enemy left in there, I think, plus Fox, my father, and that big freak. First and third doors are wired with explosives; the middle one is clear but guarded."

Jenner asked, "What about the hostages?"

"A few dead. Six, eight, maybe. The rest are seated or lying on the floor. My father and Fox are on the stage." She looked at the other men. "I want a rifle."

Zack said, "Armory. Second floor, left off the main staircase, third door on the right." Lorenzi offered to escort her up there; she handed Court his Glock back, she took Lorenzi's sidearm, and quickly she and the Ground Branch operator disappeared in the dark corridor, running in the opposite direction from the great hall.

Jenner said, "Anthem's a tough chick, but is she a shooter?"

Court said, "She's saved my ass a time or two."

"Good enough. Seven of us now. We're going to hit that room, boys."

"How you want to do it?" Zack asked.

Jenner had a plan. "We do a 'blow and go.' We move up the corridor, go to the first set of doors, set a grenade to trigger the explosives there, and then breach as a team through the smoke."

Zack said, "So . . . straight up the middle, just like at the church."

Court kept his eyes on the doors down the corridor. Sarcastically he mumbled, "Plan A didn't work, so let's try plan A."

"You two hot shits got a better plan?" Jenner barked.

Zack said, "There's a dining room on the first floor, at the back over the ground-floor kitchen just behind the great hall. It had a dumbwaiter. Saw it earlier."

"Big enough for us to get into?" Court asked.

"You, no problem. Me . . . it'll be tight, but I can do it."

Court said, "Zack and I can gain access to the kitchen. We breach the great hall on countdown, take out Zakharov, Fox, and Hines, mount the stage to get overwatch on the armed combatants. Simultaneously you guys hit through the center door, split left and right, wall flood across the room."

Jenner thought a moment. "Plan is approved, but you don't get Hightower. I'm going to have to split into two units; I want Zack as my other unit leader since Travers is walking wounded."

Hightower said, "Hooyah." Court realized it was sarcasm, but he doubted Jenner did.

"So, I go alone? Thanks, Jenner."

"Negative. Take Anthem. You just said she's a badass."

Court didn't want Zoya anywhere near her father, because he did not want her to be the one to kill him. But the four Ground Branch men had been training and operating together for years. He couldn't pull one of their number away before they did an extremely dangerous blow-and-go on a room full of hostages and gunmen.

He saw no alternative to Jenner's plan.

Jenner said, "We go as soon as Lorenzi and Anthem get back."

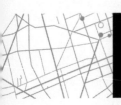

CHAPTER 65

Zakharov stood on the stage, fuming because of his daughter's escape. Slowly he turned to Fox, standing at his side. "Pick an American. Senior executive. Walk him out into the corridor and shoot him in the head."

Fox looked to Jon Hines and motioned towards a man at one of the American tables in the center of the room. Whispering to him, he said, "Dark hair, fifties. The one who looks like he's about to try something. You see him?"

"I see 'im, sir."

"Bring him up."

"Right away." Hines stepped off the stage and up to the table, slammed a hand down on the man's shoulder, then led him back to the stage to stand in front of Zakharov.

"Name?"

"Seekins. Jay Seekins."

"Your title?"

"Assistant to the deputy director of Operations." He said it proudly, albeit with some nerves evident in his voice.

The Russian smiled. "So, you work for Matthew Hanley."

"Yes, I do."

"Very good." With a nod to Fox, Hines turned the man for the double doors, and Fox followed, pulling his Beretta pistol discreetly from his jacket as he walked behind the condemned man.

Fox said, "You are free to go. Tell your friends the room is wired for explosives. If they try anything, everyone dies."

Seekins was unsure, but after a shove from Hines he began walking out into the main corridor.

He made it five feet before Fox fired once into the back of his head, sending him pitching forward onto the wooden floor.

. . .

Court had seen the man step out, but he didn't see the shooter because of the angle into the great hall.

The other men had seen it, too.

Travers said, "They're killing hostages because we're in here fighting back. That one's on us."

Jenner transmitted over the radios now. "Lorenzi, they are shooting hostages, say again, they are shooting hostages. Get your ass back here. We have to breach, now."

"We encountered hostiles on our way back. Seemed to be a two-man patrol. We've eliminated them and will be on you in two mikes."

Zoya and Lorenzi returned two minutes later. She was now armed with a SIG MPX submachine gun, and she wore a Glock 17 on her hip. Court informed her that she would go with him, back up to the first floor to try to hit the great hall from behind, and soon they were moving off in that direction.

. . .

Feodor Zakharov had relocated his guard force around the room, knowing that Zoya would be linking up with whoever was out in the hall and telling them everything she'd seen inside. He and Fox had also left the stage, and now they stood with Hines at the locked side door that led to a stairwell down to the two belowground levels of the castle.

His men stood more vigilant than before, and for this he was glad, but he worried he did not have enough guns here to stave off an attack from any large force. He ordered Fox to pick up a submachine gun from a dead security man, then he pulled his pistol and held it in his right hand while he looked at his watch. It had been only two hours since the plague had been released. He needed to stall and to keep stalling.

He also saw that it was time for his next speech. He talked for ten minutes on his sat phone to the security officials outside about war crimes committed by the Five Eyes organizations, focusing his ire on the United States and the United Kingdom. It was a short but rambling speech, and he promised another soon.

When this was done, he sat down at a table of CIA executives. "Long night, eh chaps?" he said. "But tomorrow you will all be free. No one else needs to die, on either side."

DCIA Fred Capshaw was at the table. "What side do you even represent? You're English, working with Russians. But there is no way Moscow sanctioned any of this."

Zakharov leaned towards the man. With a smile he said, "I am a rogue elephant, sir. I need no sanction." He waved his hand around. "Only men, matériel, and a plan."

"You're insane. You won't change a thing with your crazy speeches."

"We'll see," the Russian said with a bored shrug. "We'll see if anything changes when this is over. You destroyed my plague, but you did not destroy my passion."

He stood up and walked away.

. . .

Court and Zoya scooted down the narrow dumbwaiter; it was tight with their weapons and ammo, but they still had to use their arms and legs to keep from falling to the ground floor. Court fought the urge to press with his left hand and used his left elbow instead, which was as painful as it was inefficient.

Once they finally made it down into the kitchen, they brought their weapons to bear but saw no targets.

The rear exit was only twenty-five feet away, and they could see an explosive charge up against it, wired tightly against the door.

Quietly and slowly they picked their way through the kitchen, stepped through the larder room, and then entered a hallway that seemed to point in the direction of the great hall.

Court knelt in the dim light, his rifle in front of him, while Zoya stood behind. He keyed his mic. "Violator in position."

Jenner spoke for the five men out in the corridor on the far side of the great hall. "We're in position. We will breach when the shooting starts."

"Understood."

Together Court and Zoya moved forward up the hall, their eyes in their weapon sights, scanning as they stepped. They made a turn and saw the stairs up to the stage just twenty feet in front of them, while on their left were tables full of men and women in formal attire.

He leaned into Zoya's ear. "Please, let me handle your father."

Zoya began moving forward. "Move out," she ordered.

With just a brief pause for a frustrated sigh, Court shot forward, passed Zoya, but knew she'd stay on his heels. They'd be exposed on the stage, but they were counting on drawing the attention of all the gunmen in the room just long enough for Jenner, Hightower, and the others to push in and start eliminating threats from behind.

More than anything, however, was Court's desire to drop Zakharov the instant he saw him. He wasn't going to give Zoya the burden of killing her father. She'd probably hate him forever for depriving her of this, but he knew it was the right thing to do.

But when he raced up onto the stage, he instantly saw that it was empty. Zakharov had moved.

A shout came from across the room as the crowd saw the armed man and woman charging onto the stage. Court looked out over the great hall but saw no obvious threats in that first moment. Knowing he and Zoya would likely be shot dead instantly, he fired his rifle into the far wall, as gunfire was the cue for the others to hit the room.

The middle doors flew open forty yards opposite him, and Court shouted to Zoya, "Get down!"

. . .

As gunfire erupted from the back of the hall, everyone at the tables dove flat on the ground. Jenner and Lorenzi moved quickly to the right, back to the wall, while Hightower, Greer, and Travers went left. Immediately Hightower spotted a man aiming a submachine gun at the stage. He was one hundred feet across the room, but Zack shot him in the right cheek, blowing half his face off and spinning him to the ground.

Lorenzi found the second target, a man in the middle of the room who did not drop with the hostages but instead whipped his sub gun around towards the gunfire behind him. Lorenzi fired a burst at the man, knocking him back onto a table, the linens there instantly stained with red.

Greer fired at the third target, a huge blond man with a handgun by a small door far on the side of the room. He'd been forced to rush his shot, however, and his rounds went wide.

Before he could engage again he was under fire from his right, so he swiveled to take on that threat, while the big man disappeared through the door, and several others raced through behind him.

. . .

Jenner kept moving to the right, scanning his sector, trusting Lorenzi to do the same. He saw an armed man close to the stage and fired at him, knocking him down. Another man stood up from behind one of the bars along the wall, aimed a weapon, and Jenner shot him dead, as well.

He then shifted his aim to the right, scanning for targets, but only saw a flash of light in the far corner of the room before his head snapped back, and his world went black.

"Jenner's down!" Lorenzi shouted over the network, but the gun battle was too fierce to stop to render aid.

. . .

Court and Zoya had each fired at one target. Zoya hit a man in the thigh who disappeared behind a group of hostages, and Court hit a man in the lower abdomen, but he was on the ground, out of view behind a table, and possibly still in the fight.

Zoya had seen Hines and a group of armed men racing through the side door, and she leapt to her feet, launched off the stage, and went in pursuit of him.

Court climbed to his knees, still engaging targets in the room, but he shouted to her. "No! Wait!"

She did not listen, just kept running through the crowd as everyone began to climb to their feet and stampede for the center exit. Court leapt off the stage, picking off gunmen one by one, who were all struggling to orient themselves to the many angles of this small but disciplined attacking force.

. . .

The great hall cleared out in under one minute, save for the American operators, the wounded, and the dead. Jenner was in the latter category, shot through the mouth, and Greer had taken a subgun round through the right biceps that had him on the floor while he tied it off with a compression bandage, using his left hand and his teeth.

By now Travers had lost enough blood out of the wound in his right leg that his fight was over, as he could barely stand, and though Lorenzi had shot three Russians grouped closely together, he took a bullet through his right shin and his left foot in the process.

Zack Hightower had killed five men in the last minute, all with a single magazine. He reloaded his rifle now, ready to head towards the doorway where Hines and some other men had disappeared. But he heard a voice behind him that spun him around.

It was Hanley. He held the shotgun in his hand. "Where's Zakharov?"

"What the hell are you doing here, sir?"

He saw Brewer behind Hanley now, a terrified look on her face. *What a shit show,* he thought. All the smart suits were running away, and these two nitwits were running in.

"I'm helping you," Hanley said. "Brewer will help, too." Brewer seemed to Zack like she had no interest in helping anyone but herself, but she was here, a pistol held low in her hand.

Zack sighed. "They went into that stairwell. It seems to lead down to the basement."

Hanley started moving for it. "Let's go."

"Wait. Violator and Anthem have already—"

"Let's go!" Hanley shouted, and he headed through the doorway.

Zack ran after the two of them, overtaking them and making it into the stairs before them. With his weapon light shining he led the way down.

. . .

Court and Zoya arrived at the first subterranean layer without seeing or hearing anyone. Both wondered where the hell the squirters thought they were going down here, unless their plan was to use some other staircase to make their way back up to ground level.

This was the dungeon level; it was a poorly lit warren of rooms, formerly cells, common spaces, and barracks for the guards, now mostly used for storage. There were dozens of rooms where people could hide. Heavy metal gates hung in archways, held up by thick rope; a wine cellar had been built where prisoners once had been stockaded; and the entire area smelled to Court like it was right on Loch Ness and not 150 feet above it.

The two of them moved together for a while, until they reached a circular room with three archways leading out of it. Zoya touched Court on his shoulder. "We have to split up."

Court was afraid of this. Tactically, it made sense; there was too much area to cover to find anyone hiding down here before they could escape. But he could only now pray that he was the one who came across her father first.

He reached out with his good hand and took her head in it, drew her to him. Softly he said, "Be careful," and he kissed her.

"You, too," she said, and then, "My father. He's mine."

She turned away and disappeared in the dark to the right.

Court chose the left-side passage. He transmitted this decision over his mic, but he didn't think anyone still alive upstairs could have possibly heard him down here belowground.

. . .

Hightower, Brewer, and Hanley heard the garbled transmission, and they pieced it together. Anthem, right. Violator, left. The three moved slowly and quietly out of the dim stairwell and into the dungeon area. They arrived at the circular room one minute after receiving Violator's call, and they continued forward, under the middle arch.

. . .

Feodor Zakharov followed behind the two sleepers still alive as they pushed on through the dungeon towards the secret door that led down to Loch Ness. They knew the way, but they had a stop to make along the way first. Also, they were slowed somewhat scanning with their flashlights, checking the placement of the daisy chain of explosives that had been attached around the dungeon level. Zakharov had sent Fox and Hines off in another direction to check the explosives there. The wires were supposed to be out of the pathways, running instead along the walls, but the men who wired the subterranean level had a lot of ground to cover and little time, so it was an obvious rush job. Everyone knew that accidentally kicking a wire would set off the cigarette-pack-sized amount of C-4 the wire had been attached to, and this would kill anyone ten yards in any direction, so they did what they could to avoid this eventuality.

The Russian mercenaries hadn't brought enough C-4 to drop the entire castle, not by a long shot. But a timer had been attached to one of the devices, and all the devices were wired together. It was set for ten minutes, but now Zakharov wanted to find the device with the timer on it and speed the countdown to five minutes before getting into the passageway to the water, detonating thirty small but powerful charges down here in the lower levels to eliminate any pursuers.

Behind him he heard a distant, echoing voice. "Papa? Papa, I'm coming for you!"

Zakharov felt the twinge of fear run down his back now as he kept moving forward with the others.

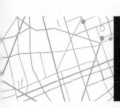

CHAPTER 66

Court moved quickly up a hallway, checking each dungeon cell with a flash from the light hanging on his rifle. Some rooms were storage now, others empty, and some rooms in this subterranean warren seemed to serve no purpose but to lead to more rooms. He flashed his weapon light on, then back off, moved forward a few feet to cover, and did it again. Over and over. It was not the fastest way to move, but it did expose him to the least amount of danger.

Or so he thought.

He knelt down behind a row of old, steel box fans in the arched stone corridor, held his rifle up, and flashed the light. Just past an archway with a massive steel gate above it suspended there by thick rope tied to a metal hook in the floor, he saw a large room and, from the quick look he gave it when the light was on, he could tell there were several mirrors in there, because of the flash reflected back on him. He was distracted by the bright light in his face for a few seconds, rubbed his eyes, and then squinted. Flashing again but towards the floor to avoid the reflections, this time he could see movement in the room, a shadow streaking right to left in the dim.

Court grabbed a flash bang grenade hooked to his belt, pulled the pin, and tossed it underhanded into the room. He ducked down quickly to avoid the blast, and as soon as the distraction device erupted he rose and ran into the room with his rifle held high.

And as he entered the room he realized the flash bang had been a mistake. The device instantly started a fire in a collection of old, dusty, and unframed oil paintings, blueprints, and maps stacked in piles and leaning haphazardly along the wall.

Shit, the last thing he wanted was to be stuck down here in this dungeon in a fire.

He looked for something to extinguish the fire with, turning to the corner on his right and shining a light to see what he could find.

And then he realized he had been wrong before. This, *this* was the last thing he wanted.

There, three feet away and closing fast, was Jon Hines. Behind him he caught a glimpse of Fox, running under a metal gate over another archway that led out of the room, a subgun in his hands.

Court got a shot off but his weapon had already been knocked to the side by Hines; a bullet ricocheted around the room with an angry multi-note shriek. The two men crashed into the hard stone floor, rolling up next to the burning paintings, and Court's rifle sling slipped off his head as the weapon slid away. He struggled up to his knees and started to reach for his pistol but didn't get it out before Hines grabbed his wounded hand and wrenched it to Court's left. This sent him down on his back in agony and short-circuited his attempt to pull his gun.

Hines got a meaty hand on the pistol's grip and yanked it free of his holster, but Court elbowed the man's hand and the pistol spun away, as well.

The fire behind Court against the wall was growing; he could feel the heat, and through the flickering firelight Court saw smoke billowing across the floor. Hines was on his feet now. Court's body still felt broken from his first two encounters with this leviathan of a man, and he knew he had little chance in another round of one-on-one with him.

"We're gonna get to finish our fun, after all, mate!" Hines said with a roar, and he launched forward at Gentry yet again.

Court threw a right jab that connected with Hines's chin but only partially slowed him down. The Englishman threw a swing of his own; Court managed to lean back away from it, but in doing so he fell down again onto his back.

The flames were raging, the smoke thickening by the second as more oil paintings ignited.

He rolled over, launched to his feet, and ran unarmed for the tunnel Fox had taken, not in pursuit of the Russian, but instead desperately trying to get away from Hines. He'd just run under the iron gate suspended above by rope attached to the floor when he felt Hines grab the back of his Kevlar vest and yank him back.

Court fell to the ground and spun around to kick at the big boxer, while simultaneously reaching out with both hands to grab something, *anything*, to fight Hines off with. His left-hand fingertips grabbed a two-foot-square wooden-framed oil painting that was fully engulfed with flames, and he Frisbeed it as hard as he could at his attacker, both to keep from burning himself too badly and to generate as much momentum as possible. He hit Hines square in the face with the burning material, but the broken bones in his hand hurt worse than ever now.

The man shouted in shock and fell back, buying Court a moment's time. He rose to his feet and ran again for the archway now, but he noticed flames raging from the ACE bandage on his left arm. He took a blow to the back of the head; Hines had thrown something at him, apparently, and he tumbled forward, falling on the ground yet again, now directly under the wrought-iron gate suspended over the archway tunnel out of the room.

He coughed in the smoke, rolled onto his back, and looked back to Hines, who was rubbing soot out of his eyes. While he did this Court ran his left arm up and down the old but thick rope holding up the gate above him, and flames immediately began licking upwards towards the ceiling.

He then covered his burning bandages with his body, extinguishing the flames, but creating fresh agony as his weight went down on his broken hand.

He looked back over his shoulder as he lay on the floor under the iron gate.

Hines was approaching, back in the fight now; he *always* seemed to bounce back.

Court rolled on his back, scooted backwards on his elbows, trying to draw Hines closer.

The Englishman's big voice boomed in the subterranean room as he advanced, paying no attention to the fire all around him.

"Gotta snap your neck and end this shite now, mate, but you were one hell of a goer, I give ya that!" Court kicked at the man, trying to buy a little more time, but also trying to keep from looking to the rope on his left that, once it burned through, would fly up, sending the iron gate down right through Court's midsection.

Hines stepped under the archway now and knelt down with a smile over the wounded American, his face glowing red from the flames. He took Court by the collar, but just as he did, Court brought his knees to his chest and shifted his legs to his left.

With all the might left in him he kicked with both feet into the rope that had been burning fiercely for thirty seconds, and in so doing he tore away the last of the fibers that had not burned through.

Hines smiled as Court's wild kick missed him and hit a burning rope, and then he heard a loud squeaking noise several feet above his head.

His eyes met Court's in the firelight.

And now it was Court's turn to smile.

The iron gate dropped like a guillotine, and the vertical shanks slammed into Hines's back, penetrating his rib cage, lungs, and heart, exiting out his chest and slamming him face-first into the stone floor.

His face just a foot from Court's, blood gushed from his mouth. He choked out one last "Fuck you!" before he died, a look of astonishment frozen into his wide-open eyes.

Court climbed to his knees and looked back into the smoky room around the body. His rifle was on the opposite wall in a raging fire, but his Glock pistol was just within reach through the square openings in the gate. He reached in for it, next to Hines's left hip, and scooted it with his fingertips back towards him. But when he tried to pull it through the gate he realized the weapon was just slightly too large to get through.

"Shit," he said. With his one good hand still on the other side of the gate he dropped the magazine from the weapon, fired off the round in the chamber, then pulled the slide back a half inch by pushing the grip back on the floor. With his thumb he pressed the takedown lever on the frame. After he pulled the trigger again, the metal slide slid off the pistol onto the floor.

Now Court easily pulled the frame through the opening next to the dead man, then reached back in and grabbed the magazine and the slide, barrel, and slide rod off the floor and brought them out as the heat began to overtake him.

Lying on his side he reassembled and reloaded the pistol, still with one hand, all the while worrying about Zoya, somewhere down here in pursuit of her father.

He coughed as he stood with the weapon, then used the flashlight on the rail below the muzzle to light his way forward.

He made it only a few feet before he saw a human form lying facedown. Closing carefully, he realized it was Fox, and he'd been shot in the left shoulder blade.

Court figured the one shot he'd managed to fire, which hadn't been aimed anywhere near Fox, had ricocheted around the room and wounded the man, who'd bled out fifty feet down the tunnel.

Just to be certain, though, Court performed a dead check, shooting him in the back of the head. The man had a SIG MPX submachine gun lying next to him, and Court hefted it, slung it around his neck, and pressed on.

. . .

Feodor Zakharov set the master timer on the plastic explosive so the entire chain of thirty explosives around the underground portion of the castle would go off simultaneously. He gave himself and the two sleepers with him five minutes before detonation, then initiated the countdown on the detonator. He and his men would be far enough down the stairs by then, and he assumed the Royal Scots Dragoons would be down here around that time looking for him.

Along with his daughter. Zoya would die, but Zakharov told himself this was something that was long overdue.

Once the timer was set, Zakharov shined his flashlight on the two sleepers. "Let's get out of here."

The men had their pistols aimed down the arched corridor they had used to get here, expecting anyone chasing them to come from that direction, but another passage ran off to their left. It had been completely pitch-black inside, until a pair of flashes in quick succession, simultaneous with loud gunshots, sent Zakharov ducking low and spinning his light towards the noise and light.

Both sleepers dropped where they stood, shot in the side of the head and neck at a distance of less than twenty feet.

Zakharov moved to turn off his flashlight, but before he could, a high beam shined in his eyes. He dropped his light on the floor. Softly he said, "Zoya, darling? Is that you?"

"It's me."

Zoya flipped off the light on her SIG MPX, allowing the illumination from her father's flashlight, now lying on the floor, to provide the only glow to the bricked room.

Zakharov looked at his daughter with a sad smile. "This will be hard for you," he said. "I feel your pain. When Feo died, of course I blamed myself; I still do in a way, and that weight has never left me. It will be worse for you, dear, of course, because you are doing this intentionally. You will carry this forever."

With a cracking voice she said, "Don't worry about me, Father. I'll be just fine after this. Better than ever, in fact."

"Your words are sold out by your emotions," he said. "My old eyes can't see in this light, but how are your stress hives right now?"

Zoya did not waver. "How are yours?"

"Why don't you put the gun down? There is a way out of here. A secret passage down to the water. We have diving equipment waiting. You and I can go alone, get away, talk."

She just responded softly again. "Not a chance."

"You should consider it. In about four minutes this entire dungeon will be a fiery grave for anyone in it."

Zoya looked around the room and saw the small box on the floor next to her father, with wires running out of both sides. The wires continued along the wall on the floor, passing into two corridors.

"Then I guess I don't have much time. But you have even less."

CHAPTER 67

Zoya shot a quick glance behind her when she heard gunfire echo up the corridor there, and in that moment, Zakharov shifted his body slightly to the right and lowered his hand closer to his waist.

Across the room his daughter shifted to the right, so that she wasn't in the line of fire of anyone coming up the hall, and she backed herself up to the brick wall.

. . .

Her father used his left hand, gesticulating with it to take his daughter's attention away from what he was really doing, going for his gun. He'd taught her this in picking pockets when she was a little girl, but he hoped she would not be thinking of her childhood right now.

He pointed at the C-4 charge. "Thirty of these, all throughout the lower level. Here, down that passage, the one next to it there." It was working; she was watching his left hand, not his right, and his right was partially shielded by the turn of his body. His hand slipped to his waistband, grabbed the pistol, and drew it slowly, while pointing down the corridor to his right. "I'll turn it off, or you can if you want. The timer is on the main device, just down that way. It's not far. You can probably see it from where you are standing if you shine your light."

. . .

Zoya did not move her gun from her father's chest, but she flicked her eyes to her right, up the hall he had indicated.

And Feodor Zakharov pulled his gun.

The concussive booms of two, three, four, then five gunshots in quick succession came from the hallway behind Zoya on her left, sending her to her knees and hefting the gun in front of her. In the dim light her father jerked, spun, and staggered backwards against the wall behind him. A pistol in his right hand fell to the floor, and then his body came crashing down forward.

She spun the gun towards the hallway just as Court stepped through, his Glock pistol still sighted on the body lying crumpled across the room, his SIG submachine gun hanging from his chest.

"No!" Zoya screamed. "No! He was mine!"

She pointed her gun at Court, and he lowered his back down to his side.

"You son of a bitch. You had no right!" she shouted at him, but he just flipped on the light on his weapon and shined it on the floor.

He said, "There are wires running all over this place. They look new."

"I fucking hate you!" she shouted.

"Later. The wires?"

Zoya's head cleared a little, remembering the imminent peril they were in. "C-4. Thirty bricks. Daisy-chained and on a timer. Three minutes." She jerked her head down the corridor. "He said it's down there."

Court said, "What if it's not?"

Zoya turned for the passage her father had indicated and started running. "Follow the wires in the other direction. Just in case."

Court ran back up the hall, his light leading the way, following the wires. A group of people appeared at the same intersection where Primakov's body lay, but quickly he recognized them as Hightower, Hanley, and Brewer.

Court said, "C-4 all over this place, no time to get back to the stairs. The timer is either back with Zoya or down one of these lines." Court shined the wires on the floor and saw that they split and went down passages to the left and right.

Zack said, "Well, I guess I can stop worryin' about dying from plague."

Hanley took charge. "Zack and I will take this way. You and Suzanne go that way. We engaged some Russians, dropped some, but some others got clear of us a few minutes ago. They're probably still down here somewhere, so keep your guard up."

Court ran up the passage, Brewer right behind him. But as they ran she asked, "Where's Zakharov?"

"Dead."

"Where?"

"In a chamber behind us."

She slowed.

Court stopped and turned to her. "What?"

"*That's* where your detonator is," she said.

Court winced. "Shit. We didn't check the bomb in there."

He turned and began running back, and Brewer followed.

Forty-five seconds later he knelt over the bomb by Zakharov's body. The dead man's flashlight had burned out, leaving the room completely black, but Court shined his pistol's weapon light on the device and saw the digital readout that told him this was the master detonator.

"Oh boy," he said.

"What?" Brewer asked anxiously.

"Ninety-six seconds."

"Can you disarm it?"

As he examined the casing he said, "One-handed, no tools, amped from combat and beaten half to shit. Sure, Suzanne. No sweat."

Brewer transmitted over the radio, although all the broadcasts had been so choppy as to render them useless for the last few minutes. "Violator is working on the timer. We've got ninety seconds. Everybody get out of the lower levels or find some cover."

Court heard Brewer moving away from him now. "Except you, Brewer. I need you to hold the light so I can dismantle this."

"I don't have a light."

Court handed her the Glock with the high-lumen SureFire on the rail under the barrel. "Step over here, to my left, keep the light pointed on the wall in front of me, that's all the light I need. Do *not* point that fucking weapon at me, you copy?"

"Right." She moved a few steps to the side and lifted the weapon.

Court turned back around, adjusting his SIG subgun on his chest, pushing it to the side so he could lean closer over the device.

Brewer pointed the pistol at the wall above and in front of Court, but the flashlight's flood gave Court the light he needed to work.

He knelt down even farther and picked at the wires in the box on top of the bricks of C-4, following them to their terminations.

"Hurry," she said.

Court hushed her; the bomb seemed pretty straightforward and he was well trained on deactivating IEDs like this, but he wanted to make certain there were no trips in the wiring, little fake-outs the bomb maker had installed to ensure that, even if someone tried to dismantle it, nothing would stop the weapon from fulfilling its one sole purpose.

Behind him the light shook. Brewer's nerves.

Softly Court said, "Hold it steady. It's okay. I need thirty seconds more, tops. We're gonna be fine."

. . .

Suzanne Brewer held the light as steady as possible, which she found challenging because of the adrenaline and emotions coursing through her.

How the fuck had she gotten herself involved in combat? Into the middle of a wet operation surrounded by blacker-than-black operators who ran serious risk to herself, the other members of the IC in the building, and the very nature of Five Eyes itself?

Standing feet away from a bomb seconds away from exploding in some dank godforsaken foul-smelling basement.

She wanted to vomit.

This shitstorm was a disaster for Brewer, personally and professionally. She would be radioactive now to the seventh floor of Langley, where the top brass worked.

Her right hand wavered, fatigue making the muscles in her shoulders twitch and causing the flashlight's beam to move.

"Hold it steady," Violator repeated. "I just about have it." He knelt huddled in front of her; all his attention was on his work.

The realization came slowly to her, but it did come. There was an opportunity here. Anthem and Romantic were still alive, for now, anyway, but Violator was the main element of Poison Apple and was facing away from her and she had a pistol trained just two feet away from the side of his head.

Could she wait for him to dismantle the weapon and then just shoot him? Hanley said there were still armed Russians down here in the dungeon; all she would have to say was that someone appeared from the dark and fired at them both, but only poor Violator was hit.

Hanley would believe her; Hightower would believe her. She didn't know about that bitch Anthem, but she didn't really care. Hanley would keep her in check if he wanted his precious program to survive.

And if he did want to shelve the entire thing when Violator died? Well then, so much the better.

Could she shoot Violator right now in the head? She asked herself this one more time, and then she realized that in this absolute disaster of an operation, this had turned out to be the most perfect confluence of events she could possibly hope for.

Her luck had finally changed. Right here, right now. And it would be so easy.

Violator looked up from his work, still facing the wall, and heaved a long sigh.

"It's safe?"

"It's safe," he confirmed.

"Excellent."

She shifted aim to the right, putting the front sight on the left temple of the Gray Man.

Violator had just begun to stand when a flash of light and a boom erupted in the room.

. . .

Court heard the gunshot, thunderous in the stone basement, and then everything went dark.

CHAPTER 68

Quickly Court recognized that the gun held by Brewer had fallen to the floor, triggering the weapon light's off switch.

He rose to his feet and swiveled on his heels, hefting the MPX as he did so. He had his finger on the trigger and his sights rising to the general sound of the gunfire, directly behind him.

A weapon light in the adjoining room told him where the threat was coming from, and a flash showed him the shooter was still firing.

He felt Brewer tumbling into him, then down onto the floor, and he got his barrel over her falling body, just as a third gunshot rang out. Court sighted on the origin of the tactical light and the muzzle flash, and he returned fire, spraying an eight-round burst directly through the archway from where the shot came.

Even in the flash of his own weapon he was unable to see the shooter clearly, but he did register that the form fell back out of the doorway, crashed onto a heavy round table in the middle of the room there, rolled backwards over it, then fell off on the other side, out of his line of sight.

He dropped his slung rifle back to his chest and knelt down over Brewer; before he could even check her he heard movement out in the hall, and then a shout.

"Friendlies! Comin' in!" It was Hightower's voice.

"Brewer's hit!" Court answered back.

"What's her status?"

Court felt around for his Glock, because the light was so bad he was unable to scan her for more injuries. He gave up after a few seconds and lifted Brewer's head. He felt blood on her neck and shoulder.

Court answered Zack back. "Assessing now."

He spoke to her. "Brewer?"

"I'm . . . I'm shot," she said weakly.

Court looked up in the dark quickly; he could see the glow of Hightower's weapon light as he approached through the next room. He was nearing the table where the attacker fell. "Hey, Zack! Dead-check the shooter on the far side of that table."

"Copy," Zack said.

Dead checks weren't exactly approved in the Geneva Conventions, but for an operator in a close-quarters battle situation, it made no sense to walk past an enemy who still might pose a threat.

Court felt around for the Glock again and found it, then he turned on the light, speaking to Brewer. "We're gonna get you out of here. Just let me roll you to check for more wounds." He shifted her onto her side; using the light now he could see that her Kevlar vest had taken two rounds on the right side of her rib cage, and a third round had slammed into her upper right shoulder, midway between the arm and the neck. It was a solid entry wound with no exit, meaning the bullet was still inside her body.

"Okay, you're gonna be—"

"Shit!" It was Hightower shouting from the other room. Quickly Court lifted the pistol up, anticipating a threat, unsure what Zack's problem was. With his light he could see Zack on the far side of the table, presumably standing over the body there.

"*Shit!*" Hightower said again, his voice plaintive now. Hanley appeared behind him.

"What is it?" Court shouted back; he lowered his gun and used both hands to apply pressure on the gushing wound on Brewer's shoulder.

When Zack didn't answer, Court shouted again. "What is it, Zack?"

Still, Zack didn't answer. Court looked up now, away from Brewer lying on her back on the stone floor.

"Talk to me!" Court implored now.

"Six. Hold fast. Don't come over here."

Now Court let go of Brewer's wound. Stood up slowly. "Why? What's going on? Who did I shoot?"

Zack said nothing.

"Who did I shoot?" He screamed it now.

Matt Hanley answered. "It's . . . It's Anthem. She's down."

. . .

Court moved slowly across the dark room, his knees weakening. After a few steps he ran forward, made his way around the table into the light of Zack's rifle, and dropped to Zoya's side. Her black track top was riddled with holes across her stomach and chest, and he could see blood on the floor around her.

Zack said, "I'll work on Brewer."

Court muttered, "GSW, right shoulder."

"Copy." Hightower was up and running to Brewer an instant later.

Hanley pulled a flashlight and held it over Court.

Zoya's eyes were unfixed, like Brewer's, but she was breathing. Her chest heaved rapidly. He hadn't taken a breath himself since he'd seen the holes in her clothes, and when he ripped open her jacket, he was terrified he'd find wounds to her heart and lungs.

Instead he saw a black Kevlar vest, identical to the one Court had put on in the armory on the second floor.

He breathed a sigh of relief but continued checking her.

He found a wound on her right hip at the pelvis, where she'd taken a single round. He felt around her hip towards her back and discovered the exit wound.

Hanley said, "How bad is it?"

"She needs a hospital, but I need to occlude the bleeding first."

Court saw her eyes open and tears stream out. She tried to talk, but he told her to lie still and quiet. She persisted, and finally he leaned forward to listen to her.

"What's that?"

"She . . . was going to . . . kill you," Zoya's weak voice croaked.

Court moved his hand from her wound, pulled off his dress shirt and then his undershirt, and jammed it hard against her hip to slow the exit wound's bleeding. He put his hand back down on the front of her hip.

As he did this he said, "No. I gave her my pistol, she was just giving me light so I could dismantle the device."

Zoya shook her head. "No," she said. "It was trained on the side of your head."

Court looked back towards Brewer, then again towards Zoya. He didn't know what to think.

He said, "Look. You're going to be okay. Those across the chest are going to hurt, and your hip is grazed, but you'll be okay."

This was a lie. Her hip wasn't grazed. It was shot, pure and simple, but he was trying to put a good spin on things.

Especially because he had been the one who shot her.

Lights filled the room as a group of Royal Scots Dragoons came running in, their rifles out in front of them.

Hanley shouted for a medic, and a man with a backpack of first-aid supplies ran over and knelt next to Zoya.

"She was going to kill you, Court," Zoya said again, and then she slipped into unconsciousness.

Court looked up to Hanley and saw the older man's jaw fixed in anger.

. . .

The Scottish military forces rendered aid to the two wounded American women, and within twenty minutes of their arrival they were on litters being carried to the ground floor.

Hanley immediately spread the word that everyone around the castle needed to get to a hospital, now, to begin a course of antibiotics, and then he was loaded into a U.S. Navy helicopter, along with Brewer, Zakharova, Gentry, Hightower, and the surviving Ground Branch men: Travers, Lorenzi, and Greer, who had all been wounded. They were flown west to the USS *Forest Sherman*, an Arleigh Burke–class destroyer just off the Scottish coast.

Everyone in the group received antibiotic infusions as soon as the helo landed, and everyone save for Hightower and Hanley had been wounded, so they all spent time in the sick bay. Court's hand was X-rayed and it was determined that he didn't need surgery, but they put a proper cast on it and supplied him with mild painkillers that made his life a little easier, though all he did was worry about Zoya.

. . .

The last surviving attendee of the Five Eyes conference received their first dose of antibiotics eight hours after the end of the event, virtually the last moment for the incubation period of the strain of plague created by Dr. Won Jang-Mi. These were followed by infusions the following day and a multiweek course of oral medicines.

. . .

The day after the attack at the castle ended, Matt Hanley stepped into Suzanne Brewer's private room off the sick bay. She was on her back in bed, her neck heavily bandaged, and she wore glasses and stared blankly at the TV.

She turned to him with some difficulty. "Hi, Matt. Nice of you to come."

Hanley entered, closed the door, and sat down next to the bed. "They say you'll be fine."

"They say I was lucky. Didn't even break any bones. But I don't feel so lucky. My own asset shooting me."

"Zoya says you were targeting Gentry."

Brewer chuckled. "Look, she made an honest mistake, I get that. She saw me with the gun and—"

Hanley interrupted. "Suzanne. We are not going to talk about this, you and me, ever again. But I want you to understand one thing. If Court dies on your watch, and I have any suspicions, *any* at all that his death wasn't in the normal course of operations . . . I send Zack over to your house. You might want to keep that in mind."

"Wait. *Christ*, Matt. You believe her?"

Hanley just stared down at Brewer.

"Matt, for God's sake, I didn't—"

Hanley interrupted again. "I'm not accusing you of anything, although I have an opinion on what Zakharova said. Next time you might be thinking about some little scheme, do yourself a favor and think about Zack Hightower, and see if that doesn't calm you down a bit."

"But—"

Hanley waved a hand through the air and left the room. On his way out he said, "Get better. I want you back at your desk pronto. Poison Apple needs to go back to work soon."

Brewer stared at the ceiling in the low light, wishing that those fucking bombs had ended her interminable misery.

• • •

Zoya was in surgery during much of the first afternoon, and then overnight she was put in ICU. She was finally rolled into a room around eleven a.m. the next day. Court hadn't spoken to her since she'd passed out in the basement, and there was nothing else on Earth that he wanted to do more right now.

He went in for another round of antibiotics and was given a bottle with sixty pills in it and told to take three a day. After he asked about her, the doctor told him Anthem had been moved to a room. Court was given directions and he descended a ladder and followed a passageway, but when he turned a corner to the room, he saw Zack Hightower standing there, wearing a U.S. Navy sweatshirt and sweatpants. He saw Court and put up a hand.

"Dude . . . forget her."

"*What?*"

"I just checked on her. She's fine, but . . . but she does *not* want to talk to you. She's pissed. No . . . she's *more* than pissed. Funny enough, it's not about the fact you stitched her up with a burst from a subgun. It's about—"

"It's about me killing her father."

"Yep."

"She wanted to do it."

"Yeah, she did. You did the right thing, but she's not gonna see that. Ever. She saw it as her cross to bear for her brother. Not yours to take from her."

"I just need to talk to her and—"

"No, man. Let it rest for now. Maybe somewhere down the road when it's not so raw you can—"

Court started to push past Hightower, but the bigger man held him firm. "I'm lookin' out for you, brother. If it's gonna work with you two, it sure as shit isn't gonna happen today. I talked to her, I saw the look in her eyes. *Nothing* good will come from you goin' through that door right now, I can promise you that.

"Stand down, Six. Let this rest."

Court looked at Hightower a long moment, and then he stood down. After several seconds more he turned and began walking away, his shoulders low.

"You outta here, brother?"

"Yep," Court replied. "Getting on a launch back to Scotland in an hour."

"Then what?"

Court stopped. Seemed to think about it. "Solo for a while, I guess. All this teamwork shit is a complicated pain in the ass."

Zack chuckled. "Watch your six, Violator."

Court turned away and headed off up the passageway again. "You be careful out there, too." He paused. Then said, "Night Train."

Zack pumped a fist into the air in excitement, but Court didn't look back to catch it.

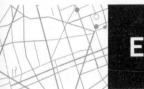

EPILOGUE

A light but steady rain fell out of the gray morning sky, over the blue and white fishing boat bobbing in the water next to an impossibly green spit of land. There was no marina here in Loch Crenen, just an old clapboard dock, half-rotten through time, sticking out barely far enough for the trawler to tie on without running ashore.

The weather here in the western coastal highlands was predictably dreary, and the captain walked around on deck securing lines to set sail without acknowledging the fact that his face and hair were drenched.

He'd been living this life for thirty years, after all, and he knew no other.

A mile or so to the southeast, a small twin turbo prop took off from Oban Airport, banked through the gray rain, and disappeared in a puff of mist.

While the captain continued preparing for the voyage, a man standing motionless on the foredeck of the trawler watched the aircraft fly away through the droplets dripping in front of his eyes off the hood of his raincoat.

Court Gentry sighed. He didn't have any idea who was on that aircraft, but he imagined it being Zoya. This was doubtful. More likely she was still on board the destroyer, or had already been spirited back to the United States on a CIA Gulfstream.

It had been a week since the attack, and he'd been lying low in nearby

Oban, eating canned food in a simple hotel room, taking his antibiotics, and sulking.

Court had been offered a ride back to the States, not on Hanley's jet; the DDO had resumed his earlier stance of remaining arm's length from the assets of Poison Apple, but Hanley had told Court he could go to Oban and fly out as soon as Transpo could arrange a lift for him.

He got a text telling him when and where, and then he'd taken his battery out of his phone and thrown it in a river.

He'd not declined so much as he just hadn't shown up at the prearranged place and time.

Court would go on to his next destination alone.

He leaned against the railing of the trawler, his spirits as dreary as the skies above.

He'd gotten this boat captain to agree to take him through the last couple miles out of this loch, to a skiff that would be waiting a few miles out in the open ocean. The skiff would take him, in turn, back to its mothership, a Singapore-flagged Evergreen dry-goods hauler. Court had arranged for transportation through a broker that he knew from his time as an assassin for hire; he knew the broker would take his fee and pay off the Taiwanese crew and secure a ride for Court, at least as far as one of their ports of call.

It was a useful service for a man like Gentry, one he used even now, though he was a CIA asset and could easily get transportation from them.

But no, he had a thing against CIA Transpo at the moment.

He felt like he was running away. Away from Zoya. He thought about pursuing her back to D.C. He could get Brewer to arrange a meeting, though Brewer and Zoya weren't exactly on speaking terms at the moment. Still . . . he wondered if he could try one more time to convince Zoya that he wasn't the enemy.

He told himself he might wonder that for a long time, because in the end, he decided to leave her in peace. She had made herself abundantly clear as to her wishes, and he would respect them, even if they killed him.

The captain leaned out of the tiny navigation bridge and told Court they'd be leaving in five minutes. The boat bobbed and Court looked to the land. The only colors anywhere in sight were blue, green, and gray, but some movement in the distance caught his attention. A white vehicle bounced on the muddy road in the distance, fast approaching the trawler tied to the dilapidated pier.

Court cocked his head. The captain had said nothing about anyone else coming along for this ride, and there wasn't a thing out here other than rocky coastline and undeveloped pasture land.

As it neared, Court determined the SUV to be a Toyota Land Cruiser that was at least twenty years old, and he had no idea who the hell could be inside it.

Hadn't they fucking killed all the bad guys already?

No, he told himself. *There are always more bad guys.*

His left hand slowly unzipped his raincoat while his right hand hovered close to the pistol on his hip. Once the coat was open all the way he knew he could just sweep it back and draw, faster than most anyone he'd ever encountered.

But he did not draw; he just watched the Land Cruiser continue forward.

"Captain?" He said it in a voice that told the grizzled older man he needed to stick his head back out of the nav bridge and pay attention to his passenger.

"Aye?"

Court bobbed his forehead towards the vehicle, and the captain said, "Not with me, mate. Haven't a clue."

Court kept watching.

"You want me to shove off?" the captain asked.

Court's training was telling him the answer was an obvious yes, but his curiosity told him he should wait and see who this was.

The Land Cruiser skidded to a stop in the sloppy mud and gravel by the side of the pier, and then the passenger-side door opened.

A pair of boots appeared slapping into the slop, with the wearer of the boots hidden behind the door of the SUV.

Court swept back his raincoat and put his hand on the butt of his pistol.

Zoya Zakharova appeared when she stood up, then turned his way. She wore no raincoat, her heavy knit sweater was dry but dampening by the second in the cool summer rain, and her brown hair tied back behind her ears shone with precipitation in just the first few seconds it was exposed to the sky.

She walked slowly and gingerly through the mud, several steps closer to the pier, before she even looked up at the deck and saw Court standing there in his raincoat looking back. She continued up the pier, half dragging her right leg to keep from bending it on the side of her wounded hip.

When she made it alongside the fishing boat she looked up at him. With a deadpan expression and in a deadpan voice she said, "Surprise."

Court could come up with no reply.

"You are wondering how I found you."

Slowly he nodded, glanced quickly to the boat captain, and saw the man was back inside the closed navigation bridge and looking at some charts. He was well out of earshot.

Zoya stepped a little closer; the Land Cruiser sat at idle behind her. The driver was a man who appeared to be in his seventies, and Court wondered if Zoya had hitchhiked here.

She said, "It seems you and I know the same stowaway broker. FYI, Antoine is not to be trusted. He has a thing for women. I called him, reminded him I'd used his services a few times, and he remembered me. I asked him about any clients in the area, and he told me about this passenger of his heading out on an Evergreen via a fishing boat in Loch Crenen."

Court hadn't taken his eyes off her. He could see the pain on her face from her hip wound, and it made him feel like shit, but the main thought going through his head right now was his confusion about what the hell she was doing here.

"Now you are wondering *why* I found you."

"I am." He realized he hadn't taken his hand off the grip of his Glock. He wondered if his body was able to detect that Zoya was indeed a threat to him, so it had stayed vigilant and prepared to react in case of an attack by her.

Self-consciously he lowered his hand to his side.

She asked, "Where are you going?"

He hadn't expected this. After a time he said, "Wherever that ship takes me."

"That's vague, even for you."

"I need a little break," he said. "When the time is right, I'll head back to D.C. I'll make my way back under Brewer's thumb before too long, I'm sure."

"Just watch your back."

Court nodded. "Will do. What about you?"

She shrugged her muscular shoulders. "I hope by me showing up like this you didn't get the impression that everything is okay between us. I'm absolutely fucking furious with you about what you did."

"Yeah. You conveyed that effectively in the dungeon of the castle."

She touched her right hip. "And I'm not talking about this."

Court nodded. "I know exactly what you're talking about."

"Good. That's good. I don't know if I can ever forgive you, to be honest. I have my reasons for that, just like you have your reasons for what you did."

Court said nothing. He wasn't going to fight with her. He figured now he'd take some abuse, and then she'd shuffle back down to her ride, and she'd leave him forever.

"But," she continued, "I keep thinking that, for better or worse, the only person out there for someone like me, is someone like you. Maybe not you . . . but someone like you."

"There is no one like me, Zoya."

She sighed. "That's exactly what I'm afraid of."

Court made a face that revealed his confusion. He had next to no experience discussing relationships, but all this sounded so obscure he couldn't make out her point, if there even was one.

Zoya continued. "And even though I'm still pissed, I wanted to come see you off before I fly back to D.C. out of Oban this afternoon."

He climbed off the boat now and stepped onto the pier in front of her. They stood a few feet apart a moment, then he moved closer and took her in his arms.

"Carefully, please," she said.

"Hey," Court said as he embraced her, "I'm still pretty beat up myself."

"We make quite a pair, don't we?" she said, and she hugged him back gently.

After a time Court stepped back and looked at her. "Please take care of yourself," he said.

"You, too. I'll see you around."

She kept the dispassionate expression up for a few seconds more, and then, for the first time in a long time, he saw her smile. It wasn't much of a smile; it hinted at anger and suspicion and trouble ahead, but for now, at least, it was good enough for him.

She reached out and touched the side of his face tenderly, then she turned away and began heading back up the dock, while Court watched her go.